SYLVERHAWK

Geoffrey W. Gilson

Clovercroft Publishing

Sylverhawk

©2015 by Geoff Gilson

Published by Clovercroft Publishing, Franklin, Tennessee.

Edited by Tammy Kling

Proofread by Andrew Toy

Cover and Interior Layout Design by Suzanne Lawing

Printed in the United States of America

978-1-942557-03-6

Like arrows in the hand of a warrior,
so are the children of one's youth.
Happy is the man who has his quiver full of them...
—PSALM 127:4-5a

To my four Ayili warriors:
Peter, Matt, Sam, and Zack.
This story is for you, and it is all true.
—Dad

Attention reader: Please see *appendyx* at the end of the book for explanation of common terms.

Please note that in old Terrasian English, many times, the letter "y" is substituted for letters "i" and "e" when between two consonants.

Prologue

Death was coming for me. Even now, I could feel it sweeping toward me, a zephyr in the high trees. I perceived it just as first light touched the western sky. It smelled like old mountain snow, cold and pure. It cascaded from the high plains over the Breach cliffs and down upon the southern forest. It danced and twirled playfully in the shadowy treetops. A single yellowed leaf caught in its caress fluttered. Silver dew, collected in its cup, tumbled from an edge. Far below, it landed icily on my bent neck. For a moment, the chill of death's kiss stirred me from my deep reverie.

I sat still as I had for several hours. Time had little meaning for me anymore. I had been a witness to so many years. My bones felt so old and they ached this morning. I sat with my head bent in deep contemplation. I looked down at my hands. They looked like they had carried the ages and it had left them all angles and dark calloused leather. Prominent vessels like worms beneath the dark earth wove winding patterns across their surface. I noticed that my wrists were so worn and brown that that they appeared to have grown from the great tree root, which served as my perch. Like wooden knots, they seemed formed from the same pulp, grain, and coarse bark as the tree, which sheltered me. I felt the aching years in them. I breathed slowly, and my pulse continued its deep, relentless throb. I was still and quiet as I waited. So complete was my camouflage, that the littlest forest creatures paid me no attention as they foraged nearby. I smiled at their busy industry.

Worn wool garments, long drained of color, and free of any adornment, hung loosely from my hunched frame. On my head was my favorite green hat, its edges bent and frayed by years of storms. Beneath its brim, my hair was thin and had grown completely white. Somehow, I had become all sinew, taut muscle, and thin bones. I waited. I recalled the decades silently. I felt the years with a swell of emotion that brought me to the edge of quiet tears. I whispered silent prayers of abiding gratitude. I absorbed the early light around me, warming and loosening in its touch. Like a long-married couple, the forest and I were quietly at ease with each other. Long ago, we had lost the need for words. We communicated now with gentle harmony and contented silences. Over the decades, we had become old friends who knew each other with an organic peace.

Though life still coursed powerfully within me as the sun rose, I felt the tug of the grassy earth upon my bones. Occasionally, the zephyr above reached its cold tentative fingers toward my soul. I was certain it would not be long now until my spirit would shrug off its earthly burden to soar. I felt no fear, just a long, steady peace.

Still, on this day, one last task was yet before me and, truth be told, I was tired by the prospect of it.

Perhaps, then, my Lord? I thought.

As the morning sun warmed the ground beneath my feet, I continued to sit in contemplation. So deep was my reverie and so distant and hopeful was my soul, that I failed at first to notice the soft thump of hooves on the thick grass. A heavy warhorse entered the glen. It was the gently spoken words of its rider that finally broke my trance.

"Hi, Pater."

I looked up slowly, the old bones of my neck creaking as I turned. With the raspy whisper of a long silent throat, I replied, "Jonam, my son."

We both smiled with deep kinship and affection while Jonam slid heavily from his horse. He was a muscular young man dressed in the royal blue cape of a captain, good steel mail, leather riding pants, and sturdy oiled boots. Blond hair in curls licked his neck, and his chin was graced with a young beard of the same hue but a courser texture. Like his frame, his features were direct and strong. His face was made of many angles, which had collided in such a way as to leave the impression of power, honesty, and integrity. It was smoothed though by playful curves of humor. He had about him, that peculiar kind of peacefulness found only in men of authority who have nothing left to prove and who have no fear of appearing gentle. His grey irises with slivers of river blue were perfect reflections of my own.

Jonam bent and enveloped me, his grandfather, in a vigorous embrace. His arms were powerfully muscled and I felt thin and brittle in his hug. His youth and vigor brought me joy. I noticed the smell of rich earth and dry grass, which clung to him. I sensed a mature peace and strength emanating from him.

We sat in silence together for a while, breathing the sun-dappled air. We retraced years of shared memories without speaking. The big horse huffed a few times in contentment.

Finally, it was Jonam's excitement for what lay ahead that made him speak.

"How have you been, Pater?"

"It seems I've become old," I said with a wan smile. "But I am well and eager to hear of your last few weeks, my son."

Jonam took this comment with a smile of his own. Though he was a man of battle, he held a deep respect and appreciation for the legendary adventures of his old grandfather. I knew that the very purpose of his visit today was to get some advice and wisdom from me.

"We battled the vulls at Kudron on the eve," he said. "It was a hard fought victory. They came out of the Breach Hills at dusk. They hardly seem to wait until nightfall any longer. Their numbers were horrible—four, maybe five hundred. Those vile beasts must breed like stink. It's clear the Defyyl Lord grows again in strength..."

Here he paused to look at me. I pursed my lips but showed no other emotion, acknowledging that I knew the evil tidings already. So Jonam went on.

"For all their fierceness, the vulls are usually quite dim. On this night however, they were different. They swept into Duvall from the west and northwest, using the cover of the low bush until the last moment. It was a well-planned, three-pronged attack. Several cy'daal were at the lead of each horde—a fearsome sight. The hand to hand combat began on the edge of Folsom Woods. We were forced to divide the squadron to protect our flanks. The fight was most vicious on the left wing. There, we lost Colonel Fassan. A cy'daal rider beheaded him, but not before he had slain several others. I fought well, and cut down my share of the horrid beasts, but was struck unconscious before the battle's end."

"Cedric pulled me from the mire, despite his own injuries, or surely, I too would have been lost. Were it not for the few Ayili, we would have taken terrible casualties. As it was, the Mynili were busy all night with the injured. A few could not be saved even by their great skill." As he said this, he turned his head and lifted his hair, revealing a vivid purple and yellow bruise split by a partially healed laceration. "I was one of those blessed by their touch," he said.

Jonam came to life, as he related the details of the battle. A spark was visible in his eyes, which seemed suddenly fiery. Jonam knew well my own history in battle. He treated me as a hero of renown. He knew that I could feel every blow that had fallen, and saw every move on the field of battle as it was related to me. He knew that I dripped the sweat, tasted the blood, and could hear the screams of the vulls, for I had lived a thousand such nights of terror. I had been the commander of the sylver-banded warriors—the Ayili—the first and some said the best.

"And, what of your brother?" I asked.

"Fredryk fights far to the south in the Pile Hills. Last I heard, he too was made captain."

"He has always been good with the short sword," I said. "The terrain of the hills permits only close combat. He will do well."

"I fear for him, Pater. There are too few Ayili in the south."

"I know, Jonam," I sighed.

"We have always been far too few." For a moment, silence fell between us again.

"That is why I have come to you today, Pater," the young soldier whispered.

After another pause long enough to make Jonam wonder whether he had been heard, I replied, "I know why you have come."

Jonam turned and looked steadily at my eyes and scanned my face trying to read the meaning behind my words. I knew that he wondered whether his hero had ever known the fluttering fear he now felt in his heart. Finally finding his courage, he spoke. "Tell me the story again, for I have decided to go myself."

"Why are you going?"

"Because I want to serve Dyos as an Ayili," the young soldier said, barely able to get the words out.

"Why?" I asked. "The costs of such a journey are terrible, and many never return."

"I know," Jonam replied softly. "Perhaps it is because I know that in the end, my life is his, and not my own."

For a long time, I looked deeply at my grandson, peering into his soul. I had grown very good at seeing into the hearts of men over the years. Satisfied with what I saw now, I smiled softly. "Very well, I will tell you it all. Perhaps, it will help."

I peered upward through the trees, summoning strength from above. My own youth seemed so far off; my strength nearly gone. I knew for sure now that the telling of his story would be my last.

"Pater" was the only name I had known for almost fifty years now. Literally, it simply meant "kins-father" or "leader." It was also a playful derivation of my "given" name, Pityr. It was the young boy Pityr who my mind now struggled to recall.

My first memories ushered in a rush of emotion. They came, not as isolated pictures, but as powerful waves full of feeling. Terror, excitement, joy, pain, regret, wonder, nervousness, first love, and passion: each flooded forth with enormous force. For a moment, I was overwhelmed and shocked by the intensity of feeling. Years had given context to these emotions however, and I had learned the power of perspective. So carefully now, I let the years wind away and allowed my mind to drift gently toward the young boy "Pityr."

I eased off the low limb, which had made my bony rear sore and numb, and slid onto the cushion of thick grass beneath. I bid Jonam join me there. Without hesitation, the young captain swept the blue cape from his shoulders, hung it across a low limb, and sat heavily down near me. His horse stood nearby noisily eating the rich greens of fall grass. Occasionally, its ears twitched at the silver-blue water flies that darted around its bowed head.

I reached out to a heavy leather sack leaning at arm's length against a heap of granite. As I did so, Jonam noticed the thick silver-white band that encircled my wrist. I saw him study it. It appeared ornately inscribed in deep relief, its tracings faintly blue and luminescent. He knew it as the band all Ayili wore. Each was different from the next, marking their bearer's unique calling. Before Jonam had a chance to observe it more closely, I let it slip beneath the worn wool sleeve once again.

From inside the sack, I pulled a block of white cheese, two green apples, grainy brown bread, and a stained wineskin. From a hidden pocket in my vest, I produced a short, sharp knife. I began to cut the cheese and then the apples with slow deliberation, handing slices of each to Jonam. Next, I tore a large chunk of the bread from the loaf and handed that also to my grandson.

"Tales go better with food," I said.

Jonam accepted the food and the comment with a secret smile, knowing my great love of food. Despite my old man's sinewy frame, I was known for my appetite. I had always been able to out-eat and out-drink much larger men half my age. My belly sometimes seemed an endless pit.

When the division of food was completed, I took a single mouthful of cider from the skin to wet my tongue, and then began my tale. Jonam had heard bits and pieces of the story as a child and as a young man sitting with the family before the hearth. It had always left him, even more than the others, stunned and shaking. I knew that sometimes he had been unable to sleep for days. I was certain that as he anticipated it in its entirety now, he felt a hint of uncertainty in his gut. My adventures had ushered in the beginning of a new age for the people of Terras. I had seen the depths of the Defyyl Lord's kingdom, and been among the first to cross its lands. I knew now that soon the adventure would become his own.

In respect, and desperate to learn all that he could, Jonam humbly bowed his blond head and bent forward so he would not miss a word.

Chaptyr 1

Nobody knows for sure when the first vulls came out of the northern hills. Perhaps, there was a time, before the current ages, when there were no such unnatural creatures, and man lived in peace and harmony with the world around him. But the vulls have always been a part of our lives and story, a constant threat to all we believe to be good and right.

In the many years since the Great Battle, the vull hordes had begun to roam the southlands once again. The blessed peace we knew for a few years after the war was gone now. We were desperately hopeful that defeat of Malthanos had been final. But that proved sadly untrue. Like a dormant plague, he had proven frustratingly virulent and resilient. The defyyl creatures were growing again in numbers and voracity.

My father told of a time when they would shrink even from dim moonlight, attacking only on the darkest nights, in small hordes of twenty to fifty. Now they swarmed in hordes of hundreds, even thousands, and had been seen within minutes of sunset. Accompanying the vulls have always been the fearsome cy'daal riders with their milky yellow eyes, and a bite of certain slow and terrible death. Their numbers also had grown. I had heard reports of as many as thirty riding at once.

Now, from the north, came stories of even more horrifying beasts that had been seen in battle. Skinless, winged creatures called "hyss" whose scream brought death first to the mind and then to the body. I knew well such evil spawn, for they were as old as the ages. I had met them and their kin myself long before. Though all these wretched creatures had crept for ages through the dark depths of the defyyl lord's kingdom, of late they seemed once again more free to roam above. Their rapid growth was again bringing death, pestilence, and a great foreboding.

I was barely six years old when I saw my first man infected with the dregs. He was caged in the square like a rabid dog, eyes turned bloodshot red like a vull. Foaming yellow muck poured from his mouth, he paced back and forth on all fours across the cage built to contain him. Since the Mynili had been healing, no one ever saw men in that stage of the dregs anymore. Back then however, it was all too common—as common as the bite of a cy'daal. And the healers of the time were helpless before such pestilence. The man in the cage was my father's good friend, a farmer named Kirus.

My older brother Samuyl was fourteen at the time. He had witnessed the fatal shot. I still remember the fear in his voice as he related the story of the good farmer's fall. He had seen a cy'daal perched, as usual, on the back of a vull, calmly drew an arrow from its sheath, placed the arrowhead in its vile mouth until it dripped with a grey pus, notched the arrow, and with a smile, shot the farmer in the back. Though the arrow barely penetrated the farmer's thick mail, the deadly mucus worked its horrors. Within days, nothing of the kind and gentle man remained.

The Exarchate Consul, with Desmodys at its head, voted to burn the young farmer in his cage. I had never heard such screams from a man. They were riveting, agonizing, and soul piercing. As the flames lit the night, I could not escape their dark terror. They filled many dreams and beat down upon my young soul long after the ashes were cleared from the square, and their echo had faded. I would feel their chill so many years later.

Even many years later, the Mynili still couldn't heal a man poisoned by the cy'daal, but they could lessen the viciousness and agony of his demise to almost nothing. They healed many wounds with surprising ease. Indeed, so much had changed with the coming of the silver-banded Ayili. The world of my childhood was one of terrible superstition and fear. We seemed powerless against the growing evil, all the more so because we did not understand it. The exarchs, the healers, the scribes, none could ever adequately explain these creatures of the night. Though we did not know it then, we were still yet veiled to Dyos'bri and were caught in the blindness of the defyyl.

Great advantage in battle came from understanding your enemy. In our blindness, we were weak and vulnerable. We had noble fighters, some of the toughest, but they had not the bless of the Ayili-nosterli. We inevitably lost several strong warriors with each battle, more than a few to the dregs. It was a time of hopelessness and numbing fear. All the good people of Terras could do was build higher walls around their towns and teach their sons and daughters to fight.

I was barely ten when my father took away my toy weapons and gave me a real sword of my own. It was so heavy my skinny arms could barely wield it. Like all boys, I trained for hours a day until I had mastered the basics of sword work with both the long and short steel. Later, I moved on to the hammer, the bow, and the pike in quick succession. I spent so many late afternoons with my father and my brothers in mock battles. I had a little natural skill, but this would suddenly evaporate whenever I imagined a vull before me. I was left feeling weak, drained, and hopeless every time I recalled the poor farmer with the dregs. All the stories I had heard, all the horrors my young eyes had seen, combined to overwhelm any spark of courage. I fought well in mock battle, but as soon as the teeth of a vull or the yellow eyes of a cy'daal crept into my thoughts, my balance would go, my muscles would contract, and a cloud would pass before my eyes.

I never told anyone about these life-sapping fears, but I think my father knew. Though he never spoke about the sudden changes in my skill and demeanor, he was uncharacteristically gentle with me at these times. Instead of belittling me, he would often say, "Your old man needs a rest." I knew well, from the lack of sweat on his brow, that he was just being kind. Perhaps, for a moment, he also remembered being a child in a world of such horrors. It was not until years later that I found the true skill within. Nonetheless, I believe he was aware, even then, of my potential. In his wisdom, he let me confront my fears myself rather than beat them out of me. Though his love was seldom public and sometimes rough, he had a far more sensitive manner than the fathers of most of my friends. I knew he loved me in his quiet way.

I had just begun my fourteenth year when I was sent to Toss Rydigg as a mason's apprentice. My first two years were spent largely as a beast of stone burden. I moved rock piles, cleared old foundations, dug holes, worked the pulleys, built scaffolding, and mixed mortar. Slowly, I grew strong from my labors. Muscles appeared on my arms and legs. My shoulders began to stretch my jerkin, and my hands turned as hard as the stone I worked. By the time I had been apprenticing a year, most of the town's bullies had learned to leave me alone.

One day, Toss gave me a simple shaping job. He was surprised to see me perform it with ease. When he expressed his astonishment, I confessed my secret. For over a year, I had been taking tools home with me along with discarded blocks of stone. After dinner, by the firelight of our hearth, I had practiced the skills I had witnessed that day. I think my enthusiasm endeared me to him; from that moment forward, he took me under his wing. He began to teach me his beloved trade in earnest. He taught me the balance of the heavy and light hammers, the diversity of the various chisels, and the particulars of the fine shaping tools. He taught me how to read the grain and texture of the stone with my fingertips as I worked. Under his mentorship, I learned to sense each stones' inherent strengths and weaknesses, their brittle angles and hidden fissures. I spent days blindfolded, caressing each new block he would pass me, and reading their internal tensions.

Many say rock is not alive. It is alive, just on a different time scale. Holding live, malleable rock between my fingertips, I could often feel its infinitesimally slow heartbeat. I learned to taste the mineral content of each new piece. As I chiseled, my lungs filled with the dusty exhalations. Toss taught me to delight in color and texture. Whether we were working with common speckled granite from the foothills of Ardmoor, pink Deluvian quartz, or green marble from Parthis, he taught me to tease from it a shape, which exposed its true hues.

Rockwork brought me freedom from the chaos of my nightmares. It rooted me solidly back to the earth, and helped me combat my childhood superstitions. Truth be told, I had natural skill with the stone. Toss, I think, started to see me as the son he did not have. He seemed to take true pleasure in bringing my potential to life. All my brothers went to work in the family leatherworks, but my father chose stonework for me when he apprenticed me to Toss. He must have known that something in me was made of stone when he made his choice.

It may seem from all this work and battle training that I had little time for play. In truth, it never seemed that way to me. I was always running off with friends in the evenings no matter how hard the travails of the day were. Of course, Restdays were also my own time once Communals were completed. Usually though, we would have to escape to the Great Woods or the Flock Grasslands for our fun on these days. We were sure to get the "dark eye" from the stricter adults, along with whispered complaints to our parents, if we ever seemed to be having too much fun.

In those times, Restdays were filled with strict ceremony, fear, and forced solemnity. There seemed a thousand rules for what passed for proper behavior on Restdays. I can recall many a good villager spending a day in the locks for laughing too loudly, or being caught picking vegetables on this day of Ex-archate ordained rest. So we were careful to go far afield for our play, and for the most part avoided all but the occasional complaint.

Though we often played in large groups, I had two special friends with whom I spent most of my free time. In the later years, we became an inseparable trio. The first was Thom, a plump blacksmith's apprentice, and the other Mryyn, a washer's girl, and Thom's cousin. We spent far too much time hunting frogs, building tree forts, and creating mischief, to cast a critical eye on the world.

Thom was the comic of our group. At fifteen, he stood a full six and a half feet and weighed well over twelve stone. He had a big square-ish head, small lively blue eyes, and a full lipped mouth with a great deal of straight, white teeth. Thom's nose had been creatively shaped by the hoof of a horse at age six, and pointed a bit toward his left ear. Though he had the appearance of plumpness, he was muscled like a bull. For one so big, he was surprisingly quick and amazingly strong. Fortunately, he was charmingly oblivious to his strength and size, the way a child would be when suddenly given the body of a giant. He seemed to dress the part as well. His mother had long ago given up trying to keep up with his growth, and his clothes were always several sizes too small.

I am sure that Karpp Poston, the blacksmith, had no end of frustration with Thom. Despite the asset of his great strength, Thom was a daydreamer and a joker, and was usually unable to concentrate on any task longer than a few minutes. His mind raced from one idea to the next with hardly a pause. Yet, it was impossible to stay angry at him longer than a few moments. So infectious was his laugh, that even the most serious infractions rarely earned him more than a stern word from the adults. Thom took on life with a gentle joy. His affability came from a childlike fascination with the world around him. There was simply no place in his soul for deviousness or wickedness. He had carelessness and forgetfulness aplenty, but not a hint of malice.

As a friend, Thom could hardly have been better. He was the mastermind of our most creative pranks, and all our best games. I am sure he spent his time at the smithy just going through the physical motions of work, while his heart was far afield, planning the next day's adventures. Thom was always the best fort builder and war game strategist, and you always wanted him on your team for *Bullball* and *Endrun*, but he would inevitably forget to bring his lunch and usually left his shoes at the swimming hole.

I met Thom when we were six, and we'd been fast friends since. I had long ago gotten used to his quirks, and was always sure to pack extra lunch in anticipation of his wandering mind.

In many ways, we made an unusual pair. Where Thom was affable, I was more reserved. Where he was impulsive, I was intentional. Where he was careless, I was exact. Thom always challenged my comfort zone, and the safety of my introversion. I found this threatening at first, but I knew instinctively that I needed it to grow. Though I hardly understood it at the time, there was a spark within me that Thom fed.

I am not entirely sure what Thom found in me. I surely kept the daydreamer anchored solidly to earth, somehow without compromising his initiative. Often, I was able to add to his skeletal plans, allowing his ideas to come alive. Perhaps I provided security for him in my rootedness. Without a solid grounding, Thom's mind would sail away like a kite on the wind. Whatever it was that sealed our friendship, it bound us tightly through many years.

A third perspective was introduced into our friendship with the arrival of the young woman who would complete our inseparable trio. Thom's cousin came to Duvall in the winter of my tenth year. Her father had been a bow captain in the Sinrik patrols who had been an archer of great repute. While in battle, his horse had tumbled, crushed him, and broken his back. For six months he had struggled to recover, until finally he had succumbed to the rasp. Unable to keep their small farm going alone, Mryyn and her mother had moved to Duvall to live with Thom's extended family.

In the early days, Mryyn would sit quietly, watching us play. There were not many children our age among Thom's neighbors, and she was naturally drawn to the sound of our mock battles, laughter, and pranking. We had no need or wish for additional playmates, but we abided her silent company. Mryyn was two years younger than both of us, skinny, and outwardly shy. She had short-cropped hair like a boy, with an athlete's gait and stance. Indeed, the first time I saw her, I thought she was a boy. At that age, only her long dark eyelashes hinted at her femininity. If her form contradicted her girlhood, her nature, overtly defied it.

One afternoon, Thom and I were deeply absorbed in a game of marbles, while Mryyn, as usual, watched silently from her stoop on a windowsill nearby. We had become so accustomed to her silent presence over the months since her arrival that we hardly noticed her anymore. Thom had won a very prized blackwolf marble in a recent game against one of his schoolmates. I was trying desperately and unsuccessfully to steal it from him. In the process, I was losing some of my best marbles. I had already given up two green knights and a firecat when my luck changed. A bold strategic roll, which even Thom did not think possible, won me the pitch black monster. I was whooping and laughing and dancing around with the marble upraised, and Thom was rolling on the ground clutching his belly in mock nausea, when I was struck.

I never saw it coming. I was knocked sideways and the marble went bouncing out of my grip. Sedge Fal stood over me laughing. His big yellow teeth, red face, and orange hair were like a nightmare to me. Sedge was a year older than Thom and me, fat, precociously large, and mean. He had earned the reputation as our schoolyard bully. Neither of us had seen him watching our game. While I tried to gather my composure and tried to figure out how to retaliate, Sedge walked over and retrieved the blackwolf and slid it into his pocket. Thom was starting to get up now, but also looked unsure of his next step. Sedge slowly backed away with a look of intense mockery, knowing we were too afraid to actually confront him.

He lifted the marble into the air between his finger and thumb and announced, "Thanks for the marble little boys.... whoooph!"

His words trailed away and ended in a big huff as the wind

was knocked from his lungs. Thom and I stood there too stunned to speak. Sedge had twisted through the air backwards and laid trying to breath and clutching the hand, which had previously held the marble. Mryyn stood astride his enormous gasping bulk. Somehow she had flipped him backwards and twisted the marble from his hand in a motion too quick to see. Sedge was no longer smiling but almost seemed ready to cry.

"That wasn't very nice Sedge," Mryyn said softly, still straddling him.

He looked at her in utter disbelief, apparently shocked by her calm and fearless demeanor—I'm sure he had never encountered a creature like her before and to be truthful, neither had we.

"You can go now," she said, stepping aside.

And go he did, like a beaten dog. Thom and I still stood in shocked silence.

Calmly, and playfully, she walked over and handed me the marble and with a lighthearted voice asked, "Could I maybe play too?"

We were a trio from that day forward.

Mryyn became known as the toughest wrestler in town as her reputation spread. Indeed, she proved her skill on more than one occasion until nobody challenged her anymore. She also had amazing skill with the bow. Her father had seen her athleticism at a young age and taught her well. At the wiry age of thirteen, Mryyn won the Harvestfest archery contest against Duvall's best archers. Though she wasn't as strong as the grown men and could not pull the bow for the long shot competition, she won the short competition by splitting a thread thrice at sixty paces. When she repeated the feat the following year, the Exarchate ruled that no one under sixteen could compete. They were finding that being beaten by a little girl was quite discouraging to the bowmaster ranks. Secretly however, many sought her out for private instruction.

The best way to describe Mryyn at that stage in her life was "spirited." She was a power-pack of energy and enthusiasm, a tiny vessel overflowing with life. She was quick-witted, joyful, and playful, though it took almost a year after her father's death for this joy to fully resurface. Though she was rough in a tom-boyish way, her heart was soft toward all living things. Mryyn was an unconscious protector of all that was good and right in people and creatures. Just as I witnessed her nurse an injured bluebird back to health and independence, so I witnessed her bind the weaknesses and nurse the strengths of those around her. Though she loved to talk and had a singsong voice, she was the best of listeners. She had a way of opening the most secret of personal doors, to join you there in smiling silence. It was with this same innocent power that she wove her way into our friendship until she was inextricably entwined.

Mryyn did not remain forever the wiry creature we had known. While the years changed Thom and me, it was Mryyn's transformation that seemed the most abrupt. Almost overnight, a rush of femininity seemed to settle upon her with stunning glory. I will never forget the day we were all riding together in the Flock Grasslands, when I suddenly realized Mryyn was beautiful. Her up-tilted eyes, golden-brown in the sunlight, were shadowed by lovely, long, dark lashes. I saw full healthy red lips smiling shyly at one of Thom's jokes. Her white teeth were per-fect. A noble and brave nose, graced with an exquisite feminine curve, led these fine features. Her hair, which had always been short, had somehow grown without my noticing, and now hung in chestnut brown curls, shot with gold reflections. She looked over at me and her smile grew even more. Suddenly, I couldn't seem to swallow, and my face felt hot. I had always enjoyed her company, now suddenly; I wanted to be much closer to her. I was stunned and more than a little confused. Never before had

I consciously noticed a woman's beauty. My inexperience with these emotions led me later to pull Thom aside for insight. He laughed at my confusion, and reminded me that perhaps I was changing as much as Mryyn was.

It was a strange time. Though the three of us were changing in ways we did not understand, we were still filled with the playfulness of children. We sensed the great wind of adulthood sweeping in upon us, and we fled from it to the fields and streams and hills. Here, for a time yet, we could still be free.

The tree forts and frog hunts gave way slowly to long gallops and games of strategy such as Jingo, Catch-the-Asp, and King's Corner, but it was all still play. Perhaps we were selfish and shortsighted the way most children are, but it must be understood what we were hiding from. Adulthood was a frightening prospect for us. It meant, ultimately, moving from a world where hope still reigned, into a darker world of responsibility, cruel reality, and real suffering. The horror of the vulls was a symbol for us of this transition. They and the other creatures of darkness were growing in number and power. The blessings of the Nosterli and the Mynili were not yet known. Men had no vision for the future. Every vull attack brought more pain, and more lost sons and fathers and brothers. It was clear that the darkness of the defyyl was slowly destroying our lives.

Chaptyr 2

It was on one of these last days of freedom that an encounter changed everything for us. A new spring was in the air and the birch forest was wet from a heavy rain the night before. We had been sent to hunt mushrooms by my mother with instructions to fill the three small tins we carried by dinnertime. My mother's cooking was rich in the fungi. We were all accustomed to this hunt, having done it many times before. So, in the way of children, we made a game of it, points for each prize. A *blackcap* was worth two, a *speckled bird* or a *pinkspur* three, and the rare and delicious white *fattop* earned the hunter five points. We were hunting in the deadwood along the west road. I flipped an old rotten log hoping to find a fattop and instead discovered a large black and yellow salamander buried in the mud. The abrupt disappearance of its roof caused it to scurry off, and I stumbled back a few steps in surprise, letting out a yelp as I went. Thom and Mryyn came immediately to my aid, but by then, my heart had slowed its fearful gallop, and I was chasing the poor lizard. Once they comprehended my intentions, they both joined the chase.

The patterned yellow critter skittered out of the roadside brush and across the hard-packed surface. In a noisy rush, we pursued. We were just about to burst into the open, when I noticed a lone horseman in the distance. I signaled a stop, and Thom's full weight slammed into my back, knocking both of us to our knees. Mryyn, in her graceful way, sidestepped lightly and came to a crouched halt. The rider was still far off and slowly approaching. He sat on an old palomino that looked tired but friendly, a far cry from the big gray war horse my father rode. The man was not large or thin or fat but well-proportioned, with strong shoulders, and well-defined forearms. Hood thrown back, a simple brown woolen garment hung from his shoulders. He wore old low-cut leather riding boots. His face was thin but strong with prominent cheekbones. He had a short, yellow-brown beard. It was hard to see the color of his eyes, for in that moment his horse stepped into a pool of white spring light that had found its way through the dense leafy canopy above.

Suddenly, the whole figure of horse and man shone with a spectacular brilliance. In that moment his simple garbs became the incandescent golden robes of a king. He sparkled with a sunlit aura. His hair shown with airy fire like a crown set upon the head of royalty. The old palomino was transformed into a glittering white stallion. He seemed surrounded by pillars of the purest white fire, which curled around him. Slowly and deliberately, he turned his face upward to bathe in the light. I remember feeling my jaw drop, and my knees begin to quiver. I thought for a second that I heard trumpets and a distant chorus. I felt a prickle of power against my skin, like the moment before lightning strikes. My heart raced, and it seemed impossible to breathe or even blink. From high to the left, a sylverhawk swept down with a cry toward the glorious figure. It circled twice in the blazing light just above the crowned head. So pale were its feathers, and so glorious the light, that it appeared at moments to be sailing aflame. The rider raised a strong arm in salute. The fiery hawk cried again in echoing praise, then swooped away into the sunlight and clouds. Then, just as suddenly, it was over, and the rider passed back into the forest shadows again. The light disappeared, the majesty evaporated, and the commoner returned. The woods were silent.

I rubbed my tearing eyes, and wondered whether I had dreamt the vision, but a quick look at the stunned expressions of Thom and Mryyn confirmed I had not been alone. Slowly, the rider passed. Though we were well hidden by the heavy brush, I felt exposed, almost naked. A small smile appeared on the kind but hard features as the man rode by. Finally I could see clearly that his eyes were of the darkest blue. I am sure he was aware of our presence, but he continued on without a look in our direction, and like a phantom, disappeared around the bend. The soft footfalls of the old horse could still be heard after he was gone. For a long time we all stood still and silent, deeply aware that something fundamental had forever changed, but not sure at all what it was.

It was just before sunset when we returned to town with our three full tins. The rest of our hunt had been performed in silence. Each of us had been too preoccupied with our own thoughts to continue the competition, and we had collected solemnly. I could make little sense of what I had seen, figuring it to have been some bizarre play of light. Yet even as I tried to rationalize it, I knew that what I had seen was magical. Even more frightening, was the certainty growing within me, that we had been meant to witness this spectral transformation.

As we passed beneath the great arch of the west wall, I noticed the Red Guards in full mail. Their spears were erect, which signaled the closure of the heavy iron gates for the night. The massive chains rattled, the counterweights fell, and the thick wood doors swung shut behind us. All the outlying farm families had been counted as they returned to town for the night. It was folly to stay beyond the walls at night. Only heavily armed war parties roamed the countryside at night risking an encounter with a horde of vulls. At that time, the scouting system was not as sophisticated as it would eventually become, for until the Ayili, few men would travel the darkness alone.

As we traveled deeper into town, we passed a small inn called The Wayfarer. I noticed the old palomino hitched to the inn's post, its head hanging in a basket of oats. I saw candlelight in a top room and thought again of the mysterious rider. These thoughts preoccupied me the rest of the way home. During dinner I was quiet and reflective. Afterwards, I sat with my father before the great fireplace, watching the flames dance, and slowly fell asleep with the ever distant sound of trumpets filling my dreams.

In the morning, I ran the short distance to the Quarter Hall. It was a clear and brilliant day, the blue of the sky uninterrupted by clouds. The morning shadows were still long. The Hall was Toss' current project, a large stone common house commissioned by the Exarchate. Toss had won the contract on merit. He was clearly the most skilled mason in town, and the best for a job of this magnitude. There were a total of ten of us now working the stone. Two weeks ago, Toss had assigned me the task of molding the arch stones for the east and west doorways. Since this was traditionally a submaster's job, requiring great skill and precision, I was truly honored.

Typically stonemasons work for a decade or more before being entrusted with such a job. I was determined to prove my worthiness. On workdays, I would arrive a half hour after sunrise to begin work. Long before the others arrived, I would be knee-deep in chippings. Toss would smile at my enthusiasm, check my work, slightly adjust my grip on the hammer, or the angle of the chisel, and move on. I was touched by his confidence in me and enjoyed my independence. We were working with fine green-streaked marble that was challenging to shape.

On this day, I had only the keystone on the west arch to complete. This was the most technically daunting piece, for it was the primary support of the structure, and had to be perfectly shaped, without flaw. I selected an excellent block I had set aside for this purpose. I felt its solid surface and inherently knew that it was without hidden weakness. I had grown to sense such things in the last four years. Patiently, I selected the course chisel and began working.

I was deeply immersed in my work, and covered in stone dust, when I began to sense Toss' presence behind me. I completed a blow and then turned to receive his instruction. With him stood a strong but plain man in a brown wool shirt. I knew immediately whom I was seeing, but my mind reeled at the surprise. Before me stood the mysterious rider, his dark blue eyes smiling, his hand outstretched. I was stunned

"Pityr, this is Yakum, a master mason all the way from a village in the far south near the coast. He'll be joining us for the rest of the job. I wanted you to meet him and familiarize him with the arch work here."

Unconsciously, I reached out a dusty hand and felt his rough grip tighten around my own. "Welcome," I croaked.

I am not shy by nature, nor timid, but until that moment, this man had seemed more a vision to me than a living being. Now I looked at him and he seemed so solid and real. I felt the calluses of his hard worked hands and looked into his eyes. I was rattled in a way I could not understand. My mind could not seem to bridge the gap between the magical events I had witnessed the day before and the reality of this moment. I felt as if I stared for way too long before Toss broke the tension again with his gruff voice.

"Perhaps, you could show him your work, Pityr, and then get him started." With that, he trotted off, leaving the two of us.

I turned and shyly exposed my work.

"It's the keystone," I said stupidly, for any master or even the lowliest apprentice could have identified this uniquely shaped piece.

"You have worked it beautifully," he said as he caressed one of the edges.

"Are you going to use wedge or box form for its fitting?" he asked. His voice was soft, deep, and powerful.

"Wedge," I replied.

"I'll let you finish the detail, then perhaps we can fit it together," he said and sat back to watch me work.

I thought I would not be able to continue, that my hands would shake, and I would split the stone. Unexpectedly, I felt a quiet peace settle upon me along with a fresh confidence. I began again to chisel and found myself working the stone with greater skill and ease than I had known before. Yakum sat quietly and watched, a small piece of the marble tumbling in his hand. When I had finished and brushed away the dust, he smiled a friendly smile.

"You have great talent with the stone for one so young. It's no wonder Toss trusts you with the arches."

"Thank you," I replied, sheepishly.

With these formalities completed, we began to work together in earnest. Fitting the keystone is never an easy task and the two of us toiled the rest of the day fortifying the two arch sections, fitting the finished piece and beginning the detail work on the

now self-supporting structure. My initial unease at meeting Yakum was slowly resolved. As we worked side by side, I began to
forget the strange transformation I had witnessed just the day
before, and I gained a different kind of respect for this man.

Yakum, without a question, was a high master of stone craft.
I watched as he wielded each tool as if it were an extension of
his own graceful fingers. I had always admired the great skill of
Toss; few could match him for technical workmanship. Nevertheless, as I watched Yakum, I knew I was witnessing an entirely
new level of stone working skill. He had clearly passed beyond
technical mastery into a stunning realm of brilliance and artistry. Never had I seen stone appear so alive and malleable. Yakum
could complete in minutes, complex shapes and ornamentation
that would have taken even Toss a full day. He seemed to draw
a deep, intrinsic beauty from the rock, as if he understood its
most intricate and personal structure, and could speak its ageless language coaxing out the loveliness at its core. It was almost
haunting to watch him work his magic in a cloud of sparkling
dust.

In the next days, I occasionally saw Toss standing at a distance, entranced as he watched Yakum work. More than once, I
saw a glimmer of jealousy cross his otherwise hardened features
as he realized no amount of training or effort would ever make
him an artist of Yakum's stature. One could not help but appreciate this humble, hard-working man, who never complained,
and who produced such stunning work. Yakum always treated
Toss with quiet respect, and never overstepped his role as an
underling.

Indeed, Yakum spoke sparingly, but when he did, it was rarely about himself. He had a natural humility and gentleness, and
his words typically involved the encouragement of others. He
was a wonderful teacher, and taught in such a way that I never
felt as if I was being taught. My stone working skill flourished

under his patient mentoring. Another and more profound transformation occurred within me during these months as well, and Yakum was also my teacher here.

Though he often worked in a contemplative silence, Yakum would occasionally speak to me when we worked together on projects. He proved to be a keen observer of human nature, and would speak metaphorically of the truths he had discerned.

One day he and I were working the south wall, precisely fitting the great stone pieces. I was mixing mortar in a large metal vat while he shaped the slabs. He turned his blue eyes my way, considered my work for a moment, and asked, "Pityr, have you ever considered that you and I are much like this wall we build?"

"What?" I said, confused.

"A man is made of two things," he said. "We are blocks and mortar just like this wall. Our strengths, skills, passions, talents, character, hopes, and dreams are stacked upon each other forming a wall of manhood. As with this wall, it is the rich mortar of our faith in Dyos, that determines whether our wall will be strong and lasting or as fragile as a pile of loose stones. It is not the strength of each stone, but the quality of the mortar that makes a man. A man without faith in Dyos is naught but a pile of rocks and sure to tumble."

Though his parable became clear later, it was not then. Yakum often spoke of Dyos in a way that was entirely new to me. To me, Dyos had always been a symbolic figure for nature's unapproachable, sometimes vicious power. I had always heard Dyos spoken of as a distant, elusive god with little apparent regard for his tiny human subjects. If he was there at all, his wrath appeared as variable as the wind. For this reason, faith to me meant fear, and my prayers were directed solely at appeasing Dyos' anger. We all knew him as a Lord of strict rules and severe ceremony. Everyone understood that the Exarchate Consul was his voice and his earthly interpreter. The consul's role was to enforce the laws of Dyos, written long ago, and thereby to ensure his angry eyes were turned from the people of Terras. Obedience, ritual, and sacrifice were our only hope, and the consul ensured these were done appropriately.

I had always felt that if I performed my ritual duties, I would disappear into the mass of humanity that did the same, and I could safely hide from Dyos in my obscurity. Yet, at the same time, I had often seen what appeared to be a random wrath from Dyos, dealt upon the most unlikely of gentle souls, while the viscous and wicked roamed the earth unhindered. I feared Dyos because he was fearsome, unpredictable, and demanding. But beyond that, I thought of him little. Truly, the vulls seemed a more real and tangible threat.

For this reason, I at first could not understand Yakum's words when he spoke of King Dyos in this most unusual way. He described a radically different lord from the one I had been taught about by the consul. Yakum spoke of Dyos in human terms such as *personal, merciful, patient, long-suffering, alive,* and *powerfully loving.* These were words I could not imagine.

I asked Yakum where he got such strange ideas about Dyos.

"Because I know him very well, my friend," he replied simply.

"Were you once trained by the Exarchate?" I asked, not aware of how anyone could learn about Dyos otherwise.

"No," he said with an ironic smile.

"The Exarchate Consul, as well as the people of Terras, have been blinded by the darkness of the defyyl. They no longer see or know Dyos as he really is," he continued.

Again I was confused. Like all people of Terras, I had heard of Malthanos or Mael, Lord of the Defyyl. He was perceived to be the ultimate evil behind the vulls.

"What do you mean 'blinded by the defyyl'?" I asked.

"The defyyl blinds the heart and the eyes to the truth," Yakum explained. "Over the centuries, people have lost the ability and the will to hear the voice of Dyos."

As I grew to know Yakum over the next few months, it became clear that he worshiped his Dyos. I enjoyed these fantastical stories, though somewhere in the back of my mind, I wrestled with their heretical nature. The more I listened, the more I began to fear the potential instability of all I knew. I was puzzled, for so much of what Yakum said during those long months began to make sense to me. It was like opening a magic box of gems and scorpions, dangerous for sure but utterly fascinating. Each day, I couldn't wait to share what I had learned with my two friends. I needed their help and insight to make sense of all I was hearing and seeing. They too struggled to process the strangeness of this man and this Dyos he spoke of.

Part of the reason Yakum's words had such an effect on me was because he lived as he spoke. He talked of loving and serving others in joyful celebration of the King's own love for him, and indeed, I never met a more selfless man. He spoke of the purulence of pride, greed, anger, and selfishness as a disease, ever more consuming. At the same time, never was there a man more humble, selfless, patient, and trusting.

Yakum began to create quite a stir in Duvall, for I was not the only one with whom he shared his unorthodox views. Always distrustful of strangers, the people of Duvall began to talk about Yakum and his foreign views. Rumors began circulating through the community, including many terrible distortions of what I knew to be his beliefs.

Several times over the next two months Yakum created quite a stir at the Evening Festyves—the informal evening gatherings of families to gossip and discuss the issues of the community. On one occasion, Veltross, a baker and the owner of several stalls selling baked goods, started raising complaints. They involved a vagrant Veltross had seen near his stall on several occasions just before several loaves had gone missing. He was convinced that this "wicked and sneaky man" had stolen his bread. Several others murmured at this report, confirming that they too had seen the skeletal man creeping near their stalls as well, clearly intent on thieving some apples or melons. A consensus arose that this evil fellow ought to be found and placed in the locks for a few days to teach him not to "bother the good folks." As usual, several Exarchate Consulors were present in the rear of the room. There, no doubt, to gather the valuable secrets and gossip of the community.

In the midst of this discussion Yakum stood.

"If you would, Veltross, and you others who've been offended, make your settlement with me. I'll cover your loss," he said softly.

The crowd hushed, stunned at Yakum's offer.

A bit perturbed that he had been undercut, the rich baker rose and announced, "It is not the financial loss that concerns us sir, but rather that such rabble runs free in our streets."

Others muttered their agreement.

"The man's name is Ponnis," Yakum said. "He lost his wife to the rasp a few years back, and his little daughter died in a fire that also destroyed his pottery shop in Parthis. He's not been quite right in the head since then, and he has nothing left to live on. The crime we should be discussing, my friends, is how a community so rich in all things—especially bread, could let a man die of hunger without even bothering to learn his name or his story."

The crowd was stunned.

"Dyos loves Ponnis in his brokenness, my friends, and so should we."

Such incidents drew attention to Yakum. One day, Yakum was pulled from the job for a rebuke by two consulors in long purple robes. I could not hear their words, but they were angry, superior, and reproachful. Yakum appeared sad and contemplative as he returned to work

"The people of Duvall and all of Terras are dying," he said, "and the consul treats their illness with more deadly poison." He stopped and said no more for a long time. Then, "Pityr, spit out their defyyl poison, and know Dyos for the king he truly is."

For my part, I remained silent, not knowing how to respond. This man whom I had come to admire so much also filled me with fear. He had challenged everything I knew and had stolen my comfort. The Exarchate had always been the earthly representation of Dyos, and demanded the people's fear, respect, and obedience at the risk of punishment or ostracism. Desmodys, who stood as High Decar of the consul, was a fearsome and powerful man. The consul's judges were the recognized authority. The people of Duvall trusted completely their interpretation and manifestation of Dyos. They alone had protected the people of Terras for generations. They were the last bastions against the dark invaders of the night, rousing battle forces, organizing scouting parties, financing wall construction, and blessing the dead, and Yakum saw them as self-preserving manipulators.

I had certainly witnessed harsh justice at the hands of the consul. Indeed, I had often imagined myself slobbering in the last moment of the dregs, seeking their mercy, and finding only fire. Yes, I feared the consul, as I feared Dyos and Mael and indeed all things supernatural. I had never considered that they might be wrong. With so many years of tradition, ceremony, and scholarship behind them, they seemed so infallible. Who was *I*, a simple stonemason, to recast history?

Yakum challenged me to recognize that Dyos had indeed provided me with a mind—a pretty decent one at that—to contemplate, observe, and judge the world around me. He argued that I should never be satisfied with another person's interpretation of the world, including his own, without my own deep consideration.

One day, as he completed some intricate ornamentation, a delicate pattern of flowers and leaves, I commented on the beauty of his finished product.

He said, "Pityr, why is it that you find beauty in shape, color, form, and texture?"

I remained silent, not knowing how to answer.

"It is because Dyos appreciates beauty. Indeed, he is the creator of it, and he has built this desire for beauty into you. Dyos is the artist of the sunset and the thunderhead, the lily and the northstar. He chose us to delight in his masterpieces with him. No other creatures he made appreciate such things. Tell me, how does the consul explain beauty and tenderness, music and love, joy and mercy? How do these things fit with their concept of Dyos?"

I knew I could not answer, for there was too much truth in what he said.

As spring moved on into summer, I found myself understanding more of Yakum's vision of Dyos. Though I didn't know it then, as my mind was grasping these new revelations, my heart was also being transformed.

Thom, Mryyn, and I spent hours by the campfire discussing Yakum's views, and their growing effect on the Exarchate. On days off, they would come and watch me work. Yakum would delight in their presence and bring them into our discussions. Thom especially seemed able to quickly discern the truths apparent in Yakum's words. In the way of many young people, we were not afraid to challenge authority. This willingness to question, once the idea was placed in our heads, allowed us, for the first time in our lives, to pursue truth. We were free of the routine and habituation that adulthood often brings, and we were full of a young idealism. Had we known then what we know now, we perhaps would have been more careful. Nevertheless, as Yakum's troubles with the consul began to mount, we found our hearts beginning to soar with new ideas and a powerful new perspective on life.

Chaptyr 3

Something that occurred that fateful summer brought all this tension to a head. At the age of eighteen, and now well trained in basic battle technique and skilled at riding, my time had come to face the vulls with the other men of Duvall. Like most young men at that point in their lives, I was filled with a strange mixture of pride and terror at the thought of going to battle. Up to that point, I had never personally seen a vull, and had only heard the horror stories of my returning brothers, and seen the torn remains of many soldiers as they were borne back to town. Nonetheless, my childhood dreams had been filled with their tusked snouts and horrid screams and the terrible yellow eyes of the cy'daal riders, mouths dripping dreg poison. Like any person about to confront their greatest horrors and their darkest nightmares, I was numb with fear. But strangely I was also proud that my father had considered me ready and that my time had come to be a man.

So it was with an anxious heart that I rode out through the north gate, one cloudy summer evening between my father and brother Samuyl. Shortly after starise, a scout from Bricker's Knoll, with horse afroth and nearly dead, rode into town. He had spotted a large horde of vulls across the river coming rapidly south. He reported three cy'daal riders at the lead. The alarm spread quickly through the town, and within minutes two regiments were mounted and ready to leave, my father's blue corps among them. Since this was my first time in battle, my role was to be primarily observant. I was to stay well in the rear and well protected. Many novices froze or fainted the first time they witnessed a vull horde. For this reason, novices were not called to fight in the first few battles they attended.

As we crested a hill just north of town, I was able to see the whole regiment, torches aloft, below me, and my pulse quickened as I thought of what lay ahead. Samuyl, already having gained repute as a fierce and powerful fighter, rode to my right. My father, wearing the blue cape of a corps commander over his dark mail, had moved ahead to take the command position. We rode through the eastern edge of the Great Forest, the soft-packed earth deadening the sounds of two hundred men on horse, and turning it into a low rumble. As we raced to flank the vulls and meet them at the river crossing, we were forced to travel a winding and circuitous route. At one point, we were riding three-abreast through a narrow valley, flanked on each side by low rock cliffs and knotted dwarf trees. The long serpentine line of torches wound into the distance, its head just entering the great, flat plain at the edge of the river where the battle would be fought. In that moment, violence struck.

Suddenly, from each side, a screaming roar arose. From the rocky walls great black shapes hurtled down upon us. We had been ambushed at the moment of least defense. I heard a horrible crunch, as my brother was swept from his horse by a seething mass of hair, black hide, and vicious yellow teeth. For the first time, I saw a vull face to face. It crouched on four thick legs, not more than two feet from my horse, hunched over the crumpled and unconscious form of my brother as if protecting its private feast. Its dead red eyes reflected the light of my torch. Its ragged, razor teeth dripped a frothy, yellow slime. Its vicious flat snout puffed pungent steam into the midnight air. In that moment, it screamed the unnatural cry of a dying baby, and I found myself unable to breathe. So fierce was the evil of this beast, and so black was its cry that my body went numb and my mind went blank. This creature was a grotesque mix of bear, rat, and man—an abomination of nature. Two long, dark orange horns crowned its horrific brow, and they dripped with my brother's blood.

All around us a fierce battle raged, but I was caught in a bubble of solitude, horrible focus, and strange quiet. In a moment, this darkest of beasts lifted its barren eyes and peered at me. It saw my helplessness, knew my heart was frozen, and knew my child's soul was dying. With an indifferent guttural scream, it laughed at me, delighted at my meekness. Then it bowed its head and sunk its vile jaws into my brother's shoulder.

Though the chaos of the ambush raged around me, in that moment, I was all alone. Then from the deepest depths of my soul came a spark. At that time I understood nothing of what this was, nor did I have time to think about what was happening. This spark became a focused blue flame that defrosted my paralysis. It brought me fiercely alive. With all of my strength, I swung the torch I held in a blazing arc upon that unnatural beast. I felt the impact upon its bowed skull, and the crunch of black bone, and finally the give of death. The vull crumpled to the ground beside my dying brother. Its oily black fur burst into flames, its claws clenched in seizures of death, and its mouth regurgitated slime and blood and fell into a black silence. I felt the dampness of the grass against my cheek and then nothing.

I awoke in my own bed unscathed, a damp cloth on my forehead. My mother was across the room tending my brother by candlelight. He was torn and feverish, vull poison coursing in his blood from the vicious bite to his shoulder and two horn punctures. Occasionally he would mutter or groan incoherently, and froth would collect at the edge of his mouth. My mother would carefully wipe it away. She was crying silently.

My father lay asleep in an exhausted heap on the floor, his robe beneath his head, a woolen blanket wrapped loosely around him. He was covered with scratches and blood, but appeared unhurt. He slept the sleep of a wrecked man.

I remember feeling strangely warm at that moment. It was not the sickly heat of a fever, but a richer warmth of something forever changed. I was not at all afraid, but rather felt numb and quiet. I remembered the tiny, blue flame that had burned for a moment inside me, and I fell asleep again.

I awoke again at midday, my father at my side. Over the next few hours, I heard the story of the night. We had suffered terribly. Five townsmen were dead, and my brother too would soon die. Never before had the vulls been so clever and strategic in their moves. The ambush had been a complete surprise and a deadly trap. The two regiments, which had ridden out late and arrived after the fighting had begun, had been able to outflank the vulls, but even so, it was only our superior numbers that had saved us. My father told me that I had become the rallying point for killing a huge vull as a novice. I had been struck in the head by the butt of a lance and had fallen from my horse. My horse had been killed and partially buried me in the mud as it fell. In the aftermath of the battle, my father had found me. For a time, the poor frantic man thought he had lost two sons.

There was nothing to do for Samuyl. His blood loss had been

great, but worse yet, the vile bite had become infected. Yellow-green foul-smelling pus seeped from the wound. Its edges were turning black, and his entire right arm was hugely swollen and purple. He had not regained consciousness. His lower chest had two symmetrical puncture wounds from the sharp vull horns, which had struck him there. One had likely pierced a lung, for his breathing was raspy and deep, and he would occasionally cough up blood and froth. His body was otherwise unmarked, pale, and covered in sweat. I could not believe that this was my brave and vital older brother who had ridden at my side as a protector the night before.

As strange as it may seem, my father sent me back to work with Toss that same day. I could not understand it at the time. Part of me wanted to be at my brother's side until he died, but I later came to realize that my father understood me better than I did myself. He knew how overwhelmed I was and how desperately I needed to return to a routine. In a single night, my childhood had been blown away, replaced by a shocking adulthood I was not yet ready for. He promised to call if my brother's condition deteriorated, and he promised that I could be at the consul death blessing that afternoon.

The handling of stone that day did bring me back from the terrible depths of my nightmare. Stonework is routine and paced. The beat of the hammer against the marble, steady and rhythmic, calmed my tortured soul. Yakum worked at my side. In silence, and with an expression of compassion, he listened as I related the night's horrors. He had not been at the fight for he had not yet been issued a warhorse and armor since his arrival. Nonetheless, it was clear from his knowing expression, that he was no stranger to battle and had witnessed much suffering.

It occurred to me at that point that though I had been working with him for almost two months, I had never inquired about his past, and his sudden arrival in Duvall, nor had he brought up the subject himself in all our discussions. When I was done relating my story, he placed his coarse hands on my shoulders and reminded me that though I was prepared to accept my brother's death as inevitable, I must remember that Dyos was in control and would be the one to decide my brother's fate. In truth, this was little consolation to me as I had seen the gravity of my brother's wounds and had smelled the purulence of his infection.

When the town bells struck four, and I had not yet received notice of my brother's death, I set aside my tools and prepared to go home. In an hour, my brother would be blessed for death by the consul, a rite reserved for the terminally ill. I had witnessed two such rites before for both my father's parents. The ritual was long and solemn, and brought formality to death. Yakum saw me collecting my tools, and asked if he could accompany me home to offer his respects.

Though I had come to consider this man a great friend and had tremendous respect for him, I felt a moment's panic at his request. Yakum had earned a reputation among the townsfolk with his strange views of Dyos, and in the process he had angered the Exarchate. On several occasions, he had confronted consul members who were publicly teaching what he considered lies and hypocrisies. As consulors were not used to having their authority challenged, this created quite a stir. Twice now, Yakum had been censored by the consul judges for "proclaiming heresies" and "inciting anarchy." The second censure had earned him a day in the locks, which he spent in absolute silence, his head bowed in prayer. This earned him a grudging respect from many, for the locks twisted the body in unnatural ways and the pain was intense. Townspeople now quietly debated his teachings, much to the chagrin of the consul. Throughout it all, Yakum had remained humble and gentle, but true to his convictions.

So, needless to say, Yakum's request gave me a moment of trepidation. I envisioned an argument erupting at my brother's deathbed, which would have been a disaster. In the end, my respect for Yakum won over my anxieties. Perhaps there was even within me a desire to see the consul challenged. At that point, I had not yet admitted to myself that Yakum's vision of Dyos was slowly becoming my own. And so it was with a heavy heart and mixed emotions that I walked the half mile to my house that afternoon with Yakum at my side.

We arrived at the house to the sound of wailing, and I knew my brother had just died. It is impossible to describe how my heart broke in that moment. Up until that time, a part of me had believed somehow my brother might pull through. I had begun to believe that Dyos was listening to my tearful prayers, and that perhaps he actually cared about my brother's sufferings. At the moment I heard his wailing, my childish faith dissolved. Yakum also knew this fateful sound, and I saw him watch me with open gentleness as the reality of the situation became apparent. He put his hands on my shoulder as I began to cry. I noticed that he shed quiet tears for my pain, and I knew in that moment how much he truly cared for me. It was he that finally encouraged me to enter the house.

The people of Duvall had never been shy about showing emotion, and few things are more tragic than the loss of a young life in such a horrid way. Many of my parents' friends, neighbors, and relations had gathered to comfort them, and the house was filled with wailing women and men in solemn huddles. My parents each looked worn and heartbroken. My mother was weeping. A few of the women were wailing in the ritualistic manner expected of the women of Duvall. I had always hated that sound, and tonight it made me feel sick. I was the youngest one present. As a child I had always snuck away from such events, but now I was expected to be a man and share in the ritualistic grief. My older sister and her husband stood in one corner, his broad shoulders clothed in homespun were wet from her tears. People stood in clusters, huddled against the reality of death.

Off through the cooking area, I could see where my brother lay, surrounded by a hundred burning candles. Two Nuys women in their dark red gowns were placing flower garlands around Samuyl's quiet head in final preparation for the burial, which would come after the ritual of death was complete.

Just to the left of my father stood Desmodys, the Chief Exarchate, and two elders. The candlelight sparked off the gold edging of Desmodys' purple robe. The black swath signifying death hung across his shoulders. His head was bowed as he spoke to the elder at his side. Desmodys stood a head taller than everyone in the room, except perhaps Collas, the lanky tailor. His wide shoulders, thick neck, and square face gave him an aura of power. Long black hair, a short, cropped beard, dark seductive eyes, and a hard mouth with perfect teeth, made him darkly handsome. Though there were many important men in that room, there were none who commanded respect, and inspired fear like this man—the earthly mind and fist of Dyos.

As we walked fully into the room, Desmodys noticed our entrance. The grim and almost fierce attention he paid sent chills across my skin and made me want to shrink until I disappeared. I had always felt a terrible fear in the presence of Desmodys, but never so much before that moment, had I felt the dread of his personal attention. I did not like it. I had feared him because, like the Dyos, I had known he was fearsome, powerful, and often harsh, but now I felt something entirely new. I instinctively felt his wickedness. This revelation hit me with such unexpected suddenness, and so blind-sided my sensibilities that I almost crumpled under its weight. Where did such a feeling arise after so many years of obedient, blind respect?

It was in that moment that I truly began to realize that Yakum's words over the months had irrevocably changed me. I was no longer the naïve young man I had been. I had begun to see Desmodys as a manipulator and a hypocrite without knowing it, and tonight, as I looked into his eyes, it was as if I saw the beast unmasked for the first time. He had always hidden within the camouflage of his royal robes and noble carriage, and my youthful mind had never cared to look deeper. Yakum had changed that. I felt enormously uncomfortable in his presence.

I began to realize that though he had noticed me, his gaze was focused over my left shoulder where Yakum stood. I let my eyes slide surreptitiously to the side and saw Yakum returning the stare with fiery intensity. I also saw something I had never witnessed in Yakum before: unbridled anger. The two men stood this way for another moment, and then Desmodys, with a barely perceptible nod and a coldly seductive smile, broke the tension and averted his gaze.

In that same moment, my father noticed me for the first time and he signaled for me to come to him. As I watched this hard and simple man fight to hold back his brimming tears, I could not contain my own emotions. I ran into his firm embrace, openly weeping. My father had rarely shown me affection as a child, but this embrace was as gentle and as full of love as any I had ever had from my mother. He knew the dark visions that haunted me even now.

After him, a sea of relatives, neighbors, and weeping women engulfed me. They all had heard the story of that dark night and wanted to share their pride in my heroism and their sincere sadness. As I stood there accepting their kind words, it occurred to me that in the end, my heroics had achieved little, for my brother lay still, surrounded by candles. I felt weak, tired, and sick. I prayed to Dyos for the strength to make it through the rest of the night.

The two elders called the people to solemn order for the ceremony of death. Desmodys stepped onto a low platform brought for the occasion. All eyes were upon him. The sound of wailing died at his raised hand. In the moment before he spoke, I could hear sniffling; the shuffling of heavily booted feet, and the rustle of clothing. I had lost Yakum. He no longer stood at my side.

Desmodys' deep voice, impossibly smooth and strong, woke me from a quiet reverie. "In the eyes of Dyos," he started, "we are all dust."

And the people replied in synchrony, "We are all dust in the eyes of Dyos."

"To dust we return."

"To dust we return," they repeated.

"No one can turn back the hand of Dyos," said Desmodys.

"We cannot hold it back," agreed the people.

"Dyos has taken as he pleases, and reaped as he will. Praise Dyos."

"Praise Dyos!" the solemn cry arose.

So began the ritual of death. I fell into its rote pattern, but my mind was numb and cold. It was a dark and empty ceremony reminding all of the invariable hopelessness of death. As I listened to the meaningless chanting, my heart grew dim, and my mind slipped away into the mist of exhaustion. Soon I would fall asleep. I wanted to just escape into the cool night air and run from that horrible experience.

Suddenly, the chanting stopped. The whole ceremony typically took over an hour; surely, it had only been minutes. I looked up. Desmodys stood silently on the platform. He stared with a fierce, black gaze over the heads of the people to the back of the room. I heard a gasp, and then another and turned to see the source of surprise.

For a moment, my mind could make no sense of what I saw, for it was impossible. There stood Samuyl, my dead brother, with Yakum at his side. Though clearly confused, Samuyl was very much alive, and from what I could see, unscathed. He appeared as strong and healthy as the moment we rode out of town together. He wore the plain grey robes of death and a few flower petals still clung to his shoulders and hung tangled in his hair. His skin had a healthy tan without the myriad cuts and deep bruises I had seen that morning. His chest was free of blood and infection, and he breathed with casual ease.

I heard at least two bodies tumble to the floor in pure faint. My mother cried out and rushed forward to embrace her son. He returned her embrace with intensity and vigor.

Yakum stepped forward, lifted his hands to the sky and announced with authority, "Today, Dyos chooses not to reap, but to sow his mercy. Praise Dyos!"

With these words, I felt the walls tremble and the air seemed filled with blue light. An unspeakable power passed through me and shook my bones. I thought I might die from its piercing. Then, just as quickly, it passed.

Yakum bowed his head, turned, and walked out the door into the darkness.

CHAPTYR 4

The room exploded with noise. I saw two elders slip from the room in pursuit of Yakum. From the corner of my eye, I caught a sweep of purple robes as Desmodys left in a barely concealed rage, an angry hiss on his tongue. People rushed toward Samuyl, touched him, and felt the miracle for themselves. Samuyl began to weep, clearly confused and overwhelmed by all the attention and commotion. Relatives thrust questions at him faster than he could answer. It quicky became clear that he remembered nothing after riding out of town that dark night, until he awoke surrounded by candles and the morbid chants of the ceremony of death. My mother was weeping uncontrollably, gasping for breath, and clinging to his side, unable to handle the cascade of emotion. My father supported her, swaying a bit himself.

I can hardly say how I felt at that time, for it was pure emotional overload. A loud rushing filled my ears. I felt my heart pounding in my chest, but it was strangely distant. It seemed as if I were a sleepwalker, waking from a somnolent journey to find myself somewhere totally unexpected. Colors and sounds seemed somehow out of place, the air was liquid-thick and strangely opaque. Several times I thought I was fainting, but I somehow kept my feet. Clearly we had all witnessed a miracle, I was acutely aware of the bigger forces at play in the room that night. I had never felt such power before, in fact I had never even been aware that such power existed, but I had seen it and I knew what it was. I had witnessed a raging spiritual flood. I had felt the flows of power and was left deeply transformed. It was as if a gaping rift in reality had opened before me for a moment, exposing a frightening endless world that existed just alongside my own. As Yakum left the room the rift had abruptly closed again

I was reeling in the aftershocks. I was intrigued and horrified with my new awareness, not at all sure what it meant. I had very little concept of what was happening to my world and only understood that it was forever changing and that Yakum stood at the center of this transformation.

I never found sleep that night. Duvall was abuzz with feverish speculation. Rumor, gossip, and fantastical stories spread through town. Everywhere pockets of people gathered to tell again their ever-changing perspectives on the story. It is in times like these that ignorance, fear, and bigotry—which live normally in the undercurrent of every society—are suddenly loosed and run free in the dark of the night, infecting all with their pestilence.

I overheard so many versions of the night's miraculous events that I began to question what I myself had witnessed. Yakum was variously described as a saint, a demon, a magician, a warlock, an illusionist, a conman, and a heretic. No one could deny that something remarkable and mysterious had occurred, for many had seen my brother bleeding and dying the night he was carried back into town. Now they saw him without blemish or disease, strong and healthy. But in the way of people everywhere, when confronted with the incomprehensible, they responded with fear. And when the evil brew of fear and ignorance is given time to ferment, the results can be deadly.

The Exarchate Consul, for its part, remained officially silent, noting only that it was investigating the events of the night. Many elders however, spoke privately of dark magic and deception designed to draw the people away from their true religion. Unfortunately, my brother was unable to give further insight into the miracle as his memory of the night never returned. Some even looked at him with suspicion as if he were a co-conspirator in some evil plan.

Yakum could not be found anywhere. After walking from the room, he had disappeared. None of the Red Guard had opened the gates that night for anyone leaving town, and certainly anyone crazy enough to walk the lands beyond the walls at night would have been remembered. Nor could Yakum be found within the town, despite an exhaustive search by the Red Guard. He was wanted for questioning.

Desmodys had been publicly humiliated and was furious. For two days afterwards he was often seen racing from point to point in the town on his great jet-black stallion, eyes like raging fire.

For my part, I once again became rooted in reality. I did not deny what I had witnessed and experienced, but somehow time allowed me breathing room and the ability to sort through all that had changed. Thom and Mryyn were very much a part of all this as well. They had been present that night and had unusual insight into all that had happened. We had, over the years, become like one extended mind and knew each other to the core. They immediately comprehended my struggle, for they shared it too. Together, we were committed to pursuing the truth no matter what the cost.

The events were clear in my mind. My brother had been miraculously healed by Yakum and he had claimed Dyos and no other, as the source of this miracle. He had not sought glory for himself, but given it all to Dyos. I had felt the awesome power of a spiritual presence in the room, and somehow the raging battle of good and evil. I had known Yakum for months now and had never witnessed in him a hint of pride or wickedness. The power I had felt that night was different, only in degrees from the power that came from his unwavering faith in Dyos every day. The mystery of Yakum grew with every passing day.

It seemed that we were almost alone in our growing convictions. My parents were not critical, just bemused. The whole town, however, seemed ready to attack what they did not understand. Only Toss vocally defended the man he had watched for months and whose words he had surreptitiously considered. He had come to respect the integrity and artistry of Yakum, and could not believe that the humble man harbored dark intentions. He was not afraid of public sentiment and spoke openly of the good he had witnessed in Yakum.

Over the next dozen days, the town slowly began to return to normal and the search for Yakum stopped. Somehow, he was gone.

About a week before the Orange Moon Festival, a jibe named Dart arrived from Parthis with his contingent of jugglers, mimes, acrobats, and stuntmen. At that time, Duvall was not large enough to sustain a full-time circus, and only at festivals could we enjoy visiting shows. Dart was a tall and strikingly skinny fellow shaped like a coiled spring of muscle. In the way of the best jibes, his speech was entrancing, and even the most simple of stories became a fascinating tale. This strange man, with a face that could contort into a thousand distinct characters, brought news that unfortunately fed the fire of Yakum's mystery.

Dart told how a stonemason calling himself Yakum, had been chased from Parthis—a small town on the south coast months ago by angry crowds. Apparently, this man had infuriated the local consul by calling himself "Dyos'Lei," the mysterious Sylver King foretold in the oldest writings of the consul. According to legend, this Dyos'Lei would come filled with the power of Dyos himself to destroy the power of the defyyl. Some Exarchate scholars expected Dyos'Lei to be some great warrior wizard who would rise to fame crushing the armies of Mael. These days, however, most scholars imagined him as a symbolic figure only—a myth told to schoolchildren. I had no idea how Yakum fit that role.

In Parthis as well, the people spoke of mysterious healings, fire from the sky, and storms in a drought-stricken land. The infamy of Yakum grew with every word. He became a much larger figure, and the people's fear of him grew. I prayed silently that wherever he was, Yakum would be safe from the brewing public sentiment. Even as I prayed this prayer, I sensed that Yakum was safe and not that far away. It wasn't even a thought, but rather an undercurrent in my heart—a certainty that my journey with Yakum had only just begun. Nonetheless, for now, despite the new and mysterious news, life seemed to quietly return to normal.

It was with the great mystery of Yakum slowly fading from memory, that Duvall celebrated the last full moon of summer. Ever since I was a child I had always looked forward to the Orange Moon Festival with eagerness. For three days, culminating in the full moon, the people of Duvall enjoyed the fruits of a summer's hard work, for a moment laying down the spade and sickle to delight in the bounty of the harvest.

Wonderful musicians from all over Terras delighted the

crowds almost continuously. Singing and laughter filled the air. Children played games of Wicket, Horse and Hoof, and Bag-the-Lamb, while adults competed in games of skill, horsemanship, and bowmanship. Contortionists and acrobats performed stunning displays of human agility and jibes entranced the public with fantastical stories of kings and maidens, fairies, serpents, giant sea monsters, and gorgons.

Dart was a master. For three successive nights, crowds of hundreds hung on his every word as his magical tales carried us all away to other times and distant lands. With the ministrations of his body, contortions of his face, a mustache here, and a hat there, he became the very characters he described. The audience screamed at the horrible villains, cried openly with the brokenhearted lover, and laughed hysterically at the bumbling fool, all within minutes as Dart wove his wondrous tales.

He spoke no more of Yakum, sensing perhaps that the people needed release from their real troubles. For my part, I longed to probe his memory and hear every word spoken about my mysterious friend. No fantasy or concocted story, no matter how fascinating, held more meaning for me at that point in my life than Yakum's. I hungered for resolution and answers, and yet I knew somewhere deep inside that Dart did not have any to give. And so I kept my mouth shut and listened instead to his contrived stories.

At that time, so much of Terras was unexplored and even unknown; its landscapes and strange creatures existed mostly as myths in the minds of the jibes. The vast western Grasslands, the Icicle Seas, the Seer Mountains, and of course, the unknown spaces beyond the Breach Cliffs and Haules Gate Temple, though real places, had always been the stuff of children's fairytales. We were not a traveling people. Far too many adventures existed in our own little corner of the world for us to seek them elsewhere. And of course there were always the vulls, roaming the darkness and keeping us safely at home. Most of us had not even traveled to Cos or Minas—just over the hills and only, perhaps, a dozen of us to Parthis. Only Desmodys had traveled extensively, even as far as Kasakar. He was gone often for months at a time. The rest of us were homebodies, satisfied with our small place in this world. For now, we were content to travel vicariously through the tales of the jibes, who always brought us back home safely.

That year, my nineteenth, the excitement as the town prepared for the festival was more urgent than normal, as if the people sensed a distant storm beyond the horizon. If one stopped for a moment in the midst of the chaos and motion and turned one's ears beyond the laughter and singing, one could almost hear its low rumble. I felt giddiness and a subtle anxiety even as I enjoyed the start of the festivities.

Nevertheless, like most people, I shoved the nagging unease deep into my subconscious and set my heart on having fun. Thom, Mryyn, and I reveled in our freedom and dove head first into the great celebration.

On the last evening of the festival, as if by magic, a great orange moon rose above the dark trees. Several large bonfires illuminated the celebrants. Delicious smells of roasting mutton, hot corn cakes, and mulled pear cider filled the cool evening air and made even our treat-filled stomachs growl. A few yellow and brown leaves, the first to fall, spun in twisting whirlwinds in the open fields where the games continued. Piles of early pumpkins sat waiting for the pumpkin roll, near the bales of drying hay that had been auctioned off earlier.

As the band began to play, Thom asked if he could borrow a pence to play Kings with a group of young men nearby. He gave me a barely perceptible wink as he said this. As usual, he had forgotten his coin sack. I noticed, as I caught the meaning of his wink, that he had a long purple streak along one cheek, a remnant of the blueberry tart he had just consumed. I smiled, and for a moment reflected on the strange juxtaposition of manly form, genius mind, and childlike playfulness that was my friend. I did not begrudge yielding my last pence, as I knew his strategic mind and card-playing mastery would generate many more at the card table that night. He trundled off, anticipating the challenge.

Mryyn and I sat side by side enjoying the night and the celebration around us. She was silent, but the small smile on her full lips told me that she enjoyed having the moment alone with me. After a while, she asked me to dance.

The band was lively and full of rhythm. Some of the instruments were foreign to me. Our fellow dancers were full of brewed cider and were caught up in the mood. We danced several fast tunes consisting of many low jumps, twirls, and spins. With her usual agile grace, Mryyn led me through a twisting, complex pattern of footwork. We ended with a rapid rhythmic cascade of steps that left us both breathless and hot. The next dance was slow and melodious, just two wind instruments playing to the beautiful night. I led now, Mryyn's body barely touching mine. In the firelight, I could see her brown eyes sparkle; her thick and very long lashes were up-tilted. Tiny beads of perspiration had collected just above her lip. Her high-boned cheeks were flushed. I touched her soft chestnut curls. They smelled of lavender soap. My heart beat like a drum in my chest.

It had been almost three years since that fateful day in the grasslands, that I had first noticed Mryyn's beauty. Even as our friendship had continued to grow, I had felt new stirrings within me. I was falling slowly and hopelessly in love with Mryyn. She was quite aware of my growing affections, and would tell me years later that she had known from the moment we met, that we were fated for each other. She did not shy away from what she knew to be good and true. Thom knew as well, and seemed to delight in seeing his two best friends fall in love. I suppose it could have been an awkward strain to our threesome, but somehow it all seemed healthy, honest, and good. Mryyn was first and foremost my friend and would always remain as such.

That night as we danced, I felt the blooming of our love. I pulled Mryyn a bit closer until our bodies touched. I could feel the firmness of her full curves and the rise and fall of her chest. I ached with joy at having her so close. Her neck glistened with cool sweat. I could see her pulse beating heavily in one of its fire-lit curves. I dared not look into her eyes, those beautiful honest eyes, for fear my heart would burst with passion. But then I couldn't resist, and found warmth, laughter, gentleness, and yes, love. She turned her face upwards and opened her mouth just slightly. Her breath was fresh. We kissed gently. It was our first. I felt her tremble. Her mouth tasted like sweet cider, salty sweat, and warm smiles. We kissed again, this time longer and then for a long time afterward, we just held each other.

"How I've waited," she said with a playful, thankful smile full of love.

We danced, barely moving, until the music stopped. The great moon was turning pale as it rose. I felt like screaming with joy. I could just hold her like that forever.

And then I heard the bell toll in the cool night.

Oh, how I hated that sound, how it shattered my joy. The clanging alarm echoed off the hills that very moment of all moments. How painful to pull away from that warm embrace, from my newfound love, to be called to war and maybe death. The people of Duvall knew that dreaded call to battle arms. Once again that night, they would send their husbands and sons and brothers off to possibly die. The vulls were on the run.

Chaptyr 5

Controlled chaos ensued. I turned to head for the stables, furious at the injustice. Mryyn grabbed and kissed me fiercely and passionately.

"I love you," she said, and looked down, "and I know you love me. Come home."

"You make sure that you're there to welcome me," I replied with a small smile.

I knew Mryyn would have joined us for the pursuit if she had been permitted. "I promise," she said and pushed me on my way. I soon caught up with Thom and we raced to the stables through the crowd.

The horses were lined up and ready when we arrived. Three stable hands were always on duty and charged with preparing them for battle within moments of an alarm. Hundreds of torches were hastily lit and passed around. We quickly mounted, and as the harsh bell tolled on in the night, the five corps formed and the march began. We passed through the great western stone gates five abreast. The huge warhorses were hungry for the battle. In truth, now we were all in a mood for a fight that night. It was rare for the people of Duvall to take the time to celebrate and dance, and we were all angry at the interruption of our moment's peace. My own bitterness was especially strong. I achingly recalled the feel of her against me as I rode off into the night. Her kiss still tingled on my lips. The light scent of lavender hung in my memory.

Thom rode beside me that night. He had seen only a few more battles than I, but had already gained a reputation as a fierce fighter of exceptional strength. This was the first time we had ridden into battle together. He wore a great broadsword strapped to his side, which he and Karpp Poston had forged together as a lesson in steelwork. I had tried it once, and could barely lift it, but Thom wielded it as adeptly as I did my short sword. Every time he looked at me as we crossed the grasslands, he laughed out loud at my love-struck expression. I slapped him on the back of his head to still his teasing, and he laughed even louder. My hand stung. As usual, his mood was contagious. I finally saw the hilarity of my love-dazed demeanor and yielded to the laughter.

We rode almost due west toward the foothills. The now white moon lay at our backs and cast long tangled shadows across the dewy fields ahead of us. I could just see the distant torches of the advance regiment, which raced ahead to uncover any ambushes and to set the battlefield. We had learned our lesson well; never again would we presume that we had strategic superiority. We had paid all too dearly for our mistake months before.

Tonight, the scout teams had spotted three vull hordes on the eastern rim of the Great Woods, near Blue Lake. They were heading toward Duvall. If everything worked as planned, we would meet them in the foothills in open battle lines. Our archers were most valuable in open formation. We raced at a full gallop now to make our goal.

One would have guessed that after my experience at the ambush, my fear of the vulls would have intensified, but as I rode into battle that night, I felt different. The fear was still there—anyone would be a fool not to fear the vulls—but it no longer immobilized me. Instead, I felt energized. I had faced my worst childhood nightmares, and in a sense, had conquered them. Although, the vulls were more dangerous in reality than in my fantasies, they were finally real to me, and I could somehow handle that better. I remembered words Yakum had once told me as we worked the stone. "Pityr," he had said, "almost all of the power that darkness holds over us exists only in our minds and our fears. If we confront our enemy and unmask him, a good part of our battle has already been won."

That night, as I felt my confidence growing, I knew this was true. How I wanted to crush this evil that haunted the night, destroyed families, and drove men to madness.

The vulls were just the surface of the vast evil that sought constantly to consume us all. How truly helpless and lost we were against Mael without Dyos behind and before us. What a simple fool I was. That night, such insights were as yet far off, and I rode to the battlefield convinced that with enough determination, we would someday wipe these beasts from Terras.

Far ahead, the very alive Samuyl rode at my father's side in a position of honor. He bore the blue corps flag, three blue seven-sided stars against a field of white, which danced gloriously in the torchlight. Our gallop slowed just slightly as we approached the Wind River. The sound of two hundred war horses rumbled in the night. The creak of saddle leather and the clang of metal on metal lent a musical melody to the deep rhythm. I looked up and saw a few high clouds lit by the moon, but the night was otherwise clear and getting colder. It would be a good night for war.

We crossed the shallow river in a shower of mud and cool water that made the horses steam. At last, we crested a hill, and saw below us the battlefield. It was a wide grassy field bordered on both sides by tall and dense woods, which prevented a flanking attack. The advance guard had drawn the battle line here. A line of torches illuminated the field. Just as we arrived, a river of black shapes crested the far hill and poured down upon the plain in a putrid, evil flood. Snarling and unnaturally high-pitched screams abruptly filled the night. I caught the scent of feces, gangrene, and rotten meat carried on the light wind. The black forces formed a ragged line roughly paralleling our own about two hundred paces off. They hissed at the torches, abhorring the light. I felt my hatred and dread swell, but tonight it set fire to my limbs and gave me strength.

As the last horses arrived, we fell into ordered formation. The bowman formed a straight line in the front and awaited command from above. Silence fell on the battlefield. The two armies faced each other across a gulf of hatred. I could literally feel the evil of the vulls and their hunger to devour all that is good, and my courage grew.

"Pull!" the command broke the silence, and the bowmen crouched, raised their arrows toward the enemy, and pulled their strings taut in anticipation of the command to fire. The tension was as palpable as the tightly-stretched bows. The battle was set to begin.

Suddenly, a deafening explosion rocked the night. A blinding bolt of lightning struck the field between the two lines. Its wall of power slammed into me and almost knocked me from my horse. For a moment, I could not find my breath. My eyes were blinded by the brilliance and I saw only spots. As my night vision slowly returned, I saw a large circle of blackened earth ringed by lightly burning grass. No one spoke. No sound came from across the plain. All were stunned by the force of the blast, and helpless to explain its sudden appearance in the cold, cloudless, moonlit night.

Soon however, all eyes turned to the woods at the northern edge of the field. From its dark depths, stepped a huge white stallion. On his high back sat a king robed in brilliant ethereal gold. Somehow I knew this majestic figure was a king, and it was obvious to all. Upon his grand horse he seemed ten feet tall. He was broad-shouldered, and his head was crowned with jewels and what appeared to be a ribbon of silver fire, which illuminated his majestic figure. A great sword of sparkling blue steel was clasped in his strong hand, which he held aloft. The stars seemed to dance in its metal. As his horse stepped forward, it made no sound.

I saw the vulls cringe and shuffle back with a hiss as he advanced to the center of the field. The majestic figure was both terrifying and awesome. The vile creatures were repulsed. I felt an irresistible power, which made me bow my head in shame, while simultaneously filling every corner of my heart with hope. My horse beneath me trembled and shuffled back a few steps. The night was as brightly lit as the day as the white stallion stepped into the ring of fire.

In that moment, I knew who stood before me: it was the fantastically transformed horseman Mryyn, Thom, and I had seen so many months before while hunting mushrooms. Thom, I knew, also made the connection, for I heard him draw in a sudden breath beside me. It was unmistakably Yakum who stood before us bedecked with brilliance and fire—Yakum, the King. My mind reeled at the implication of this.

Helpless to resist the impulses within me, I climbed from my horse, knelt, and bowed my head to the damp grass. I heard Thom step down beside me and do the same. Within moments, every rider great and small had bent his knee before the King. And still, he had not uttered a word. Then, with a voice like thunder, he spoke.

"Dyos'Lei, your King, brings light!" he said.

I felt the ground rumble in reply.

He turned and pointed his glistening sword at the black seething hordes, which likewise seemed strangely bent in humility. It was as if they too recognized the authority of the King.

"Paccas dopo nu va Dyos!" he roared in a grotesque and guttural tongue.

Suddenly, his sword seemed to glow intensely. Within a moment, blue fire burst from its tip, leapt across the night with the speed of lightning, and the front two lines of vulls exploded in flame. They were consumed in a breath. Ashes fell to the earth. The hills rocked. With horrid screams, the remaining vulls fled for their bitter lives, rat-like tails between their legs, their heads bent to the ground. Three cy'daal lay smoldering among the heaps of crisp black flesh. Thunder rolled in the clear night. In the distance, I saw the last of the vulls limping over the crest of the hill, and their screams faded into the night.

Then something truly strange happened.

The day's brilliance slowly faded, and the night settled back upon our bent forms. All became still. I looked up to see Yakum, simple stonemason, sitting head bowed on his ragged palomino. The ring of flames around him burnt themselves out into red coals. Men struggled slowly to their feet, with the creak of leather and the slink of heavy maile. No one spoke for a very long time. The horses shuffled and huffed. Yakum looked up slowly and silently, looking deeply at the men before him. A bold soldier down the line let out a half-hearted victory whoop. Within moments, the entire line broke into open celebration and clapping, still clearly in shock. None knew what to make of the simple man before them. None could explain what they had seen. Within moments, a tide of warriors swept forward and lifted Yakum high into the air.

"Praise the King!" they roared in unison.

Yakum turned his head toward me, stared for what seemed a long time, ending the look with a brief, warm smile. I felt naked before his eyes, as if my very soul had been judged and found wanting. I was filled with shame, deep and painful, but the smile brushed away my grief and filled me with peace. I was shaken by this paradox of emotions. I was lifted up in that very moment, and silently changed. I felt as if another gear had clicked solidly and mysteriously into place in the machinery of my soul. I praised my King.

Yakum was led toward town in slow royal celebration. Though none of it seemed conscious, and no orders rang out in the cold night, all fell into formation. The five-battalion banners were raised in honor before him. The commanders rode in a tight wedge behind him. The advance guards, swords raised, lined the path from the woods' edge to the gates. Messengers were sent far ahead. By the time we crested the last curving hill before Duvall, the crowds had gathered. The townspeople stood on the wall, and on rooftops, and in a great audience to welcome the King. Songs of praise spontaneously lit the air. Above, the now white moon had reached its zenith and shined its reflected glory down upon the scene.

At the gate sat Desmodys atop his great black stallion, surrounded by a dozen Red Guards. At that moment, he appeared far nobler than Yakum. In fact, the juxtaposition was confusing to the people. They knew not what to make of this common man on his old horse, whom they had been told was some new champion. None but the soldiers had seen his miraculous transformation and had felt the awesome electric power as he struck the vulls down. The townspeople continued to cheer, but the celebratory air was mixed with a palpable bewilderment. After all, was this not the very same man hunted for being a heretic just days ago? All eyes were turned toward Desmodys for guidance. The people had long ago learned to follow his lead. Ageless habits reign especially in a society dreadfully uncomfortable with change.

Desmodys stepped his massive beast before the gate and signaled for the train to stop. He and Yakum sat facing each other for a moment. The celebration and the scattered singing ceased. I knew already the depth of animosity between the two men. The town was completely silent, waiting to hear the exchange that would follow.

Desmodys spoke first. "Yakum," he said, "we have been awaiting your return. The consul wishes to discuss the many curious events of the last few weeks with you."

His voice was slyly mocking, and barely hid the restrained anger, which was evident to all near him. There was little respect in his address. This was certainly not a greeting fit for a champion and never for a king. I thought how what a mistake he was making. Any moment I expected Yakum to again miraculously transform, and perhaps rebuke Desmodys for his mocking tone, but he remained silent and common in the moonlight. The crowd was bemused. Even the soldiers, who had seen Yakum in full majesty, did not know how to take these new developments. I think we all felt that a true king would not tolerate such a challenge to his authority. Where had our fierce champion gone?

As Yakum remained silent before this rebuke, I could almost feel the sympathies of the crowd turn at that moment. I was close enough to see Yakum's face in the torchlight. Flashes of blue fire burned within his eyes, his face remained nobly aloft. His jaw was tensely clenched against words that ached to escape. But they did not. And then I saw a slow transformation. The sinewy muscles of his face unbound and an exhausted sigh escaped his lips. His eyes turned skyward and far away and a visible peace settled upon him. He mouthed some words silently to the night sky and closed his eyes. I saw a tear coarse down his cheek. Without a word, he urged his horse forward. He was surrounded instantly by Red Guards who led him quickly off into town. After a long look across the crowd, Desmodys followed in their wake tall, stiff, and dark. I tried to grasp what had just happened, but I could not.

Mryyn met Thom and I with a fierce embrace after we crossed through the gate. Once we had dismounted and rubbed the horses down, she led us to a private corner so we could all talk. We quickly updated her on all the strangeness we had seen that night. We talked late into the night, trying to sort through our confusion. The townspeople were again thrown into turmoil by the peculiar events and the people speculated widely on the implications of all they had witnessed. The soldiers vocally defended Yakum before them, but even they could not make sense of the scene at the gate.

Yakum was taken into the Exarchate Court, a huge, high-pillared building on the north end of the central square, the dominant building of the city. This grey stone mammoth was the private home of the consul. Its outer walls were without windows except for thin slits just below the roofline. Day and night Red Guards stood before the small dark arch, which was its only access. This hard and faceless building housed only the top Exarchate elders. The rest took residence in an adjacent dormitory. Within its thick walls were rumored to be a vast library, scribes' study rooms, and a worship hall. Even the most elite townspeople had never entered this exclusive sanctuary. Before that night, I had always seen the Court as sacred and mysterious—an appropriate dwelling place for the servants of Dyos. However, in those months, thanks to Yakum, my perception of Dyos had changed. To me, He was no longer distant, cold, and exclusive, but real, vibrant, and merciful.

That night I realized for the first time that the imposing and cold structure did not fit my evolving concept of Dyos. I could not imagine how the King of light could inhabit such a dark, heartless space. In the moonlight it looked like a prison of shadows. As Yakum was led into its arched entrance I recalled again the King robed in brilliant splendor that I had seen stepping from the woods that night. I was again struck by the paradox of this man I thought I knew. How could even these high stony walls restrain such power?

For the next two days, no official word came from the Exarchate, and the Court doors remained tightly sealed. Rumors spread among the people. Some reported strange red light, filling the high windows, and reflecting in the night sky over the court. Others noted low rumbles and even audible groans carried on the night air. No one truly knew what was happening, for anyone who ventured within a block of the Court was quickly met with a silent Red Guard and redirected. By the evening of the second day, the city had reached a fever pitch of anticipation. Nothing like the events of the last few months had ever happened in Duvall. To a people comfortable with routine, those times were both exciting and deeply unsettling.

The mood of the skies seemed to mirror the mood of the people. Just before sunset on the third day, a line of black clouds could be seen over the Breach Cliffs to the north. It was the first of the great autumn storms. When the light finally faded, a chilly wet wind swept through town. The wall of clouds followed shortly, snuffing out the moonrise. Clouds of dust and leaves swirled in the street. Even the oldest trees bent under the power of the gale. People rushed to shutter their windows, just as the first thunder rolled in the distance. Within minutes, the night was filled with terrible lightning, pounding hail, and sheets of icy cold rain.

Thom, Mryyn, and I were caught off guard by the abrupt ferociousness of the storm. We sought shelter in the partly finished Stone Hall, my workplace of so many months. Only the central Great Room had been roofed. The east and west wings lay open to the violent sky. Even here, there was no glass yet in the great arched windows, and the rain swept through in swirling torrents. Whipped by the wind and soaked to the core, we proceeded to the back corner of the hall. Once there, I led us into a small room, a narthex really, which had already been completed. This cozy nook had no windows. Its west and north walls had ceiling-high shelves, which would eventually hold books. While we were building, this room had been our storage closet. My tools, which had become so familiar to me over the last years, sat on a high shelf in one corner in a worn leather pouch. On rainy days, we would do detail work in there on large blocks of stone. The room was well stocked with oil and lamps. A hind of dry salted beef hung in the corner. I cut several slices from the tough slab. We sat for a moment listening to the thunder, and chewed the spiced meat. We sat and talked about all we had experienced over the last few weeks, and how our lives were changing so quickly. The lantern cast a flickering glow, which made the shadows seem long and strangely alive. Occasionally, the room would fill with the brilliance of lightening, and the shadows would scatter back to the corners.

What did it all mean? Who was this mysterious man, and why had he come into our lives so suddenly and with such power? Was he truly Dyos'Lei—and if he was, what did that mean for us? Was he a real king for the people—for all of Terras? Not for centuries had the land had a king. Thom knew the legends and history best, but even he would admit he knew little.

In that time, the consul held tight control of all the people's history. Its written record lay "secure" in the great black depths of the Court. It might as well have been as far away as the stars, for the public had no access to it. Most of the history we knew had been pieced together like a puzzle by the jibes and orators of our time. It was dredged from the parallel, but unwritten history of song and tale. No one knew how much myth and poetic license had twisted the truth.

Thom had had a crippled great uncle Mias, who, in his youth had held a low rank in the consul. He had been struck by a runaway cart in town at the age of thirty and lost the use of his legs. At the time, he had been training as a scribe. The injuries were so debilitating that even though he retained a strong mind, the consul passed him over for election to the elders. He was forced to return home to his family for constant care. As a young boy, Thom had heard Mias tell what he knew of the Southlands' history. It was the stories of Dyos'Lei that Thom struggled to recall now. As the night sky poured its violent grief on our little cave, he began:

"Mias had access to only small segments of the great scroll. It dealt with the corruption and fall of Aster Sypiros, one of the great silver-eyed magan of the last age—he who became Mael, lord of the defyyl. These tales described the horrible destruction and defilement of the land, the devastation of the seven kingdoms, and the great final battle that literally tore the land asunder at the Breach. The details though, were sparse.

"Some scrolls, however, seemed to prophesy the coming of a King Dyos'Lei—(translated Light of God), who was like none before. He was described as a king who, by his power, would destroy the power of the defyyl, and set the people free again to serve their God, Dyos. The prophecies, according to Mias, were confusing, however. Sometimes they spoke of a king who was glorious, all-powerful, and who, with a sweep of his hand, could wipe out entire armies of darkness. But other prophecies seemed to describe him as meek, gentle, compassionate, humble, and unremarkable in appearance. It was this paradox that seemed to suggest some

kind of mythic character. Mias suggested that most of his supe-riors and teachers in the consul understood these prophecies as poetic rather than literal.

"As to how this Dyos'Lei would destroy the defyyl, and usher in a new age, the prophecies could only hint. 'A sacrifice of perfect light' was a term found often in these scrolls, but no one appeared to know what they meant. Beyond these very sketchy references to the prophecies of Dyos'Lei, Mias had very little insight."

Thom concluded with this somber note, and for a long time no one spoke. Up until the recent events, most of the people of Terras saw these ancient scrolls as a mix of legend and myth. We too, had always thought of them that way. Dyos'Lei had always represented allegorically the hope of the people for free-dom from the troubles of this world. He had been our banner and source of courage in times of darkness. Few of us had ever assumed that he might be a true king—the promised Son—re-turning to conquer his father's lands after so many long years. And now, here was Yakum, a simple stonemason claiming to be the savior of the people. How could it be? His paradoxical na-ture, simultaneously majestic and humble surely seemed to fit.

Even as these doubts ran through my head, my heart screamed to be heard. It proclaimed that all was well, that some-how, somewhere, Dyos was solidly in control. It announced as well that Yakum, though cloaked in humility, was indeed the great king he claimed to be. My mind could not tell me how it could be, but I knew it was, and reassuringly, so did Thom and Mryyn.

What had Yakum said about Dyos all those months ago? He had claimed that Dyos was a living God, endlessly fight-ing a battle with Mael, for the hearts and souls of his lost peo-ple. Though He had been tilling the soil for years, I had never sensed his hand at work in my life. Nonetheless, He had planted a seed of peculiar love, and tonight, I felt the tiniest seedling burst forth. In its small way, it sprung from the dark earth of my soul, and began its long stretch to the sky. Dyos, who would be its source and life and energy, shined down upon it.

I believed Yakum. I had seen the man live, and I had felt his pain for the people. I also had seen his cloaked majesty revealed on three separate occasions now. Most importantly however, I still felt him even then in the narthex, drawing me evermore gently and forcefully to his side.

Why did he come in common clothes? Why did he not bring the people to their knees with his majesty? These were questions that had no answer for us that night. We knew suddenly though that we were his alone. We prayed that his fire would consume our doubts, and be our guide for the dangerous days ahead. We placed our six hands together in pledge between us. The lightening splintered the darkness, the thunder roared, the rain pounded. We felt the power of history prickling our skin, and Dyos, our Father, sealed our hearts for eternity.

When we released our hands, the power dissolved, and a peaceful exhaustion descended upon us. I leaned my back against the wall. Mryyn fell heavily asleep against my shoulder, contentment draped across her face. In the dancing lamplight I dreamed of myself as a great warrior, cloaked in silver regalia, my sword lifted high, leading the King's armies in battle against the monstrous consuming shadows. Light shone about me, and I felt the energy and passion of a just fight filling my bones. I fell asleep with the rumble of thunder in my ears, like ten thousand horses galloping into war.

CHAPTYR 6

Thom shook me awake. The room was quiet and filled with a dull grey light. I listened but heard no rain. A cool, damp breeze smelling of burnt wood came through the open door. I could see grey clouds reflected in the smooth pools of standing water that now filled the main hall. I kissed Mryyn gently on the forehead, and she opened her long-lashed eyes. She smiled when she saw my face so close to her own. My heart leapt a few beats at the warmth of her good morning smile. I wondered what it would be like to wake up every day next to this beautiful woman before turning away.

We collected our belongings and slogged through the main hall to the street, chewing on dry salt beef. The town was hauntingly quiet. Debris littered the street. The night's storm had torn limbs from trees and clumps of thatch from the rooftops. The clutter lay in small heaps, whipped together by wind and rain.

Huge puddles filled the street. Thousands of feet had created muddy ruts in its center. I wondered why so many had already walked this way so early in the morning. The sky was grey and sodden. Wood smoke trapped beneath the heavy clouds, settled damply on the town. Just then, the distant sound of a crowd reached us over the rooftops. The noise was coming from the square.

Thinking perhaps that Yakum had finally come out to declare his kingship, we slopped through the mud towards the square as quickly as the mud allowed. As we approached, we could see the great crowd gathered, silent as could be. All eyes were set unswervingly on a tall, red platform, which had been erected before the Court. Desmodys stood on an elevated step, flanked by three purple-robed elders. He was speaking as we arrived at the back of the crowd. His voice was thunderous in the high-walled square.

"Dyos reigns above all!" he said.

The people loudly and automatically replied in kind, "Dyos reigns!"

For a moment Desmodys paused and scanned the crowd as if assessing its mood. Then he continued, "Two days ago, as all here know, the man Yakum rode into town proclaiming himself as none other than Dyos'Lei, our long-awaited savior." The crowd murmured.

"To those on the vull battle lines, Yakum, for a time, appeared in splendor—as would a king. Unfortunately, none from the Exarchate were present at this event to witness this transformation. Nonetheless, in the days since these events, the consul has been working continuously to unravel truth from deception. As all of you know, the Exarchate has always been the protector of the people." He paused here for effect. "Dyos has ordained us with the task of Truth, and we have been faithful to this call!"

Again, Desmodys paused, while the echo of his voice beat at

the people from all sides. "After extensive investigation we, the Exarchate, have concluded that the man Yakum is a deceiver!"

The crowd erupted. Calls of "How could this be?" and "We saw him!" could be heard in the tumult. Desmodys raised his steady hands, palms down, and the people, so long used to obeying their leader, fell silent again.

"As the people know, evil has been growing in the land. The vulls have grown in numbers and boldness. Now, it appears Mael attacks us with a new and subtle wickedness, by playing upon our very hopes. Yakum is such a manifestation—a powerful wizard by the evil one sent to blind the people with miracles and seduce them with twisted words. He appears to be the strongest magan we have ever seen on Terras, able to create mass visions. Only the great skill and combined power of the consul elders is strong enough to resist his dark magic. Only we now stand between this master demon and the people."

He paused again for dramatic effect. I saw a mother clutch her young child tightly to her side. The tone of the crowd noticeably changed as the people realized they had been so easily duped. Angry cries arose. Anyone still faithful to Yakum now kept silent.

Desmodys went on.

"Yakum stands accused of the following crimes against the people of Duvall: one, inciting rebellion against the Exarchate— the authority of Dyos; two, the terrible heresy of applying to himself the name of Dyos'Lei; and three, practicing the dark magic arts."

Here I recalled the guttural words Yakum had used against the vulls on the battlefield before he destroyed them.

The crowd exploded with angry yells. Nothing riled the people like the thought of having been fooled—led like sheep to the slaughter. Now they wanted blood. Desmodys had played it masterfully. With just a few words, he had ended the debate. The three of us stood shocked and silent, barely daring to breathe.

Desmodys let the poison of a broken trust burn in the peoples' minds for a few more moments before he began again, this time speaking more softly.

"All three crimes against the people are punishable by death. Do the people consent?"

"Kill him," a voice rang out, then another, and another...

Within moments, the crowd was screaming for his death. I stood tight-mouthed against the great tide of fear and resentment, feeling weak. As I looked around, I saw a few quiet souls, humbled into silence by the vengeance driving the crowd, and I knew that Desmodys' adept oratory had not fooled all. Nonetheless, the crowd, which just two days ago had proclaimed Yakum their King and savior, now roared for his blood.

Desmodys again slowly raised his hands, and the tumult died. He spoke now with relief in his voice. "And so it is done, it will be as the people wish. The deceiver and heretic Yakum is sentenced to death. Today at noon, after the lashings, Yakum will be escorted to the Ruins and left as a blood sacrifice for the Solyss"

The crowd fell completely silent at this unexpected turn. The name sent fear through everyone. The great black beast of death, which guarded the Ruins and the Breach, was renowned in legend. None there had likely seen it, for it had been almost a hundred years since such a sentence had been handed down. Only the most evil, violent, and heartless of criminals, those without remorse, were sentenced to this unimaginable death. It was the stuff of nightmares. None in the crowd could hear the name of the Solyss without resurrecting their own nightmare imaginings.

The consul had made it clear that Yakum would be an example to all who might come after, and Desmodys had so efficiently manipulated the emotions of the people that they now had no recourse but to agree to this most painful of deaths.

"We will let Maels' Solyss feed on the deceiver! Praise be to Dyos!"

And the people returned a solemn, "Praise Dyos."

I felt utterly sick, dirty, and violated. Guilty in my silent submission and hating my weakness, I fled from the wretched scene. Thom and Mryyn followed, clearly just as distraught. We were haunted by our faithful pledge of the night before. We slogged through the sticky mud with heavy hearts back to our private refuge in Stone Hall. Mryyn was weeping openly, the tears made muddy rivulets on her dirty face. I envied her release, for my welling tears were sucked dry by my black heart.

"How can this happen?" Thom asked. "I just don't understand…"

Mryyn and I did not answer, for we were both wondering the same thing. The very savior-king we had just pledged our lives to was going to be executed as a heretic and evil wizard—a chief of demons, no less! My mind roiled as I tried to make sense of all the conflicting thoughts in my head. I felt angry, afraid, betrayed, and even guilty; a strange pudding of emotions that made no sense left me nauseous and hollow. How could we have been so wrong?

Even as I asked myself this question, however, I knew we hadn't been wrong. There are some things that can be faked and wizardry can certainly twist reality, but one cannot work side by side with a man for months and not see his true nature. I had seen Yakum's proclaimed love for Dyos lived out every day. He spoke what he believed was the truth and accepted the consequence of his words. He was a model of natural humility and integrity, always living what he preached. He had opened my heart to the true nature of Dyos not by some deceptive wizardry, but by life example and words expressed in love. Thom and Mryyn and I had been persuaded by the inherent power of his life and words. I could not explain all that had happened in the last two days, but I was sure that Yakum was not the demon that Desmodys claimed he was. Besides, my perception of Desmodys and the consul had begun to change ever since I began to open my eyes. I had seen the conflict between Desmodys and Yakum over the months and found it hard to believe that Desmodys' motives were pure.

"Yakum is not evil," I said. Thom and Mryyn looked at me with uncertainty. "I don't believe what Desmodys said about him."

"Nor I," said Mryyn quietly, and Thom nodded in agreement.

"But what do we do now? They're going to kill him." Thom sighed.

We all bowed our heads in shame. Even if Yakum was who he said he was, he would soon be dead. All our promises of serving the King seemed empty now. What could we do to change the future? At noon Yakum would be publicly whipped then dragged from the Court behind a horse through town and out the north gate. If he survived the five-mile journey to Haules' Gate, he would die a nightmarish death. As we sat in dimness of the narthex, we all imagined the horrible end. The images that filled my mind made me sick. Yakum was my friend, and if I listened to my heart, my King.

In times like these, hopelessness consumes the soul, overwhelms it, and drowns its spark. So unbelievable was the situation, and so helpless were we to alter its course, that we became utterly immobilized. Our sense of impotence was, for a time, paralyzing. We sat in a ragged line, our backs against the cold wall. Those stones seemed the only stable thing in our lives at that moment, and our bodies clung to them like an anchor. We stared silently at the weak yellow flame dancing in the glass bowl of the lamp. The air felt heavy and thick. I could hear slow dripping in the main hall; perhaps the rain had started again. I put my arm around Mryyn in an attempt to comfort her, but I think neither of us drew much comfort.

It suddenly occurred to me that I was no longer a child. I had stepped into adulthood without even noticing the change. I knew in that instant that childhood was forever behind me now, and that our little world had permanently changed. The great storm of adulthood that for so long had hung on the horizon had swept in overnight. A pounding storm of forced maturity had swept over us. The three of us lay wrecked and beaten in its aftermath. These terrible realities haunted me, and though it was my faithful friend Yakum who would die that morning and not I, my focus was largely on my own misery.

The three of us continued in silence for a while. I saw the lamp flicker in the dimness. It made me blink, for I had been staring at it. I rubbed my eyes thinking that it was my own tears that had distorted the flame. But even when I cleaned away the tears, the flame continued to seem strange. At first, I could not tell what had changed about the lamplight, but then I knew. It had changed color. Whereas before the lamp had burned with a low yellow flame, it now seemed a clean white, perhaps even bluish, and slowly growing brighter. I noticed Mryyn rub her own eyes in disbelief and Thom sucked in a surprised breath.

The flame suddenly grew tremendously brighter; its glow filled the room. The corner shadows fled and I suddenly felt heat. The three of us pushed backward solidly against the wall, fearing the lamp would burst at any second. Instead, its light continued to grow. Soon, we were shielding our eyes from its brilliance. Bright blue beams shot from the lamp and danced on the walls. An audible hum filled the room, its energy making the tiny hairs on my head stand on end. I felt the sordid waste of my melancholy singed within me by clean blue fire. Mryyn gasped beside me as the heat and power coursed through me. The doubts, fears, and frustrations from the moment before were consumed by the fire as if it fed on them like fuel. My mind seemed strangely clear and fresh, my muddled emotions swept away in a moment. I thought only of the pledge before Dyos the night before and I felt its certainty again, even as the blue fire incinerated the confusion which had so polluted my soul.

Then, just as quickly, the brilliance was gone, and the three of us were once again staring at the meager yellow flame. Nonetheless, the atmosphere had changed. The air smelled clean and pure, and I felt richly alive when I breathed it deeply—like the first warm day of spring. I realized my heart was beating heavily in my chest.

"What was that?" Mryyn blurted.

Neither of us answered because there were no appropriate words, but we all knew.

Somehow, the next steps seemed obvious now. In fact, I had a hard time understanding what all the confusion had been about just moments ago. The three of us leaped to our feet with a sense of urgency and duty. None of us needed to ask where the others were headed, for we all obeyed the same call.

"See you two at noon," Mryyn said and sprinted off through the doorway, splashing lightly through the puddles.

Thom looked at me and shook his head, a bewildered but delighted expression on his face. "In a while," he said and trundled off toward his home.

I stood in the open street for a moment and looked into the impenetrable grey sky. We were going on a trip, and I needed to prepare.

It was still hard to understand what exactly happened in the room that morning, but it was clear each of us felt Yakum's command in our hearts. It was not the panicked or fearful cry for help of a tortured man. Rather, it was the clear and authoritative call of a king—the kind of order one races to obey. And so we did.

Chaptyr 7

We met again outside the north end of the square shortly before noon. Mryyn had a spring to her step and a rosy sheen on her still dirty cheeks as she came bounding up beside me. She gave me a quick peck on the cheek to say "hi."

"You look beautiful," I said.

"I feel so excited," she replied. "It's almost like an adventure…but I'm a little afraid, too."

"Me too," I said. At the same time I wondered at the strangeness of our upbeat mood considering that we were about to witness the public torture of our Yakum. The call to action offered a powerful break from our melancholy, but the task before us was tragic indeed.

Thom trundled up as I was pondering this great irony, splashing heavily through the mud. His broadsword hung at his side and a heavy leather pack bent his shoulders.

"My, you've been busy," I said.

"Busier than an ant in a bowl of sugar," he quipped with his lopsided grin. Then, losing the grin, he said, "I feel kind of weird, like I'm playing a character in some jibe's play."

Mryyn and I looked at him and silently acknowledged that we understood the strange sensation. We had all left the room heeding some mysterious call to action. What would happen next, none of us knew. We were really simple, practical people like most of Duvall. The magic, mysteries, and miracles that had begun to influence our lives since Yakum had appeared were still new and foreign to us. This sudden spiritual awareness was often as frightening as it was exciting. Many times in those first few months, I felt like I was going crazy. If it had not been for Thom and Mryyn travelling these new realms with me, I would have been convinced I was insane.

I was feeling a peculiar and ominous excitement. These feelings carried me back a decade or so.

I had been a happy, naïve seven year old, gangly and uncoordinated. I had been sent on an errand by my father to purchase some silver needles he used in his leatherwork. My task took me to the eastern edge of town. I felt proud to be sent on such an errand, but a bit afraid as my journey was taking me into neighborhoods I had not known before. As I walked, I held in my hand a bright twopence piece my father had given me to cover costs, and I was admiring its sparkle. As I rolled it over and over in my hand, the sunlight flashed on its silvery surface. I had hardly seen anything so beautiful. I was so caught up in the glistening coin, that I failed to watch my step. With my head bent, I struck a human wall, and stumbled backwards landing on my rear. When I looked up, I saw a heavy boy of about fourteen standing above me. His wicked grin, splotchy freckles, and red-straw, short, cropped hair betrayed him immediately as trouble. I knew his ilk, but had always been able to avoid a chance meeting.

Somehow, I still held on to the twopence, despite my tumble.

"Give me the coin, you twit," he snarled.

Instead, I climbed to my feet and stared up at him silently.

"If you want to be able to walk back to your mommy when I'm done with you, you better hand that over now," he said with that malevolent grin so characteristic of his breed.

I held my ground, peered at him, and kept my mouth shut.

I didn't even see the first punch coming, and it blasted the breath right out of me, knocking me to the dust, helplessly trying to find my lost breath. That's how I felt so many years later as I awaited Yakum's public punishment. As I lay in a crunched ball, drooling in misery, a fury grew within me, a fury at the terrible injustices of the world—a world where bullies like that freckled beast picked fights with children half their age—wielding their violence with a smile. In that moment, I vowed to fight such evil no matter what the cost. I knew that within minutes, I would be pummeled, but somehow it didn't matter. I was numb, my blood coursed through me and roared in my ears, and I was furious. I knew I would survive, move on, and be wiser for it. I would not walk again with my head down or be distracted by foolish things. I would fight the evil that produced the bullies of this world.

I fought valiantly and drew blood but paid dearly for my stubbornness. By the time an adult noticed the skirmish, I was practically unconscious, and I needed to be carried home. My father, who was called, cradled me in his arms all the way home. Because I was delirious, he had to pry my hand open to get that twopence free. In the days afterwards, he treated me with a new respect, but his counsel to me was simple.

"Son, pick your fights carefully…few things are worth fighting for. But when you find one of them, fight with all your heart."

As I saw them drag Yakum from the black yawning arch of

the Court, I knew what my father had meant all those years ago. The odds against us were terrible, as they had been for me all those years ago. We were prepared to assume a tremendous risk, and yet the very idea of it intensified our stubbornness and commitment to the cause we knew was right. Perhaps, if we had known the full extent of our calling at that moment, we would not have been so sure. But Dyos is often kind that way; he sometimes gives us just enough of a view to handle the moment. And so we stood there, confused but prepared to fight for our cause.

Yakum was bent and haggard. His clothes were rag-like and bloodstained. A jagged open wound thick with dried blood traversed one blackened eye and extended almost to his chin. He was missing some teeth between his swollen lips and he fell twice as two Red Guards pushed him across the square.

The crowd went wild when they saw him, cursing, spitting, stomping their feet, and calling for blood. They were soon satisfied. Yakum was led to a heavy wooden rack; his hands were bound above his lolling head. A giant Red Guard with bulging muscles and a hungry grin stepped forward from the ranks. I thought, as I watched him gleefully unwind his whip, of the redheaded bully all those years ago. I had always assumed that eventually such vicious creatures ended up imprisoned or dead, but now I knew the truth. My resolve hardened.

At a nod from Desmodys, the whipping began. Public whipping is the clearest possible evidence that at heart, man is an animal. I looked around me at the crowd as the whip snapped chunks of meat, and eventually chips of bone, into the air. It almost seemed a horde of vulls danced before me screaming in delight at the bloody show. I wondered at how so subtly Mael's heart had become our own.

I was too numb to feel sick. Thom vomited heavily in the mud at his feet. Mryyn sobbed on my arm. My heart turned to stone, as I watched the whip tear my King into raw shreds of flesh and expose his ribs for all to see.

Finally, it was over and the whip fell one last time. The crowd fell silent wondering whether Yakum was dead. It was not clear for a long time, but finally, he lifted his bloody, pale face. His eyes were stunningly alert. They traversed the crowd from one end to the other. The vulls were silent before his gaze. They shuffled their feet and looked at the mud. Yakum said nothing, but his eyes were filled with forgiveness.

He looked at me once. I felt his gaze lock in. He held me with his look like a vice. His eyes clenched my heart and I felt completely broken, filled with shame. Then, as I held his gaze, I thought I saw tiny blue flames dancing in the dark mist between us. Somehow, they made me feel strong and safe and sure. Just as quickly, they were gone. When he released me, I felt like falling on my knees, but the tight press of the crowd on all sides denied me.

Yakum was cut down and brutally tied to two long poles by his hands and feet. The poles were lifted up at one end to rest on a brace between two huge plow horses so that his head hung inches above the mud. I saw a thick stream of blood staining a puddle beneath him. He looked up at the grey sky, silent and unmoving. I thought he might be paralyzed by the great trauma to his spine.

The people lined the streets on both sides all the way to the northern gate. Men, women, and children, many of who had stood on the walls celebrating his triumphal entry to Duvall now watched silently and angrily as he was dragged by. All that was left as the parade turned a distant corner were two deep ruts in the mud among the hoof prints and a thin, red line of blood between.

Our mood was black, but our resolve was stronger as the three of us raced from the square obeying the quiet and sure

GEOFFREY W. GILSON

command in our hearts. Thom, Mryyn, and I sprinted through town running parallel to the train, but several blocks to the east. We climbed the town wall a good three hundred yards east of the North Gate, dropped down, and raced through the wet grass. It was about a half mile to the woods' edge, and we covered the distance in record time. I was quite sure no one had seen us creep through the field. The crowds were completely focused on the gory parade exiting the gate.

A dozen paces into the shadows of the forest we found the two beasts of burden Mryyn had brought there earlier that morning. They were contentedly munching on the tall, brown patches of grass, which grew among the tree roots, oblivious to the events occurring less than a mile away.

We knew these mules well as "Hoofer" and "Possum." They were owned by Thom's father and had often been our companions on short day trips we had made to outlying farms for supplies. Bulging leather packs hung from the backs of each, and they were saddled. We added to their burdens our weapons and the other items we had packed earlier. We expected to be away for several days.

The thought of spending a night outside the safety of the town walls was terrifying. Only the boldest scouts took such chances. I knew we would be safe as long as we avoided roaming vull hordes and did not advertise our presence with a fire. Nonetheless, just the thought of being alone in the darkness made me want to scurry back home. These fears competed for attention with the pulsing blue fire that had begun to beat within me, like a forge in my soul. Its warmth comforted me, soothed my anxieties, and left me feeling undeniably safe despite the odds. Earlier that morning, when the celestial blue lamplight had filled our hearts, we had each heard the words, "You will witness the glory of your King." We did not know what to expect, but we were prepared for that witness.

I had spent a good portion of the morning writing my father a long letter explaining our intentions. Of all people, I expected him to understand my need to obey the call most. I had caught a quick glimpse of him in the crowd at Yakum's whipping. His disgusted expression and downcast face were enough to confirm my suspicions. This was the man who had saved his son. None of our parents would miss us until tomorrow evening. At sunrise, it would be Restday. The three of us frequently spent nights at each other's houses so we could get an early start at Restday freedom. My father would not find the letter until he went to work again in two mornings, as it was buried beneath his work belt. By then, I expected, we would be on our way back to town, to await our punishment.

"I can't believe we are doing this," I said.

"My father will beat me until I can't walk," Thom agreed.

"That's assuming the vulls don't find us first or, worse yet, Desmodys and his red bullies," Mryyn said with a sarcastic smile. As she said this though, we all fell solemnly silent. We were taking a terrible risk. I saw in my mind the contented smile gracing Desmodys' face as the whip fell again and again on Yakum's back. He would have no mercy for those allied with his enemy. The forest suddenly felt cold.

"Let's go," I said.

The three of us mounted and began the five-mile journey to the Stone table and the Breach Cliffs. We knew the way because we had made part of this journey almost three years ago. As we began our winding trek through the forest-covered hills, all three of us were thinking back to a certain time…

Children are the same everywhere, always daring each other to greater and greater challenges. In the Duvall of our childhood, there existed a rite of passage that no adolescent could ignore. Every youngster knew that, before his older peers accepted him, he must find a piece of red rock. Not just any rock, but a piece of the Ruins. Red marble is not native to the southern territories. In fact, it can't be found anywhere in Terras. In earlier times, when the creatures of myth and legend roamed the earth, the red marble was brought from a distant land—some say across the impassible northern seas. It was brought by unknown people, the legendary Venili, to build the massive arched temple that once had been Mael's tomb. Those few who have seen the crumbled ruins of the temple say they must have been erected by giants or by some fantastic magic. When it stood intact, the gate's main arch of solid stone would have reached almost a thousand feet into the air.

According to legend, it had once been a glorious temple to King Dyos, the center of all worship in the seven kingdoms. But it had been overtaken and corrupted by Aster Sypiros, who released the defyyl on the land. In the Great Battle that ended the last age, he had been imprisoned by the few surviving sliver-banded mages. Though it cost them their lives, they had together cast one last spell, which had bound Aster, by then known as Mael, into a death sleep and entombed him in the temple.

Here he had lain imprisoned for almost a century, but as the defyyl spread and consumed the land, the power of the spell waned, and he returned again to life. Now there were none left with the power to challenge him and he broke free in the great cataclysm of the Ryyft that destroyed the temple and severed the land east to west forming the Breach Cliffs.

So great was the force of the Ryyft that massive pieces of red marble were hurled miles into the air and strewn upon the land. The years have buried much of the stone beneath layers of earth and brush. Only if one was courageous, or stupid, enough to journey into the valley where the ancient temple had once stood, could one be sure to find a piece of red marble.

All the children of Duvall had heard the rebuke at least once:

"If you don't start behaving well, I'll have you sent to the Ruins."
It is a terrible thing to say to any child, but it worked. We all
knew well that just beyond the blasted rock at the base of the
high cliffs—laid the Ryyft seam.

It was the first and biggest seam bored into Terras from the
depths where Mael and his hordes reigned. Ever since the Ryyft, these portals to the dark depths had been appearing. Since
then, evil had been pouring to the surface like pus from a deep
abscess. It was through this, and other smaller seams, that the
vulls surfaced when the sun sat on the land. Here however, at
his main gate in the south, Mael set a watch—the Solyss, a beast
of unimaginable terror.

Only two men had ever seen the Solyss and lived to return
to Duvall—and they had gone crazy. It was said that they had
been driven insane by insomnia. Neither of them slept for almost two weeks after they had wandered back to town mumbling about what they had seen. Both had been scouts—men
not easily frightened.

Just three years before we found ourselves on this journey
headed for our worst nightmare, Thom, Mryyn, and I had accepted the challenge of red marble. We had found our way trembling to within a mile of the ancient ruins before we found what
we were looking for, a chunk of glistening red stone brought to
the surface by the massive roots of an old oak. We had waited
for the brightest spring day to hunt for our prize. Nonetheless,
by the time we found a piece we could carry, dusk had settled
in. We became frantic, and for a time, lost the path back. Terror
began to fill us, and we started to argue. Thom threw me to the
ground in anger and Mryyn began to cry. We screamed at each
other. Finally, we found the path, as the shadows were growing
long. As we raced back to town dreading the thought of a night
in this dark wilderness, we heard a distant rumbling scream
echo off the cliffs. So craven was its aching cry that we felt death

touch our young souls. The three of us had horrible nightmares for almost a month after we returned. I once awoke suddenly in a pool of sweat with the sensation of having avoided death by seconds.

And so we proceeded now with fear clutching at our hearts.

"I know what you mean," said Thom. "I was so scared I almost killed Pityr."

"No kidding," I said. "We never even got close enough to see the gates. Still, I felt like I was going to die of fear. What will it be like now?"

"I don't even want to guess," said Mryyn.

"You know," said Thom, "I feel scared too, but somehow it all seems different than the last time we came this way—almost like...well, I guess I just feel stronger. I don't know, maybe it's just my imagination, but there's a part of me that knows we'll be okay."

"No, I feel it too," Mryyn confessed. "It's as if that strange blue light did something to me and, you know, changed me somehow."

We all knew what she meant. I feared our journey, but I felt strangely protected, as if an invisible shield surrounded me. I could see, hear, and smell the damp forest all about me, but it did not threaten me. I had an abiding sense I would be safe.

It would be many days before I would come to understand the power that was indeed our shield. Though I couldn't put a name to the feeling then, I would come to know that Dyos'Bri— "the breath of Dyos"—the Slyverhawk—flew within us that misty fall day as we obeyed the call of the King.

Chaptyr 8

We raced as fast as we could through the cool, damp forest. It was essential that we stay well ahead of the procession. We wanted to be well hidden before the horse train arrived in the valley, so time was precious.

Our route was poorly marked. Only the tiniest path wound through the hills, disappearing at times, swallowed by the forest. We knew the major landmarks well, and were careful to keep the dim afternoon sun to our right. The Red Guard would be following the main road, a more indirect and level path to the gates. We were cutting directly across the low foothills of the north, which grew like waves meeting the shore until they crashed into the great Breach Cliffs, the northern border of the Southlands.

The grey light cast no shadows in the thick woods. Heavy moss hung from some of the larger trees. The burrows' steps made squishing thumps on the sodden forest floor. Mist occasionally wound like phantoms through the trees. The birds were ominously silent as we progressed, but the tree frogs filled the dimness with a croaky dirge; soggy, earth-smell rich with rotting leaves and pine filled the air.

Thom rode in the rear on Possum, the sturdiest burrow of the bunch. He suddenly exclaimed, "Quiet!"

We stopped. I heard a heavy stick break somewhere in the dark mist behind us and then only the forest sounds as before. Was someone following us? Certainly no one had seen us make our escape. Who else would know this way? And if someone had discovered our secret plans, why were they hiding back in the dimness?

"What is it?" I asked.

"I thought I heard footfalls behind us," Thom replied.

"It must have been our own steps echoing off the trees," he said, looking like he was trying hard to convince himself.

It made no sense. I was convinced that in our nervous state, we were letting our imaginations run wild. Nonetheless, we all listened carefully as we once again set off. Twice more as we progressed, I thought I heard a footfall, but the more I listened, the less certain I became.

Later, we crossed a small stream clogged with soaked, brown leaves. As we peaked the hill beyond, I looked back and thought for a moment that I saw dim movement among the grey trees, but then all was still again.

Soon, the forest became thinner; bare rock protruded from the earth in spots like bones popping up through skin. I saw a chipmunk dive beneath a fallen tree as we trundled by. It occurred to me that this was the first creature we had seen on our whole journey.

Abruptly, the forest gave way to a wide open field of patchy, low bush. Ahead, the field sloped downward, but two large grey boulders stood on either side of the path. My heart began to beat faster. Soon we would reach the spot where we had found the red quartz three years ago.

"We are almost there," Mryyn said.

I felt cold beneath the weak sun as we continued across the field. I looked back, the brush soaking my pant leg. The forest edge was empty and in shadow. Was there something hiding in the trees back there? I shook off my fears.

We wound down between the two large boulders; the distance between them was barely large enough for our heavily laden burrows. A wide grassy valley opened up before us. At its base the main road cut a muddy path through the green grass. The great, smooth, black cliffs of the Ryyft lay directly ahead, filling the sky to the north. They rose well over a thousand feet, like a great black wave about to crash on the land.

We rushed down the valley to the trail's edge. A quick look at its un-trodden and overgrown surface assured us that we were not too late. We paralleled the path well up the valley careful to leave no sign of our passage. We passed a low pile of red rock protruding through the grass. I realized that we had already come further than we had on our previous journey into this valley. Worried looks from Mryyn and Thom confirmed their awareness of this fact. We continued on, more slowly now. The black wall of the Breach Cliffs filled more and more of the northern sky until everything lay in its heavy shadow. I estimated that we were less than a quarter mile from the ruins now. None of us spoke above a whisper. We all sensed that we were being watched as we crossed the valley, but saw nothing to confirm our suspicions.

As we reached the midway point of the valley, I motioned for Thom and Mryyn to stop. I scanned the rising slope to our right and made the decision to leave the path. I quietly explained my plan to the other two. We dismounted and turned eastward, away from the trail, beginning a gradual climb up the valley walls. We scrambled over loose rock and around low scrub pines that dotted the hillside. After several minutes of an ever-steepening climb, we crested the ridgeline that marked the valley edge. We crouched low and scuttled over the edge aware that we were most in danger of being seen by anyone in the valley when our silhouettes stood out against the afternoon sky along the ridgeline.

Just to the other side of the ridge we continued northward on a parallel course with the trail, which was now hidden from view. We continued this way for some time, falling ever deeper under the shadow of the great cliffs. At one point I peered over the ridgeline toward the south. I thought that I could just make out the advanced guard entering the distant edge of the valley. We hurried on careful to stay hidden beneath the edge of the ridge.

I would occasionally peer over the edge to ascertain our position relative to the trail. I saw a huge crumpled pillar of red rock rising about a hundred and fifty feet into the air out of the valley's depths. It ended abruptly in a jagged tip as if the sword of a giant had sheared it off. I saw another similar pile across the valley in line with the first. No pillar rose out of this one however. Instead, it lay partially buried on the valley floor pointing to the southwest. Huge pieces of red stone, as large as houses, lay haphazardly scattered across the valley floor like pebbles tossed by a child. Great rusted rods of iron rose like tentacles from some of the larger heaps.

It took me several seconds to understand what I was looking at, and when I did, I began to tremble. I was peering down at the ragged remnants of the temple. I saw, as if in a vision, the red temple as it must have been: impossibly strong, towering across the valley in a great arch, holding back evil from all Terras. As I stared down at this ancient scene, I could almost hear the echoing rumble of falling mountains of stone. Unimaginably powerful forces must have been at work to wreak such destruction. My blood ran cold at the thought of an evil so strong as to wield such terrible power.

With dread, my eyes slid further down the valley until they reached the place where the cliffs met the valley floor, where a terrible blackness lay. A jagged fissure like a wound split the valley floor. Midnight seemed to dwell in its impenetrable depths. As I stared helplessly, entranced by the abyss, a terrible sense of foreboding filled my heart. A thin yellowish-brown wisp of steam rose from its depths. Just then, the wind changed, and I thought I could smell the sickening stench of sulfur and rotten meat. Suddenly, my mind was carried back a dozen years to the central square in Duvall and the smell of burning human flesh. The screams of the dregs-poisoned man burning alive filled my ears once again, and I felt like crying. Instead I covered my ears and turned abruptly away from the dark vision beneath me.

It was then that I noticed that Thom and Mryyn had joined me at the crest and were peering down at the same scene, both appearing entranced. Tears ran silently down Mryyn's cheeks. Thom had a terrible black look etched in his agonized features.

"Look away," I said. After neither of them responded to my command, I roared, "Turn away!"

Mryyn slowly looked at me as if from a dream. Then slowly her eyes began to focus.

"Oh Pityr," she cried, "it was horrible."

"I know," I said and pulled her into a firm embrace.

Thom was still glaring down at the gapping abyss.

"We have to help Thom," she said.

Together, we forcefully turned Thom away from the seam. This was by no means easy because at first, he fought us. With one great swipe of his arm, he cast me to the ground causing me to tumble a bit down the slope. Mryyn ducked his swipe at her. The whole time, his gaze remained upon the black Ryyft seam. Finally I made a short running tackle, which knocked him heavily to the ground. He looked around startled, and then snapped back to reality.

"What happened?" he said.

"I don't know," I said. "It's as if just looking at the darkness of the seam lulled us into some kind of trance."

"All I could see was Kipper drowning. I was helpless," Thom said. "He was screaming for my help, but I couldn't do anything. Then I saw them pull his bloated blue body from the water, just as if I had been there." Thom began to cry softly. "It was so terrible."

When Thom was just six years old, he had had a three year old brother nicknamed Kipper who had drowned in Green Pond. Thom had not been with him at the time, but he had seen the blue body as it was carried into town.

Mryyn hugged Thom as he wept.

"I think we need to pray," I said.

And so I began in the simple and honest way I had seen Yakum do. *"Dyos, we are small and afraid. We do not understand the powerful events that have swept us up. We believe though, that your hand is in it all and that you have called us to be bold and faithful in the midst of it. Please make us strong when we are weak and give us peace despite the terrors all around. We love you..."*

Thom and Mryyn looked at me and nodded. Together we bowed our heads and clasped our hands and spoke honestly. For a moment it seemed that our prayers could not rise through the heavy shadows of the valley. Suddenly, however, I felt my heart leap—a pulsing pure and fresh power seemed to fill our circle. At first, I had felt helpless and fearful, and now I felt calm and free of the dark thoughts cluttering my brain. Thom stopped crying, and his breathing became deep and smooth. I felt as if Yakum himself sat among us. Slowly, the evil that filled the valley below seemed distant and less threatening but still real. We stayed this way for a time, enjoying the quiet peace of the moment. A gentle whisper in my mind finally lifted me from my reverie.

"I have come," it said.

At first it meant nothing to me but then I rose quickly and rushed to the ridgeline and looked south. Red Guards swarmed in the valley below.

Moments later I saw the two great war horses drag the ragged form of Yakum into the valley. He was silent and lifeless. Even the fierce, battle-hardened Red Guard seemed unusually subdued. All were hesitant to approach the rubble-floored ruins. I saw the party stop just beyond the closest pillar. The dozen or so guards who stood at its base looked like ants at work beneath a towering tree. I marveled again at the temples' superhuman dimensions.

Desmodys stepped forward and gestured authoritatively at a large flat boulder that lay several hundred feet beyond the pillar, roughly midway between where the gates once stood and the black depths of the seam. The boulder had been carved into a rough table. Its top was smooth and level. Heavy rusted chains lay loosely coiled on its surface like so many sunning vipers. This was Stone Table. Here, Yakum would be offered up as a sacrifice to the Solyss, the ancient guardian of the Underlands, and the physical manifestation of the defyyl.

The horses were brought slowly forward until they stood only paces from the massive table. They were skittish and seemed anxious to flee. Yakum was cut from the long wooden rods, which had been his support on the journey, and flopped heavily to the ground. Three of the largest guards were instructed to carry his limp form to the table. They proceeded hesitantly, not because of their bloody burden, but because of the haunting surroundings. Most of the deeper valley lay in shadow now; coolness fell from the great heights of the cliffs. The three guards kept their gaze always on the black abyss before them. They were like children tiptoeing into the den of a sleeping bear. Only the vicious verbal threats from Desmodys made them advance at all. Once they reached the table however, they moved with quiet efficiency.

They threw Yakum's floppy body onto the flat rock and fastened the massive chains onto his limbs, pulling them tightly until he lay face up and spread-eagle upon the flat stone. Twice I saw Yakum roll his head from side to side though no other signs of life emanated from his broken body. The bulky guards ran like frightened children back to the relative safety of greater numbers. Desmodys' black gaze followed them as if they were disobedient children.

Yakum lay on the rock, his eyes barely open. Blood pooled slowly beneath his back in an ever-widening black shiny circle, running in a viscous sticky rivulet off one edge of the table, stretching into a long slow drip.

The valley became silent. I heard a high screech and looked into the grey sky. Three large black birds like none I had seen before swept in from the north beyond the cliffs and began to circle in lazy loops. Their unnatural look made my skin crawl. I realized that they had been drawn by the scent of blood and would feed on any remnants the solyss left behind. Perhaps, I thought, there was one thing we could do for our king. We would fight these wicked birds for the right to bury him whole.

The light began to slowly fade, and shadows consumed the valley. Evening seemed to fall unnaturally fast beneath the great Breach Cliffs. The black birds swung in hungry circles and I could almost feel their evil eyes upon me.

"Those things give me the creeps," Mryyn whispered. "I can't wait until one of them gets close enough to stick an arrow into."

"Poor Yakum. Do you think he's still alive?" asked Thom.

I looked down at the lifeless man lying in a pool of his own blood, and I could not tell.

Desmodys and a dozen guards moved to higher ground across the valley. They climbed up to a ledge of rock which jutted out of the steep valley wall about fifty feet above Stone Table. It was an easily defended position from above and below, the perfect spot to witness the night's proceedings. The rest of the guard and the other members of the train started home. They all but galloped out of the valley glancing backward as they went. Those that remained moved around haltingly uncomfortable with the dubious honor of being chosen to stay. As I looked down on the scene, I noticed that two especially large Red Guards stood on either side of Desmodys. They wore black metal helmets ornately inscribed, and each had a double black swath running the length of their red robes. I had never seen their like before. I thought this quite strange, since there was not much in Duvall we had not seen. Only those two stood silently and unmoving in the lengthening shadows. The others seemed to avoid them. Desmodys stood regally between them, a fierce look in his dark eyes. In just that moment, I saw his head turn upward toward our ridgeline, and those dark eyes made a sweep. I ducked quickly beneath the rocks and pulled Mryyn down with me. I wondered, with breath held, whether Desmodys had seen our movement or somehow sensed us. I waited to hear the alarm echo across the valley, which didn't come. After several seconds passed, I peered carefully over the edge. Desmodys' full attention now seemed to be directed at the dark seam.

With a quickening heart, I noticed that the steam, which rose from its dark depths, was growing thicker. I smelled the sickening sulfur smell once again, but another change in the wind swept it silently away. Over the next half hour, light disappeared from the valley as if it were fleeing the midnight darkness creeping forth from the pit before us. A cold breeze fell from the cliff heights carrying with it the distant smell of snow.

Mryyn's teeth began to chatter, and I looked at her in the dim light.

"I'm scared," she mouthed silently, as if speaking it would make it worse.

I pulled her in close and covered her with my own woolen cape. She received it thankfully clutching it closely at the collar. I looked over at Thom. He was staring intently down at the scene below. "Look," he whispered.

I peered over the edge. Below, several of the guards had lit torches against the advancing night. Following loud orders from Desmodys, two guards with panicky looks made their way down again to the valley floor, each bearing two torches. They nervously placed the four torches around Yakum so that each of them stood upright in a stone sconce placed concentrically in a square around Stone Table. No doubt, these had been put there eons ago to illuminate the terrible sacrifices that had occurred over the ages. The two torchbearers scurried back up the rock face like frightened animals. I noticed as I looked across the valley at Desmodys and his crew that their horses were acting strangely. They were stamping and snorting blasts of steam into the cold night air. Our own burrows also began to scuffle, and buried their heads nervously together. I looked just down the slope at Hoofer who was closest. His big donkey eyes were stretched wide and white in fear. I felt the small hairs on my arm stand slowly to attention, and a sense of doom crept upon me.

Over the next hour, we watched a deep yellow three-quarter moon rise above the valley walls. Its light was the color of butter and seemed to make the gathering mist glow. Twice I saw the horrid, black-winged creatures sweep across the moon like aerial demons, but no further sound came from their hungry beaks.

I looked back down the valley floor. Yakum lay still and pale in the yellow light cast by the flickering torches and the jaundiced moon. In the peculiar light, his blood made a black pool on the table surface, giving the illusion that he floated above a deep hole.

Suddenly, a long guttural cry resonated across the valley. "Dakken puraa..."

I averted my eyes to Desmodys. He stood precariously near the ledge edge facing northward to the impenetrable darkness of the seam. The horrible chant came from his lips. He repeated the words once again and then stood quiet. My skin crawled at its vile sound. I realized in a sudden haunting moment what Desmodys was doing. He was somehow calling the Solyss from the depths to his meal. It must have been some ancient chant he knew. It made me want to vomit.

Several minutes of complete silence followed the eerie invocation. Then, out of the dark pit a heavy hissing column of sulfurous steam rose into the night air. Then the rumble came.

So deep and haunting was its quality that I had to strain to be sure that I had heard anything. I wondered if it was just the cold wind slipping down the cliff walls. Then I noticed the panicked shuffling and neighing of the burrows intensify. I knew then that something dark and evil had joined the night.

The second time, I heard it more clearly—a low, melancholy groan echoed deep within the depths of the seam.

The third time, I was certain I had heard it, because suddenly the groan rose to a deafening crescendo that rumbled down the valley like low rolling thunder. I froze in fear. Mryyn let out a terrified, "Oh Dyos!" and Thom cursed loudly.

By this time I was looking directly at the seam. The yellow moonlight fell impotently into its blackness illuminating nothing. My fingers tightened on the rock edge in terrified anticipation of what would come next. As much as I wanted to avert my gaze, I was helpless to do so, as if the night had developed claws that pinned me to the spot.

Yet another loud hiss filled the valley, and a huge puff of steam vented from the abysmal depths of the fissure. I saw a massive black shadow rise in the steam. Three blood-red orbs seemed to float within the terrible dark mass: eyes. As I watched, a huge black claw rose out of the steam and planted itself with a rumble ten feet from the edge of the pit. Another followed. Then the whole form of the Solyss stepped out of the mist and was illuminated by the yellow moon.

I stopped breathing; my throat closed in spasms of horror. I felt nailed to the rock. My mind was barely able to comprehend what was before me. I heard and saw nothing but the abomination that now filled the valley.

The Solyss stood almost thirty feet tall, half its height a grotesquely huge horned head. Three eyes, sickening red balls the size of fists, peered in all directions above a snub snout. Razor teeth each as long as a finger and dripping with foul, steaming smut filled a cavernous mouth. The beast walked on four trunk-like legs like a grossly magnified vull. It dragged a skinless rat-tail that was white and slick with glistening grease. Most of the vile monster was covered in dense black hair, but its underside had a sheen of scales.

As I watched, the snout opened wide. A pink tongue wet with slime slithered out between the fangs and stuck out straight. A screaming roar rocked the valley and I felt the stones beneath my fingers tremble. My ears filled with the sound of a thousand childhood nightmares. I thought my young heart would stop its frenzied beating and fall still forever. Truly, in that moment I was sure death was upon me. Soon that trio of bloody eyes would find me—a mouse hiding in the rocks. A clawed hand would snatch me from my perch and my bones would snap in those foul jaws.

In my living nightmare, I had all but forgotten Thom and Mryyn, who were busy living their own nightmares. I had forgotten about Desmodys and his heavies and even Yakum. The Solyss however, had not. It smelled the sweet stickiness of blood in the night air. Its eyes fell on Stone Table. With surprisingly quick lunging steps, it raced to its feast.

I saw Yakum moving now. His head was lolling heavily from side to side. A low groan was growing on his lips. He struggled helplessly against the chains. His arms and legs made grotesque patterns in the mess of sticky blood that covered the flat top. The Solyss bent over and sniffed its meal. It lifted its huge head into the night air and rose on two legs. Its mouth opened again in a ragged grin. It was so tall as it rose on its hindquarters that its tooth-filled snout reached just below the ridgeline. I looked down its gapping throat into the depths of agony. Suddenly, it screamed again at the night. I was knocked backward by the power of its roar. Its hot stinking breath burned my eyes and made me gag involuntarily. I screamed at the top of my lungs, but I could not hear myself over its deafening bellow.

As I lay stunned on my back, time seemed to slow. I was absolutely numb and unable to breathe. The darkness began to swallow me, flowing like ice in my veins. I begged for death to hurry me away from this eternity of horror.

The roar stopped. The ground beneath me ceased its shaking dance. Forever passed. I felt my heart tentatively resume its faithful drumming. Then my lungs sucked in a breath. A blue haze seemed to fill my brain. I let myself rest for a time in azure peace. Slowly, I began to feel warmer. Finally, I was able to move. I took another gasping breath and rolled over. The blue fire filled me now. A wave of uncontrollable nausea swept over me and I vomited, expelling all the vileness from my soul. I crawled weakly to the ridgeline again and looked below.

The Solyss had placed one heavy clawed foot on Yakum pinning his writhing body to the rock, like a cat toying with its catch. It bent low over him and its mouth opened wide and yellow muck dripped onto Yakum.

Suddenly, a brilliant flash of blue light erupted beneath the great bent beast. The beast recoiled as if slapped and stumbled backward. Yakum stood suddenly free of the chains, which had miraculously fallen away. His bleeding wounds stood out clearly against his white flesh, but he seemed filled with power and strength. He held aloft a sword dancing with silver-blue fire. Distant stars glittered in its shining surface. White light lit the valley into day. Rivulets of blue lightning skittered across the tabletop. The Solyss, stunned and hammered by the fist of light, had taken several steps backward. Infuriated, it now advanced and rose again on its hindquarters until it towered massively over Yakum. It roared in anger and frustration. Its snakelike tail whipped in a long arch and hit the edge of the great rock table with stunning force. The flat-topped boulder moved several feet to one side. Yakum stumbled as his foothold was knocked loose, but his sword arm remained aloft. The grotesque razor-toothed mouth dove in for the kill. The foul jaws engulfed the raised arm whole. I heard the crunch of bone as the teeth sunk into Yakum's shoulder and he screamed in pain. The Solyss arched backward in sudden agony. Jets of azure flame shot from its three eye sockets a hundred feet into the night. The vile head exploded, burning chunks of black skull meat flew into the air. Its dying scream was cut short by the all-consuming fire. The now headless body tumbled heavily to the ground twitching and spurting black steaming blood. Finally, it lay still and silence again filled the valley.

Yakum knelt now. Blood ran heavily from the ragged stump that had been his sword arm. He appeared to be in a trance but still unbelievably alive. The blue rivulets of lightening danced more lightly around him now. Their frizzle was the only sound in the night air.

Then I heard the command, "Loose!" echoed across the valley.

I saw the figure of Yakum shudder twice. He fell forward heavily onto the stone surface. He lay still, now clearly dead. In addition to the myriad whip wounds, which crisscrossed his back and the amputated arm, two long arrows were buried to half-shaft just below his shoulders. The blue fires sizzled out and the light faded from the valley. I turned slightly and looked across the distance. Desmodys stood nobly on the edge of the ledge. His two Red Guards standing on either side were slowly lowering their spent bows.

It was over. And it was just beginning.

CHAPTYR 9

I leaned back against the great tree with a sigh. "My mouth is dry from the telling," I said.

I reached for the cider-skin and took several slow deep swallows. I ended with another sigh and a sweep of my almost numb hand across my lips. I cut two more large pieces of cheese from the yellow hunk and handed the larger to Jonam who accepted gratefully. All the while, the young man's gaze never dropped from my face. Jonam was speechless and shaking. Many times before, he had heard snippets of my story, which were known by everyone in Duvall. Nevertheless, I was sure he had never heard such detail and never felt such a part of the adventure. I could tell it shook him to the bones.

The late afternoon sun was high in the treetops now and the shadows had grown long. I had talked for several hours without a pause, and yet it seemed just moments. Jonam wrapped the blue cloak tightly around his chest. I imagined that he felt a chill as visions of the Solyss' horrific form danced again through his mind. I knew he had seen it all as I spoke, as though he had been magically transported back through the years and stood with me on the cragged ridge above Stone Table. He peered intently at me now as if he was trying to imagine the frightened nineteen year old beneath my old skin. Finally, his gaze settled on my eyes. There he found what he sought – Pitir's own scared eyes. I knew what he thought.

These are the same eyes that saw the Solyss fall beneath the blade of Yakum. What will my eyes have seen by my sunset years? Finally, when I knew I had him captured with me in the adventure, my old face old face creaked into a grin.

"You look as if you have seen a phantom, my son," I said, teasing him.

"Your words shook me," Jonam said. "And so they should," I chuckled. "Even in the retelling, some of the terror of it remains. The years have taken much of it away, though. Dyos heals even the deepest wounds with time."

The years truly had brought me peace and I knew it was infectious. Within moments, I could see Jonam's confused thoughts slowing, and could tell that his pounding heart took up a more patient beat. He chewed hungrily at the cheese.

Suddenly, I sprang to my feet. I moved fast for one so old and frail. I leapt over the low limb like an acrobat and skittered off into the woods. I disappeared behind another tree. I had no choice.

Jonam looked around in panic, wondering what evil was about to fall upon him. When he heard the wet splatter of my urine hitting the ground, he relaxed with a chuckle. I returned, slowly buttoning my jerkin.

"Sorry," I said with a big smile. "It sneaks up on me without warning these days."

I creaked back into his seat with a staccato of cracks and pops.

"Now I must tell you more," I said, "before this old body gives me up completely."

I cleared my throat loudly and began speaking again. Within moments, Jonam was lost again with me in the distant past...

Thom, Mryyn, and I knelt silently on the ridgeline utterly overwhelmed with emotion. It was over. Yakum lay silent and unmoving, facedown in his own dried blood. The headless hunk of black flesh that had been the Solyss lay steaming in the cold night air. Charred chunks of the head had been strewn across the valley. Two large pieces had been hurled over the ridgeline and lay behind us just below the burrows. We were shocked and speechless by the horrors we had witnessed. If this was some kind of victory, it didn't feel like it. We felt utterly destroyed. It seemed for a time that those few moments of pure terror had simply erased us and left us but ghosts of what we had been.

Several summers ago, Mryyn, Thom, and I had found an ancient towering sugar maple that had been gutted by time and insects so that the three of us could rest quite comfortably within its rugged core hidden from the world. We would sit for hours within its bowels safe from rain and prying adult eyes, a lamp between our feet, telling tall tales and playing games. One day, we returned to the spot, eager to hide in its embrace only to find that a late summer storm had brought that hollow behemoth tumbling down. Its tallest branches lay touching the green waters of the pond. I remember thinking then that it seemed an awful end for such a powerful and ancient life. It had been slowly eaten away at the core until it was a hollow shell of itself. Where once it had been strong enough to weather the worst gales, it had been transformed into a fragile shell. In the end, it was weaker than a sapling, no longer able to bend. Its brittleness and hollowness was its death.

At that moment on the ridge, I had a hint of how it must have felt for that old tree to come crashing down. I felt as if I had been cored and left but a shell of myself. So great and powerful had been the battle raging before us that we all felt hollowed out. Our little childhood lives, our games, and the commonness of daily life seemed to have no place in a world with such awesome horrors. The events we had witnessed that night and our own petty lives before that time could not even be compared. It was this strange brittle sense of hollowness that kept us speechless and silent for a long, long time.

We watched, trance-like, as Desmodys and his remaining guard remounted and prepared to leave the valley. It was clear that even these hardened soldiers were shocked and overwhelmed by what they had seen. They gathered quickly and silently into ranks and began the march out of the valley. Desmodys and his black-swathed personal guard remained behind. They sat atop their great mounts for several minutes on the valley floor unmoving. The main guard contingent had left the far end of the valley before Desmodys moved. Slowly, he dismounted and made his way to Stone Table. He seemed huge as he stood over the torn and lifeless body of Yakum.

I watched numbed, as he fiercely kicked Yakum in the ribs with a heavy black boot and watched for even the tiniest response. Satisfied by the certainty of Yakum's death, he abruptly turned and made his way back to his black horse, remounting it. I saw him turn and look down the valley as if to insure himself that all the guards but his two henchmen had evacuated. Then he turned slowly to face the seam once again.

He sat like that for a long time. Suddenly, I heard him hurl a command across the valley, but I could not make out its words. It seemed made of the same guttural, even gagging, language I had heard him use to summon the Solyss from the pit. Nothing seemed to happen for several moments, but even within my trance, I felt a twinge of fear and sickness at the unintelligible words. Then as I looked below, I thought I saw new movements on the valley floor.

At first I could not discern what it was that was moving in the darkness. Slowly though, it became quite clear. I watched as the large hunks of Solyss' skull and meat that had been blasted across the valley began to shake. The movements were subtle, but they rapidly changed. The pieces seemed to bubble and turn in on themselves. With a sickening crackling sound, grotesque limbs sprouted from the transforming pieces of flesh. They seemed to quiver and squirm as the budding limbs grasped for solid ground. Finally, snouted heads popped from the black shoulders, and to my horror, I suddenly watched as huge, fully formed vulls stood erect. There were hundreds of them scattered across the valley floor, one where each piece had fallen.

Somewhere deep within my trance, an alarm bell rang. I was still trying to sort out the purpose of its clatter, when I heard a high-pitched scream beside me. I looked over to see Mryyn with eyes wide open, an expression of horror distorting her face. She was focused down the ridge behind us. Then I saw the source of her terror. Two huge vulls, mouths agape, were bounding at us out of the dark. I had forgotten the two pieces of Solyss' skull that had landed just behind us in the explosion.

I saw Thom move with incredible speed as his heavy long sword made an arc in the darkness. The first beast to reach us was literally cut in half by his blade. But the other was coming too fast. My own sword was well out of reach and Mryyn's bow was still hitched to Hoofer. I dove in front of Mryyn, but she was quick and had already rolled away. I saw the wicked snout venting steam from two gaping nostrils and two vermilion eyes seemed to fill the sky as the ugly beast hurled through the night toward me. I heard a grotesque thunk, as metal slammed against bone, and suddenly the yellow eyes went blank. The stinking beast tumbled upon me, limp and unconscious. Stunned, I pushed the vile burden off me. A heavy stone cutter's hammer lay half sunk in the creature's crushed skull. I looked at Mryyn and Thom who were just regaining their feet, but they were just as surprised at the beast's sudden demise. Then, out of the darkness, stepped a huge cloaked form, its face hidden in shadow. As the strange figure moved toward us, its hand reached up and swept the hood from above. I heard Thom gasp. Then my eyes saw what he saw. Toss stood before us. Toss, my boss and mentor. Toss, who had watched Yakum so silently all those months.

Before we could ask any questions though, several vull screams echoed from the valley reminding us that we were not out of danger. The four of us now crept again to the ridgeline. What we saw succeeded in shocking us once again even though I thought by that point that I was beyond all surprise. Desmodys and his bodyguards sat on their mounts surrounded by scores of barking vulls. At first I thought they were under attack. I quickly realized however, Desmodys was speaking to the evil spawn and that they were listening. He sat coolly, directing the creatures—several times pointing down the valley to where the road wound back toward Duvall. To my astonishment, the hordes obeyed and, with a crying scream, rushed like a black wave of poison down and out of the valley. Their haunting screams faded into the night.

Once they had disappeared toward Duvall, Desmodys took one last long sweeping look around the valley. His gaze seemed to pause on our hiding place as if he could see us in the dark, but then moved on. Apparently satisfied, he turned his great black beast in a wide dancing spin and trotted off toward the south, far behind the now distant vulls. His two guards flanked him to the right and left.

Thom was the first to speak. "What in Maels' hell was that?"

"Oh Dyos, what a night," Mryyn added. "I feel like the world has just been turned upside down."

Desmodys, the undisputed leader of our people, the high consulor of the Exarchate, had conjured a fully-formed vull army out of charred flesh and then directed them in an attack against his own retreating Red Guard. All the while, he had looked as calm as if he were directing a Restday service.

Until that moment, I had been able to imagine some coherent reason to explain the events of the last few days—some way they could fit into a sensible world, but now...now my strained attempts to make sense of it all simply collapsed. The very foundation of our lives, even the most fundamental truths by which we had lived every day, seemed suddenly like nonsense. It was as if Desmodys had been the keystone to one of my solid arches and with this lie, the whole supported structure had come tumbling down. I struggled to comprehend the implications of all we had seen and the reality we were left with was worse than any nightmare.

Several things were quite clear: Yakum, the self-proclaimed Dyos'Lei, was now dead. At the point of his greatest victory over evil, he had been slain. Meanwhile, Desmodys, by some black magic, was able to coax the Solyss from the pit, transform dead flesh into living vole, and then command such creatures of darkness. I felt as if we had witnessed some colossal and cosmic shift that had forever altered the fundamentals of our world. I felt puny, scared, and sick.

I looked over at Mryyn. She was standing near the ridge edge gazing steadily down to where Yakum lay. I watched as a look of anger and grim determination grew on her face. She spit at the ground beneath her feet as if expelling some poison from her lips. She whirled, sprang down the slope, and grabbed her bow off Hoofer's side-pack along with two long arrows. Within moments she was back at the ridgeline. In a single fluid motion, she swept an arrow into the bow, pulled the string taut, and let the arrow fly. She hardly seemed to aim at all, but I heard a high piercing screech. I dove to the edge and peered down on the scene. While I had been gathering my thoughts, the two winged creatures we had seen earlier in the night had landed for their feast. One now lay dead, an arrow piercing its throat. The other, with a screech, was taking off into the night air. As I watched though, it seemed to tumble in midair. The screeching ceased and it fell in a ball of greasy feathers to the ground, an arrow through its gullet.

I suppose it was that small victory that galvanized us all and brought us boldly into the new reality of that night.

"Beautifully done," I said and gave Mryyn a grateful smile. I turned to Toss and welcomed him, thanking him for my life. "How did you come to be here?" I asked.

"I followed you," he replied. Finally, our perception of having been followed made sense. "At the whipping I saw your obvious disgust and wondered whether something was up. To be honest, I felt the same as you. I was ashamed of my weakness. I knew Yakum was not the man Desmodys had labeled him, but I was too afraid to speak up. Truth be told, some of it was jealousy that kept me quiet. That good man down there—he motioned to the valley floor—he had a way with the stone I will never have and a way with people I can hardly understand." Toss looked down solemnly. "Anyway, I'm here," he finished loudly, not used to having to explain himself.

"And grateful I am for that," I said, patting his back in thanks.

"It seems we've stepped into quite a mess," he said with a grunt as he calmly bent and pulled the huge hammer from the crushed skull of the stinking vull.

"What do we do now?" Mryyn asked.

It was clear to us all that at least for the night we were stuck in our hidden perch. Any attempt at leaving the valley in the dark risked a confrontation with the vulls. I had already experienced enough vull hospitality for one night.

"We'll make camp here and leave after sunrise. We can bury Yakum in the morning. If there's anything left after the vulls are done with him."

Whatever mood of confidence that had slowly been growing since Mryyn struck down the flying creatures, I succeeded in dampening with these words and the reality of Yakum's death hit us all anew. What it all meant, none of us really understood, but we knew its implications were great and possibly horrible. It was impossible to believe, but it seemed that evil had indeed won the night.

We settled into a glib circle. Though it is hard to imagine how sleep could have tempted us at such a time, it did indeed. A million black thoughts flittered here and there within our disturbed minds like so many flies feasting on a corpse. At least the surety of sleep represented something known and comfortable. Even its nightmares were at least familiar and less frightening than what we were living. The terrible highs and lows of the last few days had left us emotionally exhausted. Sleep was an escape we welcomed.

We huddled together for warmth with Mryyn leaning against me. Toss offered to take the first guard, until moonset, still hours off and said he would wake me then. We agreed we would be safe on the ridge from the returning vulls if they did not catch our scent.

I heard Mryyn's breathing transform almost immediately into the steady deep breath of sleep. I looked up at the stars to assure myself that at least they had not changed. The ox and the bear, low in the autumn sky, looked back at me just as they had every fall as long as I could remember. I thought of Dyos placing each pale spec of fire in its place across that great black palate and my soul calmed. Toss palmed the great hammer as he sat at the ridgeline. His form seemed to float strangely near and far as I watched. The night closed down upon it from all sides until only a wisp of his presence remained. Finally, even this was gone, and the black whisper of sleep swallowed me whole.

I awoke with a lurch; a lost corner of my mind told me I had slept too long. I looked around trying desperately to orient myself. Mryyn, who had stirred at my lurch, mumbled and then found the peace of dreamlessness once again. A quick inventory of our surroundings told me all was well. Toss had fallen where he had sat, clearly eaten alive by exhaustion. He snored contentedly on his back with his mouth wide open, the heavy hammer on his big chest. *Only he could sleep with a forty-pound hammer on his ribs,* I mused. Thom was curled up like an overgrown baby among the packs. The burrows were quiet and stood with heads bowed together in an equine trance. Something though, was different. I rubbed my leather pack. Dew, heavy and frosted in places, soaked its skin. The sky was clear; the ox and the bear had set long ago to continue their battle over distant lands. The moon too was long gone. A hint of pale light glowed to the western sky. It was about an hour before dawn.

Gently, I lifted Mryyn's lovely face from my shoulder and let it fall softly onto the wool jerkin for a pillow. I arose stiffly and walked to where Toss lay. With considerable difficulty, I aroused him from the rhythm of his snores. When he was fully awake, he told me that shortly before moonset, he had seen the vulls rushing back into the valley. They had circled the slain body of Yakum for a time, sniffing and barking. None however, had dared to approach his fallen form. Finally, as if by an unheard command, they had all turned and fled toward the seam and dived in twos and threes into its impenetrable depths until they were all gone. He had felt it safe to let me sleep after that and had quickly fallen prey to the lure himself. I thanked him for letting me sleep. He accepted my thanks with a grunt, rolled over, and started snoring again almost immediately.

I walked to the ridge and sat on its crest. Now with the moon gone, the dawn was barely a whisper in the west. The valley was filled with night shadows. Its floor lay in darkness, and a heavy fog had settled in its cup. The mists whirled slowly like some wizard's brew. I leaned back against the rock and watched the morning come. How I needed the comfort of its light.

My mind had somehow shuffled the wondrous and terrible events of the night before while I slept. Though still confused and worn, I felt far steadier than I had before. I did not like this new world I had woken up to, but I knew it was the real thing. In fact, in some ways the past already felt like a childhood fantasy. Nothing was as plain as I had once thought. There were forces at play so much greater then I had ever imagined. I wondered silently in the early dawn, how I had not seen them before, for surely they had been there all along.

It occurred to me that until I had learned the trade of stone, I had been oblivious to the wonderful forces of energy and angle, weight, and balance, that were on display all around me in every arch, column, and peaked roof. I had never before that time considered how lie and shape, grain and structure, made all the difference between a great hall and a pile of stones. To most of the world these were hidden forces even though their wonder danced just before their eyes every day. So too, I thought, were the great forces of good and evil that had suddenly been so clear the night before. They had always been there but rarely recognized for what they were.

The western sky glowed the deepest black-blue while my companions slept soundly. Toss' snores had a buildup, reached a growling crescendo, and then dwindled to a low gurgle over a dozen breaths. Other than that, the dawn was silent. There was no wind or creature noises—just the soundless swirl of thick mist in the valley.

Over the next hour I sat patiently through many snore cycles and watched the world awake. The highest wisps of cloud caught the light of the sun first and were set ablaze with crimson fire. The deep-hued reds changed slowly to pinks and fierce oranges, and at last quiet yellows. Finally, the first dancing rays hit the highest peaks and, within minutes, flooded our ridge. Grays, deep blues, and blacks of the night shadows were burned away and the rich browns, greens, and slate blues of the high hills glowed forth. With the arrival of color and dewy light, my lonely heart swelled. I thanked Dyos for making this land a place where darkness only reigned for a time before light returned to reclaim its right. In the end, the sun, now full above the western ridge, dipped its light into the smoky mists below, making them glow like a yellow sea.

I looked down at Mryyn. The warm morning sun showed full on her resting face. Her thick lashes and the curve of her nose cast a soft shadow across her cheeks. She breathed smoothly and easily and I looked at her lips, full, moist, just a hint apart. I felt a stir of longing to meet them gently with my own.

You are so lovely, I thought. *And so bold.* I recalled her anger with the scavenging creatures from the night before and her swift and steady action with the bow and I felt my longing for her swell all the more. I wanted to hold her tight to me but I let her sleep away her ragged exhaustion.

Thom lay further down the slope, twisted among the baggage as if he had been wrestled to the ground by an army of marauding packs. Even now, as he slept, a sly smile crossed his face. I wondered what merry trick he was playing in the land of dreams. It seemed that joyously devious mind never stopped its plotting and planning. I recalled the vull shorn asunder by his massive blade—a strike of almost unimaginable strength and boldness—unhesitatingly dealt. What a juxtaposition my good friend was: man and boy, giant and child. Once again that morning, I counted myself grateful to be his friend.

Just below me lay Toss, reaching the crescendo of yet another snore cycle. He lay among the stones as comfortable as if he rested upon a bed of feathers. Even as he slept, he clenched his hammer tightly, as if it were just another appendage of his rocky hands. His immensely thick chest rose and fell like a great bellows. He was a man as hard as the rock he worked but with a core of gentleness and truth. Thus he had walked unafraid into the darkest of nights. I thanked Dyos for bringing him here among us and for his quick action on my behalf last night.

I looked back down the valley where the mist was now rising in fiery yellow curls; its vaporous fingers twisting toward the sky. As the sun rose higher, I could begin to make out the valley floor. But what I saw made me grow very concerned.

Stone Table looked splattered with molasses in the new light of morning. Dried blood lay thick upon its surface. The heavy chains were coiled as if someone had carefully wound them in neat piles, one at each corner. I thought I could make out a square sack sitting on one edge of the table, but Yakum's tattered body was nowhere to be seen and my spirit stumbled. I wanted so desperately to believe that our presence the night before had served a purpose, even if it was only to bury our King in his terrible defeat. It appeared now that even this solemn task would be beyond our capabilities. Evidently, vulls or other scavengers had finished off the Desmodys' destruction the Solyss had begun. Though I knew Yakum had felt nothing after his death, I hated the thought of my King being devoured bit by bit.

The great stinking mass of black fur and scales that had been the bulk of the Solyss still lay in a grotesque bloated heap surrounded by a giant pool of putrid black blood. As the last mist rose from the valley, its twisting tendrils carried the scent of a slaughterhouse.

I heard a groan and turned. Thom had woken and was

stretching among the packs. He rose slowly and shook the clinging baggage from his arms and legs.

"Mornin'," he said. I managed a smile in greeting. "By Dyos, it's good to see the sun," he said.

"Sure is," I agreed.

"Everything ok?" he asked, observing my somewhat furrowed brow.

"He's gone," I said.

"Who?"

"Yakum," I replied. "His body is gone. Someone...something must have fed on it last night or dragged it into that black pit." Thom seemed upset but not surprised.

"It sure doesn't seem the right way for a king to be treated— to be picked at by a bunch of overgrown vermin."

"I know," I said. "It makes me sick to think about it."

Mryyn and Toss both slowly awoke. I related to them both the most recent bit of discouraging news and they were equally distraught.

For a while the four of us stood on the rocky lip and looked below, believing that perhaps, if we looked hard enough and with sufficient yearning, Yakum would magically appear. But he did not.

"What's that?" Mryyn asked, pointing with her finger outstretched toward Stone Table.

"Looks like some kind of package," Thom said. "I don't remember that being there last night, though."

"Nor I," I agreed.

"Well, the least he deserves is some kind of monument to mark where he fell," Toss said. "We can perhaps give him that."

Over the next half hour, we ate a quick breakfast of salt beef and corn bread Mryyn had packed the day before. We all ate ravenously. We had been so caught up in the events of the last days, that none of us had eaten since Yakum's whipping.

We bundled our packs and headed back down to the valley floor. The plan was to make a quick pile of rocks, say our respects, and flee the valley. We wanted to be long gone by noon from the shadows of those high cliffs. I led the way back down to the valley floor. We stepped carefully and wound our way to just outside the nearest pillar. Standing so near the massive structure, I was struck again by its otherworldly size. Toss too was astounded that such huge blocks of stone, each the size of a large house, could have been moved, much less piled one on the other until they reached a thousand feet into the sky. Nothing in the Southlands, even the once great halls of Parthis, could rival the scale and intricacy of the towering column before us. I could only imagine the awesomeness of the full gates. Even more incredible must have been the power that had destroyed them. Fallen fragments of column lay strewn as far down the valley as the eye could see. The partner column lay crumbling from the ages and half-buried several hundred yards across the valley floor from where we stood. I felt small and weak in this world of giants.

We advanced tentatively through the gates until we stood beside Stone Table. It seemed much larger now that we stood so close to it. Its top was at chest level and it lay somewhat off kilter having been knocked off its base with the force of the Solyss' blow. I could not believe that the huge quantities of dry and sticky blood that splattered its surface could have come from just one person. A horde of grey flies had gathered to feast on its rusty richness.

The great chains, each as thick as a man's wrist and certainly terribly heavy, lay neatly coiled like hibernating blacksnakes. On the far edge, I could make out the strange object we had seen from afar. It was a box about two feet square. Thick leather had been hammered to its sides and had long ago worn to a cracked paleness, almost the color of doe hide. I could see two large hinges from where I stood, but could not make out its front.

We made our way quickly around the table until we stood before the strange box. I searched around beneath my feet and along the tabletop for any sign of Yakum's remains. Nothing was left. The blood-soaked earth was rough with vull prints and an occasional boot print from the guards. Several huge three-pronged holes marked the Solyss' heavy tread. Its giant headless corpse reeked beyond all imagining. I found myself having to breathe through my mouth, unable to tolerate the stench. Even then the bile rose into my throat.

"Uggh," Mryyn said, looking green.

I looked at the box carefully. This was clearly the front as it was without hinges, but no lock or keyhole was evident on its rough surface. On its top was a peculiar insignia in golden hammered metal. Its shape was like none I had seen before. It resembled a triangle with a smooth cut taken from each of the three corners, each of the pieces removed slightly but not yet missing. Axis lines were drawn from each corner and met centrally forming three of the prongs in a seven-sided star.

"That is a Triliset," Thom said.

"A what?" the three of us asked in unison.

"A Triliset. I saw one of these before in one of Mias' books. He told me it was a 'Triliset' and said it was the kingdom-seal of Dyos. He said that the authors of legends tell of a time during the Old Age when the flag of every nation had a Triliset within its design acknowledging Dyos' supreme reign over all things."

I reached tentatively to touch the box. I was not sure I could trust anything in that accursed valley, especially something that had appeared mysteriously in the night.

The leather of the box was rough and worn, cracked in places and stiff with time. The metal trimming was strangely warm to the touch, despite the chill of the morning. It too had the mark of ages. Dark mineral stains had spoiled much of its sheen. The Triliset itself was smooth and shined brightly as if someone had spent hours polishing it for just this occasion. The morning light was curiously reflected on its hammered surface giving the illusion of a thousand tiny rainbows. Whether by its strange cut or the angle of light as it hit the design, the central star seemed to glow eerily blue and float a hairsbreadth above the surface. So strong was the illusion that I ran my hand across the floating star prepared to feel its raised edges. Instead I felt only the smooth surface of the design.

As the shadow of my hand passed across the image however, I heard a discernible click deep in the box, as if tiny gears slid by each other. I waited for something dramatic or explosive to follow the little sound but all remained still.

"Can you open it?" asked Thom.

I touched the lid gently and applied pressure to test its lock. To my surprise, the lid lifted easily, almost by its own accord, as if the box was hinged with tiny counterbalanced springs. I realized that by moving my hand across the star, I must have triggered the lock's release.

As the box opened, I heard the hiss of in-rushing air. It was the sound of a millennium rushing by in an instant, an ancient dusty inspiration.

The lid lifted itself until I could see the contents of the box. Whatever I had been expecting, it was not what I saw. I looked into the box and stared back at myself. For a moment, I was terribly shaken by the idea that I had somehow fallen in this peculiar box and was now staring out at myself. The effect was strangely vertiginous. Quickly however, I realized that I was looking at a mirror and a simple reflection of myself. Thom, Mryyn, and Toss gathered quickly around me in a tight bunch peering into the box over my shoulder. Now it appeared as if some four-headed creature had made the box its home. Carefully, I grabbed the edge of the box and drew it slowly toward me. The mirror seemed to shift and ripple slightly with the movement, then fell still again. I tapped the side of the box lightly with my knuckles and again the ripples shivered across the surface.

"It is liquid," Mryyn said, "like silver water."

A liquid mirror—who's heard of such a thing? I wondered. I reached gently into the box with one finger and carefully touched the shining surface. The tiny ripple spread again. I felt no heat. Was this some strange magic, to make silver melt without fire or heat? I drove the tip of my finger in to the knuckle. Besides a delicate tingling, I felt nothing. The silver water was neither cold nor hot. I withdrew my finger and peered at it. It did not appear wet or stained in any way; it still tingled just a bit. The feeling was not bothersome, rather strangely comforting—much as one would feel stepping out of a hot spring on a winter's day.

More confident now that this silvery water held no danger, I reached deeply into the box to feel whether any hidden objects lay in its depths. As I sunk my hand in further feeling for the bottom, I felt only more tingling, nothing of substance. It seemed strangely deeper than it appeared on the outside. I peered again at the box's dimensions and pushed my hand in until my forearm was half sunk in its depths—nothing. Still, I could feel no bottom. I moved my hand to the edge, sinking it all the way to the elbow in an attempt to feel the hardness of the wooden sides. I looked again at the outside of the box and tapped the side with my other hand, hearing clearly the dull resonance of leather-padded wood. It seemed from the way I had my right hand buried in the depths that my entire forearm and hand should have been sticking out of the side of the box. Were my senses tricking me? Where was my hand going? I felt a bit dizzy at the peculiar disparity of my senses, unable to sort out what was happening to my hand in those silvery depths.

"What do you feel?" Thom asked.

"Nothing," I said. "I feel nothing but water...liquid silver... whatever this is. From the inside, the box doesn't seem to have sides or a bottom. They're... just not there."

I pulled my hand out to assure myself that the limb had not been painlessly removed just below the surface, thus explaining my inability to feel, but there it was, intact and dry, tingling in the morning air.

"What is that?" asked Toss.

"What is what?" I queried.

As I was speaking however, I saw what Toss was referring to. So quickly had I removed my hand, and so focused had I been on seeing the wiggling fingers still attached after the strange sensory confusion, that I had not noticed the obvious change on my wrist. The skin itself was intact, but wrapped around its girth was a pale silver-white band—a bracelet—about three fingerbreadths wide. I stumbled back, a bit shaken by the sight, realizing that somehow this foreign object had appeared on my wrist. I moved my fingers and all the bony joints of my hand, massaging it with the other just to confirm its reality. It seemed fully intact and in working order. The bracelet felt smooth against my skin and non-binding, not hot or cold, rather like it had always been there. I examined it more closely. Thom, Mryyn, and Toss gathered around, equally curious.

"How did that get on your wrist?" asked Mryyn.

I confessed that I did not know. Clearly, it was too narrow to slip over the widest parts of my hand; I had not felt it slide on. It seemed made of pale silver-grey stone or even ceramic without obvious texture or grain, like the finest marble but without its coldness. No crack, fissure, or joint broke its smooth surface. It had no obvious beginning or end and no apparent mechanics. Its pale surface was entirely flat except for a pattern a single fingerbreadth wide running around the entire band. The pattern was made of three parallel lines. Their jagged course looked like fine lightning bolts cut delicately into the surface. I stroked the simple design and could just feel the texture of its edges when I focused my most delicate senses to the task. The others, equally intrigued, ran their fingers across its pattern as if by touch its mysteries would be known.

Shocked though I was, I was strangely unafraid of the band's gentle grip. It felt smooth and comfortable and peculiarly un-threatening. It had a gentle weight. I tried once to slide the ring-let from my wrist, but it stuck fast at the base of my hand and it would not come off. I supposed that I would have to shatter it to remove it, and I felt strangely reluctant to attempt such a thing. There was something definitely comforting about its solid weight at my wrist that I could not explain. For now, I was contented simply to leave it alone.

Mryyn was the first to turn her attention back to the box. I saw her peer into its reflecting depths.

Suddenly, as if by impulse, she drove her hand into the glistening waters. The silver ripples swallowed her limb whole as it had mine. She moved her arm around in a concentrated search for the wooden bottom and sides just as I had. A look of confusion furrowed her beautiful brows. Like me, she quickly drew her arm out to visually confirm its continued existence. None of us were surprised to see a band like mine encircling her wrist when she lifted her arm anew into the morning air. One thing was different, however: the design. While the pattern of lines around my band were angular and sharp like the rip of lightning, the three lines twisted in delicate overlapping waves around her own. It brought to mind strings of mist twisting in the breeze. Beyond this mysterious difference, the two bands appeared identically fashioned. Her band fit the slim lines of her graceful wrist with the same naturalness as my own.

After this, Thom and Toss were quick to follow suit. They rolled up their sleeves and dropped their arms deep into the reflecting waters. Each also bore a band when they lifted their wrists to the sky.

Thom's was a similar grey to ours, but instead of parallel lines, his seemed inscribed with a singular line of continuous figures, which wound around its surface. All of us looked closely at the strange script, attempting to make sense of the writing, but it was clearly foreign. It spiraled like the runes of some ancient text—a language long forgotten.

Toss' band had perhaps the strangest look of all. Like ours, it was smooth and three fingerbreadths wide but was unmarked silver-white, without pattern or inscription. For some reason, the blank look of his band made us all fall silent, unsure what to make of its emptiness. Its lack of design seemed somehow sad and lonely but also strangely peaceful. I was unsure how a simple grey band could elicit such feelings in all our hearts. Nonetheless, we were all struck, for a time, with a haunting solemnity as we gazed upon its plainness.

For a long moment, we stood in a circle, hands outstretched, wrists together, peering wondrously at our magical tokens. I felt my heart lifted toward Dyos even in the depths of the valley; my soul seemed mystically carried to the heights. I thought for a moment that I saw the intersecting bands on my wrist dance with an azure light, as I felt my spirit soar. The fears and horrors of the night before were silently swept away as we stood thus. And when the moment passed, and the delicate blue faded, we all felt fresh and clean.

What was happening to our world? Whereas before it had seemed so solid and simple, overnight it had become filled with mystery, miracles, fantasy, and magic—both wonderful and horrible. Events that just a month ago I would have called impossible were becoming almost routine occurrences. I think I might have questioned my sanity if not for Thom, Mryyn, and now Toss. Even so, there were many times over those days when I questioned whether I was caught in some elaborate dream or hallucination.

Of course, Yakum had been the beginning of it all. Only since I had known him had my world become so fantastical. Now it seemed that his passing was not the end at all, but only the beginning. I knew that above all, Dyos was in control, and that it truly was the spirit of Dyos'Bri in our hearts and minds that allowed us to function at all. Strangely enough, it was Toss, solid and earthly-simple, who seemed to adjust most quickly to the realities of our mystical new world. It's possible that Dyos'Bri had been at work longer and more deeply in our solid friend than we all suspected. After all, it was to him in all of Duvall that Yakum first came.

A cold breeze slipped down the great cliffs and whipped through our huddle, breaking our communal reverie. We turned quickly to examine the box more thoroughly. Perhaps there were other mysteries within its edgeless depths.

The box was gone. The box, which had sat just moments ago on the lip of the great stone table and had appeared so strangely, had disappeared. We all stepped back and examined the ground to all sides of the table. We wanted to make sure that the sudden breeze had not somehow knocked the box from its perch onto the blood-soaked ground. None of us had heard it fall, and indeed not even a fragment of it could be found. It seemed it had gone just as mysteriously as it had come. It struck us that it may have been silently carried off, and we all reacted to this notion with a simultaneous turn outward, and a visual sweep of the valley. No creeping creatures or misty phantoms slipped behind the rocks or back into the depths of the seam. The valley lay hauntingly empty. In some strange way, I might have been comforted at that moment by the sight of a slinking enemy. Instead,

I suddenly felt terribly small and vulnerable in the vastness of the valley, and the nearness of the seam was quite disturbing.

Thom, no doubt feeling equally small despite his size, suddenly said, "Let's finish this monument and get out of here before something bad happens."

As if with one mind, we all stooped and began collecting large fragments of red marble to make a grave marker.

Mryyn rose abruptly and looked into the distance with a squint.

"What is that?" she asked. I stood and peered in the direction she looked. I quickly realized however, that she had not seen anything. Instead, she was listening intently to a faint sound, eyes afar. I quieted my own thoughts and turned my ears to the distance. At first I heard only morning sounds—the breeze sweeping softly by the cliffs and the occasional drip of dew off the higher rocks. Then, as I continued to listen, I heard it—a distant crackling sound just below the senses. It sounded something like the aching crack of black ice in a spring thaw, only far more faint. In a moment I knew the sound. I looked over at Toss, sure that he too would recognize the noise. Indeed he did, and his eyes went wide.

I had first heard the sound during my initial chiseling lessons with Toss years ago. He had been teaching me the hidden secrets of stone. He had had me put the light-shaping chisel to a huge block of marble that seemed impossibly solid. Carefully taking my hand in his own, he had guided the point of the chisel precisely to a spot off-center on its smooth surface. I could not see what surface feature had led to his choice, but I went along with the lesson. He instructed me to hit lightly with the hammer. I did so and turned to him for further instructions.

"Wait," he had said.

I turned back to the great stone block and waited for more instruction or something to happen. It was then, like now, that I had heard the sound. I had watched in amazement as the block, after a long pause, had literally shattered into a thousand pieces like the most brittle glass. The sound I had heard, and which I heard now, was the sound of a million hidden fissures cracking apart in the chaos of released energy. The very being of the rock had been ripped apart by its inherently imbalanced forces. My pinpoint blow had only been the catalyst; the rest had been the tensions of ages released in a sudden explosive burst. Somehow, with one look, Toss had known the dark secrets of that great block.

I looked at Stone Table before me and saw that it had been fashioned from a single massive block—it was tearing itself apart. Somehow we had triggered the catalyst. I stepped back, drawing Mryyn with me, shielding her with my shoulder. I yelled for the others to take cover. The crackling grew until it was almost deafening, then with a thunderous thump, the blood-soaked table splintered, hurling debris a dozen paces in each direction. Several small pieces struck my back and stung, but did little damage.

The dust settled slowly. The table was a heap of fragmented stone rubble. The heavy chains, bent and broken, lay twisted in the pile. When all was quiet, I walked slowly toward the table wondering what sudden force had caused such destruction. It was then that I noticed the glint of shiny metal in the dusty heap.

Chaptyr 10

I looked more closely and saw again a bright flash amongst the rubble.

"What is that?" I said, pointing to the sparkling object.

The others looked where I directed but none stepped forward to investigate. The many surprises of the morning had made us all timid. Finally, consumed with curiosity, I wound my way among the scattered rubble until I stood just feet from the shattered remains of the table and the peculiar bit of sunlight in the dust. As I came closer, I could see a long, metal cylinder protruding from the heaps of stone. I reached out tentatively and grasped its end drawing it from the debris. Mryyn, Thom, and Toss came quickly to my side, now too curious to resist. Together, we marveled at the strange and foreign object I held in my hand.

I had pulled from the rubble a long metal tube almost the

length of my arm but thinner around than my wrist. It was made of some fabulously reflective metal the color of the purest silver. Its surface was remarkably polished and unmarred by scratch or dent, as if it had been made just moments ago. One end was flat and finished with a delicate filigree; the other was rounded to a ball the size of my fist and inlayed with gold designs. The rod seemed heavier than one might expect for its size. I bounced it gently in my hand. Despite its weight, I could just perceive a deep resonant hum when it struck my palm. "I think it's hollow," I said.

"It must be worth a fortune," observed Thom.

"I have never seen metalwork so fine," Toss added. "This is not Southlands workmanship."

"Where did it come from, then?" asked Mryyn.

"Your guess is as good as mine," Toss replied. "I suspect it was brought here by the same people or thing that made the magic silver waters and these bands, and probably those monstrous gates," he continued, motioning toward the colossal red pillars. But as to how it had been imbedded in a solid piece of marble, no one could guess.

As he spoke, I continued to fondle the glittering staff, running my hand over the intricate pattern of the ball. On a whim, I twisted the ornate ball on its axis—at first gently, but then with greater force. I felt it budge. Then with the gritty grind of ages, it began to turn more easily. I continued to twist it, holding the staff firmly. Finally, after several turns, the ball twisted free with the audible pop of in-rushing air.

"You've broken it!" cried Mryyn.

"I don't think so," I assured her, showing her the fine ridges in the staff that allowed the two pieces to twist together securely.

"What's inside?" asked Thom, peering eagerly into its black throat.

I flipped the staff over and tapped its end. Nothing tumbled onto the ground as I had expected. Instead, I saw something protruding from the tube's end just slightly. I grabbed it between my fingers and drew it out. It was a tightly rolled parchment scroll bound with a single purple thread in its middle. It felt as light as a feather in my hand and terribly delicate.

With Thom, Mryyn, and Toss breathing excitedly over my shoulder, I laid the scroll gently on the ground, broke the fine thread, and patiently unwound the fragile roll. Time had sucked all the moisture and substance from the paper making it almost translucent. It crackled like the dry leaves of winter as I tried to smooth it, and I was sure it would crumble if I pressed too firmly. But amazingly, it held together. When I had finally gotten it to lie flat, I moved to the side taking my shadow with me. The morning sun fell in its ancient designs and brought them alive.

It was a map. I recognized quickly the Southlands at the lower left of the beautiful rendering, but the rest was completely unfamiliar. It seemed much of the great land mass portrayed extended to the north beyond the reach of the Southland borders. I had never seen a map that made any more than a general reference to the lands beyond the Breach Cliffs, and certainly none with the detail included here. I was pondering this curiosity when I heard Mryyn gasp and let out a small fearful cry.

I looked at her and saw that she was staring near the bottom of the page at some ancient indiscernible text. I was about to ask her what had frightened her when I realized that the text was actually readable. Though ornately transcribed in a wondrous script like none I had seen, it was not foreign but had just appeared so at first glance. Still, this did not explain Mryyn's sudden fear. As I began to read, I heard Thom gasp as well, and suddenly, I knew the source of their panic. The text read:

Creation has waited patiently for this age to come.

At the moment of its birth pains
When a great heat burned in the deep
Rock ran in rivers of fire
Here I buried these my words before man I made
In time, I lifted my words towards the sky in the guts of the
mountain
Later, I brought them low again with ten thousand ages of
rain and wind
There they slept beneath the skin of the land

Out of the nations now long made, I chose one
A craftsman skilled in stone
A great block of marble he chose
And from its heart a table of sacrifice made
My words within still

Here I chose to fight my greatest battle
And won

Be not fearful at the sights of your eyes
Know there is much you see not
Quiet the beat of your hearts
So they may see where your eyes cannot
My children, I call you beyond your fears
You must tremble at naught but I
Your obedience will witness my faithfulness
In the darkest of lands, you will accomplish my will

Remember, before the day the night is
Yet in the dark, the moon stands defiant
Swearing of the Sun to come

My kingdom seal is upon you, You are

Pityr, my power
Mryyn, my touch
Thom, my wisdom
Toss, my strength

I thought the terrible and fantastic events of the last two days had made me numb and prepared me for just about everything, but when I read those hauntingly personal words, I was truly shaken. My mind struggled to comprehend the eternal mystery of these words. I wasn't exactly sure how to deal with a personal correspondence authored by the Lord of all creation and dated a thousand millennia before my own birth—when the stone table was still liquid rock.

Suddenly, my whole concept of time and space seemed precarious at best. The incredible implications of those words were beyond belief. Essentially, they spoke of a Dyos of near infinite majesty, very involved in even the smallest details of his creation, and frighteningly personal. Though his majesty and comforting words quenched the fires of fear within me, I thought for a time that I might very well drown in the flood of their awesome power.

It was obvious that the others were equally shaken and struggling desperately to hold on to any remnant of reality. The four of us stood in a silent contemplative circle. With my eyes closed, I heard someone start to cry, and within moments we were all weeping. We shed tears of great loss, for gone were the fragile fantasies of childhood. We shed tears of guilt, for the attention of the almighty was a heavy burden indeed. Finally, we shed tears of joy and celebration in the knowledge that King Dyos loved us with such a wonderful timelessness and from before we were known to anyone but him. It was a strange series of emotions. After so many days of uncertain change, it was a great release to share these tears together.

As we wept for a while, we felt the awesome and gentle presence of our King. Even though we could not see him with our eyes, our hearts knew the comfort of his love and the assurance of his absolute control.

After a time, the emotions ebbed, and we were left with a quiet and deep peace. The shared experiences of the last days were bringing us ever closer together. Even Toss, who, until the day before had not been part of our group, was slowly being grafted into our friendship. It already seemed that his presence was natural and necessary.

It was with this new sense of peace and companionship that we turned our attention back to practical matters. The more we read the ancient words before us, the more we realized that Dyos was calling us to a great and terrible adventure. The words were vague, but the intent was clear. It seemed our King was sending us over the cliffs to the Northlands on a journey into the unknown. The map had a dotted line that curled across the unknown territories beyond the cliffs into realms with fantastical names that spoke of danger and mystery. Just as the command that had brought us here, this new and ancient call seemed irresistible.

We talked for a long time, pondering the meaning of each line and the wonderful details on the map. It was Mryyn that first noticed how the sun now stood high in the sky above us, already past its zenith for the day. We would have to act fast unless we wanted to spend another day in that dreadful valley. It was then that we realized the enormous challenge before us.

"How are we going to get up those cliffs?" Thom wondered aloud.

We all gazed at the towering rock face before us and wondered the same. From far away, the cliffs had seemed impossibly sheer, closer now, and we could see cracks and uneven channels crisscrossing the vertical walls but nothing substantial enough to accommodate a man or even a small child. We were only about two hundred yards from where the cliffs began their steep climb, but we could see no place to start our journey. As we stared intently at the base of the cliffs, we were reminded again of our proximity to the deep blackness of the seam. Even in the bright afternoon sun, the evil darkness of the pit seemed a menacing presence. We had the sense that at any moment, its deadly night waters might overflow their edges and flood the small valley. These thoughts coupled with the stink of the bloated Solyss carcass instilled in us a sense of urgency.

"I think we should split up and search the cliffs for a way up," I suggested. "The sooner we get started the better."

"I'll get the burrows ready," Mryyn said.

"You'll need to get rid of some of those bags if those beasts have any chance of making it up these walls," Toss said. "Even then, I doubt we will find a path they'll be able to climb."

I was quite sure we would not, but I said nothing.

"I'll do my best to pack them light," Mryyn said.

I rolled the map up carefully and slid it back into the sparkling tube. The gold inlayed ball screwed on easily and I handed the staff to Mryyn. "Pack this well, it's our only hope once over those cliffs," I said.

Mryyn stepped forward and kissed me gently on the lips. She whispered her love and told me to get moving.

Thom headed up the eastern rim of the valley, curving his way toward the cliff base. Toss headed back up the western rim we had come down that morning. I realized with a growing dread that I was left to search at the foot of the cliffs directly ahead, which meant a closer look at the seam.

Slowly I made my way around the putrid heap of the Solyss' flesh and oily fur. I could not avoid stepping in some of the sticky black blood, which stuck to my boots like heavy molasses; its stink making the bile rise in my throat. The beast's long pink tail, naked and glistening, wound like a great oily snake toward the seam; its tip dipping into the darkness and not visible. I approached the pit, skirting as wide as possible its eastern lip. In total length, it stretched barely twenty yards, and was perhaps only half as wide, but it seemed a horrid gaping wound upon the land. I knew it led to a vast underworld of dread and evil beyond reckoning, and I shivered as I walked by.

Try as I might, I was unable to keep from peering into its depths. It held a terrible fascination and seduction. Even that one moment had a cost however, because almost instantly, I was gripped with an uncontrollable panic. One glimpse into its dark depths filled my mind with terrible images of slaughter and death.

I saw thousands of slain bodies scattered across a battlefield, many without limbs or heads, a grey rot already setting in. I realized as I walked among the carcasses that I knew faces. Some were friends, even distant family. The land around was ravaged by blight, war, and fire. The sky glowed eerily red. Large black rats were the only living things roaming this terrible vision. I saw smoke blackening the sky just over a rise, and I made my way in my mind toward the ridge. As I walked among the bodies I saw that even in death they were all skin and bones, terribly frail, and the rancid smell of disease hung upon the field. Only a few skinny horses lay among the bodies. A rare vull carcass, and other strange beasts of evil I had never seen, also lay scattered in the red dust. I looked down and saw my father among the dead.

He was starved and riddled with sores, and a cy'daal spear stuck him to the ground. I tried to scream, but no sound came forth. I looked beyond the ridge down at the remains of Duvall. Black smoke rose from the ruins, not a building stood intact. The town wall had gaping seared holes, as if great bolts of lightning had melted away the rock. I saw more bodies scattered at the wall, women and children among them. I heard a sucking sound and turned. Two vulls were feeding on the bloated carcass of a woman. I screamed again. Though I could not hear myself scream, the two vulls lifted their heads at my cry. They laughed with a human voice, terrible and mocking. I realized I knew that laugh—it was the laugh of Desmodys.

All went black.

I awoke gasping for breath on my hands and knees mere inches from the seam. Mryyn was shaking me and calling my name. Nothing in the world could have sounded so sweet. She stood with her face away from the pit and helped me, trembling, to my feet.

"I heard you scream," she said. "I thought you were dying. I came running and found you in some kind of fit crawling toward the seam's edge. You were caught in a trance or something. It was almost as if the darkness was drawing you toward itself." As she spoke to me, she held my face tightly in her hands, not letting me turn toward the abyss. "Look only at me," she commanded.

Helpless, I obeyed.

I noticed that she had strapped the staff to her back with a cord over her shoulder. Though she could not see it herself, I saw that it seemed lit by blue light. Her hands felt hot and remarkably steady as she guided me from the edge. I felt an incredible sense of power and control sweep into my mind—the same azure fire we had all felt before but of greater intensity. From the corner of my eye, I sensed a spark. Mryyn did too. She held on tightly, but we both turned our eyes to the band on her wrist. The dancing wave design inset in her bracelet shone with a bright blue fire. I was sure I could feel its healing pulse burning away the nightmarish vision. Where a moment ago it had been as vivid as any reality, it seemed to dissolve into a misty vagueness in her tight grip. She guided me far beyond the seam before she let go. Neither of us dared to turn our eyes toward its darkness again.

"I am alright," I said, giving her a grateful smile.

"Yes, you are," she replied with a radiant smile of her own.

"Oh, Mryyn, it was horrible. I saw Duvall. It had been burnt to the ground...and all the people slain...our families...and I saw my father..."

"Peace," she said. "It was a nightmare, nothing more. There must be something about the seam that causes trances. Remember when we were on the ridge and we had to tackle Thom? There is terrible evil here; its vapors must somehow infuse our minds and make us crazy. We need to get out of here soon."

"I almost crawled into the pit," I said. "I felt its pull."

"I know," she said, turning away. "I could feel its tug too."

"Thank you for saving me," I said.

"I'm not letting you get away that easily," she said, laughing.

I felt calm at the sound of her laugh. "What happened to your band to make it glow like that?" I asked.

"I don't know," she replied. "I just felt I had to pray hard to Dyos for you and when I did, I felt suddenly strong and warm, like I was full of power. And then the band became almost fiery hot. It was all I could do to hold onto you. Then the more I held on the more I felt the power leave me and go to you. It was really strange, but I felt like I could see right into your mind, into the parts that were suffering. I know it doesn't make any sense, but they had a different look from the rest...even a color. They were darker, and I saw little flecks of grey-green fire, like some kind of disease at the edges. If I concentrated, I could make the blue fire focus on those parts, and it would burn them away and make the sick parts look clean again. You probably think I am crazy, but I think this band made me able to see inside you so that I could heal you."

"I don't think you're crazy," I said. "Whatever you did, it did heal me. I felt the power of the vision dissolving as you held me. Even now I can barely remember the details, and the fear is gone."

"Pityr, so many new things have happened in the last few days to all of us. I don't know if I can make sense of it all. Sometimes I feel like I am caught in some bizarre dream, or that I am slowly going crazy. The thing that frightens me the most though, is that I am not as scared as I should be. The beasts, and the evil, and the magic, and the terrible things we have seen... they make me afraid on the outside, but somehow I am not really that afraid on the inside. Sometimes, I even feel calm. I don't understand what's happening to me."

"I know what you mean," I confirmed. "I have felt the same. I think the person I was a month ago would have died of fright, or certainly gone insane if he had seen the things we have seen. Something has changed. I know Dyos is protecting us. I never knew he did such things, or even cared about me...then again, I think there is a lot I didn't know about Dyos until Yakum came. The words on the map make it pretty clear that we should fear nothing but him. We can bet that when we get over the cliffs there will be a lot more challenges to face..."

"Oh, I'm sure," she said, giving me a lopsided grin. "It is nice to know though that I am not the only one that is crazy." We hugged long and hard, assuring each other of our solid presence in this new world that did often seem so dream-like.

As we turned to begin our survey of the cliffs, we heard Thom's deep voice calling our names. It was urgent, but not fearful. We made our way slowly back past the seam, carefully avoiding even the most cursory glance into its depths. We found Thom pacing excitedly near the burrows. I think he was anxious that something had happened to Mryyn. In her speed to respond to my cry, she had dropped a saddlebag on the ground, spilling its contents on the ground. Like anyone just arriving at the scene in this accursed valley, we would draw the same conclusion Thom had—that Mryyn had been snatched away without a sound.

Thom was so relieved at seeing the two of us safe that he forgot to ask what had happened. Instead, he began right away with the news he had come to tell.

"I think I've found a way up," he said. "Just above the ridge, there is a fissure that looks as if it might run all the way to the top. I can't tell for sure, because the cliff face takes a turn about three-quarters of the way up. Either way, it's going to be a tight climb. It looks like most of the path is only about two or three feet wide and pretty steep."

"Well, let's see what Toss finds," I said. I wasn't too keen on trying to drag the burrows up a path two feet wide.

We didn't have to wait very long. Within minutes, Toss came huffing back into our camp looking discouraged.

"Nothing," he grunted. "The rock face is as smooth as a polished piece of marble over the ridge for as far as I could see. There was only one break, and it started a good two hundred feet up—don't think it'll be much good to us."

"Thom thinks he has found a path," I said.

Toss peered into the sky, judging the light. The sun had passed toward the western ridge. It looked to be about mid-afternoon. This time of year sunset would be only about three hours away. "Whatever way we go, we better do it fast," he said. "I don't like the thought of being here when it gets dark."

Agreement was unanimous and we all jumped quickly into action. In just moments, we completed the sorting and re-packing Mryyn had begun. Thom buried the few packs that remained under a pile of stones well up the ridge in the hope that they would be missed by any wandering vulls. It was hard to believe we would ever be back that way to retrieve our belongings, but we wanted to leave as little indication of our passage as possible.

When we had trimmed all we could and re-balanced the heavy loads, we proceeded up the eastern edge of the valley. This side was steeper than the ridge we had come down that morning and its rocks looser. It was a tough climb. Every footstep sent a cascade of loose shale tumbling in tiny avalanches back toward the valley floor. Nevertheless, every bit of distance we put between ourselves and the midnight-evil of the seam and the Solyss' putrid corpse seemed a step toward freedom. Finally, we crested the eastern ridge and were graced with a view of low hills and valleys caught in afternoon shadow.

The endless ridge of cliffs just to our right seemed to cut through the hills like a massive ship's bow slicing a windblown sea. I marveled again at the unimaginable forces of the Ryyft that had ripped Terras apart, thrusting the Northlands over a thousand feet into the sky, and creating those towering walls.

Thom led us part of the way down into the next valley, and then in a long curving line toward the cliffs. As we came closer, I could see the path he had described. A great gash ran a jagged line across the stone face. It was nothing more than a wrinkle of age for these monstrous ancient cliffs, but it was our only chance of breaching the impossibly high wall. Closer still, I could see a curve in the wall that had not been visible from afar. Because of the bend, it was only possible to follow the path about three quarters of the way up the face. We could not know for sure whether the fissure ran to the top until we had rounded the curve.

At last, we came to a jumble of massive boulders heaped against the cliff face. They had clearly tumbled from the heights long ago when the fissure had been formed. Like a giant's staircase, they stepped almost a hundred feet up the wall, to the place where our path began. As we approached, I looked over my shoulder toward the east, and was disturbed to see how low the sun had already sunk in the afternoon sky.

We halted just long enough to tighten binding cords, chew some salted beef, and whisper a prayer to the almighty Dyos who had called us to that terrifying climb.

These first hundred feet proved quite a climbing challenge. Some of the boulders were the height of a man. We had to drag the heavily laden burrows up each step with ropes, at times lifting them by sheer force. I don't think we would have made it beyond this first obstacle without the combined strength of Thom and Toss. By the time we reached the beginning of the path, the four of us were exhausted and sweating profusely.

Together we surveyed the precipitous path before us. It seemed frighteningly narrow in places and especially steep in others.

Toss, who had some experience dangling off the sides of tall buildings repairing stonework, instructed us in proper belaying technique. He tied the four of us together with plenty of slack rope between which he coiled carefully. Then without evident hesitation, he began climbing the path.

We traversed the first several hundred feet without too much difficulty. The path was reasonably wide and not too steep with the burrows following closely behind us. Thom held Hoofer's reigns, leading the pack, with Possum obediently following on his heels. As long as I did not look into the vertiginous space just beyond my right shoulder, this part of the climb did not seem much worse than climbing stairs. Too quickly however, the path began to narrow, and we were forced to take every step carefully. Here, the burrows had a particularly hard time. Though we had packed them as lightly as possible, their packs scraped the rock face as they passed, pushing them toward the edge. More than once, Hoofer, who was the most heavily laden of the two, came a hairsbreadth away from tumbling.

The first true challenge came about four hundred feet up the cliff wall. Here, the path grew suddenly steeper and narrower.

Toss proceeded first, using both hands and feet to climb. When he had reached the full length of the rope, and it stretched taut between us, I followed carefully, my heart pounding in my chest. Though I did not dare to look, I could sense the emptiness to my right. The wind was quite strong and cold. I could feel airy fingers tugging at my sleeve, drawing me off balance and into a deadly embrace. Despite the coolness, sweat beaded on my forehead and dripped into my eyes, which I had to blink away because my hands were too occupied finding finger-holds. Finally, I came even with Toss. He had coiled the slack rope around a protrusion in the rock.

Mryyn followed next. I watched her move like a cat up the trail. She seemed confident and graceful, and I was reminded again as I watched her, just how much my love for her was growing. I carefully coiled the rope as she advanced. When she finally stood close again, I realized that I had been holding my breath during her whole climb. I gulped in air. She looked up at me and, understanding my concern, gave me a confident smile.

Thom ascended next. He was so wide that his right shoulder hung a few inches over the edge of the trail, even as his left shoulder scraped the rock face. Bits of the trail's edge crumbled beneath his feet, falling several hundred feet onto the valley floor. It seemed forever before they struck the jagged rocks below. I began to realize that coaxing the fully laden burrows up this stretch was going to be a nightmare.

Finally, Thom stood just below Mryyn, on a wider bit of path. Here he was able to turn around, and steady himself in preparation for leading the animals up. I looked below at Hoofer, now two score feet down the trail and at Possum beyond him. I realized with growing dread that I could barely make out the trembling form of Possum in the rear. The afternoon shadows below the valleys seemed to be filling with purple evening, while the highest ridges stood out in orange relief. We were running out of time. Thom moved fast, also realizing the need for cautious speed. The thought of spending a night on these cliffs was in the back of all our minds. It was becoming less a subconscious drive, and more a reality with every passing moment.

Thom had trouble getting Hoofer started. He coaxed and yelled and swore, but in the end it was the pure power of his tug on the line that got Hoofer to take his first hesitant steps. Once he was started, the beast seemed to make slow but steady progress. Occasionally, the packs would catch on the ragged rocks, and Hoofer would seem to waver for a moment, ready to tilt into the abyss, only to catch himself at the last moment. He was visibly trembling and strings of dirty lather hung from his snout. His nostrils flared wide blowing steam. His eyes were bulging, terrified. I could not see Possum behind him, but I was sure the picture would be the same. These were simple beasts of burden used to the field and country road. Never had they walked these heights before.

I saw Hoofer stumble the last few feet to where Thom stood. Thom grabbed the rope attaching him to Possum and began dragging him the last few steps up the steepest part. And then it happened. The trail edge gave way beneath Possum's rear hooves. Heavily laden as she was, her backside slid off the edge and she tumbled fast. The cord grew immediately taut in Thom's hands, and several feet of it whipped through his grip. The slack, coiled at his feet, sprung to life. In a tangled mess, it wrapped itself around his feet and swept them out from beneath him. Possum disappeared over the edge with a pleading cry. Before any of us could react, Thom was dragged a dozen feet down the path feet first, clutching desperately for any handhold. In seconds, he would follow Possum off the edge. In a last ditch effort to save himself, I saw Thom draw the sword from his back and swipe at his feet to cut the cord. He struck hard, and the tight line binding him to Possum split below his foot, but his momentum carried him over the edge, nonetheless.

Now I moved. I dived past Mryyn and grabbed the line attached to Hoofer, which was uncoiling at a tremendous rate—Thom's free-falling weight at its end. I jammed the slack into a small crack, which split the trail. Within a fraction of a second the cord snapped tight and held, caught in the wedge. It creaked under the tension of Thom's dangling weight but did not break. I heard the screech of poor Possum stilled with a suddenness on the rocks five hundred feet below. The cord holding Thom swung, arching back and forth. It twisted and groaned, but held.

I screamed for Thom to hold on, though I knew he dangled by his feet. I felt Toss come up behind me. He handed more cord over my shoulder.

"Wrap it round your waist," he said. "I've got the other end secured." I did as I was told.

Together, we began to pull Thom up. He hung about thirty feet over the edge. Though all of us yelled for him to hold on, we heard no reply. Though he seemed deadweight at the end of the line, Toss and I pulled with every ounce of strength. Foot by foot the line advanced. I felt my forearms cramping terribly and my heart pounding within my chest. I prayed to Dyos fervently for the safety of my faithful friend. Toss' steady strength behind me kept my panic at bay. Up the slope, Mryyn was busy calming Hoofer and insuring our lifeline held strong.

Finally, we dragged Thom's unconscious bulk onto the ledge. A deep gash ran along one eyebrow, and the area all around was swollen and purple. Thom was unresponsive, but his breathing was steady. I guessed that when the line had caught fast, he had been bounced against the cliff face upside down and knocked unconscious. Toss dragged him another few feet up the trail to where it leveled off. Even as Toss set him down, Thom began to wake up and Mryyn came down to him.

"Let me tend to him," she said. She handed Hoofer's cord to

Toss. "Take him further up," she commanded, and Toss obeyed.

Mryyn took Thom's head between her hands, just as she had mine, and furrowed her brow in concentration. The blood ran in a single scarlet rivulet from the wound over Thom's eye. It formed a small pool in the cup where his cheek met his nose. I was entranced by its redness. Mryyn did not remove her hands and her eyes were shut. As I watched, the wave pattern in her white band began to glow with the warm azure color we had all come to know so well. It seemed that the tiniest blue fires danced along the waves coursing through the delicate designs.

Thom began to groan and move his head to and fro. Mryyn's grip tightened and stilled its motion. I could see her knuckles whitening. Thom again fell silent. Suddenly, the blue light became intense like a flash. I saw Mryyn shudder, but she held on. Then, abruptly, Thom opened his eyes wide.

When he saw Mryyn bending over him, the wide-eyed panic abated, and was replaced by a calm knowing.

"What happened?" he asked softly.

"You fell, Thom," Mryyn replied. "You hit your head pretty badly against the rock." The way she said it you might think Thom had just stumbled on his own feet, not slid off a cliff face headfirst and plummeted thirty feet. Nonetheless, he seemed comfortable with the explanation.

Mryyn reached over and, with a white cloth she had produced from somewhere, wiped the blood from his cheek. I could not believe my eyes. The wound that had been open and seeping blood now was nothing more than a pale scar. The dense swelling and blue discoloration had almost completely resolved. Only the lightest tint of yellow remained where once the brutal bruise had been.

I looked at Mryyn with amazement and she caught the look in my eyes and smiled. I knew her expressions well enough to know that the smile carried some hint of self-amazement.

Clearly, she was surprised by the power she had been given.

"Just like with you," she whispered.

I knew exactly what she referred to, remembering all too well the healing intensity of her grip near the seam.

We both helped Thom sit up against the wall of the cliff. At first he seemed a bit confused by his surroundings, but he quickly reoriented himself.

"I fell off the cliff, didn't I?" he queried. I could see those mental gears grinding again. He did not look to me for the answer, sure that my silence was a confirmation.

"Why am I not dead?" he asked.

Though on one level, the answer was easy; the truth was far more complicated. I hesitated. Finally I said, "The cord caught around your foot. You only fell about thirty feet. Toss and I pulled you back up."

"And the animals?" he asked, looking around.

"Possum is lost," I said. "You saved Hoofer and yourself by cutting the cord." I looked down at Thom's sword resting safely on the ledge. He had let go of it before he fell, and it had not gone with him over the edge. Twice now, that sword had saved him. I vowed to wear my own short sword at all times for the rest of the journey.

"What was it Mryyn was doing to me while I was out?" he asked me. "It felt like I was struck by lightning, but it wasn't unpleasant."

"I'll let her explain it to you," I said. She heard me say this from where she was just up the slope rearranging her pack and came back down to Thom.

I left her to satisfy Thom's ever-inquisitive mind and squeezed by her. I made my way up to Toss who had managed somehow to steady Hoofer. The creature had clearly been terrified by his companion's screams.

"How bad is it?" I asked.

"Bad," he said. "We lost about half our food, two bedrolls, our compass, most of our rope, and Mryyn's pack. Worst of all, Possum was carrying all the water except what you have there," he said, motioning to my water bag. "I don't know when we will find drinkable water again."

"Also," he added, "it's getting on." He pointed his finger to the east.

The sun had descended into a thin line of clouds just above the horizon. We would not see it again that day. Within an hour it would be dark. Already, the hills and valleys far below were swathed in evening.

I felt the panic of our situation start to fill me up, but just as quickly, I felt a more powerful calm settle in. Dyos himself was here among us. It was he who had called us to this perilous adventure, and it was he who would carry us through. Thom was safe against all odds; Mryyn wielded miraculous healing powers; Hoofer had survived. Already, we had climbed more than half way up the impossible cliffs. It was imperative that we believe in the one who called us across all time. He, I thought, was a king worth serving.

With these steadying thoughts filling my head, I led the reorganization. We all realized the urgency of moving on. Quickly, we re-fastened our belays and began our ascent again. The trail was somewhat wider here and its pitch less intense. Occasionally, the cliff face bled little rivulets of water, which crossed the path. None of these miniature springs were heavy enough to replenish our water stores. Instead, they made the trail all the more perilous in the fading light, for where they ran, a slick algae grew. We had to coax Hoofer the whole way. He looked terribly forlorn.

We continued this way for about an hour in growing darkness. The trail at times became steeper or more narrow but never as difficult as the stretch where Thom had fallen. A three-quarter moon rose in the west but did little to light our way. Off in the east, I could dimly see that the line of clouds was closer. I feared we would have rain later that night. I knew the others sensed this as well, for we pushed ahead with even greater intensity, despite our exhaustion.

Thom seemed to be doing well. He walked between Toss and me in case he became dizzy, but his solid trot seemed as steady as ever.

Finally, we came to the bend in the cliff face that had been the limit of our sight from the ground. We all approached with hesitation, concerned that the trail would simply disappear. Toss, in the front, was the first to round the corner.

"It's alright!" he yelled back.

"Looks like the trail runs on for a bit at least. It's hard to see in this light. Steep though."

The trail did indeed curve off into the darkness and quickly became steeper again. Half way up one of the steeper stretches, I felt the first raindrop. It was big and cold and promised a night of heavy rain. It was hard to estimate how far we had come. The valley below us was deep in darkness and seemed miles away. Likewise, the cliff top appeared to stretch endlessly up into the night clouds. I was shaking with fatigue and hunger, and fear crept its way back into my heart. The prospect of continuing this dark and perilous climb in the pouring rain was daunting.

I hazarded a look back at Mryyn, wondering how she was doing. I could barely see her in the low light. She looked wan and worn but staunchly determined not to slow us down. *You are one tough girl*, I thought. As if in reply, she looked up at me. Her slight smile did more than any torch to brighten the night.

The rain fell more heavily now, and our path became slick. Each footstep had to be placed with the utmost of care. Up ahead, the trail curved again out of sight. I saw Toss turn the corner carefully and stop in his tracks.

"Hold!" he bellowed.

I wondered what he had seen. Did the trail simply stop, falling off into the night, or did it become impassibly steep? The rain was falling harder now, coming in waves carried on the high cliff winds. The roar of the rain and wind seemed impossibly loud as we waited for Toss in silence to tell us what he saw.

We did not have to wait long.

"Come slowly!" he yelled back, trying to lift his voice above the rain.

I rounded the corner after Thom and was confronted with the sight that had stopped Toss in his tracks. Ahead, the trail seemed to disappear in a wall of darkness. As I looked, Thom's form evaporated into the blackness at the end of the trail. At first I thought that he had tumbled off the end of the trail, but then I heard his steady voice bellowing above the rain.

"It's a cavern!" he yelled.

Ahead, both Thom and Hoofer also disappeared into the darkness. As I approached, I could see more clearly that the trail wound into a large fissure in the cliff face. I could see Thom, Hoofer, and Toss standing just within its dimness. Streams of water ran off the cliff face creating a thin sheet of water that shrouded the entrance to the fissure. I waited for Mryyn to catch up, and together, we passed through the drenching waterfall into the quiet blackness of the cave. I heard Toss fumbling with Hoofer's pack and then the sound of flint and metal meeting. First, there were sparks and then a brilliant flare of light. Toss held a small torch and together, we looked around in amazement.

We stood in an immense cavern created by the great forces of the Ryyft that had torn the cliffs asunder in ages past. The walls rose above us over a hundred feet, meeting somewhere far above in the gloom beyond the torches' reach. The floor was dry and covered in a fine silt inches thick. A few larger rocks lay strewn about on the floor where they had fallen. We could not see the back of the cave from where we stood, but the black emptiness beyond our sight echoed hollowly with each whisper suggesting cavernous depths. I could hear a slow plunking drip somewhere in the distance.

I saw Toss wander over to the wall to investigate something he had seen at the edge of his light and I heard him catch his breath.

"What is it?" I asked.

"Bones," he replied calmly. "Looks like a vull or some other kind of wicked thing; sure isn't a cow. Guess we're not the only ones who've climbed these god-forsaken cliffs." Indeed, it appeared we were not. The more we investigated the dim corners of the cavern, the more skeletons we found, as many as thirty. They were in varying stages of decay, some little more than dust, but all had been there a very long time. Some were clearly vulls and other dark creatures, including some huge multi-legged thing that looked made of nightmares. Several of the skeletons however, were clearly men, though some seemed exceptionally large. A few still wore shreds of cloth, which crumbled when touched. Occasionally, a rusted sword lay nearby one of these reclining bony figures.

I realized the more we looked, that none of these figures, beast or man, seemed to have died in a struggle. There were no severed limbs or piercing spears. Instead, it appeared that each had simply lain down and quietly died. Then a quiet terror grew within me.

There was no going back! This cave was the end of the line. The trail outside was far too steep and precipitous to descend. It had been hard enough to climb. All of these creatures had simply sat here in the dust until they had starved or gone crazy. Suddenly, I had no doubt that the rocks far below the entrance to the cave were littered with a thousand broken bones from those unwilling to starve or were driven crazy by the idea of slow death. The trail must not have continued in the depths of the cave or surely they all would have moved on.

My dread at realizing our new predicament was horrible. I looked around at the others and saw that they were equally stunned. None of us spoke. Toss' torch sputtered; it would soon go out.

"Oh Dyos," I sighed. "Where have you led us?"

CHAPTYR 11

The anguish and frustration we felt was terrible. How we had struggled up those ragged cliffs! We'd lost half our supplies, a good burrow, and almost seen a friend die. We were exhausted, wet, hungry, and emotionally spent. We felt impossibly far from home and lonelier than ever. I realized how it had been hope alone that had driven us beyond ourselves and given us the strength to climb those accursed cliffs. Now it seemed all hope was gone. We were caught in an impossible trap.

I thought that in the dimness, I could almost hear the bones in a mournful cry. It was a dirge filled with agonizing sadness and raging frustration.

"Join us in the dust," came the whispers.

The plunking drip, steady and low, beat a rhythmic requiem. Outside, the rain fell in sheets, its echo a dance of whispers. How many times had this cave sprung its simple trap over the ages? Its victims had had plenty of time to consider their lonely deaths. Many, I was sure, had chosen the quicker path—a swan dive into the valley below. They at least had escaped the certain insanity that would have met them in the dust.

Toss broke the solemn silence. "I, for one, don't think Dyos brought us all the way up here just to make another pile of bones of us. Seems there are plenty here already. A little stew and a little sleep might make things look a bit brighter."

I laughed, despite my mood. His curt sincerity was uplifting. How grateful we were for his simple optimism at that moment when we were feeling so sorry for ourselves.

Within an hour we were sitting around a small crackling fire. Mryyn had mixed a magical potion of smoked bacon, broth, and dried vegetables, which we had all consumed with gusto. This was our first real meal in two days. Despite the fact that most of our food now lay at the bottom of the cliff, we had elected a feast. If we were going to escape our predicament, it would likely take all the mental and physical energy we could muster. On the other hand, if escape was hopeless, it mattered little how long our food lasted. We would not know which it would be until morning.

It was with a full belly and a strange sense of peace that I lay my bedroll among the others by the embers. Somehow, I was sure Toss' faith was on the mark. It seemed ludicrous that Dyos had brought us here as company to the skeletons. Still, I knew there was more yet to come.

I lay awake watching the red light from the embers play on the walls. Monstrous bony shadows danced all about—all skulls and ribs in rickety silence. I could not hear them sing their melancholy whisper songs anymore. I was warm and dry and surrounded by those I loved the most. My ears were deaf again to the secrets of the dead. I left them then to their dance and joined my friends in an exhausted dreamless sleep.

We awoke to a cold misty fall morning. Delicate curls of fog floated by the cave mouth. The rain had stopped sometime in the night and the mist had coated the cave walls with moisture. They glistened with pale blue-white morning light. Gone were the dancing shadows of the night.

Thom had woken before the rest of us and was boiling tea over a small fire.

"Morning Pityr," he said. "I've been meaning to thank you for yesterday. Mryyn told me what you did. I can't remember much myself."

"Sure thing, my friend," I replied. "Just do me a favor. Next time you decide to go tumbling off a cliff, eat a bit less a few weeks beforehand. You weigh near a ton you fat lug. How are you feeling?"

"A little beaten up, but none the worse," he replied. "Whatever it was Mryyn did to me fixed me up just fine. Felt a bit weird, though—like she was patching things up from the inside out. I'm not quite used to this magical stuff yet, you know."

"I know," I said. "I don't think any of us are, even Mryyn."

He handed me some steaming tea.

"I've looked around a bit," Thom said. "The cave only goes back about a hundred yards. I think the wall back there is smooth—felt like it, but I couldn't see worth beans. Know what's weird though? I could have sworn that I could hear water dripping behind it like it was hollow. It might have just been an echo, but I had my ear right up to the wall and could still hear it. Also, when I turned around to come back, I banged my shin on a big rock right in the middle of the floor. When I was done cursing, I bent over and felt it. It wasn't just any rock, it was a perfectly shaped pillar about four feet tall—carved, I'm sure. Try as I might, I can't for the life of me figure out why anyone would sit back in the dark waiting to die and carve a pillar. Weird, huh?"

"Mm," I said. I looked around at the skeletons decorating the walls and imagined the last few days for these poor souls. I wondered if insanity must have come for most in the end. Some delirious fool probably thought he was building a cathedral back there. "We'll go take a closer look again when the others get up," I said.

As if on cue, Mryyn opened her sleep-swollen eyes, saw us preparing breakfast, and stretched cheerily. So expansive was her stretch that it knocked over a pack propped on the wall near her. The bag, full of assorted camping gear, slumped heavily onto Toss. He awoke startled and gasping from his snores.

"Oh, I am so sorry," Mryyn giggled.

We all laughed at Toss' sputtering surprise. He was covered in dust and big sleep creases ran across his face.

"Humph!" he said good-naturedly. "You look like a bunch of beauties yourselves."

Looking around, I realized that we did make quite a ragged foursome—weather beaten, dirty, and worn. It occurred to me then, as it has many times since, that king Dyos' soldiers were an unusually motley crew. What did he see in us that we clearly did not see in ourselves?

Thom looked directly at me. I knew the look. It said he knew what I was thinking. We had been friends long enough to have few secrets. Nonetheless, there was something a little strange about the intensity and depth of his look, as if part of his mind was far away.

"I suspect he sees the same ragged bunch," he said. "You know though, somehow I'm sure that our ugliness and weakness makes the best palate for his beauty and might. If we survive this crazy journey and make it home again, it will be obvious to all that it was the King's work. Only he can do such things."

We all stared at Thom in shock. The simple power of the

words, and his eerie mind reading shook me. I felt in them the clear ring of truth I had heard in Yakum's words. Thom himself seemed stunned that such serious contemplations could escape his own lips.

"I'm sorry," he said a little embarrassed. "I don't know what made me say that."

"I do," Mryyn replied, stating what we all felt.

We were all quiet for some time, each of us still getting used to the strange new realities of our changing lives.

"I don't know about the rest of you," Toss said, "but I, for one, can't put my mind around such things until I've had a slab of bacon in me and some cornbread." He said this to break the tension, and succeeded. We all eagerly fell to the task of making breakfast.

The seriousness of our situation hung with us however, throughout the meal. It lightened a bit when Thom explained what he had found in the back of the cave and we all resolved to investigate further.

Thom and I made thick corn cakes fried in the pork fat from the night before. We consumed these hungrily along with the last of our tart green apples and fresh icy water we had collected from one of the small pools scattered around the cave. As we ate, we were aware that except for a bit of salted beef, this was the last of our food. Even had Possum not been dashed on the rocks below, we would only have had two or, at most, three more meals. None of us had planned for a long journey; we had simply obeyed the call spoken within each heart—a call to follow our King.

Though our mood was somewhat subdued by the dimness of the cave and our grim prospects, there remained in all of us a sense of a future filled with challenge and adventure. It seemed to matter little to any of us that we appeared to be hopelessly trapped. None of us felt that the end lay here. I knew somehow that this cold corner would not be my grave.

After breakfast, we ran an inventory of our supplies. Thom and Mryyn had done well distributing the weight among the beasts before our climb. This had, in the end, saved us. In addition to the food, we had lost some cordage, three woolen blankets, several bundles of kindling, two of four water bottles, and some clothes. We were lucky to still have the flint stones, two pots, all our oil, several candles, and most of our weapons. Sometimes, it is hard to see the patient hand of grace at work in the midst of misery, but I think that morning, when we realized all that had been saved, none of us doubted the purposeful hand of Dyos.

Taking advantage of the low angle of the early morning sun, which stretched its glistening rays as far into the depths of the cavern as it would all day, we decided to investigate further. Surely, we thought, if there was any way out of this trap, it must lay in the shadowed back corners.

We divided into teams of two. With candles aloft, we examined each wall systematically, moving farther and farther back into the cave. We caressed the walls with our fingertips, feeling for tiny fissures, air currents, or seams. We searched out the origin of the various dribbling springs that slickened the rock. Most of the springs seemed to weep through tiny pores from deep within the cold stone. A few gurgled down from far above, beyond the reach of the candlelight.

Despite our careful search, the walls seemed largely smooth and solid. Wet, heavy, and cold, they responded to our probing touch with impenetrable indifference. The cavern curved almost imperceptibly toward the right and downward as we moved farther back into the darkness. By the time we met again at the back wall, the cave entrance was out of sight up and around the curve. Only a pale whimper of morning light reached that far back. I judged that we had come about four hundred feet into the heart of the cliffs.

The ceiling was low and just within reach of the yellow candlelight. Peering up into the flickering dimness, I glimpsed jagged rows of fierce stalactites like the fangs of some timeless stone beast.

There were fewer skeletons now, a pair of vull bones, and something resembling a horse but not much more, all half consumed by the dust. Most creatures, I thought, would prefer to die closer to the light—a final bit of solace in the black emptiness of insanity. I shivered.

By the light of the candles, it was obvious that we had reached the end of the cavern. The back wall was as smooth as the rest and glistened with a perpetual dampness. I saw now the strange pillar that Thom had alluded to at breakfast. It was clearly manmade and not natural. It stood roughly four feet tall, and was about two feet in diameter—too symmetrical for a natural fixture. It stood exactly between the side walls, and about fifteen feet from the back wall.

We all gathered around it shining our candles on its course surface. I had thought from afar that time had simply made it rough, but a close inspection revealed otherwise. It was covered in a delicate and twisting script, beautiful and haunting. It appeared strangely free of dust and wear, even though we had to clear several inches of silt from its base in order to see all the delicate images. Knowing stone as I did, I was quick to notice that it had been fashioned from a single block of dark green marble. Deluvian, perhaps? Toss guessed Parthian, pointing out the fine red specks that confirmed its distant heritage.

What was a several hundred pound block of Parthian marble doing in the back of an almost unreachable cave deep in the Breach Cliffs? None of us could even begin to fathom a plausible explanation, and we just looked dumbly at the pillar, waiting for it to tell us its secrets. I suppose we could have stood like that for eternity without a hint, had Thom not dropped his candle into the dust near its base. As he bent to retrieve it, he put his right hand on the top of the pillar for support.

In that moment, his wrist seemed to burst into azure flame, brilliantly lighting the cave. The shock of it sent us all stumbling backward. Thom, even more surprised, jerked his hand away, and tumbled backwards into the dust with a puff. The cavern fell dark again except for the feeble candlelight.

"What happened, Thom?" I asked. "Are you okay?"

Spitting dust and wiping his eyes, Thom rose from the silt.

"I'm not hurt," he said. "Just a bit surprised. I don't know what happened, but whatever it was, it felt pretty strange—sort of like stepping out into the sun after a long nap—a little dazed by the glory."

We all stepped forward again. Thom reached his hand out very slowly this time, touching just one finger to the pillar. At the moment of his touch, the band at his wrist again lit up. Expecting it this time, we were able to see several independent blue rivers of fire twisting among the strange script pattern on his band. He did not jerk his hand away but held it steady.

Mryyn reached out carefully and touched the stone. I could see a dim blue tinge to her band but nothing like the blazing fire on Thom's. Toss and I each followed suit, touching the stone carefully. Like Mryyn's, our bands glowed dimly but did not dance with brilliance. When I put my hand atop the pillar, I sensed a light tingling, much like I had when my arm had been in the box, but nothing more. It was quickly evident that Thom's experience was something entirely different.

I watched him closely as the blue sparks skittered among the runes on his wrist. His eyes were strangely distant, as if his mind was atop some great mountain rather than here in the bowels of the earth. He had a half smile on his face, the corners of his mouth creeping up just slightly. His jaw was clenched; its muscles tight beneath the skin. In the candlelight, I could see a small artery at his temple, beating a steady tempo. Little else moved.

I had seen this look in Thom many times before, but never had it crackled with such intensity. I had jokingly called it his "moon face." Many times, Mryyn and I had seen him fall into this trance: his head slightly uplifted and his eyes miles away as if his thoughts were dancing somewhere among the celestial bodies. It was often after he returned from one of these mental jaunts that his thinking was the clearest. Whenever I would see Thom's mind slip away thus during Aces and Jacks or other games of strategy, I knew his opponent had no chance. Time after time, we had watched him take the pot with just a hand or two, or corner his competition with just a few moves after a "moon face" trance.

I asked him once where he went on these little mental journeys. He told me in confidence that as long as he could remember, his mind would slip away like this, and he would find himself alone in a small room made all of stone. The room had no furniture or fixtures of any kind and was windowless. What light there was came from a door at the opposite end that was just the tiniest bit ajar. Beyond it must have been some brilliant light, for the brightness of the light that escaped through the crack was almost blinding. Each time he found himself there, he would take a step or two toward the door, but the distance was always farther than it seemed at first. In fact, he said, as I would try and walk toward the door, it would seem I was moving farther instead of closer. Nonetheless, he always felt this uncontrollable need to reach the door. He said that he would always wake up as he started to move away, ending up back within himself. He went on to explain that each time though, when he left this place, he would still have a bit of the light dancing around in his head, something like an echo I assumed.

"As long as it's there, it just seems easier to think than usual," he said. "Also, while the light is there, when I think through something complex and I find the answer, somehow I am certain it is right—not just confident but positive. You know though, the only thing is, I never have control when I find myself in the room."

As I watched him now, I knew he was in the room again. Somehow the whole picture was different. Usually, his brief trances had the wispy quality of a daydream. Now instead, he appeared fully absorbed, every sense aimed toward some distant hope. I saw sweat bead on his brow and drip in sparkling rivulets down his cheek to the curve of his strong chin where each drop hung, collecting themselves. The band sizzled with the intense blue.

Thom slowly slipped his hand off the top of the column until his fingertips caressed the carved runes. He used the soft pads of his first two fingers to trace the delicate curve of the script. His fingers moved left to right in a twisting spiral down the pillar. Perhaps I imagined it, but I thought I saw his fingertips glow. They seemed to leave a trail of azure phosphorescence as they caressed—a blue mist that lingered for just a moment. And then he spoke....

Around thy wrist I've woven stone
Which unlocks doors to worlds unknown

Where chaos from an infant grows
And midnight's king—in wrath he sows
The seed of death—an end he knows

Through his world's black mist and fyre
Those will come whom I desire
To lay their lives upon the pyre

From cold ashes I will raise
An army for the final days
Whose Light of faith in Truth alone
Portends my trumpet call to Home

His fingers finished their gentle blue glide and his words ceased. The cave fell silent as the candlelight flickered. The sizzling pop of the wick seemed too loud in the haunting quiet. I thought I heard the dust settle about us. No one moved. Thom's eyes were closed.

Slowly he smiled, at first achingly, but then, with a clear and free joy. He opened his eyes and they were laughing. His mirth swelled and spread among us. At first we smiled for him, and then finally, we laughed for ourselves. They were full and hearty laughs—the spontaneous expression of hearts liberated by truth.

Really, we had no idea why we were laughing at all. It escaped from inside us, as if it had been building up in there all along—an impossible joy and deep contentment. There was no other way to let it out. In the dark and heavy depths of that cave, those words of truth came like zephyrs off the mountaintops—cool, freshly pure, and irresistibly free. Dyos had spoken again and our hearts sung, even as they trembled.

Thom stopped laughing, but his smile remained. We watched as he reached out with his left hand and brushed a fine layer of silt from the top of the sculpted pillar. He then bent over and blew several times with pursed lips on the flat surface to clear the dust further. I could see now a fine ring carved lightly into the otherwise smooth stone. With his right index finger, Thom touched the ring. Once again blue light danced at his fingertip. He traced the circumference of the ring with his finger three times and it glowed brightly with the same blue light we had come to know so well.

We stared in awe as the central circle defined by the blazing ring slowly began to shimmer. I saw the image of Thom's hand appear in the circle and realized that I was seeing a reflection. The stone within the ring had changed. Somehow, it had been transformed into the same silvery water we had seen in the box. It made just a small pool about six inches across.

Thom drew his hand back, and then with a single motion plunged it beneath the silver surface. Concentric ripples spread outward. I noticed that Thom's arm was buried to just beyond the wrist—the band an inch below the surface. He kept his wrist there for a moment, no more, before he withdrew it completely. The blue light disappeared and the shimmering liquid froze over, once again becoming cool green marble. Though I looked closely, I could see nothing different about Thom's arm or the band itself. He held no new objects. There was a tension in the air as we all waited for something to happen, but nothing did.

I looked at Thom, and so did Mryyn and Toss. With our eyes, we all asked what was going on and what would happen next. He met our looks with eyes full of passion and peace—a look I had seen on Yakum's face many times. It was a bit eerie to see it now on Thom's, as if for the moment he wore the mask of another.

Just when it seemed I would burst with anticipation, I heard a low coarse rumble. With it came a gritty rasp and the sudden hiss of air under pressure. At first, because of the echoing acoustics of the cave, we could not tell where the sound emanated from. We all twisted in circles trying to focus our combined senses on the true source. Then I caught a glimmer of movement out of my right eye. I turned to peer at the rear wall of the cave along with the others. Even in the dim candlelight, there was no mistake that the wall was moving.

CHAPTYR 12

With an awesome grinding sound, a ten-foot section of the rear wall rose slowly toward the ceiling. Perhaps it was my imagination, but I thought I could hear the groan of monstrous rusted gears and the slide of huge counterweights. Plumes of dust lifted by the shifting stone wafted toward us. The great rumble of the heavy stone made the scattered skeletons shake. A few collapsed in a bony clatter.

And then it stopped. The wall was gone. Our candles hardly cut through the dust and dimness. All I could see was a black hole where the wall had been. I could hear the drip of water—a heavy plunking as if the drops fell far. There was no other noise except our own heavy breathing and the occasional dust-induced cough.

Thom grabbed the candle from my hand and, holding it aloft, stepped to where the wall had been. The feeble light illuminated the secrets beyond. A few feet from where Thom now stood was a large pool of water perhaps thirty feet across. The candlelight glowed orange across its rippled surface. Drips fell from somewhere far above, occasionally shattering the surface into a thousand spots of light. These in turn would coalesce into rings of light, which spread outward across the pool.

It was the stairs, however, that caught all our attention. On the right edge of the pool, extending out from the wall, was the first step. We could see a dozen steps climbing upward beyond the candles' reach, following the curve of the wall. Cold fresh air swept down from somewhere far above. We all knew what that meant.

Mryyn spoke first with a sly smile on her face. "Well Thom, you've sure gone and done it now." She leaned over and pulled his head down to her level and kissed its top.

We all snorted in agreement. Thom was stunned at what he had wrought. He accepted our admiration and pats on the back with wide eyes. Finally he said, "We must move quickly, I don't know how long it'll stay like this. I just followed the directions."

Toss was already moving off to collect our gear, having anticipated the urgency. I hurried to catch up to him. Too much in shock for a conversation, we sorted and packed in silence. We loaded up Hoofer hurriedly and each took a heavy pack ourselves. We left anything we were not certain to need. Toss kept a bundle of candles free for our use since the ones we had were burning low. We dragged Hoofer toward the back of the cave and at first he resisted mightily, afraid of the gloomy depths, until he smelled the fresh air. After that, he came on his own.

When we got back to the pillar, Thom still stood beside it. Mryyn stood on the first step peering upward. Her face was under-lit by the candle, and filled with hope. I wanted to hold her, but there was no time.

As a group we advanced through the doorway and up the

first few steps.

Toss had Hoofer's reigns. Thom came last, ready to act if the door began to close.

The steps were wet and slick and carved from the solid rock of the cliffs. They rose in a continuing spiral as high as we could see. Peering up into the darkness, I thought I could see faint rays of light, but I could not be sure. The walls were roughly carved and glistened with moisture. Like the cave walls, they seemed to sweat a thin layer of water.

After Thom came safely through the door and joined us, we all sighed with relief and started the great spiral climb upward. At first I worried that Hoofer would have trouble with the steps, but my fears were unnecessary. He seemed to adapt well to their symmetry, and required little encouragement to climb.

We had made perhaps two turns in the spiral when we felt the stairs begin to tremble beneath us. I looked below into the pool. Its surface shivered and my heart skipped a beat. Spontaneously, we all bent to our knees for greater stability. Hoofer groaned at the sound of a low rumble.

Toss was the first to realize what was happening. "It's the door," he said. "It's closing again."

We all peered downward as the great stone slab slid slowly back into the dust and the door closed with a thud. The symbolism of the event did not escape us. We had left our old world behind and there was no going back.

Slowly we began our climb again. In a few places, small chunks had broken from the steps. In two spots a step was missing altogether, having fallen long ago into the pool below. Mryyn checked each new step before taking the next. Nonetheless, we were all wondering who would be the first to tumble. I heard a few of the steps groan beneath Thom's weight but none broke. I could imagine what was running through his mind, having almost fallen to his death once already.

We continued our cautious ascent for what seemed like for-ever, spiraling dizzyingly higher. Eventually, we could no longer see the pool below. It seemed somehow brighter as we climbed. The walls became dryer and speckled with a pale green lichen.

We were all beginning to wonder if the stairs would continue their spiral into the clouds when we came upon a thin strip of light in one wall. A delightfully cool and fresh blast of air swept in through this tiny fissure. Mryyn placed her eye against the crack but reported that all she could see was more rock. The stairs continued further upward as high as I could see.

Toss moved forward and examined the crack more closely. I saw him trace an almost indiscernible seam in the rock, which ran perpendicular to the fissure. He tapped and sounded the rock wall. At points, a plunking hollowness answered.

"What is it?" Mryyn asked. "Is it a door?"

As if in answer, Toss suddenly drew the heavy hammer from his belt and struck the wall precisely on one of the hollow spots. We watched with delight as a large section of stone fell away and wind-swept afternoon sunlight flooded in.

In awe, we stared out at a foreign world where we could see forever. It took several moments to get our bearings. Ahead, and what seemed like a mile below, lay a rolling hill in shades of pale greens and reds undulated to an impossibly distant hori-zon. I thought that somewhere on the farthest edge of my vi-sion I could see blue-black water, and on the other edge, some purple mountains. Scattered here and there among the valleys were patches of darker brown often remarkably symmetrical. I realized with a sudden vertiginous shudder that I was looking down upon the Southlands from among the clouds.

For a long time we all stood peering through that small hole as if through the eye of a bird, at the world we had always called home. How far away and insignificant it seemed. Thom pointed out an irregular square of brown off to the southeast that was likely Duvall. From this height and distance, no single object could be discerned. Instead, it appeared as a lonely grey scar on the edge of a distant hill.

Walking through town, surrounded by thousands of busy people, and dwarfed by towering architecture, it was easy to believe that the whole world was made by the hand of man. From here however, the truth was obvious. With all our generations, and all our efforts, men had achieved little more than a few strokes of greys and browns on a wide and wild palate strewn with color and texture. All the while we called ourselves kings and princes and rulers of the world. It was clear from this view however, that this notion was as ridiculous as the ant calling the great forest around his fragile mound, his kingdom.

It struck me how Dyos, maker of all we could see, must gaze upon our ludicrous conceits and monstrous egos. How strangely patient he was with us. How he cares for his proud little ants as they scurry about across his wide lands, all the time barely acknowledging his presence. Why is it that he takes such pains to treat us gently rather than stamping out our precocious little anthills?

As I stood there, I could hear Yakum speaking again. Words that at the time had seemed so lofty, somehow now, standing with the clouds, seemed barely adequate. This wondrous perspective, looking down from the heavens, filled his words with indelible truth. I wanted to cry out and scream how wrong I had been, how blind and deaf I was. I just stood there and wept and thanked my King for the privilege of flying with the birds for a time.

Thom, Toss, and Mryyn also flew with me. I had my arm tightly wrapped around Mryyn, and I could feel her gentle sobs against my chest. After a time, we all regrouped and smiled peaceful smiles, aware that little needed to be said.

Toss, who stood closest to the hole, pointed out something

that none of us had seen before. About fifty feet below our vantage point was a brief stretch of long grass, which ran to the cliff edge. From my perspective, it had seemed that by some magic, we had indeed climbed high into the sky. In actual fact, we appeared to be about fifty feet up, right on the edge of the cliffs. The stairs, which began in the depths of the earth, apparently continued without pause spiraling upward in the heart of a tower. Without knowing it, we had passed ground level and continued our ascent.

Toss suddenly moved past me, descending the stairs again. He wound down, about two twists, and then his steps slowed. We followed, wondering what he had discovered. We found him examining the wall very closely. Finally he stopped altogether. At first I could not see what had caught his attention, but then I made out a thin cut in the rock. I could see it ran down to the step that Toss now stood upon. With a sudden quick motion, Toss flung his bulk against the wall. I heard a grinding sound and a square block of the wall gave way slightly. Thom, who was closest now, joined the fray. One more heave, with their combined weight, and I heard ancient hinges groan. The heavy stone door swung open.

Three stone steps ran down into tall brown grass. The four of us tumbled out into freedom. We had stepped out into an infinity of grass. Long and golden this time of year, it rolled away in undulating waves toward the north—the direction we now faced. On the horizon a jagged range of snow-capped mountains marked the end of the vast yellow sea. The sun stood high in a brilliant blue sky that was almost cloudless. An autumn wind, brisk then soft, then brisk again, bent the long grass in swirling patterns. Golds, yellows, and deep shadowy browns spun around us in great windy arcs racing off toward the northeast.

After the claustrophobia of the cave and the tower, the panorama was stunning. I gulped the clean autumn air and thought I could taste a hint of distant snow. I soaked up the sunlight until I felt its fire stoke my soul. We stood arms raised toward the blue heavens and twirled in the wind—a dance of freedom. I looked again at the great grassy sea before us, enthralled with its twisting color and texture. The scope of the land was out of proportion to anything I had known before. Standing in this wild ocean of yellows, the grasslands of home seemed tame and confining, though until now, I had never thought of them as such.

"Oh, Pityr, isn't it lovely?" Mryyn asked.

She had come up beside me and stood arms outstretched trying to scoop up all the color and light and freshness she could. The wind swept strands of chestnut hair in a swirling caress of her face. The sunlight sparkled on her lower lip as she turned her face upward. I hugged her from behind, wrapping my arms about her waist and under her own. I kissed the top of her head and smelled the sunlight and wind in her hair. "Yes," I said. "It's beautiful."

She peeked at me with one long-lashed eye and smiled, having caught my doublespeak.

Thom and Toss, breathing deeply, joined us. We stood on a low hill, one among a thousand sheathed in gold. Behind us, the sea came to an abrupt end meeting the blue of the sky. I turned toward the cliff's edge and had the sense that if I walked too close to the precipice, I would be caught up in the rushing current and swept in a great waterfall of gold to the lands far below.

At first I could not see the tower, and this greatly confused me, for I was sure I stood less than two dozen feet from it. Then I saw the doorway, only a thin slit now, having partially closed in the wind. It hung impossibly a foot above the ground. As I stared further however, my eyes caught one long edge and then another, and suddenly the tower's features were quite evident, making me wonder how I had failed to see them at first.

In another moment, I understood. The stone of the tower was cloaked in mirrors. A silvery metal, smooth and glistening had somehow been applied to the rock walls. So reflective was this surface, that it caught the sky and grass precisely like a mirror. The tower stood perhaps two hundred feet high—taller than any building in Duvall, and the tallest manmade structure I had ever seen. And yet, it was wonderfully camouflaged by the sky and hills.

I realized that such a tall structure so close to the cliff edge would be easily visible from below were it made of simple stone. Though I had heard whispers of strange lights and shadows that scouts had seen atop the cliffs, I had never heard reports of any towers. Now I knew why. From below, the tower might seem like a sparkle at noon, or a shadow at sunset, but never what it really was. Here and there along its height, I could see slit-like windows, like slivers of night cut into the blue sky. I imagined there were more on the far side. I wondered what purpose this great and beautiful structure served. Why was it camouflaged so? Who had been its makers, and how long had it stood peering down on our world from these windy heights? We pondered these questions among ourselves, but in the end it was yet another mystery to add to our growing collection.

It was Toss, always practical, that recommended that we take another look at the old map. After all, the faint twisting line started here at the cliff tops. It would be here that our journey into truly unknown territory would finally begin.

Chaptyr 13

I carefully unscrewed the top of the silvery cylinder Mryyn had been carrying on her back. The stale smell of ages wafted from the tube. Gently, I shook the old parchment map from the tube with as much delicacy as I could muster and spread it out on a patch of trampled grass. All of us stood quietly for a moment as the bright sunlight warmed the parchment beneath my fingers; its ancient script and faded colors came suddenly to life and we were hushed by its ancient majesty. The millennial hand, which had drawn these lines and traced these letters when the mountains were yet young, commanded a respectful silence.

It was Mryyn who spoke first and barely above a whisper. "I think it has changed," she said.

I was just about to ask her what she meant by that when I noticed for myself what seemed different about the map. When we had first looked at it, it had consisted of little more than a narrow line twisting through vaguely drawn landscape symbols, grasslands, low hills, mountains, and so on. A few scripted names had marked important spots, but all in all, the map had been remarkably simple, almost to the point of being symbolic. It had appeared almost as if the mapmaker had little or no personal knowledge of the geography and landscape and only a vague understanding of scale and distance. When I had first looked at the map, it had appeared fascinating but not particularly helpful. Now, however, some of it seemed to have changed.

When I looked carefully, I could see the path up the Breach Cliffs distinctly marked. The cave, which had been our overnight shelter, and which we had worried would be the end of our journey, was clearly illustrated. A brief line of foreign script appeared next to the cave. Even the tall, cliff top tower was clearly marked. A single word of the ancient script appeared to give it a name. The long winding path twisted across the page from this point, up to the right hand corner.

I was wondering how we could have missed such obvious indications of the path we should take the first time we had looked at the map. I had no recollection of these symbols when I had first eyed it. It occurred to me at that moment, as it did to the others, that I had not missed the markers at the first viewing but that the map had indeed somehow changed. It appeared that our passage had been recorded on this ancient scroll as if it had always been there. The map was evolving and becoming more precise as we advanced along its course. A collective sigh escaped our lips as the profound implications of our journey struck home.

As I looked at the map further, the certainty of our revelation was confirmed. The golden, grassy hills upon which we now stood were painted in hues of yellow but seemed to fade slightly farther up the page. Indeed, the farther up the page the path wound, the less illustrated the geography became and the fewer names and text appeared. Near the top right corner of the page, the line itself seemed to fade out, and the landscape symbols ceased.

Beside me, I saw Thom reach down gently and stroke the parchment. His finger delicately traced the bit of script next to the tower illustration and the band on his wrist glowed a bit.

"Shymmerspire," he said simply. We were becoming accustomed to Thom's new talents, but were still moved to hear them in practice.

I turned and eyed the sparkling tower behind me, struck again by its sparkling immensity. *Well named,* I thought.

"What does that say?" Toss asked, pointing to the sweeping text near the cave.

Again Thom stroked the crackling page. The "moon look" crossed his features for the briefest of moments.

"It says, 'Herein lies a scrollmaster gate,'" Thom replied.

"What is a scrollmaster?" Toss asked

"I don't have any idea what a scrollmaster is," I said, "but I'm willing to bet that we have one walking among us."

As I said this, all three of us turned and looked at Thom. He stared back at us with that same silly grin he was famous for. That grin had gotten him out of trouble a thousand times over the years. It seemed to say "Who, me?" with a tilt of the lip and a flash of big teeth and a sparkle in the eyes.

It was clear to all of us, including Thom, that the strange band around Thom's wrist had changed him somehow, or rather expanded him somehow. Just as the band with the wavy blue line had given Mryyn the power to heal deep hurts, the inscribed band had given Thom the ability to see what we could not in these foreign words and traced patterns. As with Mryyn, the azure power of the band seemed to fan into flame the spark of talent that was already there. Mryyn had always been a healer of sorts, and Thom, of course, had always seen patterns and strategy where others were lost.

I looked down to my own wrist and saw again the jagged lightening strips in three parallel lines extending around my wrist. I wondered what power if any, lay there, as yet undiscovered. What talents and strengths had Dyos built into me? Who did he want me to be? I felt Mryyn's hand on my shoulder. I grabbed it with my own and sunk my cheek to its softness. It was warm, and I could feel the pulse in its delicate vessels. Her fingers were slender, but strong, the nails long, clean, and shapely. I kissed her knuckles and rose to my feet. I knew she knew the questions I was asking myself. Her touch said simply, "You will know soon."

It was clear from the map that we should proceed northeast across the grassy plains and toward the roughly illustrated mountains. According to the map, only one named feature crossed the plains to the north about halfway between the mountains and where we now stood. It was a river winding down from the mountains. With Thom's help, we learned that the river was named Mylkwater. I thought I could almost see a faint black mark on the map just south of the river. When I looked closer, I couldn't be sure that I wasn't just seeing a stain or a spot that had been overdrawn. No one else seemed to notice it when I pointed it out, so I presumed it to be nothing. Nonetheless, as I carefully rolled the map back up and slipped it into the glistening metal tube, I had the sense that I had missed something important. I almost unrolled the map again just to be sure, but instead screwed the cap back on. Mryyn took the tube and slung it across her shoulder. It seemed to fit well up against her arrow sheath, and the strapped bow.

Together we turned northward. The mountains seemed sheathed in a haze of purple light. *More than a day or two walk,* I guessed as I looked skyward. The bright sun was still mid-sky. A few fast moving clouds drifted silently on the strong breeze.

We had perhaps five or six hours before we would have to make camp. Though it would be tiring, I thought this might get us well on our way to the mountains. Perhaps we might hit the river by nightfall.

We gathered up the gear, reorganizing our greatly diminished stocks. It seemed a bit frightening to be heading off on a journey into foreign lands with almost no food, little water, and a minimum of tools and weapons, until I remembered who had called us to our task.

"Be not fearful," the words on the map had said.

As I looked around at the golden hills bathed in streaks of cloud-shadowed sunlight, it should have been easy not to be afraid. Try as I might though, I could not forget the heart-wrenching scream of the Solyss, and the Yakum's blood dripping off the stone dais under Desmodys' black look. When I thought of these things, even the sunlight was not enough to quell my anxieties. A nagging question hung in my mind and tormented me even now. How could the King say not to fear, while at the same time allowing Yakum, light of Dyos himself, to perish so horribly? The last few months had allowed me to see the King as I had never known him before, but I could not explain this apparent juxtaposition. Simply put, why would the King let Yakum be destroyed by evil if he had sent him to lead us to himself?

It was with this quandary occupying my mind that I led our little contingent north toward the mountains. We walked all afternoon through the tall grass, stunned by the immensity of the high plains. The terrain hardly varied as we progressed. Low hill after low hill, the rustling grain stretched seemingly to infinity. Our only confirmation of progress was the rapidly diminishing tower and the winding trail of bent grass behind us. So unchanging was our environment that it took careful concentration to keep from walking in circles. I kept my eye on a peculiarly shaped mountain peak to the north, using it as my compass. It was a double peak with a long slope on one side covered in snow, and it stood taller than many of its neighbors.

Occasionally on our trek, we encountered wide swaths of grass, which appeared crushed and flattened. Each was roughly a dozen feet wide and stretched off to the east and west, crossing our path. I knew the others noticed these peculiar variances in the otherwise unmarked landscape, but no one spoke of them. The sea of gold had subdued us all along with the incessant rise and fall of its waves. Nevertheless, I felt a bit of a chill with each new swath we encountered. I tried my best to convince myself that these were simply wind current sculptures or some other natural variant, but my intuition was not so easily tricked. I looked behind us and saw our own path marked by a narrow path of similarly flattened grassland and tried to imagine what type of creatures shared these open places with us. I saw no footprints to confirm my suspicions, but once thought I saw a hoof print. It was hard to tell, for the ground was dry and hard, and the fallen grass lay thick upon it.

Just as water seeks the path of least resistance on its journey from the heights, the wind naturally coursed through the winding channels. Whenever we crossed one, we were buffeted by a sudden blast of wind. Had we not fought its currents, it would have swept us eastward on slipstreams of autumn air. We did resist its lure however, and trudged forward.

As we made silent progress northward, the shadows grew steadily longer and the wind settled peacefully, fading almost to naught as sunset approached. Toward the horizon, the sun fell through shades of golden orange, pink, and eventually red. The hills, now still, caught the fiery colors on their crests, while the valleys fell into blue shadow. On the crest of a larger hill, we paused to watch the drama around us. From there, it looked like a million fiery pyres, which blinked out one by one, as the sun dipped lower. Even surrounded by friends, I nonetheless felt hauntingly lonely in the vastness of this space. I tried desperately not to think about the rivers of flattened grass and the coming night. Somehow, the possibilities seemed too frightening to comprehend.

We set up camp in a shallow valley as evening set in. We had little wood for a fire and chose to save it. We shared a meager meal of dried fruit, the last of our supplies, and a few drops of warm water that had acquired the musty taste of the old skins. The hunger pains I felt upon its completion reminded me of just how dire our situation would become if we did not find some game to kill soon. I had not seen as much as a field mouse all day. No one spoke much; there seemed little to say, and we were all exhausted. The monotony of the day's walk had left us exhausted in body and mind, and the excitement of the last few days had finally caught up with us. Our energy was truly depleted. Mryyn sat warmly beside me, and I was thankful for her presence, but I was aware that she, like all of us, was feeling the oppressive loneliness of the surrounding emptiness.

I took the first watch sitting in the tall grass on the hillside trying desperately to keep myself awake. As I watched the stars blink, I found my grasp on reality slipping. It all seemed so impossible. One month ago, I had been a busy stonemason safe and content in my little corner of life. Now I roamed the Uplands, behind enemy lines on some crazy quest for who knows what. In the last week, I had seen enough strangeness to fill ten lifetimes and I felt like it was swallowing me.

In my exhausted daze, my vision grew dim and my thinking became confused. The stars seemed to waver, the shadows bent, and time became strangely twisted. It even seemed as if the ground beneath me was shaking. I put my hand down solidly on the ground in an attempt to stifle this sensation. Instead, the sensation grew stronger and the ground continued to tremble. I looked off just to the west and found my eyes playing tricks, too. A great black form seemed to rise upon a distant hill and then fall again into the valley shadows, only to rise again on the next hill. I rubbed my eyes roughly, but when I looked again, the image persisted. Now I could hear the rumble, low and steady, a deep earthly groan.

The great dark shape moved toward the east about three hundred yards to the south of where I sat. The shadow seemed made of writhing appendages, stomping hooves and glistening sweat. A cloud of dust rose around it as it rumbled forward at tremendous speed.

It took me several moments to register what I was seeing. Though it moved as one, the great shape was not a single entity but rather a mass of seething bodies—horses to be exact. They ran together so close that their limbs seemed entwined. The dry ground shook beneath them. I sat transfixed somewhere between hallucination and dream. The roar of a hundred hooves, the glistening blackness of muscled flesh, the rippling haunches steaming in the cold, and the blue dimness of starlight combined to make the vision surreal. I could not move or speak to warn the others, but strangely felt little need to do so. I was immobilized by my sense of unreality and dreaminess but felt no real fear. I could hear Hoofer snort behind me in dreamy confusion at the new smells, but he never lifted his head from sleep to acknowledge his equine cousins.

As I watched, the seething mass slowed and then stopped. The stomp of hooves settled. The steam, formerly trailing the beasts like the tail of a comet, now rose thickly above them. Near the head of this confluence of creatures, an especially large stallion stepped from the pack and lifted his huffing nose into the night air. Even hidden as I was in the tall grass, I felt terribly exposed. His loud snorts tested the night air in all directions. He knew I was there. As I watched closely, I noticed something that made my blood freeze. White eyes. Cold, lifeless, glazed eyes of stone. I cannot say, on a moonless night, that I saw so clearly, but what I saw of the haunting image of that massive steaming stallion, eyes lifted blindly to the night, terrified me to my soul.

Clearly catching the scent of our passing, the leader whinnied loudly in anger and, I thought, in fear. He swung his great head with its stone eyes and the herd moved off toward the southeast. As they turned to go, I noticed several of the creatures stumble weakly. A few had bare patches or large sores on their dark hides, and one had what appeared to be a huge and grotesque growth on its flank.

I must have fallen asleep soon after the eerie encounter, completely unaware that I had finally crossed that misty barrier into sleep. Were it not for the great trampled swath of grass or that certain vivid memory of cold stone eyes, I might have thought it was all a sad and haunting dream.

I awoke at first light with a start. I had failed to pass on my watch to Toss as planned when Grigon, the eagle's red-star beak fell beneath the southern horizon. Instead, I had slept a dreamless sleep of pure exhaustion. By the grace of Dyos our small party lay untouched and at peace. Only my heart seemed troubled as I looked at my sleeping companions. Though I had felt no particular threat from the dark beasts of the night before, I had seen the illness and fear among them and it gave me further unease about these strange lands now all around us. Something else nagged me as I thought about that great blind stallion; I had seen his like before. Somewhere in the back of my mind, I had seen him as he might have been without those blind eyes, but where, I could not recall. These were clearly noble creatures far superior in line and stature to our Southland horses. Even in the dull moonlight I had discerned their proud heritage and powerful musculature. These graceful lines made disease an even greater abomination. Like a beautiful woman with a scarred face, the disfigurement seemed somehow all the more shocking.

As I sat pondering my unease in the purple-blue light of early dawn, it suddenly came to me where I had seen their like before, and my flesh began to crawl. Desmodys, it was Desmodys who rode such a noble mount. I was no saddle master, but I had a good eye for such things. My father's brother bred the beasts and had taught me well. Desmodys' great midnight stallion had the same sweep of shoulder, proud crest, and noble carriage as these creatures of the night. I was sure, as I mentally compared my last image of Desmodys riding out of the Solyss' valley with slaughter in his wake and my dreamlike encounter of the night before, that his mount had come from among these high plains herds. My heart felt black as I pondered the dark implications of this connection. I knew Desmodys had traveled far abroad. Indeed, for months at a time, he would be gone from town without a trace. Nonetheless, I did not understand how he had come to acquire a horse from the Uplands. As far as I knew, there were no traders of such things.

The groaning stretches of my companions stirred me from my line of thought, but the feeling of uneasiness remained.

"I'm hungry," Thom said.

I smiled—so what else was new? Though my own stomach growled ferociously in reply.

"I was dreaming of a slab of ham and a half dozen goose eggs frying in butter," said Toss.

"Stop. Please stop," said Thom, "before I drown in my saliva."

"Now there's something I'd like to see," laughed Mryyn.

We all joined her in laughter, but it was a somewhat restrained effort. Our journey would be a short one if our supplies were not replenished soon.

I told them as we packed, about my eerie equine encounter of the night before, though I did not discuss my musings about

Desmodys and his stallion. The thoughts were still a jumble in my own mind and I felt it was better to stay quiet.

Mryyn stepped up beside me as we headed off and I found myself wondering how she could still be so lovely after so many nights of sleeping under the stars. She had a small smudge of dirt under one eye, a few sleep-creases on her cheek and a blade of grass in her hair, but otherwise seemed remarkably preserved. She noticed my grey mood immediately.

"What's wrong Pityr?" she asked.

"I don't know," I said. "Just wondering what we are all headed for and why."

She offered nothing in reply but a sigh filled with empathy and, I thought, love—which was all the reply I needed at that moment.

We set off northward about an hour after sunrise. We would have to make the Mylkwater by sunset or by early the next day we might well die of thirst. The dawn sun had given way to low grey clouds that were swept along at a brisk pace by a high wind. Once again we trudged along in single file with me in the lead. There was something about the immensity of our surroundings that suppressed conversation. We crossed two more wide swaths on our way north and I wondered to myself how many horses roamed these endless plains. Perhaps the herd I had seen the night before was only one of many. Nonetheless, despite our long traverse that day, and our almost infinite view across the plains, we saw no other horses or any sign of more recent passage. Perhaps they only traveled at night. If they were all blind, like the ones I had seen, daylight or moonlight would make no difference except as camouflage. There were no places to hide out here.

The hills seemed longer and taller, and the valleys deeper, as we progressed throughout the day. Our pace steadily increased as a sense of urgency propelled us forward. We shared the last drops from the canteen at a brief stop somewhere around high noon. I frequently checked our direction by the great sawtooth mountain peak, which had become my beacon. A quiet fear began to build in my gut as I gauged our progress throughout that long day. It was the consistency of the view that fed my unease. Despite our day and a half journey into the grasslands, the peaks seemed as frightfully far off as they had at our first step. My original assessment of a two-day journey to the mountains had clearly been off, but I was beginning to wonder whether it could even be achieved in a week at this pace.

I knew the others had also noticed our lack of progress, but no one commented. Perhaps they were just too parched to care. My own mouth was beginning to feel sticky, and my tongue felt a bit swollen. This high plains air was dry and the constant winds whipped the moisture from the skin. If we turned around, we would never make it back to the tower. Together, we bent our heads and trudged on.

It was in one of these moments, with my head bent in contemplative angst, that I stumbled, striking my leg against something hard. I fell head first into the grass. Mryyn ran quickly to my side and lent a hand. Fortunately, my thick boot had taken the brunt of the blow and my shin was only one layer of skin less for wear. I rubbed it roughly, cursing my lack of attention.

At first, I wasn't sure what had tripped my step, but a quick search through the tall grass revealed the perpetrator. It was a large, smoothly cut stone, blackened at one end and half melted into a petrified pool. It lay partially buried in the tall grass and the soil beneath. Toss and Mryyn gathered around and examined the rock with me. Thom took one look at it and walked away to the crest of the hill, seemingly uninterested.

"Look at this," Toss said, pointing to one face of the rock. "This has been cut and polished with some fine tools,"

Looking more closely, we were able to see a lacy design twisting into two intertwined circles cut deeply into the rock. The pattern had been worn by the ages and was partially distorted on one corner by the searing the rock had once received.

"It must have been some type of marker stone," said Toss. "I've never seen such beautiful detail work. And this," he said pointing to the pooled stone, "what could cause marble to melt?"

Having lived stone and breathed its mineral dust for most his life, Toss was familiar with the molten birth of the hard igneous rocks with which he worked. He had even told me fantastical stories of great fire-breathing mountains far to the south of Parthis, which had been seen by the sailors. There, he said, was where the earth birthed itself, heaving forth its fiery children from its deep womb. Its labor pains and rumbling cramps could be heard from great distances—even occasionally in Parthis itself. Nonetheless, he was at a loss to explain how such rock once formed could be once again melted. No forger on Terras was capable of generating the heat and pressures required for such destruction.

As if he had been reading our minds, I heard Thom speak in a low voice from the hillcrest. "Mael's defyyl-fire, I suspect," he whispered.

He had spoken the words so lightly and with such eerie certainty, that we all peered up at him, wondering what had brought this change upon him. He stood looking northward into the deep valley beyond, harsh pain creasing his brow.

Mryyn was the first to join him at the peak, and she stopped as if she had hit a wall, uttering a single exhaled breath. Toss and I crested the hill together and saw, with shock, what lay before us. Stretching for at least two miles to the north from our vantage point was a city, or rather, was the rubbled remains of a city. What had obviously once been grand halls of stone, pillared courts, and a great central square radiating a busy network of streets, now lay in absolute destruction. Colossal slabs of the fine grey marble we had just seen lay strewn in heaps, scorched and deformed as far as I could see. A few well designed arches and gateways still stood, having narrowly survived the cataclysmic destruction now many years past.

As I looked upon the destruction, I thought immediately of the temple pillars that lay at the base of the cliffs. The terrible work done there at the Ryft was identical in character. Now I understood Thom's deduction. Clearly, the temple and this unknown city had seen the wrath of Mael. None other had the power to liquefy stone, and the evil heart to wield such wrath.

We stood on the crest for a long time surveying the graveyard below and I found myself in a daze. The crumbled city seemed to waver in the golden light. For a time, I saw it as it must have been, a bustling city filled with grand architecture, colorful marketplaces, and all the noise and smells and pulses of life. By estimation, it looked to be about twice the size of Duvall, but it had grander courts and wider streets. To the east, just on the edge of the hills stood a huge structure—probably a palace of some kind—that appeared to have been hit especially hard. Almost all its wide pillars had been sheared off just above the ground, black and melted atop like so many long-burnt candles. Off one wing some stables with long arched openings still stood intact. In an open yard in front of the stables sat a large square pool once used to water ranks of horses. It now looked to be about a third full, and its contents glistened in the sunlight. My mouth spontaneously panted at the sight, and I quickly pointed it out to the others.

The sight of water finally broke our sad reverie, and we gathered our few belongings and started down the hill toward the city. As we progressed, a shadow raced from east to west across the ruins, as some high cirrus clouds crossed the line of the sun. In the changed light, the city looked even more like the skeletal remains of some colossal beast silently sinking into the earth from whence it had come. Our quick steps slowed as we came closer. It seemed the air was full of aching loneliness. A palpable chill floated among the stone bones like a grey mist. I could hear a high shrill whistle as the wind swept through the hollowed structures.

We stepped into what once must have been the main street of the city. Though finely cobblestoned, it was now overgrown with sick-looking grey grass. With inexorable slowness, the plains were filling and drowning this carcass of a city. I guessed that it had been at least several centuries since this place had had its fiery death. In another few, even its tallest bones would be buried.

We moved cautiously in a tight pack through the city. Its scale was even more impressive from street level. We passed under many high arches but most had long ago given up their fight against gravity and lay in heaps. The piercing whistle of the wind waxed and waned, sounding far too much like the moans and cries of the dying. We turned one corner and entered a small court with high walls all around. Many hollowed windows peered down from above like the empty eyes of a skull. A great mound rose in the middle of the court. It was perhaps seventy or eighty feet long and half as high. It appeared to be made mostly of dark earth and rocks and was partially overgrown with grass. I saw something shining in the light, and as I came closer, I could tell it was a helmet of sorts, made of silvery metal and laced with gold in parts. I had to clear away some of the gravely soot in order to tug it free. The helmet was only partially intact. It had been completely crushed on one side, but its fine metalwork was clearly evident. A starburst of gold shown on its crown and within it, to my amazement, was a Triliset. It appeared to be exactly like the one that had graced the box from which we had pulled our wristbands so many days ago. As if in reply, my band began to pulse softly the blue light coursing its tracings. Thom and Toss stood with me, and I showed them the mysterious symbol. As I turned the helmet, it rattled as if filled with small stones. With some care, I shook one of the pebbles out through the eyehole and into my hand. When I again opened my hand, I froze. The object I held there was unmistakable. I looked up at the great mound before me and stepped back several steps, dropping the helmet in the process. Thom and Toss looked at me, bewildered. I lifted my hand and showed them the contents. I held a human tooth.

With horrible clarity I now saw the mound for what it was—a colossal funeral pyre. It would have taken twenty thousand bodies or more to make such a heap of ashes. The wind whistled more loudly. None of us spoke. In all of Duvall there were only about fifteen thousand souls.

Chaptyr 14

It took us several minutes to move, and we all knew to speak no louder than a whisper. None of us could escape the horrid images this funeral mound evoked. My mind wandered. As if in premonition, I saw a few starved survivors heaping the bodies of family and friends in the great central square of a war-ravaged Duvall. With hopeless tears, they lit the terrible mound aflame. These images evoked the nightmares experienced at the edge of the seam only a few days ago. They also had foretold the destruction of Duvall and all its inhabitants. Were these indeed prophecies, or just disturbed thoughts? One look around the skeletal city clearly testified to Mael's wicked might and intentions. Were he to have his way, all of Terras would lie in ruins, and its inhabitants either slaves or dead.

It was a movement at the corner of my eye that broke me from my musings. Mryyn saw it too, for she pointed with a gasp at one of the empty windows, high up on the northern wall of the courtyard. I had just seen a flash of grey move across the windows' shadows.

"There's someone up there," she said. "I saw someone move in the window."

All of us watched the high windows for a long time but nothing further moved. By now, our nerves were tight, and our hearts beat fast. I freed my sword from its scabbard and I saw Toss gripping his hammer tightly. I think all of us itched for a fight at that moment. Somehow, an upfront fight with a known enemy was far more palatable than this terrible sense of evil that hung in the shadows. I felt the nervous itch of spying eyes upon me and found myself twisting abruptly in all directions to find its source.

It was Thom that spoke next. "We need to get out of here," he said. "Let's get water and go."

We moved in a tight diamond, each taking an edge, our eyes dancing around, peering into the shadows, which were growing longer by the minute. After several more turns and a tense few minutes, we found ourselves in the courtyard of the destroyed palace we had seen from the hillside. The high walls and thick columns of the main building had received a terrible blast. Little was left to suggest its ancient grandeur. The adjoining stables seemed to have been spared the most vicious attack, and there were some sections that stood completely intact. Here, the fine stonework was truly remarkable. Had we not the sense of foreboding hanging so heavily upon us, Toss and I could have spent hours discussing its details.

In the wide cobblestoned expanse before the stables, stood the large rectangular pool. It was at least half full of water. The sight of wind-rippled water, sparkling in the low sun, made me pant. I was viciously thirsty. Never had I felt such a longing to drink, such a desperate bodily need. It overwhelmed all my sense of caution and previous dread. Somehow, up to this point, we had controlled our growing thirst, but now, all powers of will seemed to dissolve. We dropped our weapons and ran forward the last few steps. As we did so, we scared a drinking crow from the pools edge. It flew off to the tip of a shattered pillar with an angry caw.

I cupped my hands and plunged them into the water, which was icy cold. I felt my body shake with impossible joy and barely noticed the blue fire that suddenly coursed along the lightning tracings on my band. For the briefest of seconds, I paused. It was in that moment that something else caught my eye. Thom and Mryyn were just bending over the water, and Toss, like me, was lifting cupped hands to his lips. The most peripheral and vague corner of my vision had sensed a movement, and for some reason, my mind signaled its import despite my thirst.

"Stop!" I yelled. "Don't drink."

Thom and Mryyn paused, and even Toss unclasped his hands not inches from his mouth. Despite the urgent plea of my body, I let the clear water fall between my fingers back into the pool. I turned to see what my mind had registered with such urgency.

The crow, jealously eyeing us from atop the pillar, had inexplicably tumbled to the cobblestones, and was weakly thrashing about. Even as we watched, its jerky movements ceased, and it died in an unnatural splayed position, its wings askew.

We looked around trying to discover what hidden arrow or cast spell had struck the creature. As we looked more closely at our surroundings, we noticed several more disturbing peculiarities. I saw two more feathered corpses in a dim corner of the courtyard. Mryyn pointed out a small curled skeleton the size of a dog near the eastern edge of the stables. But it was Thom's discovery that finally completed the puzzle. A heavy grey cloud had moved across the sun, and the brilliant sparkle on the pool subsided. Thom raised his hand and pointed out an object in the pool's far corner. It was the corpse of a small horse, bloated and pale, floating weightlessly beneath the surface.

Thirst had sapped my mind of its conscious clarity, but some deeper survival instinct had recognized certain death in these un-noticed signs. The water was poisoned, a horrible lure for the thirsty high plains creatures and wanderers like ourselves. It seemed the terrible Mael was not content with thousands of bodies in his funeral fires, but he wanted all who passed through this lonely city, even the innocent creatures, to feel his deadly grip. We needed no further urging to escape this cursed place. We gathered our weapons, and with one last longing look at the sparkling water, raced from the courtyard.

Gripped now by a deep and strange fear, my senses started to play tricks on me. Eerie peripheral shadows seemed to fade and appear around the next corner, slip into dark doorways, and peak from behind broken columns. The others seemed equally edgy, whipping their heads back and forth after sneaking phantoms. Exhausted and spooked into a state of paranoia, we fled as a group, weapons raised against the creeping darkness. Clear thinking was swept away by the wailing, moaning, hopeless wind, and thirsty panic consumed us. We stumbled over our own tired feet in our rush down the long angled streets. We drove poor Hoofer almost cruelly in our urgency, though truly, he needed little encouragement. The terror filled him as well until he was wide-eyed and foaming.

As if the sky sensed the black moods below, its peaceful demeanor changed. A thick grey mat of clouds rolled over the city from the east driving the wind wickedly before it. Within minutes, the last clear sky was being pushed below the horizon far to the west. The moan of the wind became the high piercing cry of a lost infant. We could feel the dark phantoms behind and all around causing us to flee faster still. Finally, when we had just begun to wonder whether we had been caught in some terrible eternal maze, we passed under a last crumbling arch and stumbled onto the plains. With the unshakable sense of foreboding still upon us, we pushed northward back into the grassy hills.

We lasted about a mile or so before our fatigue and thirst brought us to our knees. I tumbled to the ground, my pack still on my back, unable to move. The others fell with dry groans. My last thought before succumbing to an irresistible sleep was that we would all likely be dead of thirst by morning.

My sleep was complete and dreamless for hours. Then, as if my dying body was left behind, I sailed over the plains effortlessly to a green and lush place far away. I landed among willows on the shaded banks of a river. I knew the place immediately. It was the swimming hole where Thom, Mryyn, and I had spent so many days. I could hear the roar of the water as it fell from the low hill cliffs into the clear pool before me. I looked up and saw the foaming water tumbling down the rocks; my face tingled by its misty vapors. Effortlessly, I floated over the still waters toward the falls. The thundering of the water grew louder, and now big droplets soaked my cheeks. I opened my mouth and felt the cool pellets on my tongue. Still I floated forward, the fall's fringes poring over me. Suddenly, as if I had been pushed, I fell headlong into the foaming torrent of water. Now water rushed into my ears, nose, and eyes, and I could not close my mouth against its powerful fingers. I sought breath but found nothing but water. I gasped and choked and woke up.

The night was a roaring thunderous waterfall. Lightning split the sky, and for a moment, I saw the others sputter awake on hands and knees. The mud was already drowning my hands to the wrist. The crushing thunder came next, its force practically burying me again in the mud. I lifted my mouth to the sky and gulped heavily the icy torrent. We knelt like this for a time trying to breathe between giant swallows of water, our senses totally overwhelmed by the noise and the light and the flood.

At one point I bowed my head to breathe. As I lifted it again for another drink I looked over at Mryyn. She, like me, was still on her knees in the mud. Another bolt flashed above and our eyes locked. In the infinitesimal fraction of time the light lasted, I saw a movement behind her. The depth of my gaze shifted, and I saw what stood in the darkness.

Black as the night, tall and naked, a huge man stood behind her, his red eyes glowing faintly in the night. He held a spear above her. The lightening danced on its dripping tip. His face was cracked in a perpetual smile by teeth that were too long and sharp.

She must have seen the shift in my eyes and the terror beyond imagining, because she sunk suddenly into the mud and rolled to her right, springing to her feet. The next flash of light revealed the poisoned spear buried deeply in the mud where she had been and her short sword sticking in the neck of the smiling creature. Mryyn was already cocking her arm for another blow. As I too rolled, reaching for my sword, I felt another one of the creatures fall next to me. It landed facedown in the mud, an arrow sticking out of its back. I gained my feet and struck out madly with my sword. The rain, combined with the night and light partially blinded me, but I could see as Thom flattened the faces of two of these monstrous creatures in succession with his large fists, dropping them like stones. Toss struggled loudly with one hanging on his back, which was trying to bite him with its deadly teeth. He pulled his hammer from his belt and sunk it deeply into the black creature's skull. I spun and swung, sensing an evil breath beside me. I saw my wristband flare with vibrant blue, and the sword met its mark. I had struck the fell-spawn at the shoulder and my sword would have caused harm but not death. Instead, the creature exploded in a flash of blue fire, and bits flew everywhere. The force of it stunned me, and I slipped backwards, falling on my back in the mud. Another one was ready. Its spear dove toward my chest and I deflected the blow with my sword handle at the last second, and the spear point hit the wristband. A cry of sheer agony split the night. For a second, I thought it was my own voice released in death. Instead, I saw the demon creature before me fry in a blue bolt brighter than the lightning. Somehow lifted by a power greater than myself, I rose and lifted my sword hand to the night. Thom was taking the head of a creature with his long sword. Mryyn danced and ducked the spear points of two spontaneous thrusts. And Toss lay in the mud, blood and water streaking his brow, a tall demon man bowing for the kill. An anger deeper than the earth and higher than the skies, ancient and potent rose within me. Blue lightning burst from my sword in ten directions at once. The clouds above continued their torrent, and the night exploded. Thom, Mryyn, Toss, and I were thrown deep into the mud by the force of it. Dozens of the beasts all around simply dissolved. Fangs, bones, and remnants of black flesh sizzled as they met the mud. Ozone and static crackled in the air for a time and then it was silent.

"What was that?" asked Mryyn as she wiped the mud from her face.

"I...I don't know," I said. "My sword just exploded."

I knew this sword well. It was nothing special, except for its sentimental value. It was the same worn sword I had practiced with as a child. Over the years, as my strength grew, so too had my swordsmanship. The old steel felt balanced in my hand now. But still, it was nothing special. There were hundreds like it in Duvall, all the work of Jaivos the smith. No, the lightning and power had not come from the sword itself but from me! I had felt it build deep inside me. Somehow the band had played a part too, but I couldn't understand how.

I lifted my sword before my eyes. Even in the dimness it shone, shiny and without defect, as if it had just been lifted from the forge. Even now the faintest blue shimmer ran along its edge.

"That was incredible!" Thom said. "I've never seen the likes of it."

"Is everyone ok?" I asked.

Mryyn nodded and Thom grunted in reply, though we heard nothing from Toss.

He lay in the water facedown. Thom was the first to reach him. He rolled him over quickly and lifted him onto his lap. A deep gash ran along one temple, and blood pulsed from it silently. His eyes were shut, but as Thom held him, he gasped, coughed, and spat up some brown water. Then he was still again, looking very pale.

Mryyn took his head in her hands, just as she had to both Thom and me before. Also as before, blue fire traced the fine weaving lines on her band. Her head was bowed as she concentrated on the task. She placed one hand over the wound. I could hear her murmur an unintelligible prayer. The wound was almost completely gone when she slid her hand away. Still, she kept her head bowed and seemed to concentrate even more deeply. Toss opened his eyes with a suddenness and fierceness that made me take a step back. He stared at nothing, clearly not fully awake. Deep in his pupils, I could see the slightest hint of green, just a flash, and then it was gone. He closed his eyes again and Mryyn's hands shook. The band on her wrist danced suddenly with bright ringlets of blue, then quieted again. She gently let go of Toss' head.

"How is he?" Thom whispered.

She seemed almost unable to speak. "Well..." she replied with deep exhaustion. "I don't really know. The wound isn't too bad, but it won't heal completely. There is something... Something else in there. I don't know what it is, but it's a darkness of sorts; I can't seem to grab a hold of it. I don't think he is going to get better until it's gone, but I don't know how to beat it. It's too elusive." She said this pensively, worry furrowing her brow.

"I think he will be alright for now, but he may get worse later." Mryyn wiped his face gently, clearing the mud, blood, and debris from his features. Toss was breathing evenly and deeply now.

"What a nightmare to wake up to," Thom said, referring to the nights events.

"Where did they come from?" Mryyn asked.

"I don't know," I said. "But we're pretty lucky to be awake at all. If we hadn't been woken by the storm, we would all be stuck to the ground right now, poisoned spears through our hearts."

"I think they came from that cursed city," Thom said. "They were just waiting for the darkness to make their kill. I've heard Mias speak of these creatures. They're called demonym, and they served as Mael's personal guard in the city."

"What were they doing there?" I asked. Even as I said it though, I remembered the creeping shadows and high window eyes among the crumbling ruins. And then I added, "I think you're right, Thom. He left them there."

Thom looked at me and nodded knowingly.

"What do you mean 'he left them there'?" Mryyn asked.

"Mael," I said. "The evil bastard set those creatures up as guardians of his wickedness when he was done with the city. He wasn't content just to slay tens of thousands and destroy a city. For him, that was only the beginning. I think he knew that everyone who passed through the high plains would see the city and stop there. If the poisoned well didn't get them, nightfall and the demonym would." I sputtered, surprised at my own bitterness.

Thom and Mryyn looked at me. They were not used to this kind of anger from me.

"I think it may be even worse than that," Thom sighed. "I

think Mael set them there in greater numbers. I think they were waiting for us. I think Mael knows of our quest."

Suddenly, I knew where the seeds of blue lightning had come from. I hated Mael, and I hated what he had done, and I hated what I knew he would do. I hated the constant fear he and his minions held over Duvall, and how we all had to operate our lives by his rules. I hated seeing Toss suffering with some unknown poison. Years of suppressed righteous anger had exploded to the surface. Somehow, I thought, the band had turned it from an emotion into power and fire—Dyos' own power channeled through me.

Toss stirred now in Mryyn's gentle hands. His eyes opened again, this time more naturally. He smiled weakly when he saw us. Thom helped him struggle to his knees. From there, he was able to stand on his own.

He remembered the fight but not the blow that laid him out. He said something about nightmares but couldn't recall what they were about.

"Are you ok?" I asked.

"Sure," he said. "I feel fine now, just a bump on the head." He would not meet my eyes.

I looked over at Mryyn, who shrugged her shoulders lightly with an uncertain expression on her face.

Over the next half hour we gathered our soaked and spare belongings from the mud. Somehow Hoofer had survived the attack without a scratch. I found him just outside the camp in some kind of trance. It finally took two strikes with the switch to rouse him from his reverie.

When we began moving, we agreed that there were probably more demonym in the ruins than had shown up that night. We couldn't be sure that one of the vile creatures hadn't escaped the sword and was now signaling the alarm. None of us would be able to sleep anyway. At least the downpour had been so heavy that each of us now had a temporarily quenched thirst.

Once again we struck out northwards toward the mountains, now deeply hidden in the veil of darkness. The storm had blown over but the wind was heavy now and much colder. I looked skyward at the large irregular patches of stars between the clouds. The moon had set long ago. I estimated it to be about three hours yet till dawn. The cold air was fresh and carried a hint of snow. As we walked on in silence, my eyes slowly adjusted to the night. The patches of starlight occasionally lit the peaks far ahead. They glowed with a whiteness they had not had before. The storm, which had drenched us, had laid a first fall snow high above. I wondered how we were going to get over those tall peaks when we finally reached them.

I felt a hand slip into my own and a peace settled upon me. I put my arm around Mryyn and her head bent toward my shoulder as we walked.

"I love you," I said as she snuggled closer for warmth and returned my sentiment.

We didn't have to say anything more. She had seen the fear for her in my eyes as I had woken to the storm. She knew I would not leave her so alone again.

After what seemed like forever, I noticed the first light in the west. Then the dawn came fast. Heavy grey clouds raced to the west as if trying to catch up to the storm that had left them far behind. By full light the sky had mostly cleared, and a fall sun shone down on the plains. It was bright and white but did little to warm the earth or our chilled bones.

About midmorning we finally came upon the Mylkwater. We had walked up and down the long low hills all morning. We peaked over one particularly high hill and there it lay before us, filling the valley. The night rains had swollen it far beyond its banks. Full of silt and debris, it ran an opaque white-grey. It was not difficult to discern the derivation of its name. I was instantly discouraged. This was no streamlet but a full and raging river with a visible current. Even as I watched, a large branch was whipped by spinning miniature whirlpools. There was no way we would be able to cross this bloated river until it fell well below flood stage, and that might be days. Starvation would claim us in less time than that, if the demonym did not get us first.

Had Dyos led us on this fruitless journey only to let us starve on the banks of a grey river? We all sat down with a communal sigh. Reality had suddenly become too heavy a weight to bear. I leaned back against a large rock that stuck out of the plains.

Just as I was settling back to contemplate our situation, Thom pushed me—hard. Sometimes the oaf did not know his own strength.

"What was that for?" I groaned angrily. Hunger and exhaustion had admittedly made me a grump, and this new incident had taken me over the edge.

Thom, however, did not seem to have heard me. He had pushed me away from the stone and was down on bent knees examining it. *Not again,* I thought. *What now?*

Thom did not speak, but continued to peer closely at the stone, which, to my eyes looked no different than any of the others we had passed along the way. It was almost pyramidal in shape but looked to be naturally so. I could discern no clear sculpting marks along its edges. Something though, had clearly caught Thom's attention.

Mryyn now stood beside me. "What is it, Thom?" she asked. "What do you see?"

After a long moment he replied, "Look across the river."

We turned as a group. At first, I did not know what I was looking for, but then I saw it. Directly across the milky raging waters, on a low hill, stood another stone. It was a mirror image of the one before us in every way. So precise was the symmetry, that they seemed two halves of the same whole, separated now by the floodwaters. I walked to Thom's shoulder and bent down in an effort to see what he saw. Even close up however, I could not see any markings. Then Thom reached forward and touched the stone with his open hand. I was somehow not surprised to see the delicate script on his wristband begin to shimmer with blue. Nonetheless, the stone seemed unchanged. Toss sat off to the right, still regaining his strength from the battle.

"Another Triliset," he said. He was pointing at the right edge of the stone, which faced him alone.

We all peered around the corner. A pale blue Triliset, sparkling with fire, was clearly embossed on this face. As soon as Thom withdrew his hand however, the image disappeared. We looked at the other two sides while Thom replaced his hand, and saw nothing but rough stone just like the side facing the river.

Thom stood and looked skyward, his hands like a vice on his temples. I could see his jaw clenching and unclenching, the muscles of the mandible rippling. We all knew well enough not to speak. He was far away, walking, in his mind, toward the door ajar and then to the light beyond. This time, the spell lasted less than a minute. Then he unclamped his head, and the present returned to his eyes.

"Help me," he said with a smile to me.

I was standing closest, and he motioned me to the stone. He placed my hands on the two edges opposite his own.

"Twist clockwise when I say go," he said.

We gripped the stone hard.

"GO!" he said, and we put our weight into it.

The stone began to turn on its axis slowly with a loud grind. I heard its echo across the river and saw with amazement the stone across the way turning with perfect synchronicity. The face with the Triliset became brighter as it turned; its glow lighting up Thom and the others behind. When the stone had turned clockwise a full ninety degrees, and the Triliset faced the river, I heard a click and felt a discernible locking beneath my fingers. The stone would turn no more.

For a long time there was silence, and we all looked to Thom as if to ask what would happen next. He was facing the river now, expectantly. The milky water was in turmoil, and if anything, the river seemed even fuller than before. Across the water, another Triliset faced us, the mirror stone having also passed through a ninety-degree turn. Suddenly, the waters between the two stones appeared to bunch up as if pushed from beneath. As we watched, a distinct hump grew and grew in a straight line between the stones, the water rushing forcefully overtop. This continued higher and higher, until finally, a long and wide platform rose out of the water. It stopped as if floating, the waters now running smoothly beneath. The platform itself seemed made from a single slab of marble, and ran as a bridge from side to side, perhaps fifty feet in length and a half-dozen wide. I knew, of course, that this was impossible, since such a slab, if it existed, would weigh hundreds of tons. We stood still for a long while, too astonished to move. Finally Thom motioned for us to proceed.

"Let's go," he said, clearly proud he had figured out the puzzle.

With the burrow closely tethered, we proceeded to the river's edge. I bent and touched the bridge, running my fingers over its smooth surface. I couldn't believe what they told me: It was indeed marble, and some of the finest I'd seen, faint pink lines running through a pale grey grain. Toss bent next to me, also entranced.

"Who could cut and form such a piece?" He wondered aloud.

Thom urged us forward, and we stepped at first tentatively, then solidly on the stone. There was no give. I expected the wet surface to be slick, but course treads had been cut into its surface, and we crossed smoothly. Hoofer too, seemed without fear.

All the time the milky current rushed silently beneath. In less than a minute, we had crossed the raging flood and stood on the other side.

I squatted on the far bank, dry and contemplative. I was just beginning to learn one of the lessons that had since carried me through life: "When led by Dyos, there are no impossible obstacles."

Thom walked to the Triliset stone, and with little effort, turned the image ninety degrees to the left. Its partner across the water turned again in synchrony. Silently, the fine marble bridge slipped beneath the waters again and was gone. We hoped our enemies would not be able to access that bridge.

We stood, considering the journey that had brought us this far, looking back over the river to the hills and the city beyond. Duvall seemed a thousand miles and a lifetime away. Nothing would ever be the same. The innocence had faded, and in its place was a world bizarre and complex. Even now we had only taken a few tentative steps into its mysteries, terrors, and wonders. Where were we headed? I shivered at the thought. Mryyn was the first to turn away from the waters and the past, and lift her head toward the mountains, and she gasped.

Standing on the peak of the hill above us was a giant hairy beast. Mryyn already had her bow cocked and an arrow strung in the time it took me to draw my sword. The creature however seemed unfazed; it stood still as stone eyeing us silently. I could see now that it was a huge dog, the size of a small horse, lean and solid, and terribly furry. It panted softly. I could discern the viscous teeth behind the tongue. What struck me immediately as peculiar about the creature were the large leather sacks that hung from its back down both sides. The beast neither advanced nor retreated but continued to eye us quietly. With a sudden premonition, I motioned to Mryyn to hold, and she slowly dropped her aim toward the ground, keeping the bow taut nonetheless. The creature continued to stare at us, and then without warning, a tall figure stepped up behind it and placed his hand upon the dog's back. It was a man, lean and straight. He wore a deep green cloak tied with a brown leather belt and had a crossbow and staff strapped to his back. He had long blond hair almost as ragged as his dog's hung below his shoulders. He appeared relaxed and at ease, but even from the distance, he emanated a sense of confidence and strength.

"I've been waiting for you," he said in a low solid voice.

A small smile kinked his face. When he smiled, I could see that the skin on his face and forehead was terribly scarred and in places, deformed. Nonetheless, from beneath the jagged damage, a sad kindness shone forth. Closer, I realized that this impression had a lot to do with his clear grey eyes, which reflected a gentle but burdened soul. He lifted his hand from the dog's back, and it trotted to us completely unafraid. It came excitedly among us sniffing, and even licking playfully. Mud and grass were twisted into its thick dark grey coat so that in places it was matted down flat and elsewhere stuck up straight. And it stunk like a bog. So close, it was even bigger than it had seemed on the hilltop, coming well up my chest. As it jostled and sniffed playfully, it was all I could do to plant my feet and stay upright. If Mryyn weren't so quick on her feet, she would have been knocked to the ground immediately by the dog's affections.

"Enough, Ull," the man said as he approached. The dog immediately crouched to the ground and sat still, his enthusiasm suddenly restrained.

The man stopped before me, his hand outstretched in greeting. I took it and felt a rock-solid grip in reply.

"I'm Vyyd," the man said, his eyes crossing my own and passing on to the group. "And this…" he said motioning to the dog, "is Ull."

CHAPTYR 15

For the next half hour, Vyydrick Pye, as he was formally known, patiently told us his story, and I found myself lost in its wonder.

Up until three years ago, Vyyd had been a wheat farmer in Parthis—a small costal town south of Duvaal. He had owned large properties far outside the walls of the village and had been quite successful. Wheat was a tough crop to grow in the far south, but he had cultivated a hearty species, and few could match his productivity per acre. Each day he, his wife, and his two sons worked the fields. Harvest time was particularly tough, because by October, the days were growing shorter, but the work doubled. Just as in Duvall, none dared to stay beyond the walls after dusk as the vulls ruled the nights.

One fateful harvest evening, Vyyd and his family had worked a little too long collecting the harvested stacks into a great carriage. It was their last collection of the year.

"My good wife urged us home, but I would have none of it until we were done. Perhaps pride and greed drove me a little too strongly that night."

As they started home, night seemed to fall faster than usual. Heavy dark clouds rushed from the west. They found themselves still about a mile from the city when a great storm hit. It was no more than a quick and viscous autumn thunderstorm, but a close bolt of lightning had jarred their faithful workhorse so thoroughly that it had slipped its halter and fled into the night. The heavy carriage twisted and stalled and the workhorse galloped off around the bend deep in spook.

They delayed only moments longer, finally deciding to abandon the newly harvested grain on the road, and flee as a family toward the city. The moisture would ruin the grain, but fear now reigned. They ran in a tight alert group. They turned two more corners in the road and found the huge workhorse torn to pieces and slick with blood. It was then that the vulls fell upon his family. They rushed from the dark woods on all sides as if they had planned the whole evening.

Vyyd awoke in the healers' lodge in Parthis two full days later. His wife and boys were dead, and he was dying slowly from more than a dozen wounds. The Parthian wall guard had counted, as usual, the night's returning families. When Vyyd and his wife had not returned, a search party of armed men had been quickly summoned. They had found the family not a quarter of a mile from the gates. Twenty-two dead and dying vulls lay on the road. It had taken three strong men to pry the bloody pitchfork from Vyyd's hands, as he lay unconscious.

"The healers say that it was my anger alone that kept me from dying over the next two weeks."

It was another two months before he could walk again, and when he finally left the healer's lodge two seasons later, he was no longer the man he had been. Though he walked and talked and ate like other men, he had long ago died inside. He had become a phantom. He was irreparably consumed with anger and loneliness. No longer could he stand the company of laughing families, affable friends, and playing children. The guilt within him was like a stone, heavier than his soul could bear. He blamed himself alone for the lack of care and poor judgment that had destroyed his family.

The following year, he sold his farm and became a recluse, living in a small hut on the edge of town. With time, however, even this became intolerable for him, for he could not completely avoid the sound of children or smiling townspeople. The whispers of lost love haunted his dreams until he stopped sleeping all together.

Finally, in the spring of last year, Vyyd gathered his few belongings into a pack and headed out the gates of Parthis for the last time. A ragged stray puppy, the only company he could tolerate, became his sole companion. Vyyd and Ull became a team with only one mission—revenge. Together, they hunted vulls. They lived off the land and constantly roamed the hills, becoming quite adept at their chosen profession. They hid and watched for months until they understood the secrets and strategies of the night monsters. They mapped by day the paths of attacks and found all the local seams. And then they began to kill. With cleverly set traps, ambushes, fire, and pure soul-felt hatred, Vyyd slew his enemy.

"I must have killed almost two hundred vulls and a dozen cy'daal all in twos or threes over the next several months, but there never seemed to be fewer."

But try as he might to purge the loss from his soul, he could not. No amount of black and pungent vull blood could ever bring his lovely wife and two strong boys back. His loneliness and guilt were greater after months of nightly reaping than they had ever been.

During this time also, his wrath had not gone unnoticed by the cy'daal, and suddenly, he and Ull became the hunted. Huge vull hordes, with several cy'daal seemed to focus specifically on tracking them. They spent their nights continuously on the run, and their days resting and plotting for the next night's escape. Vyyd knew that his time on Terras now would not be long. Soon he and Ull would be caught, and the vengeance of the beasts would be viscous. He was not afraid though, of death, for he could no longer bare the weight of the soul-deep pain that was crushing him. He was done with this life.

It was with this sense of destiny that Vyyd planned one last stand. Tired of running, he led the night monsters into a rocky gully with steep sides. Earlier, during the day he had heavily soaked the entire small valley with pitch he had stolen from a mill nearby. He had then laid a dense layer of dried grass atop the mess to hide the smell and feel.

There was a large rock in the middle of the gully. Here he stood in his final moments with Ull at his side. All around, the vulls became a seething mass. They crawled atop each other trying to reach him. He lifted his burning torch into the air. Two cy'daal before him drew arrows, licked them, and strung them even as he watched, unafraid. He knew he would not live long enough to get the dregs. He welcomed the end. And, if he was lucky, he would take at least seventy of the black vermin with him. His left hand patted Ull one last time and he threw the torch to the ground. It fell into the thick grass, sputtered, briefly flared, and then died. Nothing happened. No consuming flame swept the valley as planned. A grotesquely fat vull fell atop the torch and snuffed it completely.

The cy'daal arrows flew. In the time it took for the arrows to reach his chest, Vyyd noticed a presence behind him. He cocked his head and saw a man stepping onto the rock with him. The man placed his hand upon his shoulder, and then the valley disappeared in a flash of blue and white.

"The very last thing I remembered was looking down at my chest. Time had stopped and I saw the arrow tips not two inches from my ribs. There was nothing else, just those arrows so close to my chest. Then they just burnt up. I could see them burn to dust right before my eyes. The wood just dissolved. All that was left were the stone heads, and I saw them bounce lightly off my leather armor, smoking as they fell. I saw and heard nothing more."

Vyyd had awakened hours later in the still smoking valley. He was leaning against the rock, and Ull was sleeping peacefully at his side. The vulls were nowhere to be seen, but the valley was scattered with ash and stunk. He felt his chest, and it was unscathed. He noticed a peculiar band around his wrist, with flames embossed in a circular pattern, but it didn't hurt, and somehow, it made him feel strangely secure. He heard a soft shuffling behind him and turned quickly. The man from the night before stood there. He was tightening the saddlebags on an old palomino. His back was turned to Vyyd, but he seemed quite plain wearing only canvass clothes and well-worn boots.

"Good morning, Vyyd," the man said, without turning around.

Vyyd was too stunned to speak at first. He was confused that this man somehow knew him when he was sure they had never met. He had managed to reply with a thank you. The man turned then and looked at Vyyd.

"I don't need to tell you what he looked like, since I know that you yourselves have met him more than once, or you would not be here."

The man had introduced himself as Yakum. He had told Vyyd that he had survived the night for one reason, and that was because King Dyos had willed it. Vyyd was told he had a journey to make in service to his King, and that only then would he ever have an answer to the impossible loneliness of his heart. Needless to say, Vyyd had been more than a bit confused. He had heard of King Dyos, but only in mythological terms, and had no idea how this man before him knew what he did to his privately guarded heart. What he was saying made no sense, but somehow the man himself did.

"Though I have thought about it almost continuously for the last three months as I have traveled from Parthis, I still cannot tell you what it was about Yakum that made me listen. I do know this, he stepped into my life at the moment of sure death, a breath before the end. He came with unexplainable power, and he spoke as one with impossible authority. I had no choice. All my choices before had led to nothing but death and emptiness. I simply knew that he was my last and only hope. I knew too that the man was on a mission, and that the night had been the answer to an appointment planned long ago. His mission would be my destiny."

Yakum had stayed only long enough to give further instructions. He had climbed atop his ragged horse and headed away. That was three months ago. Alone but for Ull, Vyyd had traveled to this appointment, driven by the same irresistible breath of Dyos that inexplicably had brought us here.

When Vyyd finished his story none of us spoke for a long time. I had felt the depth of his agony as he talked, and each of us knew the peculiar draw of Yakum and his life. I had spent more time than any of the others with Yakum while he was alive, but even that time seemed so brief. Nonetheless, here I was trekking across unchartered Terras, deep in enemy territory, headed toward a destiny only Dyos knew.

Vyyd had suffered horribly, and had known loneliness deeper than I could imagine. For him it seemed there was no other answer than death. He seemed to sense from our silence that we understood. For the first time in a long time, he stood among people who knew personally the hunger in his soul. This gave us a common bond that we could never have achieved so quickly otherwise.

One other thing that Vyyd and Ull brought to our group that seemed almost as precious were provisions. Dyos, who knew our needs well, had directed him to this spot and he came richly supplied. From the great packs on Ull's back, he drew cheese and bread and thick salted wild boar. Never had any fancy feast tasted so good as that simple food. It had been three days since a bite of solid food had crossed our lips. It was a time of such deep satisfaction.

As we ate, we talked and walked. An urgency and sense of pursuit drove us. There seemed a darkness behind that we could not shake. Vyyd had traveled for weeks just to reach the cliffs. He had come from the south and east, and met the cliffs where they were not quite so high. Like us, he had found a narrow trail that had brought him to the plains. A high, mirrored tower but no cave beneath also had marked this one. He had crossed the plains without incident. He had seen the city we had passed through, and reported two others to the east, which had been smaller but equally decimated. Ull had refused to enter any of them, despite Vyyd's urgings and desire to explore. In the past two years Vyyd had come to respect the instincts of his faithful canine and took a wide path around the ruins. They had arrived at the Mylkwater five days before and had camped there since. They had been given instructions only this far, and knew they must wait for more.

Just over the next rise, we came upon their camp. To Thom's delight, even more provisions were there. Vyyd himself had carried a pack across the plains that must have weighed almost a hundred pounds. He was a man hardened by death and loss, and a year and more on the run had also hardened his lean body. We

GEOFFREY W. GILSON

divided the burdens and loaded anew the burrow. Especially
precious were the two large wineskins filled almost to the brim.

While in the camp, Mryyn reminded me that we should look
at the map again. We unrolled the ancient parchment on Toss'
cloak. For some reason, I was not that surprised to see that it
had changed yet again. A faintly sketched horse was clearly
depicted on the southern grasslands. The city with a cloak of
darkness upon it was plain for all to see—even a bolt of lightning was depicted just south of the Mylkwater, which now had
a bridge across its foamy waters. To the north, the mountains
seemed higher and more detailed, and a snowflake was beautifully drawn. Between the river and the mountains, other
faint objects were drawn, a barely discernible torch, some vaporous bird-like creature, and faint shadows. The area beyond
the mountains was essentially empty except for smudges of
color and shape. I wondered again what kind of magical object this was, that seemed much more clearly a record of our
journeys than a map of our future. The way, for now, was clear.
The mountains, particularly the high twin-peaked crag, were in
sharp relief both on the crackling ancient paper, and against the
cold fall sky before us.

For two straight days we hiked northward, now in much
rockier terrain at the feet of the towering mountains. The hills
were sharper and more erect here, and we found ourselves frequently having to climb almost hand over foot to get up the
steep sides. The nights were cold and starry, and we took turns
at watch. I slept very well those nights, exhausted as I was by the
changes of life and the journey.

Sometimes Mryyn and I would take a watch together. Huddled near each other for warmth, our breath, a shared plume
of steam in the frosty air, we talked and laughed quietly, sometimes also crying for home and loss and fears. Sometimes we
would kiss, and the sweetness of her mouth, and the soft press

of her lips, and the dancing of her tongue would take me higher than I could imagine, and silence the burdens of my heart. Other times, as we kissed, my tears ran, as did hers—our ache was so strong. I would press my wet cheek against her neck, and feel its heavy pulse, and tremble. My love for her was growing as we shared this time, and I ached to make her my wife. We vowed then, beneath a silver moon that if it be the will of Dyos, she would be mine, and I hers when this journey was done.

On the fourth day of our journey from Mylkwater, a great shadow passed over our camp near dusk. I looked up and saw something that chilled me to the bone. High now, in a great slow circle, flew a winged beast. It was no bird. It looked more like a skeleton with wings, or a monstrous bat. Boney, skinless, and vile, it swung in a wider arc, a long tail dragging in the wind behind. Its snout was flat and squished, and its fangs were unmistakable. Mryyn had her bow taut within seconds, but Vyyd reached over and pressed her arrow toward the ground

"Don't waste your arrows," he said. "It's way too far."

Instead, he pressed a short steel arrow into the grove of his crossbow and with power stretched the bowstring back to its tightest notch. He then took careful aim. Just as he was about to fire, the flying beast let out a high piercing screech.

I had never heard a sound that could compare with the horror and power of that noise. It sounded suddenly as if the creature and its scream were inside my ear, up against the drum. My mind was shattered with its intensity and soul-wrenching terror. I found myself uncontrollably on my knees, clutching my ears with all my might, trying to shut the screeching out. It seemed as if all the terror of the scream had been woven into sound, and hurled like a weapon at my head. I could not think or breathe, and terrible, violent images filled my mind.

Blood and dismemberment, laughter and fangs, loneliness and death, scorched bodies and agonized souls, black hatred, betrayal... All things intensely evil resonated in the frequencies of that terrible cry. I saw Mryyn curled on the ground clutching her ears. Ull was howling miserably; his head tucked as far beneath his legs as he could go. Thom bellowed in agony on his knees, and Toss seemed out cold.

I looked over at Vyyd. Initially, knocked to his backside by the horrific cry, he was willing himself back onto his knees and struggling to lift his arms to aim. And then I saw the arrow fly. For a second, I heard the cry grow even more piercing and deadly, but then it faltered. I lifted my head skyward, my ears clamped by my hands like a vise. The beast was flying to the south. One wing bone was pierced straight through by Vyyd's arrow. The cry faded as it flew, but echoed still with black terror. My head felt as if it had been crushed beneath an avalanche of stone. Surely, had the craven cry lasted but minutes more, I would have been left a soulless corpse on the plain.

I reached down to Mryyn, who still lay curled near me, terror dancing in her eyes. When I touched her shoulder, she cringed and drew away from me. Her eyes, for a second, showed a complete lack of recognition. I grabbed her and pulled her against me, and she began to sob uncontrollably, but she relaxed and leaned against me in the end.

"It's okay," I said, crying myself. "It's over."

"What was that?" she whispered. "I was dying, and I couldn't breathe."

"I don't know," I said, running my hands through her hair. "I don't know."

Vyyd was bent over weeping. "I saw it all again," he said. "But it was worse... I saw what they did to my family after I was unconscious. I saw those damned beasts... eating them... Aaaaugh!"

He drummed the ground with his fists with impossible anger and pain, moaning and sobbing. I knew that only hatred beyond reckoning had given Vyyd the strength to stand against that scream and take aim. His deep agony had saved us all, but I did not know how to help him escape the torturing images caught in his mind. Mryyn rose with my help and stumbled to him. She clutched his head between her hands. Almost instantly, she shook, and Vyyd's eyes closed. This time, I saw a flash of blue, as brief as distant heat lightning, and then she let go. Vyyd tumbled to the ground, completely unconscious. Mryyn sat unsteadily for a moment.

"I saw it, Pityr," she said. "For the briefest second, I saw the darkness of his thoughts. I don't know how he lives. I just don't know..."

"Will he be ok?" I asked.

"When he wakes, he will not remember the images," she said. "But they are still there, along with a lot of horrible stuff. I cannot heal him. I think only Dyos can. I don't know whether he will be ok, Pityr."

I looked over at Thom, who appeared steady enough, and was helping Toss to turn on his side as he vomited heavily.

"Are you two all right?" I asked.

"I'm ok," Thom said. "I don't think Toss remembers anything; he just went out cold as soon as that thing started screaming. He's just sick."

Ull crawled over to Vyyd and laid his big fuzzy head on his evenly rising and falling chest. The dog whined softly for a moment and then was silent.

"What was that thing?" Mryyn asked.

"I think..." said Thom, "that was a hyss or soulthief."

"What's a soulthief?" I asked.

"Well, my uncle Mias always had a stack of old parchments around whenever I went to visit him. Sometimes he would leave me alone for a while while he practiced his calligraphy. I remember always being amazed by the ancient creatures described in some of the mythic stories. Like the demonym we met in the storm, they also were mentioned in these pages. Several others spoke of these hyss. They were giant bat-like creatures that were formed by Mael's evil hand sometime during the Great Battle. Apparently, they have a hidden song in their scream that poisons the soul. Many of the old stories told of great warriors left "soul-less" by the hyss' piercing scream. Warriors of great renown were sometimes found after an encounter with one of these defyyl beasts jabbering and insane. Sometimes they would have to be treated forevermore as infants, unable to feed themselves, bathe, or even speak. They were left as physical shells—living, but long ago dead. When one of these beasts would fly over a city, it was said, you could trace the path of its flight in the morning. There would be a great streak of death, miscarriage, illness, and insanity, like an arrow through the land. The few men who survived an encounter with a hyss told stories of terrible images filling their minds, and overwhelming their senses. I think I would have to concur..."

"You speak true," I said still trying to sift the vileness from my mind. "I too saw such things...as if I had fallen within a seam."

"Even the great healers of the time were unable to patch their empty souls," Thom continued. "Some of the commentaries spoke of the hyss' song as 'a false witness to the soul' or as 'breath of the accuser.' Apparently Mael used these hyss as messengers between his legions and to steal the strength of his enemies.

"Some of the later commentaries spoke of some successful battles against these creatures. One legend tells how under the terrible curse of hyss, the people cried out to Dyos for relief. Later, a few young children in the city were noticed to have a peculiar trait. These individuals, it was said, were like prophets. From birth, they could infallibly discern truth from lies. They became collectively known as the filah. Their gift known as viriteus aura—the ability to hear only truth—was in them from birth. The breath of Dyos was reported to be so clear within them that they could not hear a hyss' accusing scream at all.

"Under the direction of the oldest filah, arrows of truth were forged, which would instantly kill any hyss, and the filah were trained as expert archers. They often led armies into ancient battles. Over two generations, by the courage and marksmanship of the filah, all hyss were wiped from the land, or withdrawn by Mael. After they were gone, no more filah were born in the land either."

"I fear I am no filah, and that my arrow did little true harm to the beast," Vyyd said, slowly recovering.

"I fear," added Thom, "that its mission was accomplished, and that our position is now known."

The reality of Thom's statement struck us all deeply. No longer would our journey go undetected. The fight with the demonym had probably escalated the search for us and alerted Mael to our presence. Things were sure to get tougher.

As a group, we raced northward with a new sense of urgency.

As if to confirm our worst fears, Vyyd woke us from sleep, sometime past midnight with a motion to be silent. He had seen something far to the southeast, against the dark hills. We all crawled to the rim of the hill and looked in the direction he pointed. It was a dark night, the moon having already set and high clouds shading most the starlight. At first, I could see nothing. For too long, my eyes had been staring at the inside of my lids, then, I saw it…just a flicker, on the crest of a distant hill.

"A torch," whispered Mryyn. "Two, maybe three. From the way they're moving, I'd say they're atop horses."

Though I couldn't see half as clearly as Mryyn, I instinctively trusted the eyesight of a woman who could pick a firefly out of the air with an arrow at thirty feet.

"Why horses? And vulls don't carry torches," I inquired.

"I don't know," said Vyyd, "but I don't think we should stay around to find out. I watched them for several minutes before I woke you, and they are definitely heading toward us."

Without any argument, we gathered our gear and moved off toward the towering white glow of the now close peaks. Somehow we knew, if we reached the peaks, we had a chance at escape.

By dawn, we stood at the base of tall cliffs, broken in places by great fissures. The tops of the double tooth crags were lost in mist. The air was discernibly colder, and already I had had to pop the pressure from my ears twice as we had climbed ever higher hills. Vyyd explained to us that the sky has a weight, just like deep waters. I had dived to the bottom of Carp Pool several times as a child and knew the strange pain within my ears. Vyyd had climbed some of the high peaks near Parthis, during his year alone. The vulls, he said, never went there.

With the growing light, we had lost sight of our hunters. They had come slowly closer during the night, despite our relentless pace. Vyyd estimated that they were only a few hours behind. We hoped that the day would bring an end to the pursuit. None of us had ever known the creatures of darkness to travel during the daylight hours, but something nagged at our hearts and would not let us relax despite our fatigue. We did, however, stop briefly for a meal, and the last of the wine. Even dry and crumbly cornbread was delicious. Ull roamed restlessly, often looking toward the south, and whining softly.

From this point forward, we had to pick our way carefully. We climbed great tumbles of rock along ledges that rose from the lower hills. About lunchtime, we encountered our first old snow. It sat in thick dirty heaps, as dense as ice, in the shadows of great boulders, never having melted during the summer. Deep among the rocks ran icy streams. We could hear their subterranean rushing all along our path, and sometimes, a great crevasse would appear before us, and we could see the cold foamy waters rushing by beneath. We filled our skins repeatedly from the cascading water that rolled off the largest mounds into the depths. Those glacial droplets were like an icy fire in our parched throats. We stopped in late afternoon atop a high ridge unable to walk any further. For eighteen hours, we had fled from our pursuers, and my muscles were cramping so badly, that I could hardly feel my feet.

We had not seen signs of any trackers all day, but each of us could feel a creeping evil somewhere below us among the sharp cliffs. We had passed several impenetrably dark and deep caves on our way up the mountains' sides. Even though we had given them wide berth, at several points, I had felt the same faint seeping blackness I recalled intensely from my near encounter with the seam. I wondered, with a shiver, whether deep within this mountain, there were dark passages that our pursuers traveled even now.

By dusk, we had rested two short hours, and had filled our empty bellies with the last of Vyyd's once plentiful supplies. I had no idea how we would make it over these peaks without further sustenance. My cramping legs were nowhere near up to the task of further climbing, and I knew the others were even more exhausted. Toss, especially, seemed flat and quiet. Clearly, he was still suffering from the demonym's viscous blow and an illness was brewing in him. Ull alone seemed to have some energy yet in reserve.

With the sunset came an even greater threat. Within a few minutes of the sun's silent retreat, the temperature dropped a dozen degrees. Heavy white clouds suddenly poured over the peaks above shrouding their crags in mist. They descended on us in great billows and with a biting wind. Soon, large fat flakes of snow began to fly. We took quick shelter from the worst of the wind and snow, in the shadow of a large boulder, but even here, we couldn't retreat from the gnawing cold and swirls of snow.

Then, and only then, as if Mael was laughing, did we see the sudden reappearance of the torches just below us and hear the horrible and distinct cry of a horde of vulls in pursuit.

How was it possible? Where had they come from so suddenly? It occurred to me that my earlier musings about our pursuers following through underground passages was the only explanation. Regardless, we were shocked into action. Ull whined for a fight, but we dragged him, our whipped mule, and our exhausted bodies up the mountain. The full force of the blizzard was upon us now. It was almost impossible to look up as we traveled. The wind and flakes froze the eyes, and brought an instant and overwhelming flood of tears. And so we trudged, heads bent to the fury, leaning heavily into the mountain. Even so, we felt that at any second, the storm would sweep us, like so many fall leaves, from the rocky cliffs.

Looking back we could see our hunters now. Three horsemen with torches were expertly navigating the rocky tumble. Each was wrapped in heavy cloaks of black that danced like midnight fire in the wind. They seemed amazingly unaffected by the roaring blizzard and were clearly gaining. At the feet of the horses were at least a dozen vulls, huge even by the standard of their south-plains kin. Their harsh cry rose above the wind's whine, and even from here, I could see their teeth, hungry for the kill. We bent further into the mountain, at times reaching forward with frozen hands to grip the icy rocks as we climbed.

After a few minutes, I could no longer feel my feet. My leather boots were no match for this winter fury. Nonetheless, I kept somehow placing them one step above the other. Often, I reached out and steadied Mryyn, as the winds rushed upon us, pulling her close. If this were to be the end of our journey, I would die at her side, my sword drenched in vull blood. The mule was having a tough time with the ever steep incline and the glaze of ice beneath the snow. At one point, Hoofer lost all footing, and Thom was forced to let go of her reins, or he would have been dragged off the cliff as before. As it was, Hoofer slid until her hind legs caught in the rocks, and then she tumbled. With a bellow, she began to roll, fell off a low shelf, and landed broken fifty feet below us. She was still alive, but unable to rise, and beat her front legs frantically. Her bleating cry swirled with the snow. It was agonizing to hear.

We watched even as we continued to climb. The vulls fell upon her like a swarm. Within seconds, her cry was stilled, drowned in her own blood. This grotesque feast set the vulls wild, and they danced and howled and blood and saliva fell upon the snow. The horsemen paused to take in this early victory and the largest turned and lifted his shrouded head to our perch. He stared at us from his shadowed face, and I could feel his smile and the wicked joy with which he was contemplating our eminent destruction.

Tearing ourselves away from the horrible scene, we dragged each other upward by sheer will. Toss seemed in a trance, almost delirious, but he continued to climb with the rest of us. We reached a level stretch, now deep in snow. I paused to look below but could not see the spot where Hoofer had met her death, already, the vulls were racing up the steep rock face we had just climbed, and the horsemen were not far behind. I looked into the storm above us. The mountain disappeared in the whirling grey twists of snow, but I could see clearly the cliffs rising almost vertically upward from where I stood. We would cross this level spit, and if we could not climb further, we would make our last stand at the base of the cliffs. Already, the numbness had crept to my knees, and I was walking with legs locked, all sense of my connection to the earth gone. I yelled these final commands to the others, who had already come to the same conclusion themselves anyway, and as a group, with Ull bounding ahead, we pushed through the drifting snow. At first I did not realize what was happening as I felt the ground rushing suddenly at me. I heard Mryyn scream and I grabbed her hand, but it made no difference—there was nothing beneath us. We fell beneath the snow with a rush. Abruptly, the sounds of storm and hungry vulls were gone, and we were just falling through blackness. After a second, my frozen feet struck something hard, and my body and head hit heavily in succession. I started to slide deeper, and tumble, but the blow to my head had dazed me, and I was slowly losing consciousness. The slide ended in a frigid wetness that was all-consuming and enveloped me in an icy womb. I thought also I could see light…I thought how peculiar to have light here so deep. Perhaps it was in my head. I was so cold, and now it was so quiet…but the cold was not frightening, and the quiet was quite peaceful… and I was so tired…

Chaptyr 16

I stopped now and looked over at my grandson. I knew the young warrior was tired, but his eyes were blazing with excitement and anticipation for the rest of the tale. My own bones were weary, and my voice was dry from the telling. Many hours had passed since he first began, and now the evening shadows had overtaken the forest.

"Gather some wood, my boy," I said. "Soon we will need a fire. This old man chills too easily these days."

I saw Jonam look around startled, and he realized he had not noticed the time pass and the evening shadows come.

"Yes, Pater," he said softly, regaining his presence. He rose stiffly and began to gather fallen sticks and larger logs from among the forest debris.

I took several long drafts of cider, savoring the sweet-tart apple flavor. I would miss such things soon, but who knew what waited ahead and beyond. Even now, I felt the tug of his King on my heart and longed to go home to him. I would join his love there. I envied her now, already beyond. It would not be long. First though, my task here must be finished.

As Jonam stacked the collected timber, I divided the remaining bread into two large pieces, and cut several more thick slices of cheese. Jonam was hungry for the tale's further unfolding I knew. I had never told it like this before, with such depth and heart. I could tell he felt as if he were there, among the five, floating now in the cold blackness, with the vulls' cries echoing somewhere above. I smiled to myself, knowing that the boy was caught in the journey with me. It would bind us together now forever. Never had I told the truth of this journey with such richness of detail or emotion. This young man alone would carry the legacy to the generations beyond. It would be only a story to him though, and nothing more, if Dyos'Bri did not touch his heart and call him forth from this place. The story would have to become his own, the journey real, for Jonam to receive the blessing.

I prayed silently for my grandson, that Dyos'Bri would fill the telling with his presence and make the call irresistible.

I felt warm and safe and could sense a faint orange glow when I first became aware of myself again. There was a heavy weight upon me, but it was soft and not frightening. I could hear a faint crackling, the distant rush of water, and what sounded strangely like snoring. It was a while before I realized that my eyelids were still shut, and when I finally wrestled them open and looked around, my confusion grew further.

The five of us lay on wooden beds, beautifully carved and of solid design. I was weighed down by a huge bearskin, as were the others. Vyyd also seemed to be waking, but the others, including a snoring Ull, were still fast asleep. We seemed to be in a tall chamber, carved expertly out of solid rock, and I could faintly feel the press of a million tons of mountain above. The space was warm and lit by several flaming torches, dancing with a peculiar reddish fire, hanging on iron wall sconces. I could also hear a distant roaring waterfall or rushing river but no sounds of voices.

A flood of memories came rushing back upon me, and I struggled to make sense of our current circumstance. The last thing I remembered was falling into icy water at the bottom of a long crevasse. The distant vull screams still echoed in my mind, and the black look of the hooded horsemen gave me chills even now. How had we escaped? With a sudden panic, I wondered whether we had been captured, but I could feel that my hands and feet were not bound, and my racing heart resumed a normal rhythm. I had no sense of fear here; in fact, a great peace seemed to pervade this place. I had not moved anything but my heavy eyes yet, when suddenly a voice said, "Do not be afraid; you and your friends are safe here."

It was the voice rather than the words, which kept me from jumping to my feet. The gentle voice of a mother feeding her child at the breast could not compare to the peaceful solace this voice conveyed. Even in the few syllables spoken, I caught a strange accent, a slight lilt here, and a stretching of a word there. These plain words seemed so beautiful.

I turned slowly in bed feeling my stiff bones rebelling at the effort.

"Do not move yet, Pityr. Your body has suffered much in the long fall. Rest still, then you will be ready. Tomorrow, perhaps."

As she said this, the speaker came around the head of the bed so I could see her. My breath caught in my throat. The woman was stunningly beautiful, tall, and dressed in ghostly white robes, that flowed as she moved. She had high regal cheekbones, deep brown eyes, and golden hair swept back in a bun, with ringlets hanging down to her shoulders. I had never seen more perfect lips and teeth, and her smile eased every fear in my heart.

Before I could speak, she placed two fingers gently on my lips. They were warm and soft, and I could feel a pulse in their tips.

"Shhh," she said softly. "Let sleep come again…"

I wanted to speak and ask her name, and move around, but I suddenly felt the full weight of my exhaustion again, and could not keep my impossibly heavy lids open. I felt her fingertips brush upon my forehead, and I slipped back into a dead man's sleep.

When I woke again a long time later, I felt fully refreshed. Mryyn now sat beside me on the bed, her fingers gently stroking my hair, her smile a joy to awaken to. She bent to kiss me when my eyes opened.

"How are you?" she asked.

"I'm ok," I said, pushing myself up in bed. "Have I slept long?" I asked, noticing the others were not in their beds any longer.

"Two days or so, I'd say," she replied.

I was shocked. I felt as if I had briefly napped since I had seen the tall woman. "Where is she?" I said.

"Who?" asked Mryyn. "Do you mean the Lady?"

"The Lady?" I asked perplexed. But then I knew. Certainly, she had been a Lady—so tall and regal. Even now I could recall her beauty and gentle authority. "Where are we, Mryyn?"

"Come," she said, "you shall see."

She helped me rise out of bed. My muscles and joints only held the faintest of stiffness now, and it felt good to put my feet on the floor again. Someone had dressed me in a heavy cotton robe that was incredibly soft. A pair of thick woolen slippers sat next to the bed, and they fit perfectly. Mryyn gripped my hand and drew me eagerly into an embrace. I realized she must have bathed, for she smelled like lilac and mountain streams, and her chestnut hair gleamed.

"I missed you," she whispered in my ear.

"When did the others rise?" I asked.

"Thom and I woke earlier today. Vyyd had already been up for a while, and Toss woke just a few hours ago."

"What is this place?" I asked again, growing ever more curious.

In reply, Mryyn took my hand and led me forth out of the chamber and down a long passage lit with torches. In several places, I could see other chambers, lit and unlit, stretching down the main hall, but Mryyn did not turn into any of them. She seemed to know where she was going, so I just let her lead. Finally, we turned a corner in the passage, and it opened into a large hall. Two huge fireplaces, big enough for a grown man to enter upright, were roaring with flames. Thom, Vyyd, and Toss sat at a solid wooden table stretching along one edge of the hall between two columns. Also seated at the table were the beautiful woman I had seen in my dreams, and a huge barrel-chested man with a great salt-and-pepper beard. In several places around the hall, I saw tall, broad-shouldered men in rich blue-black robes, standing at attention. Each of them wore a hood over his head and had a large decorated sword at his side.

As we entered the hall and approached the table, the others rose. Thom stepped forward and swept me up in a bear hug.

"How was your beauty sleep?" he said playfully.

Vyyd and Toss shook my hand warmly, looking filled with new life. I did notice however, that Toss walked with a limp. I turned then to face the lady and was struck again by her astounding beauty.

"Knight Pityr, I welcome you," she said with the lilting accent. "I am the lady Karolyne, and this..." she said turning to the giant beside her, "is my husband Lord Pellanar."

I stood unmoving for a moment in front of the mountain of a man before I fell to my knees and bowed. A massive and powerful hand fell on my shoulder and lifted me effortlessly until I stood again.

"None will be worshiped here but Dyos himself good knight. You and I are brothers, and I welcome you to my home." The voice was deep and rich, and sounded as if it echoed up from a great depth. Lord Pellanar stood at least seven feet tall, and at least half as thick. He wore heavy fine-knit robes of crimson and rich purple, and his beard reached to his chest. Nonetheless, it was his eyes, deepest blue and penetrating which held my gaze like a vise. He was a man born of power, truth, and authority, clearly a natural leader among men.

"Thank you, good Lord," I replied. "I am honored by your welcome. I think however, you are mistaken—I am no knight, only a lowly stone mason."

At this, Pellanar cracked a broad smile.

"Trust me son, I am a commander of men, I know what I say. You are a knight of the Silver Order, the Ayali, for it is a knight's band you wear. Such things cannot be falsified."

I looked down at the band on my wrist with new wonderment. Even now the jagged lines danced faintly with blue fire as if in reply. *A knight,* I thought. *How could this be?*

His wife touched his arm and nodded her head toward the table.

"Forgive me," he said. "I have been rude. Let us delay no further."

We were instructed to sit at the massive table, and within moments, large platters of dripping meats, steaming bread, and a vast array of vegetables, pies, soups, and puddings were set before us. Tall mugs of icy mead were also placed before each person.

"Eat well, my guests. I know your journey has been long and

hungry. Later, we will talk. We praise King Dyos for your company and for this rich provision."

Pellanar finished his prayer and passed the food around.

Faced now with this impossible abundance, after so long in near-starvation, my body was shaking, and my stomach was cramping. The others wasted no time helping themselves to mounds of food. I thought Thom might start drooling all over the table and commented on the fact. This got a hearty laugh from all and set the mood for one of the most pleasing meals I had ever had. There were thick venison sausages baked in maple, wine-roasted pork, whole chickens on spears basted with Gustine butter, sweet-oaknut bread with black fruit jam. There were large platters of little root and sweet beans with garlic, coarse fried wittleweed, and water beets with chestnuts. Platter after platter was brought to the table by the hooded servants, and platter after platter was removed empty.

Eventually, I paused for a breath and realized that my bloated belly could hold no more. One by one, the others came to this same conclusion. Thom managed another helping of the hearty food before he too laid down his knife and smiled a very satiated smile. Even as I pushed my chair back from the table to accommodate my expanded abdomen, the servants were busy clearing the remnants of the meal. Once it was clear, they brought another platter of small, decorated cakes and replaced the mead with a rich and smooth cognac that tasted of sweet fire.

The Lord and Lady of the house watched us with delight as we enjoyed the bounty set before us. Pellanar ate relatively little considering his bulk, for he was too busy paying attention to us. I watched him even as he watched us. Several times, I turned suddenly and caught him staring at me as he had at the others. I felt no fear from his gaze, rather a powerful sense of strength and wisdom. In many ways, it reminded me of my father's

gaze—potent and penetrating, but also fair, honest, and accepting. I was sure no secrets could escape those eyes, but that was
all right because I was accepted for who I was and loved nonetheless. Pellanar, I knew could accurately discern the measure
of a man with only a brief gaze into his heart. I now know that
he was at that time pondering our role in Dyos' great plan, and
wondering whether we were ready for what surely lay ahead.

When the cakes were mostly gone and the cognac had kin-
dled a soothing fire within us, the jovial dinner banter ceased,
and Pellanar leaned forward over the table, folding his hands
before him. He looked at his lovely wife, and she gave him a nod
of consent as if to say, "Now is the time, yes."

"Friends," he began, "I know you have many questions about
the strange days and journeys that have brought you here. It
is no mistake that your wanderings in the high plains have
brought you to my home. I have known of your journey nearly
from the start, and the troubles you would face. These things
are by design, you can be sure. I, like you, play but a bit part in
its great drama. Much of what I will tell you has not touched
the ears of many mortals for almost a thousand years, and is
unknown or simply myth to the men and women of the Southlands. Nonetheless, it is a story that must be told again among
the people. It is a story of unimagined power across the ages,
and only recently has its latest and most important chapter been
written. You, my friends, are key characters in its unfolding, and
you must carry the message into the future."

Perhaps it was the sweet wine or the dancing firelight in the
great hall or the voice of deep authority, but whatever it was, I
was transfixed. The others too looked stunned, literally rooted
to their seats. I was impossibly hungry for the answers, the answers I so desperately needed to explain why my life had been
so abruptly turned upside down. Why, suddenly, had I felt the
irresistible urge to leave all that I knew behind, cross a barren

land filled with mystery and evil, struggle with thirst, starvation, snowstorms, and demonym? It was as if my sanity depended on there being reason behind the craziness of the past few weeks. Without some answers, some perspective, I was sure I would soon cross that grey line into lunacy, where the world would no longer make any sense at all. I knew surely that my hunger for truth was about to be satisfied, and I was starving for Pellanar's next words.

Lord Pellanar began, "In order to bring us to this point in the great unfolding story, I must go all the way to what must be called the beginning of man's memory. The tales I now tell were told first in the *Book of Fathers* over a thousand years hence. And they tell of times millenniums in the past. No copies have survived the defyyl, but its stories and truths were told and re-told in the courts of the Triliset kings for centuries. As the old order of kings passed, almost all memory was lost. As far as I know, the remnant hidden here in the mountains are among the last old kingdom children alive on Terras. We have sought to preserve the ancient truths with zeal. Our scribes have made the record anew, and we have eagerly awaited the promised Light of Dyos, which would break the power of the defyyl forever and set us free." He paused for a moment as though to collect his thoughts, then said, "But I am getting ahead of myself."

In the dark days of the old epochs, Terras was a very different place. Some say that there were once many chapters in the Book of Fathers since long lost, which told the earliest stories, and how the darkness first came. Nonetheless, we know mere whispers.

In that time, Terras was a land of turmoil, fear and hopelessness. Great hordes of barbarians roamed the hills, constantly at war. Seers, warlocks, giants, and pagans ruled the hordes with the blackest magic, plagues, and terrible sacrifices of blood. The people lived and breathed hatred, war, disease, slaughter, and fear.

They worshiped unknown gods of stone and fire, gold and spells, earth and wind, with names like Kroor, Zillith, and Drejj, and they slaughtered each other mercilessly for the glory of their gods. For thousands of years, this was the lot of the people of Terras.

Somehow, in the midst of these dark times, Dyos spoke into the heart of one man—a seer from a small tribe in the south named Soll Pajjah. His visions spoke of a great King God that reigned supreme above all gods—indeed the true creator of all Terras. In this way Dyos revealed himself to a pagan people. Soll's vision prophesied that this King would build a new tribe from the rubble of the old tribes, which would become a kingdom of eternal light, and his reign would never end.

At first the small tribe hardly listened to these strange heretical teachings. So, Dyos filled Soll with power. Later by Dyos' command, he made a spring rise from the desert ground and a gusher of strange silver water burst forth. Soll permitted no one to drink from this spring of water unless they bowed to his authority, and therefore to the authority of King Dyos.

The Book of the Fathers *tells that those who chose to follow, and who drank from the well, were forever changed. They grew in physical strength and had a passion to follow Soll and this new God of gods, Dyos. In addition, the silver waters caused a silver ring to appear in their eyes, encircling their irises. They became known as the Ayali-vinn, silver warriors. As their numbers grew into the thousands, they became an unstoppable force.*

Soll Pajjah led his great warriors in battle against the horrible armies of darkness, paganism, and wizardry. For seven years the battles raged, but finally the Ayali-vinn overcame their foes, and darkness was cast from the land. Many who had been sorely oppressed and beaten down in the old tribes rose up to follow Soll and became believers in the one true King. From this victory, the seven kingdoms of the Triliset grew and united.

For almost a thousand years, Dyos was invited through his

chosen human leaders to sit on the thrones of Terras. Never before or since, has there been an age like this where peace, truth, righteousness, honor, justice, hope, and freedom reigned. The land was without significant disease, fear, pain, hunger, or tears. The old gods had been long ago smashed, their last followers gone or dead. The people loved Dyos unabashedly, and the King his people. Even the lowliest servants walked with Dyos'Bri in their hearts.

There are amazing tales recorded of in this age that tell of great cities of glass and gold reaching to the clouds and chariots of fire which carried people across the sky. Art, all forms of craftsmanship, music, culture, and learning in all disciplines thrived. It is said, that the people who lived at this time knew a love and a peace that is no longer even understood, for its purity was so wonderful.

For several centuries, the consul of silver mages ruled well and fairly, carefully adhering to the whispers of Dyos'Bri. The land and its people remained largely unchanged. They knew the closeness of their eternal king for sure, and each one could feel his power deep within their hearts.

The scribes say, at this time, a man rose to power within the consul of mages who was a master scholar and magician. His name was Aster Siprios. Even as a child, he had been trained well in the magic of light fueled by the power of Dyos'Bri, and had achieved things of greatness and renown, which had benefitted all the people.

However, something happened to him as he became strong in the magics. It is suspected that he began to accept for himself a little of the glory and praise due his King. Over time, this small pride changed him, and he became hungry for more power and attention. His high position as a leader of the consul no longer seemed to him sufficient.

Unbeknownst to any of his fellow consulors, in his pursuit of power, he discovered an ancient scroll of black incantations. It had been buried in a cave before the Age of Dyos by the last dark warlocks. He knew not what they were, but it was clear they spoke of a great and ancient power, and this power was not rooted in the spirit-flowings of Dyos'Bri.

In truth, he had found scrolls of the Midnight Magics, a deadly powerful pagan ritual. These incantations were rooted in the deep earthly powers that Dyos had woven at creation to fuel the molten fires of the earth and to shape all living things—what we now call Vel'Bri (Breath of the Earth). It's at the root of all natural forces and the bonds that hold all matter together. This power was almost unimaginable but was never meant to be worshiped separately from Dyos himself. Vel'Bri alone, unless infused with Dyos'Bri (Breath of God), was just power without moral direction or a soul. The Pagans of the past however had worshiped Vel'Bri alone and sought its power, while never acknowledging Dyos. In essence, they worshiped the created rather than the creator and became skilled at using Vel'Bri for their own dark and twisted ends.

Though Aster did not understand the nature of the fire he toyed with, he saw in these incantations the expansion of power he so hungered for. As he delved deeper into the dark powers, the force of Dyos'Bri, once strong within him, became veiled to him, and this gave him an even greater hunger and new and different power that could not be quenched.

One of the scrolls spoke of a black bane that could be conjured forth with the darkest and most ancient mantras. This defyyl had power beyond belief—nearly unlimited—but was almost impossible to control. It was said that the bane would consume the very being of anyone who sought to wield it. The scrolls spoke a clear warning against its release. Even the powerful warlocks of old knew its horrible potential and feared to touch it. In his pride though, Aster was lost, and one night conjured the defyyl into *existence with the blood sacrifice of a dozen stolen children...*

Harkion Pellanar paused now in his tale. Tears were streaming silently down both his massive cheeks. This strong man was crying like a child at the images conjured by his tale. His beautiful wife, also in tears, reached up gently and turned his face toward hers. She stood on the tips of her toes and kissed him gently on the lips. I could barely breathe as I watched their deep sadness.

"Continue, my Lord," the Lady said.

And after a brief pause, he did.

The defyyl, once he released it, overwhelmed Aster Sypiros as prophesied. That night, his soul became forever twisted. Henceforth, he has always been known as Malthanos—Blackdeath—a name he chose for himself. So great was the defyyl's power that it overflowed his soul and flooded out the windows of his high keep. Carried by the wind, it descended on the quiet land and its naïve people.

It is recorded that many—young and old alike, and those who lived closest to the keep—died in their sleep that night, deep in the blackest nightmares. The evil of the defyyl was immense. Nonetheless, even it could not directly overcome the power of Dyos'Bri left to the people by their good King.

Like most banes of darkness, its power came through deception. The defyyl became like a living black shield, blocking the hearts of the children of Dyos to the power of Dyos'Bri, who had been ever-present across the land to that point. Under its curse, the land suffered from sickness and death, as the life-giving power of Dyos'Bri was shielded from it. The great crystal cities fell into slow decay. The force, which had kept them whole now dissipated. Even the knowledge of their inner workings was lost with time as Dyos'Bri wisdom faded from the people's minds and hearts.

The whole of Terras felt the terror of lonely separation from their King Dyos. No longer could they sense the King's presence so deeply within their hearts. No longer could they know the purity, fearlessness, peace, and joy that they once knew. Disease, wickedness, hate, murder, jealousy, apathy, injustice, foolishness, all these once again appeared in the land after an absence of almost fifteen hundred years. And the power of the defyyl to block the power of good grew stronger as it spread, like rot on a carcass. It seemed the Age of Dyos was at an end.

The Consul of mages, late at discovering what had occurred and now considerably weakened, and themselves afflicted with the defyyl, gathered their combined force in a final effort to combat Mael. They could not reverse the defyyl, for to break its power was far beyond their ability. In a final terrible battle of magics, the fading power of the mages was used to enslave Mael within the Great Temple, bound with chains of spiritual power. All but two of the last mages died in this effort. It was hoped that he would forever be held captive within the light-power of the Gate. However, this was not to be.

For a time, Mael was successfully enslaved, but the defyyl continued to spread across the land with devastating effects. Within a generation, the kingdom of Dyos fell apart. Its people were now barely able to hear the voice of Dyos'Bri, and they became lost in their own struggles to survive. War and destruction followed.

Out of the rubble of the next few generations, the seven cities of the Triliset barely survived, and for a time there was relative peace. All by then agreed that the true enemy was the defyyl.

As the defyyl strengthened and spread, its darkness took a physical form. Born spontaneously one day from the chaotic power of the defyyl, the Soulyss burst from the earth, rocking the foundations of the Great Temple, and breaking some of Mael's chains. The prison of the temple Gate was showing signs of failure.

Mael, now freer tapped deep into the dark powers of the earth, and fed on the defyyl's corrosive magics. He grew slowly again in power. The defyyl bane within him festered and consumed the last remnants of his human soul, and thus became a power like none known before. At the high solstice in the year 2343 e.II, just three and a half centuries ago, Mael finally shattered the chains that bound him, and with a cataclysmic burst of force destroyed the temple and tore the land asunder in the great Ryft.

Now loose upon the land again, he immediately rose up against the seven kingdoms. The lands had been ripped asunder by the Ryft and seams to the underworld opened. Vile creatures brought to life in the deep earthen-fires crept to the surface, and Mael's armies were born.

This time, he set out to completely destroy all remnants of Dyos' kingdom on Terras. His black defyyl-fire, a terrible new weapon, was unstoppable and destroyed whole armies. The seven kingdoms were weak in the power of Dyos'Bri, having long suffered under the plague of the defyyl. In short order, the seven cities were decimated and the bones of the people were stacked in mounds that reached toward the sky. It is said that half of a million people lost their lives across Terras in that slaughter.

My own great-grandfather was the King of Pentos, when Mael came wielding defyyl-fire. The city of rubble and phantoms you passed through on your way here is all that remains of once-great Pentos. In that terrible battle the king and queen laid down their own lives to save a few trying to escape.

The tale is told of one nursemaid to the Lady, Mynna Firr who saw her pregnant master slain by a demonym. Instead of fleeing immediately, she returned and slew the demonym with a flaming torch. After a prayer to Dyos, she bent before the dead mistress and slit her waist with a knife, lifting the tiny almost-born infant from its mother's womb. That baby was my grandfather, the last surviving heir of the seven Lords. Only about five hundred children and adults, the last of the seven kingdoms, escaped. We have lived here as a remnant for three centuries, awaiting the return of the King. In that time, our numbers have grown to near twenty thousand.

In the Southlands Duvall, Parthis, and Tille still barely cling to life. At the time Mael escaped his chains, they were little more than rural villages of a few families, and avoided Maels' wrath, which was directed toward the seven kingdoms of the uplands. He has hardly given them a thought, only sending a few spies, and small vull hordes to keep them at bay while he grows his dark kingdom in the north. Besides, he has largely won over the spirits of the people of the lowlands already, who only know the faintest whispering of Dyos anymore.

What Mael in his corruption had forgotten, until recently, were the old prophet Soll Pajjah's words, spoken nearly three thousand years ago in the Book of Fathers:

...when, in the final days, all seems lost, the seven horns of truth are gone, and dark fire and plague have swept the land, and the greatness of my breath is but a whisper, do not shed your tears my children. For from the last of my remnant will come the King, a light like no other, born through myself, and of my heart. Through His sacrifice the plague of death will be shattered forever and the Dark will be burned by Light. My children will be reunited with the power of My Voice, and My kingdom will live again in their hearts and it will never end...

Lord Pellanar paused now and looked us over before continuing.

As a group we probably looked pretty ragged and dazed. I am sure he wondered in truth whether we were indeed the latest characters in Dyos' astounding plan, or whether somehow, he had mistaken the prophecies. I saw him glance again at my wrist, now upon the table, and he gave the slightest nod before he continued.

"We, as protectors of truth, have not forgotten these words and other similar prophecies that speak of the coming of Dyos'Lei, Light of Dyos, his hand, sword of truth, and king's fire. We have watched and prayed with zeal for the light to come, never knowing when, but always sensing that it was right around the corner. Like Mael, we also sent spies to the Southlands, for our scholars had told us that Dyos'Lei would rise there. Idros Lancath, himself came among you as a child, an orphan.

With this statement, he motioned to one of the tall men in the shadows, and I saw him step forth, sweeping the low hood from his head. He said nothing, but smiled at us almost shyly, as if asking for forgiveness. I recognized this man. He had worked alongside Paddren at the flourmill for as long as I had known. I could not believe that all along he had been a spy from the North.

As if reading our minds, Lord Pellanar said, "Do not hold anger in your heart for Idros. He has not betrayed anyone, rather he probably saved you. He had to obey a higher calling. Imagine the courage it took for him to leave his family as a child and go to live in an unknown land. Dyos himself spoke to Idros as a child in a dream and told him of the sacrifice he must make to prepare the way. When he told the scholars his dream, we agreed to let him follow his heart. He has waited almost thirty years to see the answer of his prayers."

I recalled that Idros had never married and had no family in Duvall. I suddenly had a sense of the incredible passion it must have required to live as he had, and I could hold no anger in my heart for him. He had been but an observer, and his intentions were not malicious. All of us had also known the irresistible call of Dyos'Bri on our hearts, and we had left all we knew behind to obey that call. In the end, it brought Idros closer to us than before, knowing that we had shared such a similar calling. Like him, we had probably caused great pain and sadness to family and friends in the process of our obedience.

"Idros is a brother in his obedience to the call. We hold him in no anger," I said, looking to the others who nodded in agreement.

He smiled a deep smile now, silently conveying his thanks for our understanding.

"Idros has now relayed to us the wondrous but confusing news," Lord Pellanar went on.

"It seems a man claiming the name of Dyos'Lei for himself has appeared. By all reports, he sometimes wielded great power like a king, and at others seemed a low traveling stonemason. Further, we are told that this man caught the attention of the Exarchate Consul and somehow angered them terribly. We are told that he was publicly whipped and sentenced to die on Stone Table among the rubble of the Great Temple. Idros followed the Red Guard there and was a secret witness to all that occurred the night the Solyss was destroyed.

We looked again at Idros, who remained silent but nodded humbly. I realized now that my premonition of a secret follower in the lowland woods had been confirmed twice now—in Toss and Idros both.

Pellanar went on. "We fear Mael's spies in the south alerted him to the strange happenings, and that he recalled the prophecies, ordering the consul's destruction of this man Yakum."

For a moment, I was stunned by the revelation that Mael's spies had the power to influence even the highest decisions of the Duvall Consul, but when I recalled the eerie figure of Desmodys conjuring vulls forth with strange mantras, the absurdity of my own innocence was revealed. I looked at the others and watched this same mental process occur in the minute contortions of their faces and the blinking of their eyes.

It was Thom who spoke next, always two steps ahead the rest

of us. "Well, if Yakum was indeed this Dyos'Lei the prophecies speak of, where is the king now? He died on the stone table?"

The simple logic and terrible realization of Thom's statement shook us all to the core. Was the plan supposed to go differently? Yakum had been killed before he could conquer Mael or even raise an army. Was our journey now all for naught, and the hope of these last children of truth now gone? Had Dyos somehow failed in his promise to usher in a new kingdom? Was Yakum just an imposter?

I looked at Lord Pellanar, hoping he had the answer to these most basic questions, but he remained silent and his features indiscernible. I felt abandoned and afraid, on the edge of a precipice. All these stories, all this history of Dyos' great kingdom, the battles fought for truth, the seven kingdoms of the Triliset, they were all just empty stories if Dyos'Lei never came or if he had come and just died. For a second, my soul quivered on that great cliff that hung over the abyss of emptiness. Then I heard it, a whisper, like the lightest breeze blowing me back from the darkness of the abyss. Dyos'Bri....

"No," I said. "Yakum did not die for nothing. That was the plan."

The others looked at me like I had sprouted three heads, but I continued.

"Dyos'Bri is free," I said. "We all have felt its call on our hearts, and we have seen its power at work. Yakum destroyed the Solyss—the physical manifestation of the Defyyl..."

The other faces lit with slow understanding as they recalled the night of the storm so long ago in the half-built meeting hall, when the fire of Dyos had danced among us, and the many times since when the blue light of Dyos had burned forth to give us victory.

Thom, finishing my thoughts as he always did, said, "He was the King's sacrifice. He broke the power of the Defyyl. He slew the Solyss. The darkness no longer shields Dyos'Bri. Its power is available to us again, just like the prophecies say!"

...My children will be reunited with the power of My Voice, and My kingdom will live again in their hearts, and will never end...

We looked again at Lord Pellanar, who indicated with his nod that we had indeed stumbled on a truth that he himself had only recently understood.

"For the first time in over a thousand years, almost overnight, it seems the power of Dyos'Bri, so long only a whisper to us has now come forth like the sound of trumpets. Our scholars are suddenly grasping the truth that has eluded them for centuries. Children have had prophecies, and students dream dreams of wisdom that have surpassed anything before. Our healers are suddenly able to help even the most afflicted to a degree unheard of since the defyyl, and it is only just beginning."

"When we first noticed these signs a little more than a month ago, we knew not what to make of it, then Idros reached us with the incredible news, and finally you four have come confirming the truth."

For several minutes, we all sat in silence, pondering these incredible revelations. We stood on the cusp of a new age in history. Dyos'Bri was once again free in the land. It was both terrifying and joyous. Suddenly, we were walking in realms of power that two months ago we had no idea even existed. We had a sense of hope like none we had known but also a terrible trepidation, for everyone in that great hall now knew that ahead lay a terrible storm. Mael would soon know, if he did not already, that his only true enemy, Dyos'Bri, was once again loose in the land. Surely he would not be idle. When Yakum died conquering the Solyss and breaking the terrible power of the defyyl on the hearts of men, he began a course of events, which would clearly change the face of Terras. If the prophecies were true, the storm would not be over until the eternal kingdom of Dyos was established. Mael would never bow down again to his old king; he wanted all Terras for himself. Sitting there, I think we could all now hear faintly the terrible thunder of war in the distance.

As if to confirm my musings, Pellanar spoke again.

"We believe that Mael now realizes the terrible threat the Southland represents. Our spies tell us that even now he is gathering an army to crush the southern towns. There are already reports of small outvillages utterly destroyed by defyyl-fire, and of sightings of night-creatures not seen for centuries. Two of our scouts were found dead and scavenged in the foothills. It is believed that they encountered a hyss and were left to die."

At his mention of the great winged beast, we all looked at each other, recalling our own brief encounter with that creature of horror.

"The groaning of evil is all around," he continued. "War is imminent."

After a time, Thom raised a question we all had begun to ponder. "What, then, does Dyos want with us? Why has he brought us here?"

Lord Pellanar did not speak for several seconds, again looking around the table at us each. He seemed to pause at Toss for a few seconds, but then moved on.

"Truly, I don't know," he said. "You carry the white-band of the Ayali on your wrists. After extensive discussion with the scholars, and a look at the map you brought with you, and a review of the pertinent prophecies in the *Book of Fathers,* we believe Dyos has a higher purpose for you."

We looked at each other around the table as if we were seeing each other for the first time. Try as I might, I saw only the simple men and women I had come to know and love. What did Dyos see that I could not? Why us? Then it occurred to me that this really had little to do with us as individuals but rather about him as King. Whatever power had brought us this far on our journey, and was to carry us forth from here, came not from within us, but from the King himself. When I thought this way, for just the briefest second, I saw different people around the table, leaders, and mages, healers, princes, knights, and warriors of renown. I realized, I was seeing the future.

Pellanar went on. "We believe that your journey will continue to the north, deeper and deeper into Mael's own darklands. Even into the heart of evil itself..."

The room grew deathly still. Even the fire seemed to stop crackling.

"We do not know the purpose of your journey, but we believe it has been ordained by Dyos himself, and therefore must come to pass."

He let his words sink in for several seconds, perhaps expecting a response from us.

Though none of us wanted to hear these words, I think we already knew their truth before they were spoken.

Finally, Toss spoke up: "What about Duvall? We can't head north while our families are facing the armies of Mael in the south."

I remembered the terrible premonition of war, death, and plague I had had when I walked too close to the seam below the cliffs. Even though the room was warm, I shivered from the memory.

"We are gathering an army five thousand strong, half our number—all we can spare, which will head south to help in the defense of Duvall and the other Southland towns. We will send our best soldiers and commanders. Nonetheless, I feel that all of this will be hopeless, unless your journey is fulfilled."

I had a sense that perhaps Lord Pellanar knew more than he

was saying, but for whatever reason was not choosing this time to reveal it.

"There are a few among us who have felt the voice of Dyos' Bri clearly in their hearts these last few weeks telling them that they are to accompany you north. They are only three, nonetheless they are among our best, and I have no doubt that three called by Dyos are more effective than a thousand set together by any man. Time has come for you to meet your traveling companions."

Harkion raised his hand silently and signaled to his right.

From the shadows at the eastern end of the Great Hall, beneath a great-pillared balcony, hung with ancient tapestries of war, stepped three cloaked figures. They came forward silently and knelt each on one knee before us; their heads covered still by dark blue velvet hoods. The central figure was the first to speak.

"Knight of the White Order, we beg leave to speak." There was a long pause while I waited for Pellanar to answer before I realized that this warrior was addressing me. I knew not what to make of this honor but managed to eek out a response nonetheless.

"As you will," I croaked.

With this, the three raised their heads and swept back their hoods.

Before us knelt three very different figures.

"My Lords, I am Sennytt Pyke, lieutenant commander of the Order of War, and your servant." Thus spoke the massively muscled warrior bowed in the middle. His head was even with my own, despite the fact that he was kneeling, and he looked directly into my eyes. His face was like hard rock, rough chiseled with crags and scars, but his eyes were a vivid blue and piercingly unafraid. Along the right side of his short shaved scalp ran a deep furrow where the bone of the skull had onetime been crushed, and the top part of the right ear was gone. I knew in an instant that we had a deadly ally in Commander Pyke.

To his right, head at his shoulder, was a woman.

"I am Cynte Lass, a three-mark north tracker and huntress. I have been called by King Dyos to serve you as guide." I turned my head and looked fully at Cynte. She was taut-muscled and tanned by the sun. Her hair was cropped short above her ears, and was the color of the late autumn sun, yellow-gold with hints of orange, her face was pretty, and I was struck by an earthy beauty that seemed to glow from every pore. She had large olive eyes and full lips. I could have sworn that I heard Thom sigh behind me. With surprise, I also noticed a white band of stone like our own upon her tanned wrist. I was too far away to see clearly, but I thought I could see an extensive branching of lines like an ever-bisecting path inscribed in its stone.

Finally, in a voice little more than a whisper, the man to the left of Sennytt spoke, and in unison our eyes and ears tilted toward him, straining to hear.

"Pylos Aull is what I am called. I am chief-mage in the Order of Illadai, and serve you now through the command of my King Dyos."

Pylos was blind, his eyes were as white as eastern marble and cloudy like milk. His long hair and shaped beard matched his eyes in eerie paleness. His nose was large in proportion to his face, and he had a thin mouth with dry lips. He was the smallest of the three, frail of build, and almost arthritic in his movements. Nonetheless, it was clear that the others, including Lord and Lady Pellanar viewed him with great respect and more than a little fear.

And so we had it: a warrior, a tracker, and a mage. I looked at these three again, and all three stared back. Even Pylos Aull seemed to meet my gaze with those empty eyes that saw too much. It would be an honor to journey with these three, whose experience and fearlessness I think gave us all comfort.

After they had addressed us, I thanked them for their commitment, and Thom, Mryyn, Toss, Vyyd, and I introduced ourselves. Lord Pellanar then released them to prepare for the journey north. Plans were made for departure only two days hence. This seemed too quick for me. It had only been a few days since the vulls had trapped us on a snowy mountain ledge on the verge of starvation, and I can't say I was all that eager to resume such adventures. All it took, however, was a thought of Duvall, and the family and friends who were even now going on with their lives oblivious to the black death on the horizon that was Mael and his armies. Suddenly, two days seemed too long a wait and a luxury.

We spent the rest of the evening around the fire with Harkion Pellanar and his wife. The great hall later filled with people, many of whom were introduced to us. There was dancing and acrobatics, music played on instruments I had never heard before, and a seemingly endless flow of fine port. My body was not ready for such an onslaught of sensation after so much deprivation. Mryyn gently rested her head on my shoulder and fell fast asleep. Then the room began to swim with fire and sound, and it wasn't until the following morning that I remembered anything else.

Chaptyr 17

The next two days were an incredible wonder. Between heavy meals and lots of rest, we were given a tour of Aelikos, as the mountain city was called. And a city it was indeed! Our first impression had been of a system of several halls, large and small and adjacent residence rooms, but we were sorely mistaken. Aelikos was a vast, multistoried complex, buried in the heart of several mountains.

Our tour leader was one of Lord Pellanar's young sons, no more than twelve at best whose name was Dews. He was a tall skinny lad with a mop of dirty hair and a constant sly smile. Nonetheless we could not have asked for a more knowledgeable or thorough guide. Dews led us through level after level of passageways and great halls. We saw the vast kitchens and storerooms, forges, carpentry shops, a huge weaving works, metallurgy and armory, a multistoried healers' facility, vast libraries, schools, alchemists labs, a paper works, scribes shop, a tannery, several breweries, deep mushroom caves, an ice room, a tremendous cavern in the bowels of the mountain that was a fishery and reservoir. On higher levels, there was a theater and arena big enough to hold thousands, several meeting and feasting halls, a throne room, a hall for sword training and the arts of war, with weapons like none I'd ever seen.

Higher still were endless family and private residences, meeting halls—like the one we had spent our first night in—great pools for bathing and others for cleaning, a steam hall, powered by deep earth forces, more small libraries, vast art and music halls where many men, women, and children painted and sculpted, made pottery and tapestries, and where we met a group of young men and women known as the Curios, whose primary task it was to invent new mechanics and tools. This room, more than any other drew my attention. I was endlessly intrigued by the peculiar devices scattered around this hall, many only partially constructed, some seemingly moving by their own power and others making strange noises as their great gears creaked. I had no idea what I was seeing, but I had the eerie sensation that this hall was filled with the future.

Nothing, however, prepared me for what we saw next. Dews led us out through a long hall that twisted and turned, and suddenly ended at a door. When he opened it, I was momentarily dazzled by light, but he urged us out onto a large balcony. Vertigo quickly replaced the bedazzlement. We stood hundreds of feet in the air on the side of a cliff overlooking a vast valley between two hulking mountain ranges. It seemed to stretch for miles in both directions, and was remarkably green and lush. Dews explained that this hidden valley was the only reason the remnant had survived, and had been able to build the vast city of Aelikos over the centuries.

When the first Children of Dyos had arrived, they had

dwelled in deep natural caverns, and barely survived, their meager stores quickly disappearing. Two scouts had followed a long stream that ran through the mountain to its source, and found a passageway into this valley, which even then, though it was winter in the highlands, had been filled with an abundance of natural fruits and vegetables, game, fresh water, dense woods, and peculiarly, warm air. It was then that Aelikos truly began, for the people realized a new spirit as they understood Dyos' miraculous provision for their needs in the midst of such recent destruction. It was not for a long time however, that they came to understand the true wonder of the valley.

Dews went on to explain that the valley was forever warmed by deep earth heat. Explorers had journeyed to the great caverns beneath the valley and reported rivers of melted stone that flowed like a furnace. Even as Dews spoke, I could see several large pillars of steam rising into the sky, which I had first mistaken for fires. The valley was, in places, densely wooded and in others cleared for a vast array of crops, many now visibly early in their growing cycle despite the fact that fall harvest had come weeks prior to Duvall, and that the peaks all around were crowned in heavy snows. Horses in great herds ran across some low hills. Cattle, sheep, goats, and even some herded aurochs were evident on other pastures. Here and there across the valley, I could see orchards of various fruit trees, and great fields of waving grains. I think we were all stunned. None of us, perhaps, had queried before that point the source of supply for the twenty thousand inhabitants of this amazing city.

Dews pointed across the blue air of the valley to the high and jagged mountains beyond.

"Over those peaks is the beginning of the true Northlands; Mael's corrupted territories, the Whispering Hills, the Parched Lands, the Pestilence, and some say a waste of death that surrounds Dyy Loss—the dwelling place of the Lord of Misery and wielder of the defyyl. For centuries, the mountains, too high even for a hyss, have kept our secret well, but we fear that is ending. The sentinels high on those peaks have seen the movement of distant horde armies, and they have shot down several grotesque ravens, with fir, sharp teeth like bats where their beaks ought to be, and a single central black eye. It is believed these are new spies for the defyyl lord crafted in the hells of the north. Just the other day two were shot trying to re-cross the peaks on their way north. Thus, we fear our valley has been found"

I could tell as Dews spoke that he was covering carefully his fear. All his short life, he had known nothing but this valley and the amazing mountain city of Aelikos. The enemy of all that made this place special lay just across the peaks now. Like most boys his age his soul held that peculiar mixture of unparalleled courage, invincibility, and fear. Even now I marveled at how quickly Thom, Mryyn, and I had been thrust out of our comfortable existence, into a world filled with new and terrible possibilities.

After a lunch of rich aurochs and onion stew, cold milk, and warm bread studded with grains and lathered in butter, Dews led us back to our chambers to rest. Harkion's instructions had been very clear. We were to be fed and rested beyond contentment, for we were likely to see little of each in the north.

Later in the day, Mryyn and I were summoned to the Lord and Lady's chamber, which was not that far from our own. It was modest but richly appointed, and actually had a balcony of its own overlooking the verdant valley. The couple greeted us as old friends, smiled knowingly as we shared pale wine and cakes with them, and talked about their long lives together. Mryyn and I both sensed that they wanted to speak to us about something more private, but we knew not what. Finally, I asked plainly what was on their minds. Lady Karolyne smiled at her husband. He cleared his throat and carefully began, buoyed by her supporting gaze.

"It has come to our attention as we have watched you two that you share something more than a friendship interest," he observed. "Karolyne and I are reminded of our own courtship when we see how you look at each other. Are we…mistaken?"

Mryyn and I both laughed easily at their goodness and perception.

"You tell it right, my good Lord," Mryyn replied. "At first I knew Pityr as a child friend, now I understand he alone is Dyos' choice for me."

I was not a little stunned to hear Mryyn speak such words. I too had felt this truth, and between us an unbreakable bond had formed. Nonetheless, I had never heard her speak her thoughts so clearly.

"I wish to make her my wife soon upon our return to Duval," I said, "for I think my heart may burst if I must wait longer."

The Lord and Lady now visibly relaxed, assured their perceptions were true.

Harkion went on, "My wife and I asked you here to make you an offer. You are headed on a journey into darkness at the call of our King. Whenever we chose the path of obedience, we can never be sure of the events, but we can always be sure of the outcome. Dyos never abandons his children and never leaves them short on strength, but he often requires all we have and sometimes our very lives as well."

Mryyn and I were both hushed. We understood he was telling us we might well die on our journey. This was a fact we both knew was true, but had not let surface in our conversations.

"Together my wife and I have prayed for the will of Dyos since we have known of your coming. We also have seen the bond he has knit between you two. We believe it is indeed the will of our King that you might be eternally love bound, and we wish to offer you the chance for marriage here, before you go north.

I felt Mryyn grip my hand fiercely in her own, and my heart beat like a heavy war drum within my chest. I barely had to look at her face to see the certainty there, and I mustered the voice from somewhere to reply. "Please, my Lord and Lady…if you could, it would answer our hearts."

Harkion now rose and placed his huge hands upon us.

"So be it, then. Time is short. Tonight we will celebrate what is made at the will of Dyos."

It seemed the next hours were a dream. Mryyn was whisked away by Lady Karolyne and her serving maids, and I did not see her again until she stood before me.

Harkion took me first to the great baths. Servants led us into a round room with high pillars and a ceiling hidden in a cloud of dripping steam. A large round bath filled the room, the water scalding, deep earth boiled, and scented with oils. Here, two swarthy servants, who nearly drowned me in bubbles, scrubbed me at the Lord's command. They seemed intent on scraping the top layers of skin clean off my body. I had not known the depth of my filth until that point. A layer of grime bubbling on the surface of the pool when I was removed disgusted me. Unexpectedly, I was dunked into a frigid bath of clean water to the side of the hall, and then toweled dry until my skin tingled. Next came two old women who beat my muscles until the journey's knots were loosed and rubbed a thick scented oil into every pore. I was cloaked in a warm soft robe, and attended by an old bent man with a razor and scissors who scraped my beard growth off and trimmed my shaggy locks so I looked less like Ull. I was set to rest in a warm, dry room filled with burning candles on a thick soft mat. Though my mind was filled with a thousand thoughts, I could not hold on to any of them, and was asleep within minutes. After an hour or so, I was gently awakened, bathed again quickly in a tepid pool and led to the clothier. There, two more old women dressed me in clothes finer than any I'd ever seen. I was draped in the darkest blue fine wool coat trimmed in silver, a clean white cotton shirt beneath. A lake-blue cloak with a silver triliset hung across my shoulders and was bound by a silver clasp. Fine leather boots, tipped in steel and simmering with oil were placed on my feet. I felt like a prince sheathed in all this finery. Harkion met me then, approving of his handiwork, and commenting that he hoped Mryyn would recognize me. He led me then into a small chapel and instructed me to kneel at the alter. There, a single candle burned with a white-blue fire. I knelt before the fire and prayed silently to Dyos. Never had I known his presence so fully upon me. Time passed; perhaps an hour or more. I felt Thom kneel beside me and I looked over at him. He too had been bathed and cloaked in rich garments, though not as trimmed as my own.

"I want to pray with you, my friend," he said with a smile.

I had rarely seen him so serious and silent, and I was thankful for his presence. He and I knew that this marriage bonding would forever change the dynamics of our trio. Nonetheless, instead of loss and sadness, I could only sense joy and peace from my big friend. We knelt together for a long time.

I then felt a hand on my shoulder and stood. Harkion and Thom flanked me, and to my surprise, several other people had entered the room silently. Lady Karolyne was there and stunningly gowned. A clean pair, Toss, and Vyyd stood together. I could even see a newly groomed Ull sitting in the shadows next to his master. Cynte, Dews, Sennytt, Pylos and Idros were all there, as well as several other men and women we had met. The small chapel was full to bursting with new and old friends.

A high consulor entered from the end of the sept cloaked in ornate robes blue and black. He greeted me sternly as if trying to convey the seriousness of the business at hand. Surely, I knew this already. Then I heard a door open to the side and saw bright candles. There stood Mryyn, and I could not breathe.

Shimmering in the candlelight, she entered the room like a whisper. Her eyes never left my own. Mryyn had always been naturally beautiful and graceful. I had known her as a dirty tomboy, a fierce fighter, an expert archer, a fireside friend, and more recently as my someday wife. The person I saw before me now however, was a princess of light. She was clothed simply but very richly in a silken white gown finely embroidered at the neck in silver thread. A shawl of translucent silver hung over her shoulders, as if it had fallen from the clouds. The gown found and enhanced every curve of her stunning figure, and I found myself almost too shy to look. Her hair was bound high and ornately woven, like I had never seen it. Ringlets of auburn fire hung down and danced lightly on the skin of her neck. She wore silver earrings with tiny bells that jingled as she moved. Her skin glowed with candlelight, and health, and a rosy flush. Beneath her gentle nose, her full lips glowed a deep plum red, colored by some glistening paint, which made her smile shine. It was her eyes, though, that stole my breath and sent my heart galloping. I had looked deeply into them a thousand times, but never had I been invited in so completely. I felt engulfed by their love, and delicately tickled by the impossibly long thick midnight lashes. Her lids shimmered with a hint of silver powder and her brows arched in silent laughter. I was lost, utterly and completely abandoned, and the richest man in all Terras.

The consulor took our hands and joined them together. Mryyn's grip was light but pulsing with heat. I could feel her long shaped nails against my palm, and when I looked down I saw that they too shimmered a lacquered silver.

We said our bond-song together, our eyes never parting. In words honest and strong we confessed our eternal love before the King who holds our lives forever in his hand. The bands on both our wrists came alive with tracings of blue fire as we spoke. I took two simple rings of deep earth gold from my breast pocket and handed them to the consulor. With a stone rod, he dipped them into the blue candle fire on the altar. Together we watched as the yellow-gold was transformed into a shimmering blue-white by the fire. When they had hardened and the consulor had finished his blessing, I slid the hot ring to the base of Mryyn's third finger and she did the same to me. All those present sang the River's Prayer

Two small streams born from first rain
One among the golden plain
One among the airy crest
As if by some mistaken jest

Alone they wind their secret ways
Fed by storm and starved by sun
They seek a friend where there is none
They cry the nights and sleep the days

But high above the Master stands
He splits the mount with gentle hands
And twists the knolls till all is right
His works are done in spoken light

In the end two, too long alone
He weaves together and walls with stone
Now a river deep and pure
Floods the land and will endure

Long after the song was done, its high echo seemed to ring in the small hall. Mryyn and I both opened our eyes simultaneously not realizing they had been shut. Suddenly, I was fiercely aware that we were a new river that would endure, born of the eternal spring of Dyos.

With high and official words, it was declared so by the counsulor. Suddenly the hall rang with cheers, and I swept Mryyn into my arms. I knew I would forever feel the tingle of that kiss.

With celebratory jesting, strong pats on the back, and hugs from all, we were swept from the sept, down long torch-lit corridors, and into the great hall. It was already filled with people, most of whom I had never seen before. Nonetheless, the crowd seemed ripe for celebration, and celebrate we did. Five large fires roared in hearths around the hall. The deep reds and blues of the war tapestries had been overhung with white and silver drapes in honor of my wife. Great banquet tables laden with every food stretched along two of the four walls, and there seemed a thousand servers, winding and twisting their way through the party with mugs of mead and casks of fine wine. Musicians and singers filled the noisy hall with swirling song and high notes. People danced and ate, and laughed and sang, and ate and danced some more, until the hall was drunk with joy, and time seemed of no consequence. I realized, as I looked around, that this was much more than a wedding celebration. Though Mryyn and I had the seats of honor, and though we were congratulated endlessly by all, this was really a party for the people of Aelikos. Harkion had wisely brought his people together for a last release before the coming dark winds of war swept down upon this mountain home.

There was, for me, only one other person in that room. We sat with shoulders touching. We danced twined together, her head resting lightly on my chest. And finally, long past midnight, we said our first goodnight as a couple, high on wine and hope and joy.

I cannot tell the secrets of that first night, for there are not words with power enough to express such things. Besides, these are things best shared between two, not the whole world, and each man must find his own way there. Let me just say, that I never knew. I never knew the freedom and peace of right passion before that time. Mryyn was a teacher to me about how to really love someone more than myself. When I gave myself to her utterly and completely, with pure abandon, I was set free, and on my way home. What a difference there is between a man and woman, and what a joy in the tight joining of the two.

I knew I would never forget waking up that first morning. The softest and sweetest weight upon me, velvet skin against mine, a heart beating against my side, warm sleeping breath on my shoulder, lavender scented hair tickling my cheek. I knew this was the only place for me. Before Dyos, I vowed my all to this amazing woman.

Harkion did his best to give us at least a little time alone. Our departure was delayed two days. We were left alone to explore the baths, treated to fireside feasts, and given freedom to walk the wild-flowered acres and cool forests of the valley. We soaked up enough sun and sleep and passion in those two days for a lifetime.

It was good that this was so, because on the morning of the third day, our friends came for us with packs and boots and sharpened weapons and heavy leather cloaks and mail. It was time to leave the dream and head into the nightmare.

CHAPTYR 18

After a thick and hearty breakfast of wild boar and honey sausages, onions, fried goose eggs, and black bread with strawberry jam, Harkion gave a final word of encouragement and blessing. The eight of us sat together and listened as he spoke of the high calling on our lives and the challenges ahead. Truly, I was not far enough away from cold and starvation, thirst and sore feet, to forget that they were the commonest fruits of adventure. I am a brave man, but no fool, and certainly not crazy enough to crave a return to such things. Everyone at this table had known hardship. I looked at Vyyd's melancholy gaze across the table, and I knew, for some the cuts would never fully heal. We all dreaded what lay ahead, the uncertainty weighing heaviest of all. Nonetheless, this was our path, and none there could deny the harsh truth. Why Dyos chose this rough crew for such a task, I would never know, but call he did. Any who had felt the fire of Dyos'Bri within could attest it is not a fire easily snuffed. It grows stronger with each step forward in faith.

For his part, Harkion promised his soldiers would soon travel south to defend lonely Duvall and the other Southland towns. We all knew that the armies of darkness and the power of Mael would be overwhelming for these little towns. As so, Harkion concluded with these words:

"Where we go, and what we face I do not know. One thing I do know though is that the Light of Dyos has been loosed on the world, and is alive in all of us now. I would rather have an army of ten farmers and the power of the King at my side, than ten thousand chariots of trained warriors when I meet the defyyl lord face to face. Go my friends, and go with the King, and bear his name as you bear your swords, and nothing will stand against you."

We traveled with large packs laden with every provision we could carry. We trekked with Cynte in the lead across the fertile fields and pastures and high up into the hills on the far side of the valley. We then began an exhausting series of cutbacks higher and higher into the peaks, until we once again trudged through snow. Now, however, our feet were well protected by oiled boots and several layers of warm woolen socks. By evening, we reached the guard post on the high pass of Skylen, which permitted an unimpeded view miles into the northlands. The post was carved from solid rock, and from afar, looked part of the mountains' natural features.

Though cloaked in heavy snow, we found the Skylen post warm and well stocked. Ten men continually manned its ramparts, though it had bunks for a dozen more. A pit of red coals was kept well fed with logs, both for warmth, and as an immediate source of signal fire fuel. A fat-joweled cook with a greasy apron named Muel kept the soldiers full, and this night he served up two dozen plump, basted and dripping rabbits and a large vat of boiled greens. Also served in honor of his guests were some strange yellow fruits that were long and crescent-bent, and had a skin that could be easily peeled. I had never seen their like and their taste was sweet and peculiar. Muel called them banyas, and I could tell that he was very proud to serve such a treat. The men had other names for them and being a crude lot in general, all the names referred somehow to male genitalia.

Long used to men and their infantile behavior, Mryyn laughed right along, and I was pleased to see that Cynte too, often broke into wide smiles. She was bright and friendly but also cautious. Her eyes were constantly watching, evaluating, and taking stock of her surroundings. *A good trait for a guide,* I thought.

Sennytt was obviously well respected and feared by this bunch of soldiers, who knew the history of each of his assorted scars and respected his rank. He ate and drank heavily, but kept his words few. I never saw him shed his sword belt, even when he lay down for the night.

Pylos seemed almost to hide in the shadowed corners of the low, long room. His marble eyes were cold in the dimness. He ate almost nothing and said even less. After the dinner was cleared, he pulled a short wood pipe from his tunic, stuffed it with leaves, and lit it. The sharp odor of aged tobacco and spices floated across the room, and settled in a thick layer along the rafters.

Exhausted from the day's journey, and well aware that it might be a long time before we slept on the relative comfort of bunks, we all bedded down early except Pylos who continued to quietly smoke. Warm and tired, I was soon lost in dreams and the bedbugs had their uninterrupted fill.

We awoke to a dazzling high mountain sun and a clear view to the north. I could see tree-covered hills stretching for miles, and here and there large blue-green lakes in the valleys. Further on, the land flattened and turned brown, and stretched off into a greyed haze on the horizon, where I thought perhaps I could see another distant range of mountains. We pulled the ancient map once again and were not surprised this time to see Aelikos clearly indicated with color and detail. The north remained largely undrawn.

Cynte stood beside me also gazing north. I asked her what she had meant when she had called herself a three-mark north tracker. She explained that very few of Aelikos' people had ever traveled out of the valley at all, and fewer still had dared to travel north. For most, Skylen Pass, where we stood, and Rydyr Pass, further to the west, were considered the northern limits of the kingdom and the end of civilization. Even the boldest soldiers would not journey beyond these points into the fringes of Maels' realm. There were maybe ten people in all of Aelikos who had descended the northern side of the mountains and entered the Whispering Hills beyond. These few were known as north trackers. Each trip into the Northlands, greater than a few days, earned you a mark. Cynte lifted her sleeve and showed me a series of three arrows tattooed on her right shoulder.

"I am a three-mark north tracker because I have journeyed three times into the northern hills almost to the edge of the Sand Plains, each time for more than two weeks," she explained.

Cynte had gained renown first as a huntress and tracker and had caught the eye of a mythic ranger called Saxx Lem, who had taken her under his wing.

"Saxx was a twelve-mark," she said, "and once spent over a month north of the mountains, even traveling into the Sand Plains, a feat no other ranger would ever dare. Twice, he took me north, training me in the ways of survival, and teaching me how to hide from the phantyms, and the hyss."

I had met a hyss already, and hoped to never see or hear another. The phantyms I did not even ask about as Cynte's expression said enough. There was no reason to give myself nightmares before the actual encounter.

"Where is Saxx now?" I asked.

"About fourteen months ago, he traveled alone into the hills and never came back. After three months I went to look for him. No other rangers would journey with me, afraid of what they would find. I was able to track his path, though he'd hid it well, all the way to the edge of the Sands. There I found his vest and some blood but no other sign of him. It's possible he died on the Sands, or was caught by a hyss and scavenged, but if anyone could survive those lands it was him." As she said this, Cynte stared far off into the grey north, and I saw a tear trickling on her cheek. I realized that Saxx had been more to her than a mentor, whether he knew it or not, and she had loved him and perhaps still did.

We had a last hearty breakfast thanks to Muel, and with all the garrisons' soldiers looking on silently, we swung the heavy packs on once again and started our descent.

Muel yelled for us to pause and, in a huffing swaddle, came to meet us. He bore a dozen more banyas in his greasy hands, a last parting gift.

"Dyos go with you," he said as if he were speaking to the dead, and turned back up the slope.

Cynte led us down a narrow streambed cut deeply into the rocks. It was covered in ice and snow, but I could hear running water deep beneath. For a long while, we descended along this winding path, high cliffs on each side. Cynte explained that there were no manmade trails in the north face of the mountains, and that we would have to travel what natural paths we could find. After a while, the walls of rock got higher and higher, and we turned a corner to find a huge wall of blue ice barring our way. I thought we were stuck, but Cynte led us into a small hole in the wall no more than four feet tall. It was a tight fit, especially for Sennytt and Thom. Even I had to wiggle through, bent down and on my knees. After a short shuffle though, the tunnel opened up into a glistening blue cavern.

We were inside the ice. Here, the stream ran free and had bored a great tunnel through the glacier. All around, the walls and ceiling danced in hues of blue and white, the bright sunlight above penetrating the frozen waters. In places, great pillars and spikes of blue-green ice hung from the ceiling. Cynte led us as though she had been here a thousand times. We followed the stream in its cascade down the mountain. Sometimes we would come to what seemed like the end, but always, Cynte would lead us through a hidden fissure, or over a great ice mound, and we would once again find the stream. We continued like this for hours, slipping and, at times sliding, down icy chutes, always bathed in the strange and dancing blue light. We ate lunch next to a frigid pool within a blue crystal cathedral. The ceiling of ice was almost a hundred feet high, and in places, had collapsed so that shafts of white sun poured from above and sparkled magically on the water. Truly, this was one of the most beautiful places I had ever seen. No manmade hall could ever compare with this work of Dyos. We ate the banyas in silence, overwhelmed by the spectral beauty all around.

After lunch we continued downward for about another two hours, until the stream finally bore its way out of the glacier. Our path opened onto a wide rocky plain still quite high on the mountain. As we walked out onto the plain, I looked back up the mountain and could see the glacier stretching for miles upward. I was stunned by its size and could almost feel the pressure of its centuries-slow creep.

Cynte led us around a large, milky blue lake that had formed in the plain, and we caught the path of the stream again as it cut down from the far shore. Here, the path became steep, and in many places we had to descend backwards on hands and feet down waterfall-splattered cliffs. Come late afternoon, the slope finally eased, and we hit high, rounded hills with patches of dry and bent grass and clumps of snow. Here we could travel much faster, and by evening, we had reached the tree line, where stunted pines clung to the rocks. Here were larger and thicker patches of grass, sprinkled with deadwood.

Thom and Vyyd started heaping up the wood in preparation for a fire, but Cynte ordered them to stop. "We cannot have a fire here," she said firmly, "for it can be seen for miles around. We cannot even leave a sign of our passage or soon we will be hunted."

With these words the mood of the group became solemn, all now reminded that we traveled in the heart of the darklands, and that the freedom and comfort of the last week would be no more.

We shared several loaves of dense nutty bread, maple-dried pork and the rest of the banyas, and quenched our thirsts in the glacial water of the stream. We talked, but quietly. For the first time, I heard Pylos speak more than a few words, when he found some small yellow rocks that seemed to excite him among the jumble of mountain debris all around. He picked them up carefully as if they were fragile, and tasted them lightly with the tip of his tongue. "Flamerocks," he said with wonder. "And the purest I've ever found. These may well be useful in the days ahead."

Mryyn asked him what was so special about them. In answer, Pylos took a knife from his pack and carefully shaved a few minute flakes from one of the yellow rocks. He then took one of the flakes, no bigger than an ant and placed it on a large flat rock. He took another large rock, stood over the flat rock, and let the chunk of granite fall. When the flake was crushed between the two stones, there was a blinding flash and a crack that split the night like lightning. When our eyes again adjusted, the two large stones were crumbled like dirt, and the grass around was singed.

"These little yellow rocks have the power of the Vel'Bri within them," he marveled, as he rolled one between his long bony fingers.

That night was cold and windy but alight with a million stars. Up here, on the edge of the mountain, it seemed as if I could stretch out my arm and pluck a few from the sky. Mryyn snuggled close for warmth, and I wrapped my arms tightly around her. Suddenly, the rocky earth seemed as soft as a featherbed, and I slept a dreamless sleep.

Morning found us just above a sea of mist that stretched to oblivion. Cold, damp, and cramped, we descended into the fog. Soon we traveled among tall black pines. In the mist, they seemed like the great burnt skeletons of giants, fingertips sweeping the mossy ground. The silence was eerie and profound. Our footfalls were dampened by the soft moss and lichen, the clank of metal weapons was dulled, and voices carried only a foot or two before they became the faintest of whispers.

We traveled like this for the rest of the day, feeling wrapped in cotton and dulled to the world. Late in the afternoon, a breeze came from nowhere, and the mists swirled and cleared, and by sunset, only lingered in the deepest and most protected valleys. I could see that the retreat of the mists relieved Cynte, and I asked her about it.

"The phantyms hunt only at night, and only in the mists. Some believe they are not really animals at all, but strange twistings of the mist itself, for they are never seen on clear nights, and they cannot die by sword or arrow, for metal and wood pass right through them." I was a little sorry after that answer that I had asked the question in the first place but was certainly thankful that the mists had cleared for now.

Ull had run off in the afternoon after a wave off from Vyyd and trudged into camp now covered in blood and dragging the carcass of a small goat, one haunch already missing. We all thanked the scraggly beast, whose wild coat no amount of grooming or shaving could quell. I surmised that the poor goat had probably dropped dead of fear when hairy Ull had leapt from the underbrush. Sennytt and I set about skinning and filleting the gift. The goat was certainly peculiar. It had twisted brittle horns, a flattened, rather than snouted, face, and claw-like digits on the front feet instead of hooves. Cynte saw my concern.

"We are now in the true Northlands. All this, as well as the rest of Terras, was once the domain of King Dyos. Some say it was his most beautiful lands. For many years now though, Mael and the defyyl power have been strong here. With time, the good and beautiful things of Dyos have been corrupted and fouled. This goat here has been touched by the defyyl sickness. Its meat is ok to eat if cooked well, but its nature has become more corrupted with each new generation."

As if to prove her point, she bent over the head of the carcass and opened its mouth, stretching back its lips. Instead of the cud-chewing teeth of a Southland goat, this one had yellowed fangs, sharp as razors, and a long forked tongue.

"This one eats only meat, I'll bet," she said with not a little disgust.

Pylos spoke suddenly from the back, his voice hushed, so we all had to bend toward him to hear.

"The defyyl has a pattern to it, one that you will see as we progress deeper into the darklands. Its weakest and most distant tendrils can touch only the mind of man and animals, twisting truth, deceiving, accusing, stirring jealousies, and hatreds. In greater power, it begins to eat away at the essence, or soul, of all living creatures, first man, then beasts, then every living thing, until the internal rot alters the physical being itself. Finally all order and the very natural forces of the land set in place by Dyos himself are befouled, and chaos and death reign. This is the legacy of Mael."

As Pylos spoke, I recalled my midnight encounter with the great black stallion and his herd, and I understood the disease that ailed them.

"Enough talk of dark things, already," Sennytt grumbled as he tore a rear haunch off the carcass with his muscled hands and set to skinning it. "The night is black enough and my stomach is grumbling. Rotten goat or not, I mean to feed my hunger."

Within an hour Cynte had the goat meat roasting over a fire she had built in a deep hole between two large rocks. The flames could not be seen, but the skewered meat smelled good enough.

There was no more talk of dark things that night as we all took our fill of the goat while Ull crunched the bones between giant jaws somewhere off in the trees.

The next morning was clear. My stomach was a little queasy from the goat, and I had little appetite. The forest was damp, and smelled a little of rotted wood and pine needles. Somehow, the autumn sun seemed to make the trees even more skeletal. Cynte explained that these pines never had a full growth of needle, but always seemed to lose as many of the black spines as they grew. The ground was strewn with their debris. Late in the morning a strong breeze swept down from the mountains, and suddenly the air was full of a million falling needles. We had to wrap our faces against the onslaught, for fear of a thousand stabs.

Midday, Cynte stopped to examine a bush richly laden with deep green berries. Thom plucked a few, and Cynte fiercely slapped his hand, sending the berries into the underbrush.

"I am sorry to strike you Thom, but you mustn't touch or taste anything without asking me first. This fruit is deadly to man. They are the food of phantyms," she said, showing us a branch picked clean and clearly nibbled by sharp teeth.

"Saxx once told me that he thought these berries were the reason that phantyms have the dark powers they have. Now they just kill for fun, they don't eat their kill... We walk their territory now."

We continued on through the afternoon beneath the tall trees, mostly in shadow. At one point, seemingly without explanation, Pylos stopped in his tracks and looked sightlessly upward through the trees. For several minutes he stood there as we grew uncertain.

"They hunt us now," he whispered.

Thinking he meant the phantyms, Thom said, "I thought they only hunted at night."

"Not the mist creatures," Pylos replied. "Its Mael, he knows we come, he has sent his hunters. Even now the hyss take flight, and there are others."

He did not continue, but as if waking from a trance, he suddenly looked at us all with those milky eyes.

"We must go now," he said.

None of us asked how he knew what he knew at that time, but late that night when we finally stopped for the night I asked him where his whisperings came from, and how he was able to see without his eyes. Cynte had led us to a small cave smelling of mold. It was not comfortable, but it was shelter from skyward eyes, and we felt safe.

For a long time after I asked the question, Pylos said nothing, and I was beginning to wonder whether he had heard me, when he suddenly spoke. "I was born with these eyes, and have never known anything other. I can imagine how others see the world from what they speak, but I have never known color or light as you do. My eyes do see, but only faint shadows in the world of men. They see clearly, however, in the world of illihi, or power and spirit, what I have come to recognize as the world of Dyos'Bri."

He was barely whispering as he spoke, and Thom, Mryyn, Vyyd, Toss, and I, on the opposite side, had to bend our heads closer to hear.

"For example, I saw the flamerocks in the ground, not as you see them—yellow and coarse, I believe, but I saw pockets, shapes, if you will, of denser illihi, against a faint background. Illihi is really the flow of power that is constant in the spiritual realms, and it is this I see as others see light. The flamerocks have deep earth power. They hold in concentrated form, some of the Vel'Bri power that Dyos placed in the world when he breathed its creation, therefore they appear distinct and bright to me.

The *Book of Fathers* says, "... that all of creation cries out to the glory and majesty of Dyos." It is made by his hand, and it is this signature that is illihi, and my light and color. When the hand of Dyos touches us, and Bri power fills and transforms us, we are lit by the illihi. Some I know right away as dark, for I cannot see the signature of Dyos on their hearts but faintly. Illihi also comprises what we would call truth and wisdom, holiness and righteousness, purity, and even hope. It is the power within Dyos'Bri, if you will, his language and power.

I have heard your stories of the man Yakum who claimed himself as Dyos' Lei—the manifestation of Dyos' light. You spoke of two occasions when you witnessed a transformation as if by magic—a plain man suddenly appearing as a king. I have thought much of these things since I first heard you together speak of them. I do believe that Dyos'Bri, for a time, gave you eyes like mine, and you could see Yakum as he appears by the light of illihi rather than the light of the sun. I believe you saw the Light of the King, his truth and hope, Dyos'Lei, the very one who has broken the power of the defyyl. This is why I have agreed to come on this journey, even though I know I will never be going home again."

What could we say in response? The five of us looked at Pylos with awe and wonder. Cynte and Sennytt watched us quietly as we tried to swallow the impossible. None of us knew what to say about his statement that he wasn't coming back with us.

As usual, Thom's quick mind went to work first. "What does the defyyl look like to you?" he asked.

Pylos considered carefully before answering, "The defyyl looks like mold or rot in places, and like a dark covering in others. On created things, when I am close, it appears like a sickness or corruption, spots of shadow on the illihi light of a thing. When I look distantly, or across space, it appears as a dimness, or even full darkness. Sometimes the defyyl covers completely what I am trying to see."

Mryyn asked, "What did you see when you looked toward the sky this afternoon and knew Mael had sent the hunters?"

"I saw rays of shadow across the sky, dark toward the north. The creatures of evil were still far off, but their release momentarily shadowed the illihi even here. They will arrive on the morrow."

I looked long at Pylos' creamy pale eyes, and I thought what a blessing and a curse it must be to see as he did.

"I know what you are thinking," he said as if he could see our thoughts. "But it is the only thing I have known since childhood. It is not any stranger than light and darkness must be to you after years of sun and night, color and shade. I have learned to navigate well by the light of illihi, and Dyos has graced me with ears, and a nose that senses what others do not. I knew the flamerocks by their bitter smell as well, and I can hear the closeness of solid things."

After he spoke these things, Pylos fell silent again, and I wondered whether he was listening to our thoughts, or smelling our sweat. After a while though, he pulled out his pipe, and filled it this time with a faint cinnamon blend, and practiced his smoke rings, while the rest of us fell into an uneasy sleep.

We woke shrouded once again in mist, and this time, it did not clear, but only seemed to get denser and wetter as the day progressed. Even breathing seemed hard, for it filled the lungs with cold, moldy, vapor. Cynte tried to keep us on high ground, but several times, we were forced to dip into long valleys barring the way, and several times we had to round great black lakes. How Cynte knew where to go or when to turn off the circumference of a lake in such heavy mist, I could not decipher. In the early afternoon, Cynte pulled a hemp line from her pack, and bound us together, for the mists had thickened to the point where a handbreadth from the face, the world ended in a sheet of white.

Sennytt sang a few bawdy tunes to himself as we went, and the distant voice raised our spirits a fraction. But even this was not enough as the light began to fade. I could tell Cynte was not at all happy that we were still on low ground as night came on. We had rounded a lake about an hour back, but weren't yet making any uphill progress. At one point, Pylos yanked on the cord and stopped us all. He alone seemed oblivious to the mists, and as surefooted as ever. The rest of us had each stumbled several times on roots and rocks, and tall Thom had been slapped in the face by a branch and bore a nasty welt.

Pylos shushed us. I bent my inferior ears to the task at hand. I felt it before I heard it, like a whisper of death—the faintest scream of a hyss, far above the mists. It passed and was gone, and the feeling of dread left me.

"The fog protects us today," said Pylos.

"It will also be our destruction if we do not get free of this valley," said Cynte.

With ever-greater urgency, Cynte dragged us forward and the night got darker. Next I heard the splash of water and realized Cynte must have stumbled on another lake. Her curses however, suggested otherwise. Somehow, we had wound our way back to the lake we had first rounded two hours ago.

"We are in trouble," she said in a voice shaking with barely controlled fear.

That was when a wind passed my ear and Thom was knocked to the ground next to me. The length of cord binding us jerked, causing me to drop to my knees. Mryyn screamed nearby, Sennytt cursed, and I could hear Thom groaning.

"Cut the rope!" Cynte screamed.

Without thinking, I drew my sword and swiped at the cord that had dragged me down. I struggled to my feet and reached for Mryyn's voice. A textured wind moved beneath my hand, and I felt a searing pain in my forearm, and the wetness of blood. Suddenly a swirl of wind twisted the mist away, and I could see our attackers. Thom was pinned to the ground by a pale catlike beast twice his size. He was reaching for its throat to thrust it away, but his hands were passing right through the phantym. Its claws and teeth were inflicting damage though, and his face and neck were sprinkled with blood. Sennytt was dodging and swiping at another similar beast, but his sword cuts would have been more effective against the wind. I saw Mryyn sidestep the closest beast, smaller than the others. She avoided its claws, which had swiped me in the pass, but fell on her back when another mist beast swept Vyyd down in a heap, and the cord binding the two of them tugged her off her feet. The sudden absence of mist startled the creatures. The one nearest Mryyn turned toward me, and barred its fangs, I froze in terror. Its eyes were black holes in a dead, empty skull. Thin trails of white pus dribbled from the sockets down its face. It turned its head back and dove its teeth for Mryyn's bare throat. I screamed in anguish. Mryyn rolled beneath its feet. All around were the voices of my friends and companions crying out in terror and pain. Ull howled. A force of immense power and weight struck my back. My breath left me in an instant. I felt claws piercing my back. I rolled with all my effort to the side, and stared into a dead, rotting mouth filled with fangs.

Without warning, a wind of fierce power, warm and dry and filled with the smell of late summer grass, swept over me. I had to squint at its force, but in my squint, I saw the form above me shift and roar in anguish and in a final smoky swirl, whip away into a silent clear night. The weight upon me was gone and the sky above was filled with an impossible number of sparkling stars. I could hear moans and whimpers of pain but could barely move. My feet, I realized, lay in the lake's edge, and I felt the gentle lapping of wavelets against my pant leg. Care for Mryyn, who was laying next to me, filled me as my mind crept from the dullness I was swimming in. She was not conscious, but her pulse and breathing were strong. Except for a thin trail of blood on her temple, she appeared unscathed. I felt a hand on my shoulder and turned to see Pylos standing next to me.

"They have gone," he whispered.

I knew, as I looked at him, that he was the reason they had been swept away in the night, but I asked no questions then, and he had no more words to give.

He gripped my hand with surprising strength for one so thin and pulled me to my feet. I rushed to Thom who lay facedown in a bloody heap, and Pylos walked almost casually over to Toss and Vyyd, who were groaning but moving, and Sennytt, who was vomiting on all fours at the edge of the lake. It wasn't until then that I saw Ull standing in the water up to his haunches, bleeding from one eye. He gripped Cynte's collar in his mouth, her head listlessly hanging in his bite, while the rest of her body remained submerged. As I moved toward Thom, Ull dragged Cynte slowly to shore and dropped her gently. I realized he had saved her from drowning, for she coughed now, and water flooded from her mouth and nostrils. She took several gasping breaths, rolled over and also retched.

Thom, when I turned him over, was barely breathing. He had been cut deeply in the neck, whether by fang or claw, I could not say, but even now, the wound pulsed rich dark blood. The pool of precious blood beneath him was frighteningly large. I hurriedly tore his cloak and pressed the cotton against the wound, temporarily staunching the flow. Pylos came beside me silently. From a black leather pouch at his side, he removed a small jar, and twisted its top. Inside was a pungent black tar, thick as clay. He scooped a large heap of it with his fingers and thickly applied it to Thom's neck. The black clump stopped the flow of blood, and Pylos let Thom's head down gently.

"He will be okay but has lost much blood. He will need more ministering later. For now we need to gather our things and make a large fire. The spell does not last, and the mist will come back before long."

Even as he spoke I could see a wall of mist all around, stretching tentative tendrils into our pocket of clear night.

Toss and Vyyd recovered enough to help me gather some sodden logs and rotten branches—not the best fuel, but Pylos pulled yet another packet from his sack and sprinkled some powder on the wet wood. I didn't see the rest, but before long the wood was ablaze, and the fingers of mist kept their distance.

Mryyn slept peacefully for a while. I lay her head upon my lap and wiped the blood from her temple. There didn't seem to be any gash beneath, just a bruise. Even as I watched though, the bruise faded, and her paleness passed in a flush. I saw the pulsing blue weave of her band burning brightly on her wrist and realized, that Dyos'Bri was coursing in her veins and healing the injuries. In moments, she yawned, and her eyes fluttered. She started to speak, but I stopped her with a kiss.

"The others are okay," I said in answer to her question. "We were attacked by the phantyms. We're all beat up some, but Thom got the worst of it. He's lost a lot of blood, but Pylos got it stopped for now."

I took her to Thom once she had steadied. He lay shivering and frightfully pale in the brown grass next to the fire. For several minutes, Mryyn bent over Thom, running a practiced hand over wounds and bruises. When she was done, the band's fire faded, and she washed Thom clean of blood and mud with water from the lake. He woke then, but was almost too weak to speak, and his skin remained pale and sweaty.

"He almost died from the blood he lost," she said. "I can heal the wounds, but I can't replace the blood. It will be several days before he is able to travel."

"Maybe I can help," Sennytt said, speaking loudly from the fire's edge. We all looked at the soldier, who was streaked with blood and dirt, but looked as formidable as ever.

"I'll need some bloodroot though, some oil and salt. I've used the mix myself near death, and it works."

We all looked at him without speaking. His face was stretched with scars, and I had no doubt his torso was a meshwork of the same.

"How can I help?" I asked.

In the end it was Pylos who returned from an hour in the mist with several big deep red roots, freshly torn from the ground.

"It was harder to find than I expected," he said, barely above a whisper, thereby ending any further inquiries.

Cynte had a bottle of oil among her things, and it was she who made the broth at Sennytt's instruction. It bubbled in an iron pot on the fire, the salt donated by Vyyd. The stuff smelled dangerously foul. When done, it was as thick as syrup, deep brown-red, and stunk of an animal long dead.

It was Cynte who held Thom's half conscious head, pinched his nose, and fed him the sludge without as much as a grimace.

Perhaps she saw it as her penance for getting us lost in the mist, but I thought more likely she was quietly beginning to care for Thom. Regardless, she managed to get almost all of the broth down Thom's throat before he threw some of it back up, and it came out his nose. Sennytt assured her that he had kept enough down, but even then, she waited until Thom was quietly asleep before she went off and retched herself.

A strong and determined woman, I thought with a smile.

Mryyn had made the rounds of the others, healing cuts and scrapes, concussions and cracked bones, before she came tiredly again to my side. She lifted my torn shirt and gasped at the deep gashes on my back. I also showed her the torn skin on my forearm. She healed them gently with her blue touch, and then fell deeply asleep, her head resting against me. The healing had sapped the strength within her. The fire burned brightly, and Pylos sat guarding against the night, seemingly without fatigue. It wasn't long before my mind grew blank, and I let the flames' dance take me away.

Chaptyr 19

Morning came in shades of pale pink and yellow. The sky was clear, and the mists of the night before had crept back to the darkest recesses of the forest. We woke with aches and groans. Thom seemed to have benefitted from the bloodroot brew. Some of his paleness had receded, and though unsteady, he was able to walk unsupported. Cynte also had recovered fully, and I saw her watching Thom with a quiet concern. I knew Thom was fine when he growled for breakfast with a crooked smile.

The rising sun revealed the reason behind our confusing return to the lake in our attempt to flee the night before. Unlike all the other lakes we had passed, which were eerily round, this lake was shaped like a horseshoe, bent in a great three-mile long "U." Unknowingly, we had rounded its far edge, walked across its inside, and then encountered its other arm, which lay before us now. I think Cynte was relieved to see that her instincts had not been entirely off, as she took Thom's barbs with a smile.

We ate as hardy a breakfast as we could afford and bathed in the clear waters of the lake before we set off again. There was higher ground visible all around now, and we felt confident we would be able to reach it by early afternoon. Pylos alone sat quietly in the pale sun, amidst our activity, frequently staring off to the north with those haunting eyes.

We did make good progress, and the day remained clear. A wind rose by the time we climbed into the forest once again. It animated the hanging branches of the black pines, and they seemed to reach for us as we passed beneath. Grey needles spun in the wind's twists with a subtle hiss. The forest was otherwise strangely absent of the scampering and fluttering of little creatures.

For two more days we traveled this way along the high ridges, only occasionally traversing the misted valleys when absolutely necessary, and as fast as possible. Night always found us above the fog now but without a fire. Cynte and Pylos both agreed we did not want to advertise our presence to any spying eyes.

For my part, I doubted anyone was watching, and our good progress had lifted the other's spirits as well. The terror of the phantyms was far below in the mists, and the sky was bright with starlight. Pylos insisted on watch each night. It was hard to tell his moods, but he was clearly worried about something. Whatever was bothering him, he kept it to himself.

I slept well during his watch. Having my new wife against me, with her scent and pulse so close, gave me fresh joy each night. I wondered how I had ever slept before, alone and cold. Pylos never seemed to sleep. The one time I awoke in the night to relieve myself, I could see his pale eyes staring northward, circles of spiced smoke slowly rising from his dark form.

Late the next afternoon, we were hiking along a high rocky

ridge spiked with dead pines, when Pylos halted us all with a loud whisper.

"We need cover. NOW!" he growled to Cynte.

She looked around at the sunlit afternoon trying to find the threat for a few seconds before Pylos grabbed her arm and shook her.

"Now!" he said.

Instead of asking what for, she led us at a run, off the path, and into a cleft along the ridge edge. Here, a deadfall of trees littered the ground. They were thrown atop each other like so many sticks. Before I had a chance to wonder what natural force had ripped the trees up and dashed them about, Cynte led us crawling on hands and knees beneath the tumble.

"What are we hiding from?" Sennytt asked, echoing our own thoughts.

"Hush!" Pylos said viciously.

Even the warrior in Sennytt had a fear of Pylos and his eerie power, and he shut his scarred mouth tightly at the rebuke.

Within minutes, I heard it. High and distant the haunting scream of a hyss echoed across the highlands. It was answered moments later by another right above. It was all I could do to turn my head toward the sound. I could see small specks of sky through the tumble above. A dark shadow slid across the filtered light and swept off southward with another cry. Like the first, it seemed to numb the mind and blacken the soul. Speech was all but impossible and a dreadful hopelessness lingered with the echo. Far away the second one answered again, and then they were both gone. Beneath the rubble of wood, I felt as vulnerable as a mouse hunted by the great eagles of Pirth.

After a few minutes, when the terrible screams had lost their edge, Vyyd whispered, "Pylos, is it safe to leave cover, or must we wait?"

We all crouched in a muddled heap beneath the scattering of

rotten wood and it was hard to see each other's faces.

Pylos gave no answer.

Toss, who was closest to Pylos, finally whispered, "He seems asleep. His eyes are closed, and he breathes shallowly."

In all the time we had been traveling together, I had never once seen Pylos close his eyes or sleep. It scared me to think that something was wrong with him. Though the smallest and physically frailest, in many ways he had become for us a pillar of strength.

I crawled first from the rubble heap, happy to be breathing fresh air, hyss or not. I saw none of the beasts however, not even distant shadows to the north, and I ordered the others out of cover. Sennytt in particular, not used to hiding from enemies, seemed eager to come out. Thom and Toss dragged a limp Pylos behind them into the light. He was even paler than usual and seemed to be barely breathing. Mryyn ran to his side and laid her hand upon his forehead. She withdrew it with a gasp not a second later, as though she had been burned. The band on her wrist was afire. Pylos opened his eyes just as suddenly, and his breathing became regular. Mryyn slid away, afraid.

"I am sorry," he said. "I should have warned you never to use your healing hand on me. Others cannot see what I see, even for brief moments without great pain."

Mryyn nodded, looking at him with fear and rubbing her hand. I don't think I had ever seen her truly afraid of anything.

"What was wrong with you?" Thom asked. "Why were you asleep?"

It was a few moments before he answered. He looked all around the sky and tilted his head slightly as if listening to a distant voice.

"I was not exactly asleep, but was in more of a trance," he replied just above a whisper. "It was self-preservation. I saw the shadow of the hyss long off, and I could hear their cry in the distance. They are on the hunt for us. My eyes and ears are very sensitive to such things—too sensitive, really. Were I to hear a hyss cry close, or confront its darkness face to face, I would perish quicker even than you. The trance is something I learned from others with the gift of illihi sight. It closes me off to the world, and is my only protection. Come. We must move on, and tonight find better shelter. These flying demons will not give up the hunt. They will be back."

We spent the rest of the day in a fast hike to the end of the ridge, and down into a deeply forested valley. It was not so low that it cupped mist, nor was it as exposed as the higher ridges. I felt caught between two certain perils. We were cursed if we wandered into the misted realms of the phantyms and cursed if we walked the open ridges of stone from the hyss above.

Cynte found us a perfect cave for the night, where a bear had once inhabited; its dried bones were curled up in a corner. Again, we made no fire, for the smoke would have found the sky, even if the flames were not visible from above. Supper was subdued. We all felt oppressed and hunted, and the carefree progress of the last few days seemed at an end.

After the meager meal, I asked Mryyn for the map. She handed us the shining tube, and I carefully removed and unwrapped the parchment. None of us were too surprised this time to see many changes to the map. Aelikos was depicted now in fine detail and color as if it had always been there. The great blue glacier was evident, and even the "U" shaped lake, at one end a swirling dark depiction of mist, meant to illustrate the phantyms' attack. The road ahead was, as always, faintly laid out, and stretched far yet up the parchment, with only a few markings and smudges—hints of what was to come.

It may seem peculiar that a map that only revealed the path already taken with clarity, would be of any value at all, but it was. For us, it offered an acknowledgment of all that we had already accomplished. The path stretching from the cliffs now far to the south of our current spot on the journey was marked with many adventures and victories. It was also helpful to see that we had come more than halfway to the journey's end at the top corner of the page. Though the path's end was faint and shrouded in a shadow without discernible features, it represented an end nonetheless. So wearied and worn were we by this point that any end, even one so ill-defined seemed something that brought peace.

We woke to a grey drizzle. We were all aggrieved to leave the veritable safety and dryness of the cave. The forest was damp and depressing, and the drizzle made the rotten needles underfoot smell with each squishy step. Nonetheless, we made quick progress until late morning when we came upon a wide river. The forest was split in two by its rocky gorge. The water ran rough and foaming among great boulders, broken rocks, and old tree trunks thrown in among the tumble. The great fissure was maybe one hundred and fifty feet across, and both sides had sheer rock walls dropping thirty feet into the roaring water. Any other time, I would have found this setting quite beautiful. Now however, I found it an aggravating and dangerous inconvenience.

Cynte led us along the edge of the gorge until we found what seemed like the best place to cross. Here, the tumble of boulders and dead trees was not too thick in the river, and the rock walls had a few apparent handholds. With the help of thick hemp rope, which Vyyd had been carrying all this way, we made it safely to the riverbed. The rocks were slick and moss-covered, and in places, we had to jump across deep foaming pools. Cynte led the way, and I must say, she was as surefooted as any mountain goat. Even Pylos seemed to jump without trouble.

How or why it happened at that moment, I will never know, but just as Cynte reached the far side while the rest of us were strung out across the river, I heard a terrible groan and a *CRACK!*

I looked upstream just in time to see several large tree trunks break free from a huge clutter of debris pinned between two boulders. The swift green current of the river shot the trunks downstream like spears upon us. None of us were able to take more than a few steps before the thick logs struck us. Pylos was knocked off a slick rock, and I saw his head land with a sickening thud against another, his body going suddenly limp, half in the foam. Mryyn dodged some branches, slipped, and fell but was up again quickly. Thom pulled her up onto the safety of a high boulder. Vyyd, Toss, and Ull who were all midstream, were thrown into the river, and I saw their heads disappear beneath the green water. I was knocked to my knees by several branches as they passed, but the larger logs missed me. Once I regained my feet, I was able to reach over and drag Pylos to my rock and Cynte helped me lift him onto its flat surface. He was bleeding from his left ear, and I wasn't sure he was breathing. I felt at his neck for the beat of life. It was there, but faintly. I looked downstream for the others. Vyyd had managed to pull himself onto a log sticking into the river, and looked unhurt. Ull was climbing out of the water on the far shore. I could not see Toss anywhere. Sennytt sat not far from me on a rock, pulling a broken branch as thick as his thumb out of his left thigh, and cursing.

This time, I saw their shadows before I heard their cry. The two hyss were upon us. Somehow, they had found us at our most vulnerable point, and with complete surprise.

They flew a low pass, slowly arched one after the other and descended into our midst. The whole time their terrible empty moan echoed along the riverbed. The rushing of the waters was silenced and the wind and creaking tree branches were gone. The daylight grew dim; all senses were dulled. All that existed was the low haunting heart-tearing groan of the giant creatures.

One landed heavily on a pileup of trunks fifty feet downstream. It flared its wide wings, and arched its black neck. Its darkness shadowed the whole area around. Beneath it, the river turned black. Its death moan reverberated and rose.

As I looked into its shadow, I could barely discern movement among the tumble of brush where it stood. I realized that Toss lay there broken but moving. The beast had seen him there and had come for the kill.

Even as this thought reached me, I felt darkness hit me like a wall from behind. I was knocked to the rocks, all the breath punched from me, all thought sucked away by an empty wind. I rolled just barely onto my back and saw the second hyss above me; its talons deeply dug into a great boulder midstream. Cynte, Mryyn, and Thom also lay stunned and immobile, scattered within the beast's dark shadow. This hyss now answered its brother's pleading, hellish moan, and the world around me died. An abyss of midnight emptiness consumed all sense of life, hope, purpose, and courage. The creature's moan, rumbled within me, freezing my blood, numbing my mind, and filling my heart with death.

I saw the creature turn its head. It looked right at me, but there was nothing there. Its eye sockets were empty and black, and I saw the depths of hell within. I knew then that I would die. I turned my head to avert its eyes, and I looked downstream. I saw Vyyd loose his grasp on the log and slip beneath the water. Then I saw Toss. The hyss above him had dragged him from the scattered logs with its massive beak. He fought weakly even now, but it was clear he was dying. His legs were limp and bent backwards at an awkward angle, and I realized later that his back had been broken in the original tumble. The hyss lifted him like a rag toy and arched its head skyward. Its moan deepened in rumbles of evil. Its beak was around Toss's waist, twisting the two hundred pound stonemason like a cat with a rat in its jaws.

Suddenly it dropped him, and it seemed Toss lost consciousness, twisted among the trunks below. But the hyss was not
done. It drove its beak like a spear and pierced Toss's abdomen
through. Even as I cried out for my friend and mentor, I saw
something amazing. Seconds from death, Toss twisted his right
arm and reached behind his back. He grabbed the handle of his
twenty-pound war hammer and swung it with his last breath.
The wide metal head sunk between the empty eye sockets of the
beast, and its hollow skull shattered like pottery dashed on the
rocks. The hyss went down in a headless heap atop the logjam,
its moan suddenly silenced. Toss died hanging in the branches. Though he was distant, my vision seemed magnified and I
could swear he seemed to smile before his breath stopped.

It was that smile, I think, that changed everything, for somehow, in the midst of terrible death Toss had found peace. I knew
then that Dyos'Bri had met him there. The moan of the hyss
above me had grown to a roar with the destruction of its broth-
er-spawn. The blackness of its cry reached with wicked talons
to crush me forever. I was already near death, so great the darkness within me, and paralyzed in terror. I could not fight as the
black fingers strangled my soul. Except for that smile.

Suddenly, I felt a faint spark within me, and the spark lit an
explosion. Blue fire rushed in my blood; its roar drowning out
the hyss' moan. I had energy not my own now, and I moved like
the wild raging fire I had become. I rolled and sprung to my
feet. My legs felt suddenly like tree trunks, solid and steady. I
drew my sword from its back sheath, and it burned in coursing
blue flame. My whole arm, band and all, seemed enveloped in
azure lightning. I did not think; I just became the weapon forged
within me. I danced across the rocks separating me from the
great beast, and I felt the darkness part before me. I confronted
the surprised hyss with a series of moves I never remembered
having learned. I feinted left, cut low right, arching up again to

the left. The blade cut a swath of fire across the massive black chest of the beast, making it scream in pain. I swung low then rose up, the blue blade ahead. I became a terrible flaming spear even as the hyss dove its beak to kill. As my blade buried to the hilt in its long neck, the power exploded, and I was thrown from the rock into the water.

It seemed a long time before I could find the surface again through the icy bubbles, and when I did, I gulped a giant breath. The air was fresh, the darkness was gone, and the sun shone on a roaring river finally at terrible peace.

Chaptyr 20

We stood together on the river's edge—those of us who could stand anyway, and lifted a final prayer to Dyos for our fallen friend. Thom and I had dug the grave in the dark soil. Toss lay now beneath the roots of tall trees and layers of black pine needles—his war hammer atop his chest. I had folded his right arm across his wide breast as we laid him in the hole, and for a moment, I had touched the smooth band upon his wrist. It had been cold and hard, the band of a chosen servant, and I now knew, a martyr. Toss' journey on Terras was over and his forever was just beginning.

I knew I was not alone in feeling a bit envious of our good friend at that moment. All of us had seen the gentle smile he still wore when we had pulled him from the river. I had never seen him smile like that in all the years I had worked by his side. Surely it was the smile of a man finally home after a long, long wandering. Toss, I knew had journeyed well, and now stood in the courts of his King, his duty done. We would miss our quiet brother, and I my mentor in stone, but we thought also of the duty ahead of us yet, and silently yearned for the peace he now knew.

By evening, we had again found high ground among a grove of trees. The river's roar was a faint whisper now. Even the dance of a blazing fire however, which we chose despite the risk, could not banish the cold within our souls. Though the slain hyss lay in the river, and in the past, the wounds they had inflicted in our souls still ached as fresh as ever. The hyss' cry was a wail of doubt and depression, fear and hopelessness, depravity and lies. No man or woman was left unscathed by its darkness.

Both Vyyd and Pylos had been unconscious at the time of the attack and seemed the least affected spiritually. I had felt the purging fire of Dyos'Bri in battle, but when it had left me again, had felt an all-surpassing sorrow fall upon me. Cynte, Mryyn, Sennytt, and Thom were hardest hit and seemed to be wrestling with dark beasts. I knew that the enemy was fear with many names, for at the peak of my azure frenzy, I had seen the dark spirit behind the hyss' deadly song. Even though the blue fires had destroyed the beast, our small band now seemed almost immobilized by fear and hopelessness. Our conversations contained doubt, trepidation, and insecurity. In short, we were all ready to quit this crazy journey and go home. We knew with certainty, we were doomed to failure. We were eight—now seven weak souls against all the evil powers of Mael—and we were walking steadily toward his lair no less. What fools were we?

Pylos was especially quiet after the attack on the river. His scalp wound was not dangerous, but I imagine it hurt him quite a bit. He listened intently to our speech around the fire but spoke no words at all. Before we slept though, he came to each of us alone and laid his pale hands upon our heads. I heard him mumbling something under his breath as he gripped my temples between his hands. I remember thinking his grip was surprisingly strong for one so frail. And suddenly, it seemed impossible to keep my lids open, and I slid into heavy darkness.

My sleep that night was dreamless and amazingly restful. The others seemed also to have recovered well by early morning. Yesterday's horrors seemed somehow numbed and distant. Toss' loss still tore at us with an empty and aching hollowness. We already missed his steady courage and rocky solidness. Breakfast seemed dull and bland. The future was so daunting, but somehow less hopeless with a deep night's rest. The sun shone pale through a high haze dulling the forest's fall colors. We lingered a while overlooking from high the river where we had lost so much despite our victory over the hyss. I said a long silent goodbye again to my friend and mentor. I thought I sensed a quiet assurance that we would someday feast side by side again. I lifted a fist in salute.

Finally, driven by a terrible and unspoken urgency, we set off quickly, and were afoot before the mists cleared. Our path seemed to slowly descend now, and the high pines progressively yielded to groves of birch, red crest, and silver maple. We crossed two more rivers, both smaller than yesterday's without event. We rested at noon on a grassy hillside so that Mryyn could minister more to Sennytt's throbbing leg, and so Pylos could rest. He still seemed nauseous from his blow to the head, though he never complained.

Mryyn brought down a large wild boar with a shot between the eyes late in the afternoon. Cynte found a patch of blacktop mushrooms, and I, a few wild onions. We cooked the aromatic stew for hours, and that night, ate better than we had since leaving the mountains.

Over the next two days, we traveled about forty miles. We moved fast, with a sense of urgency. Pylos reminded us that

Mael had not given up the hunt. When his hyss did not return to their lairs, the hunt would intensify. Nonetheless, it was not until the third night from the river that we saw even a hint of the enemy. That day we had taken a long break at lunch beside a small lake. Cynte had managed to trap seven large trout, and we paused to grill them with the last of our cornbread. We were all bone-weary, and all of us, except Pylos, had fallen asleep in the low grass beneath the warm noon sun. We had decided to continue late into the night before stopping again.

The night was bright with a three-quarter yellow moon, and we had no difficulty seeing our path. About two hours before moonset, we came upon a horrific scene. We entered a grassy glade, strewn with blood. At first, I could not figure out exactly what I was looking at, but slowly, comprehension took hold. The patch of open grass was drenched in black, congealed blood, torn limbs, entrails, and strangely, white bones. The stench was unimaginable, and Ull began to howl as if in horror. It appeared as if two large bears had been cornered by a pack of vulls. Several vulls lay broken and half devoured; the bears were almost unrecognizable except for their fur and the size of their strewn limbs. Their heads, even their skulls, were gone.

The gore of the scene was enough to give anyone nightmares, but it was the thought of the vulls here, literally in our path, that sent chills deep into all our souls. There was no doubt in any of our minds that this was a hunting party sent for us. The bears had just been unlucky victims. From the state of the carnage, Cynte estimated the vull horde had passed here the night before. We also saw clawed footprints signifying the presence of cy'daal among the horde. Fearing ambush, we decided not to travel further that night and made camp about a half mile upwind from the battle scene where we found a low cave on a hillside. Its entrance gave us a good view below, and it was crowned with an impenetrable thorn thicket, making a silent approach from above impossible. We set two watches all night, but still, none of us slept well.

The next day, we could not move from the cave. The dawn had brought thick clouds, and a waterfall-like downpour that no rain garment could keep out. We could not even see more than five feet out of the cave. Travel was useless in these conditions. We could not afford any sprained ankles, fevers, or falls if we had any hope of reaching our destination alive, and this was a day made for such things. Our only consolation was that even our pursuers could not hunt in this weather, for the scent would be lost. They were likely holed up in some black seam somewhere. None of us felt like talking much, and the mood in the cramped cave was as grey as the rain. We passed that day and night in a series of naps, quiet contemplation, and a few unsatisfying meals of dried and salted auroch meat and water.

My wife laid next to me on the damp floor, dozing fitfully. Sometimes, we talked in whispers about our future together. Even though we both knew it was very possibly fantasy, it took us away from the dark cave and the solemnity in our hearts. I noticed Thom and Cynte sat close. She seemed overly interested in his face and his stories, and for his part, the big oaf was clearly smitten. I loved my large friend and was delighted to see him enjoying Cynte's company so. Sennytt and Vyyd talked quietly among themselves while Ull guarded the entrance to the cave. In this weather, I trusted his canine senses far more than any lookout's. I don't think Pylos said a single word all day; nonetheless, he seemed content to sit blindly in the corner sending aromatic smoke rings spiraling toward the ceiling. All of us were emotionally and physically beaten down. And although the cave was depressing and dreary, the rest was clearly recuperative.

The heavy rain changed overnight first to sleet and then into a heavy wet snow, all of which was blown away by a cold clear wind before dawn. The pale sun that morning lit a boggy and muddy plain with patches of melting snow still in the shadows. The land now before us was made up of long low hills with patchy glades and brush. The thick forest we had traveled in for several days was behind us now. The grass here was coarse and grey green, thorny, and sickly, even the few glades seemed composed of stunted and gnarled trees. Cynte explained that as we headed deeper into Mael's territories, the land suffered more corruption and sickness from the defyyl. Indeed we saw fewer and fewer creatures as we progressed. Large round rats, fat and ugly with long yellow fore-teeth, however, inhabited these lands. In our desperation for fresh food, Mryyn shot a few, but when we grilled them over the fire, the stench of their flesh was foul. The oily strips of meat seemed half decomposed even though the kills were fresh. Only Sennytt and Thom were hungry enough to try small bites of the most burnt pieces, and for their troubles, both lost the little breakfast they had eaten earlier. From that point on, we depended on our meager stores of dried food and boiled water for our sustenance.

We hiked through this depressing land for two more un-eventful days. Twice, we came upon muddy patches trampled by the many footprints of a vull hoard, but in each case, the prints were days old. Pylos seemed to be constantly looking off toward the north, scanning the land ahead with his illihi vision. I noticed him stumble a few times over the rough ground and I began to wonder if the blow to his head back at the river had done more damage than I'd thought. I asked him about this as we walked.

"No Pityr," he said. "It is not the effects of the blow. The truth is, I walk now in a dusk-like darkness. Ever since we left the mountains I have noticed a very slight dimness to the illihi all across the land now. Never before have I experienced this de-gree of darkness, and I am not used to navigating in such dimness, even at night."

"It's the defyyl then that you see?" I asked.

"Yes," he replied. "It is the defyyl shadow clouding all. As I look further northward, it is as if I am looking into a nightmare."

Pylos was clearly disturbed by what he saw. He was a master at hiding his emotions, but even I could sense the tension in him. I suddenly realized that he had always seemed so stony because he likely had never learned to express himself with his face. Just as a deaf person never learns to speak clearly, because he never hears a word, Pylos had never seen a facial expression, only the illihi patterns emanating from a man. This realization helped me to relax around this man who had always seemed so stern; however, I made a mental note at that moment to never lie to Pylos.

We made camp that night without a fire, as had become our custom, and set a watch from the nearest high knoll. Mryyn took first watch, and Ull accompanied her to the hillock. Though I missed her beside me, I had no trouble dozing off, so great was my fatigue.

It was sometime around midnight when I was awoken by something wet and soft brushing against my face. Because of my sudden fright, I was fully awake in seconds, on my feet, and grasping my sword before I realized the friendly wet awakening had come care of Ull. Moments later, I heard Mryyn urgently whispering to me from the nearby hill. I now understood she had sent Ull to wake me. The others, strewn around the camp, continued to sleep the sleep of deep exhaustion. I noticed Pylos, who was sitting up against a rock, turn his head toward me as I began to move off toward the hill.

When I joined Mryyn, I asked her what she had woken me for, and she pointed off toward the south. At first, I could see nothing in the direction she had pointed. The land was lit by a clouded half-moon, now low, and I could see the coarse hills stretching off far to the south. We had, by luck, picked a highpoint to camp, and the view of the land from there was good. I was about to ask Mryyn again what she had seen, when I noticed a large black shadow slowly cross a distant hill and two faint sparks seemed to follow. Now that my mind began to wake, I realized that what I saw was a large group of vulls, far enough away as to seem a single shadow, followed by two torches, probably riders. The image gave me a chill, but what bothered me even more was that they were following the exact path we had come earlier in the day. They were not wandering aimlessly, but had caught our scent and were coming for the kill. My mind suddenly flashed to the blood-strewn glade we had come upon days earlier where the great bears had been mauled, and I trembled.

Mryyn and I turned back toward camp to warn the others, and there they all stood, fully garbed, not ten feet away. Pylos, seeing me leave, had woken the others, and sensed the coming danger.

We fled at almost a run. Cynte led us well over the dark ground, and after a half an hour of fast pace, we came to another high hill. We were all winded. I was convinced that we were moving fast enough that we might outdistance our pursuers, and therefore was stunned to see the riders far closer than before. Now if I held my panting breath for just a moment, I could hear the distant vulls howling. We had no choice but to run still harder. The ground seemed rockier as we proceeded, but it was uneven and made for twisted ankles, and we had to slow a bit to keep from stumbling. Cynte, who was just cresting the slope ahead, let out a sudden yelp, seemed to slide, and I saw Thom reach for her, as he too skidded to a stop. Seconds later, I stood where they stood and was almost unable to believe my eyes. The others came sliding up next to us with great gasps and exclamations of despair.

We stood on the edge of a sheer cliff, two hundred feet high. We looked out on a smooth, barren plain. I peered over the edge to the ground far below and stepped backwards in a vertiginous rush. I turned back the way we had come and saw the vulls less than two hills behind like a black poisonous flood sweeping toward us. Behind them rode three torch-bearing riders. Though these could have been any cloaked riders, I knew I had seen these three before, especially the one in front who rode the large black stallion. I felt as if I could almost see into the shadows of that hood.

Suddenly, Pylos shook me from my reverie.

"Jump!" He was yelling. "Jump!"

I wondered how I could jump as I turned back toward the cliff. I could see us all splattered below. I knew we had to make our stand here, but Pylos was bellowing now.

"Jump!"

I felt Mryyn grip my hand and squeeze hard. She ran to the edge mere steps away, dragging me, and I now heard the pounding feet of the vulls jut behind. I saw Thom and Cynte, hand in hand, leap.

Pylos once again yelled.

I took two huge bounds, Mryyn at my side, and leapt into the night air.

I felt myself falling, and was strangely peaceful about the death to come. As I sailed through the night air, I was supremely aware of the stars above, the glowing white sands below, the whip of the wind in my ears, the warm hand of my love beneath my own. My heart was quiet but powerfully sensitive to the seconds preceding death. I anticipated the crushing blow within moments, but still, the expectation held no fear.

I was therefore shocked when it did not come. Instead, with a sudden deafening whoosh, I felt myself underwater. I gasped and got a mouthful of hot water. Then, just as suddenly, and without effort, I found myself thrown to the surface as though I had become supremely buoyant. In my panic, I began to wave my arms and legs, terrified of sinking, weighed down as I was by sword, clothes, and a pack. Where, just moments ago I had been awaiting death with quiet peace, I now fought it with a vengeance. For all the terrible foaming about me I could not see or hear. I had lost my grip on Mryyn upon impact and could not find her anywhere. My heart was in a terrible frenzy. Each breath was an awful sputter of hot water and an impossible flood of fizz. Despite my chaotic flailing, I did not feel like I was sinking, but rather felt unnaturally light, and pushed along by some deeper current. Finally, my many years of swimming instinctively took over and I began to relax, stretching my limbs wide and letting the foam lift and carry me. At last, I could get a deep breath now and then. My surreal dancing foamy ride had lasted seemingly forever, when I abruptly felt my feet drag through sand below. Soon, I was able to stand on my own above the bubbles, and I stumbled onto a white rocky beach. I sunk to my knees in a terrible watery retch but was up again quickly looking for my companions.

Ull was licking a coughing Vyyd not ten feet from me. Thom was starting to climb from the foam. Mryyn was floating on her back slowly toward shore. I could not tell if she was conscious. When I stumbled back into the foam and grabbed her, however, she twisted and clung to me and her joyful eyes were quite alive. I saw Thom hugging Cynte by the time we had crawled to the beach together. Once we had regained our breath, we found Pylos standing silently, like a statue further down the beach, peering up toward the cliff top. I turned to follow his gaze, and could just discern a single rider with a torch lifted high, on the rocks far above. As I watched, he turned his horse abruptly, and disappeared.

"He knows we yet live," Pylos said with a bitter edge I had

never heard from him before. "The hunt will continue."

"How exactly did we live?" Thom asked. "That fall was well over two hundred feet. Even on water we should have splattered like eggs."

Though Thom's imagery was not pleasant, I knew the same question was on all our minds. How could we all have survived such a fall?

It was a while before Pylos answered. But finally he did, saying, "We lived, because we did not fall onto smooth water, we fell into bubbles."

The simple truth of his statement suddenly made sense of what had seemed impossible just moments before.

He went on. "This lake is a vent from the deep earth, where Terras belches her gasses and stomach juices in one endless burp. The water is hot, and in a constant upwelling rush. It is also high in minerals, making it more buoyant than regular water. We fell into a great cauldron of foam, otherwise, as you so nicely put it, Thom, we would have indeed splattered."

"But how did you know what lay below?" Cynte asked, well aware that Pylos had never been here before.

For a moment I thought I saw Pylos smile, and then he answered, "I guessed. I could see the Vel'Bri uprush, and the rest I guessed."

The group of us stood there, stunned. This man had gotten six people to jump off a two hundred foot cliff with him on a hunch?

Then Pylos posited a query, which I will never forget, and which, in its simple truth has forever changed the course of my life.

"Do you think," he asked, "that Dyos, having led his children to the edge of a cliff, would not give them a way out?"

None of us could respond to his simple statement of faith. We stood dumbstruck and humbled. He was right, of course; it was Dyos' journey we traveled now. Our security rested in our King's hands, not our own.

And so, it was in contemplative silence that we collected our sodden garb, packs, and such that had washed up with us on the sand. We rung out our garments and repacked for the journey. We did not move again that night. Wet and weary, and content to let Pylos keep his watch, we lay together for warmth beside the bubbling lake.

I awoke just as dawn was piercing the sky with yellows and pinks. The surroundings, which had seemed so ghostly in the starlight, now stood out with intense clarity. The cliffs, high and white, towered above us. The foamy boiling lake, which had caught us so gently, stretched at the base of the cliffs for a quarter mile in each direction. It gushed into the mountains of foam nearer the cliffs spreading tall waves concentrically outward. These waves diminished to bubbly ripples near the shore on which we now stood. The great forces, which had split the land ages ago at the Ryft, and thrust these cliffs into the air, had loosed some deep rivers of steam. These somehow vented to the surface beneath the lake.

The beach on which we now stood was filled with sparkling pillars ranging in size from a few inches to a dozen or more feet high. Clearly, the core minerals that bubbled up from deep below had crystallized over the millennia into these unique statues. They were salt-white, sprinkled with streaks of blue, gold, and rusty iron red—stunningly beautiful in the dawn light, arrayed as they were like a vigilant army around the lake. Before us, at the outer edge of these pillars, and stretching forever, was sand, hills, valleys, and more hills, without interruption. The sun, which had at first seemed like a welcome friend, suddenly seemed deadly to me as I peered out over that eternity of dunes.

"Welcome to the Sand Seas, or as Saxx used to call it, the Dry Rim of Hell," said Cynte with an uncharacteristic bitterness. I had not heard her approach from behind me, but turned now and watched her big round green eyes, long lashed as they were, peer out defiantly at the enemy she saw ahead. I realized that to her, these desert hills represented more than a guide's challenge, but they represented friendship lost. As I recalled, it was somewhere near here, on the rim of the sands, that she had found Saxx's bloody garments. She had not seen him since. Her mentor and friend had been consumed by these white waves of sand.

I watched her for a few moments as she stood and looked off into the heat mirages. She spoke without fear, however, when she commanded us onward.

"We must start now," she said, "before the sun gets too hot. We will not be able to travel at midday."

She instructed us to collect as much water as we were able. The lake we had fallen in was warm and metallic in taste, and smelled a bit rotten, but Cynte assured us it would do. Every available wineskin, bottle, and pot was filled, and we carefully packed the lot to prevent any spillage. In addition, Cynte wound torn cloth around our heads in such a fashion that a portion hung down the back of the neck and covered the forehead. We looked ridiculous, not unlike a group of jugglers from south of Parthis I had once seen perform. She instructed us to cover all exposed skin and liberally wiped a white cream on our faces, hands, and necks. When Vyyd balked at the absurd makeup, she chastised him, explaining that if he did not wear it, the skin of his face would bubble and peel off in a matter of hours in this sun. He readily and enthusiastically applied it thereafter. Ready now and looking like a troop of miserable clowns, we took our first steps into the Dry Rim of Hell.

The scorching monotony of those next few days would be painful to recall in years to come. The long sand hills and valleys came one after the other as relentlessly as the waves of the ocean. Most of the time I felt only a terrible dry boredom. It was too hot to talk or sing. My mouth was pasty and my tongue swollen, and I frequently felt the crunching of sand particles between my teeth. At the peak of each hill, I would clear the crystallized dust from my lids and peer far off toward the north and west in hopes of seeing some change in the landscape, but it was like looking again and again at the same dusty beige image. We were as careful as possible with the water, but our supply dwindled quickly.

The nights on the other hand were frigid and brilliantly star-lit. Sometimes with the dehydration and hunger, vertigo came and it seemed as if we hung above a giant black bowl filled with sparkling lights. It felt as if I might let go and fall into this forever-er sea, floating in the ethers lit by a billion stars.

After two days, we got in the habit of traveling from sundown to midmorning, then setting up tents half dug into the edge of a sand hill for a camp. This might have been restful except for the bugs. Within seconds of sitting on the sand, scores of pea-sized, eight-legged white bugs would emerge from the sand and viciously nip any exposed skin, drawing blood. These tiny pests seemed remarkably adept at burrowing between layers of cloth-ing until they found blood. I became so irritated and sleep de-prived from these viscous sand bugs, that even when there were none on me, I could still feel a dozen squirming beneath my robes ready to bite. All the others were equally affected, and our combined thirst and hunger and irritation made it hard to en-dure any but the most cursory conversation or companionship. We each withdrew into a dry world of sandy, windswept silence, wrapped as tightly in our garments as we could get. I remember with horrible clarity, the dread that would come on me when my body signaled the need to void my bowels. Even though it was infrequent due to the lack of food, it was still too common. For every episode meant stripping to a bare bottom and a dozen new nasty welts as one crouched over a hole in the sand.

Who knows how many days it actually was that we endured this misery. It was at least five, perhaps as many as seven. I became increasingly sure that I would die in this parched hell and that my bones would quickly be sucked dry by armies of these little white demon bugs. It was at the pinnacle of my despair when something very unexpected occurred.

We were once again struggling to erect our miserable cloth sunshades one mid-morning. The night before we had drunk our last water, and we were all pretty sure that one or more of us was going to die that day. Thom and Cynte actually appeared the worst with deeply fissured lips, chapped fiery skin, and unstoppable shakes. I didn't realize until later that several days before they had made a mutual silent pact to secretly hide their own empty water bottles in order to keep us from having to sacrifice our own supplies. I loved them for their sacrifice but hated them for being such martyrs. It was unfair to have to watch your friends suffer so.

I had given up on Dyos. Days ago, I had stopped caring about this journey altogether, wanting nothing but an end to the miserable monotony. My faith, what was left of it, had shriveled and dried up just like my water skin. My heart felt barren. My pain at my friends' suffering was so great and my inability to help was so profound that I turned in bitter half-hearted prayer to Dyos once again. Simply put, there just was nothing else to do. Though I had heard a thousand times the curt phrase, "In our naught Dyos is all," it had never meant much more to me than mere words. That was the moment in my life however, when those words finally came alive for me.

I was propping the ragged cloth over Thom and Cynte, who were arm in arm in an attempt to stop the racking chills, and who were both slipping in and out of consciousness. The hellish little spider-bugs were once again nipping at my exposed hand, but I had finally begun to accept them as part of my short remaining life. I was so dry that they hardly drew any blood anymore. Out of the corner of my eye I saw a movement—a quick blur—and turned to see what had crossed the periphery of my vision. It was a bird, large and brightly colored in blues and greens. As I watched, astonished, it danced on the sand and pecked intermittently with its beak, happily nipping up the sand bugs. I was sure I was hallucinating until I saw Mryyn and Sennytt both watching the creature as well. For its part, it appeared oblivious to us. It hopped around for perhaps another five minutes and another score of bugs then jumped into the air and fluttered off. Mryyn, thank Dyos, took off after it. She raced to the top of the hill and then watched for a long time as it flew off toward the northwest.

She came back quickly and, with unexpected enthusiasm and authority, commanded us to rise and follow her. It took us another half mile to find where the bird had gone, and when we did, we knew Dyos had brought us to paradise.

Hidden in the endless sand hills was a remarkable canyon. Several hundred feet beneath the sand flowed a raging river. For thousands of ages, it must have burrowed a great cavern beneath the sand and bedrock, hidden from the sun. In this magical spot the rock roof had collapsed for a quarter mile stretch, and a deep ragged canyon had been exposed. Over the years the sun and seeds, carried on the wind, had filled the vast space with a profusion of green. Great leafy trees, winding vines, and a jungle of flowering bushes fought for space along the river at the base of the canyon. Peering down into its depths, we saw a swarm of twisting colors, and soon realized the valley was also filled with thousands of birds, twisting and fluttering and squawking among the verdant growth.

It all seemed so unreal that at first I was sure we were experiencing some type of communal hallucination induced by our state. The longer we stood there however, the more real it all became. I could feel the damp coolness billowing up out of the canyon and on its wind came the smell of leaves and soil and flowers. So many days had I spent with nothing but sand and arid heat in my nostrils, that this aroma seemed dizzyingly fragrant.

We found a rockslide that breached the cliff edge, and were able to half carry and half slide Thom and Cynte, ourselves, and our meager stores into the valley, and ultimately into the quiet pools that swirled at the river's edges. I have never forgotten the power that water holds over my life. That moment of absolute ecstasy when I drenched my hot head into the icy pool and gulped my fill was a moment I knew I would never forget. "In my naught, he is all."

I didn't think any of us did much more than sleep in the cool shallows or in the soft moss and grass shade for the rest of that long day. Toward dusk I forced my aching frame to move and, with Sennytt's help, gathered all the deadwood I could find. Mryyn, ever true and accurate, arrowed a half dozen of the big birds. Pylos, with his magic powders gave us a blaze even though the wood was damp, and that night and for many more, we ate our fill.

In the days that followed, we found a small perch in the deep pools, some berries, fruit, water lettuce, and a wide selection of roots and mushroom to add to the endless supply of birds. Fresh water, shade, sleep, and good, abundant food had a transforming effect on us all. Even Thom and Cynte, who had been so near death, with Mryyn's healing touch and the reviving fruits of the canyon, sprung back to life.

After a few days, we explored. At each end of the canyon were dark and wet caves that echoed the water's rush. From one the river emerged, and into the other, it again descended. Bats, crayfish, and the occasional reptile frequented the caves, but there was no other sign of life. In the sun however, life and color were plentiful. The birds, we realized, had a patterned day. In the early morning, they would almost all fly away to the desert hills and eat their fill of the white demon bugs as we came to know them. Around midday, they would return in a great squawking cloud. In the dusk, the bats would swarm, and the colorful birds would rest.

For many of the days in the desert, we had come to operate on sheer determination and primal need. Nothing so isolates a person as starvation and hunger and hopelessness. We had found ourselves dwelling more and more in the selfish dark recesses of our own misery. Not only did the blessings of the verdant valley free us from our painful physical cravings, but it freed us from the selfish bondage of those days. For the first time in a while, we had expanding and outward-focused hearts. We ministered to each other's pains, and grew to know each other better. Many nights we spent talking, laughing, and wondering at the incredible transformation in all of us over the last year.

Mryyn and I, whose marital bliss had been set aside in the last weeks of pain since we had left Aelikos, now found again the intense passion of our love for one another.

It was a moment of magical light in a very dark period of our lives. Had we known then how much darkness and pain lay ahead, we never would have had the courage to leave that paradise. Even later though, in the midst of great pain and misery, I was able to recall this time and submit to an almost impossible hope that kept me going.

We finally did have to go though. Thom woke one night in a terrible shivering sweat. He had had a dream—a horrible prophetic vision. From what little he was able to share, his seemed remarkably similar to the dark images I had seen when I had journeyed too close to the seam all those long weeks ago.

He described cresting a hill and seeing Duvall destroyed and fire blackened below. Bloated and plague-ridden bodies lay scattered about, and many others had terrible and fatal wounds. His nightmare had ended with the horrific image of two cy'daal slowly disemboweling and eating one of the fallen souls. The vision had been so vivid, it caused him to weep at its retelling. It had carried with it the peculiar sensation he said that it was a glimpse across space, as if he was actually seeing what was happening in our home at that moment.

I had never related to him the details of my own vision, and was therefore horrified at the similarities. Whether these visions were real-time images, prophetic, or merely nightmares, none of us could say. Nonetheless, we could no longer ignore the clear message they spoke. We could dawdle here in this sanctuary no longer, but must finish the strange journey we had begun.

Even so, it took us two whole days to gather from the abundance of the valley, provision, repair, and pack before we were ready to move on. By consensus, we had agreed that a further attempt to traverse the desert would certainly lead to death. In addition, Pylos, with his illihi eyes, had described a growing blackness across the desert ahead, dimmer and deeper than anything he had known. No longer mere shadows, the portents of evil had become a flood of midnight darkness. Cynte assured us that there was another option: the river.

Logically, she determined, the underground river had its origins in the higher hills and mountains from which we had descended, perhaps even in the glacial tunnels we had journeyed. Likewise, it appeared to course beneath the desert for some time yet, until it inevitably came again to the surface somewhere far ahead. I hoped Cynte's reasoning stood the test of truth and that this river did not continue to dive deeper and deeper into the bowels of the earth, never to surface again. Skeptical as we all were, we had come to trust the experience and instincts of our guide, and now, by her lead we would travel yet again into a new world of shadows.

Chaptyr 21

The fire burned low now as the dark forest grove filled with night sounds. The trees closest glowed an eerie orange. The grass was heavy with midnight dew. I paused for a deep breath of cold air. My grandson shivered beside me despite the warm coals and his thick cloak. The tale had him entranced clearly. I had watched him slipping away into its enveloping arms, much as one is woven into a dream, or as the case may be, a nightmare. I knew that at this point, the tale seemed far more real to him than the dark forest all around.

Jonam looked at me. He was clearly struggling with exhaustion, but the coals' soft light glinted in his eyes.

"Are you ok, Pater?" he said to me. "I fear the telling may be too much for you."

"I am old and tired my son, but I have a story yet to finish before I am done." I replied.

He smiled now, softly.

"Pass me the skin, my son." I said. "My voice is drying up in this chill."

Jonam passed me the half-empty skin and watched as I swallowed several gulps of apple wine. "Ahh, much better," I said, my voice slightly less raspy.

For a while we sat together and stared at the fire. We were silent until finally I spoke again.

"This next bit is hard for me, Jonam. Even after all these years I can feel it like it has just passed."

"Its ok, Pater. We don't need to go on if it's too hard for you." Jonam said this I knew with a silent fear that I would stop now and the tale's end would not be spoken.

But I knew his thoughts. "I said it was hard my son, not impossible. Over this long life, I have learned one or two things worth sharing. One of them is the value of suffering in Dyos' greater plan, another is the *scarcity* of true impossibles." Jonam had nothing to say to this and nodded.

"I speak of these things that pain me so, because you too, if you are to become a banded Ayali, must make this choice. Will you journey with Dyos to a place where suffering brings freedom, and faith makes impossibles possible?"

Again Jonam answered with a nod of respect.

"Stoke the fire my boy, for the night is bearing down hard upon me." I whispered honestely.

So it was, on the quarter moon, after two weeks of unbelievable rejuvenation and revival, we descended into the giant western cavern's gaping darkness. We were guided by the constant sound of the river's rush and the dim light that Pylos was able to draw from a palm-sized glass ball he drew from his waist pouch of surprises. I had seen him set the ball in a hot fire's coals for hours earlier in the night. When he had drawn it out, it was glowing, but cool to the touch. When I inquired about this peculiarity, he had explained that the glass had minute fragments of sand imbedded in its structure. This unusual sand had the strange nature of absorbing the heat of the fire as energy, and somehow it never became hot. Instead, he explained, it emitted a faint light that lasted for days before it dwindled. I marveled again at Pylos' deep knowledge of all things natural and supernatural.

The river ran a deep and winding course beneath the desert. After wandering more than a few turns into its path, all natural light was gone. Only the flamerock's faint fire lit our passage. The walls dripped moisture and seemed coated with a green-black residue, which glistened like the skin of a snake. Bats, in hanging clusters, opened their beady eyes at our approach, but remained largely unimpressed by our passage. Rats twisted and scurried beneath our feet, often slithering away into cracks, or slipping into pools bordering the river. The tunnel was wide enough that along most of its course, we were able to follow dry, rocky paths along either side of the river. Sometimes, we would have to walk through knee-deep water for a while around twists or rock falls. Pylos led this careful procession, as he alone could see clearly in these deep caverns. His light was for our benefit. For those in the rear—Thom and me now—it was too dim to guide us safely. I had to follow carefully every one of Vyyd's steps before me to avoid stumbling on the slick rocks. Even so, I had cracked my shins and knees a dozen times and twisted my ankle twice by the time we finally stopped for supper.

Pylos had found a large flat outcrop of rock overlooking the river, just where the water tumbled ten feet in a raging torrent. The chamber echoed with the rumble of water beating stone, but the spot was remarkably pleasant. We had carried enough dry wood for a small fire and had plenty of fresh food. Something about all the rocks above and the steady power of the water and the firelight combined to calm the soul. I found my spirit caught peacefully in these deep earth rhythms. I had no idea whether it was dawn or dusk far above on the dry sand wastes, but my body told me we had already walked several miles, perhaps as many as ten, along the river's course.

We all conversed quietly and ate hungrily, feeling sleep's caress draw us one by one into its embrace. As usual, Pylos smoked silently a few steps away from the group. He was peering far off into the darkness, quietly watching the strange world only he could see.

Some inner cycle woke us all at nearly the same time, and after a quick bite we were off again along the slick paths. Occasionally, we had to climb down ledges bordering roaring falls. Twice, we had to ford the frigid waters to find a passable path. For the most part though, the day consisted of the constant monotony of each slippery step, one following another. I think Pylos pushed us a little farther this day, for by the time we stopped again, I was thoroughly exhausted and bruised. He never spoke of any concerns, but he seemed to lead us with an increasing urgency as he peered into the dark.

We continued like this for two more days, constantly picking up the pace. All of us were beginning to wonder if this twisting darkness would ever end. All our clothes and provisions were soggy. Mold had suddenly sprouted on some of our food stores. My skin became chafed from the rub of wet clothes. My nose began to run with yellow mucus no matter how often I would clear it. At times, I even found myself dreaming of the desert sun longingly. I was even ready to suffer the demon bugs to feel its bright warmth again.

Sometime during the fourth day, we entered a colossal cavern. The river cut across its width, and continued on in the direction we were headed. Another deep tunnel met this cavern perpendicularly, and headed off again on the opposite side. It was a crossroads of sorts. Pylos led us rapidly across the chamber along the river. He made us traverse its entire length even though on both sides there were large open spaces of rock where the two paths crossed. When Cynte questioned him on this, and suggested that this might be a good place to rest, he hushed her harshly.

"Do not utter a word. Make no noise, and move fast!" he whispered.

Not used to seeing Pylos agitated, we did as he commanded. Only after we had turned two corners beyond the large chamber did he let us speak.

"What stirs your soul so, my friend?" Vyyd asked in a whisper.

Pylos peered back from whence we had come.

"The darkness moves," he said.

"Mael's spawn are on the march, and they come this way."

After carefully instructing us to maintain absolute silence, he led us back a bit around one turn in the river. He made us crouch on a ledge and peer around the last corner before the chamber. We could see the crossroads dimly about four hundred feet ahead.

"Pray to Dyos that the scent of our passage is disguised by the river, or this day will be our last," he whispered.

He extinguished the flamerock by removing it from his staff and slipping it into his pocket. The caverns fell into complete darkness. None of us knew what to expect next. No one would query Pylos, as all of us, even the warrior Synnett, were afraid of his wrath. Thus we squatted like this in absolute silence and darkness for what seemed like almost an hour. Then I heard something in the dark.

When the senses are completely deprived of all input, they invariably generate their own. Therefore, when I first heard a deep thumping against the background rush of the river, I thought I was hearing my own pulse, or that my ears were playing tricks. Then Mryyn grabbed my arm in a fierce clench that bespoke her fears, and I knew I was not imagining. The pulsing thump grew louder and deeper, echoing in the caverns. There were war drums and the tromp of thousands of heavy feet.

I watched in disbelief as the dimmest of lights began to trickle into the chamber from the northernmost tunnel. The light grew brighter and the terrible thumping louder and louder until my heart did indeed pick up its haunting rhythm. Then I saw them.

Scores and scores of vulls and cy'daal entered the chamber from the left and marched across to the passage on the far right, heading south. But they were only the vanguard of an even more terrible force. A hundred huge bear-like beasts with leathery hides followed, walking upright like men, but twelve or fourteen feet tall. They bore studded clubs and torches. I realized that they were hellwyyn, another felspawn we had heard described in Aelikos. Like the vulls and demonym, they were spawn of the defyyl fires and ancient incantations Mael used to birth monsters. Next came beasts like giant aurochs, but horribly malformed. They dragged huge carts of provisions. Thousands of demonym came next. They were naked and black as pitch. To a man, they were grotesquely disfigured, but marched powerfully with muscles glistening in the torchlight. Each bore a spear or bow. I had never imagined such numbers in the service of Mael before, and I found this new reality extremely disturbing. Where had they come from, and how had they chosen to serve this Lord of darkness? A few looked toward us, and I saw that they had the same red-eyed stare as the cy'daal and the vulls. Later I would come to understand that the demonym were dead men re-birthed into evil in Mael's black furnaces.

For what seemed like forever, this terrible army of defyyl spawn marched on. My blood was pulsing in my ears to the beat of their march. I was shaking, chilled more by the evil passing before my eyes, than the chamber's dampness. By the time the last tail guard of vulls and cy'daal had left the chamber by the south tunnel, I was sure I had seen an army of fifteen to twenty thousand.

I felt as if I had not breathed during the whole horrible apparition and gasped now for air. My arm, where Mryyn had grabbed hold, was numb and throbbing. My pulse continued to thump that terrible drumbeat and cold sweat drenched me.

Somehow, we found the energy to crawl and stumble our way around a few more bends in the river by the light of Pylos' partially masked flamerocks. Finally Vyyd spoke.

"I don't understand," he cried. "Why would Mael send such an army after us?"

No one replied, though I could tell Pylos knew.

Finally, Thom spoke. "They are not after us, are they Pylos? They're headed to Aelikos and on to Duvall and the Southlands aren't they? He asked, staring at Pylos.

It took Pylos several long seconds to answer.

"Yes," he replied quietly, almost in a whisper.

"What you have seen is only a fraction of the force Mael now sends against the Southlands. They travel in the dark earth passages and will rise through the seams to sweep down upon our homes."

At this moment, the horrifying vision I had seen when I had passed too close to the seam, once again flooded my mind as if given new life. The scourged land, a burnt Duvall, the bloated and dead bodies of friends and family, vulls feeding among the carnage, such dark images filled my head. The bile rose within me. It had been not just a nightmare but also a prophecy, a terrifying vision of what was coming. Our homes were targeted for destruction, and the armies of darkness were rising.

In the south, I was sure, life went on. Planting and building, playing and dancing, the pulses of life continued as they always had. Duvall and the southern cities had no idea of the monstrous evil descending upon them. The force I had seen that night would crush any defense Duvall could raise. The entire population of my town barely equaled this fraction of Mael's force. How could it be? We had no hope against such an army.

"The people of Terras will be quickly consumed by such an army," Vyyd said, echoing my own thoughts.

Pylos again paused before he replied. "It is true. Were the battle ours alone, we would be unable to withstand such a force. Let us not forget though, this battle belongs to Dyos, and in the realm of the illidi, all is not lost. Dyos'Bri is once again loosed on the land, thanks to the sacrifice of Yakum. It is the very power of Dyos breathed into every man and woman. Do not underestimate its power to affect events."

I found this answer faintly reassuring, knowing Pylos' usual obtuse style.

It was Mryyn who next expressed the sentiments of us all. "Why do we go north when the battle lies far to the south?"

"We follow the commands of our King. It is not for us to question his wisdom."

Even as Pylos said this, I watched his milky eyes staring off into the darkness ahead. Though his words were strong, and without a question, true, I saw for the first time fear in the set of his face. I knew he believed these words, but in his heart he was questioning his King, and he feared the future. He already had told us he knew he was not coming home from this journey. Perhaps now he was pondering the costs of his own obedience. He appeared more human in that moment than I had ever known him. As we pondered our own souls' struggles, we turned as a group and shuffled off.

It was another day and a half along the dark course of the river before we noticed the faintest of natural light. Two long turns later at a slipping and stumbling run, we entered a large cave mouth that opened onto a broad wet plain. After so long underground, even the gloomy light of a foggy morning seemed dazzling. Before us, the river divided into a thousand rivulets, which ran out into an endless swamp. Drained of its energy and playfulness by the flat plain, the water became sluggish and stagnant. The stench of rot was heavy in the fog. Nonetheless, I found its potency and richness peculiarly refreshing after the all-encompassing darkness of the caves.

We paused for an hour or so at the edge of the swamp. It was good to see the faces of my friends in the light once again. We had become quite a soggy and ragged lot. We all looked pale, worn, and grimy. As I watched the others though, I was struck by a common determination that was clearly shown on everyone's faces through the grime and exhaustion. We were a sorry looking but stubborn team. Mryyn caught my eye while I was making these silent observations. Her tired and loving smile told me she knew my thoughts, and agreed.

Cynte spent a long time staring off into the swamp. I knew she pondered the task before her with trepidation. Guiding us through this horrid bog was going to be a true challenge. There were no paths to speak of. Countless muddy pools, ripe with stagnation and overgrown with algae stretched off toward the horizon. Where the mud barely rose above water level, great clumps of sharp bog grass, thorns, and glens of dead trees seemed to create an almost impassable thicket.

We all dearly wanted to rest at the mouth of the cave but the recurring visions of the dark armies marching off to our unsuspecting homes would not permit any delay. We knew not what lay ahead, or how our small band of warriors would influence the course of events, but we did know the constant quiet voice of Dyos' Bri in our hearts. It prodded us forward into the ever-darkening lands to a fate only Dyos knew.

Before heading off, we all drank our fill of the cold river and filled our skins to bursting. The lands ahead, though rich with water, were likely as barren of potable water as the desert we had already crossed. We started off into the muck with Cynte's explicit instructions to follow precisely in her footsteps. She warned that a step to either side could sink us in mud to our necks, or leave us dying of a snakebite.

"Don't wander, don't take your eyes off the path, don't touch or eat anything unless I say it is ok. And Vyyd, keep a close reign on Ull, the journey will be just as treacherous for him," she said.

These were unchartered wastes, with untold dangers. The seriousness of her responsibility was clearly weighing heavily on her.

"You've done naught but lead us well, Cynte," Thom said gently. "Dyos has blessed you with a tracker's eye and senses. We trust you with our lives."

"Thanks, Thom," she replied with a smile that spoke her gratitude and perhaps a bit more.

All that morning, we battled the mud and slime. It gripped at our feet like a thousand cold hands. Each step was a sucking, straining effort. Often we sunk to our ankles, sometimes to our knees. Occasionally we were able to traverse short courses of dryer land, but here we fought the knifelike grasses and brambles with inch-long thorns. Cynte stopped several times and surveyed the swamplands before us. To my eye, it all looked like the same mucky mess, but she saw subtle distinctions, which determined our next steps. The bigger members of our crew, Thom and Synnett, had the toughest time of it. Their weight sunk them deeper into the mud and made their struggle even more exhausting. Pylos was right in front of me. Several times I noticed him stumble over roots and step heavily into ruts. I was not use to seeing him stumble at all. When I asked him quietly if he was ok, he huffed and grimaced and turned away. Later though, he came alongside of me. "I did not mean to be gruff," he said, as though he were speaking to himself. "I know you were worried for my health. It's not my health that is the problem though, it's my vision. These lands are very dark. There is little illidi light here. We move ever closer to the realm of Mael, and his darkness overshadows these lands. I now walk in a deep dusk, the only bright lights are you, my companions."

His words troubled me deeply, but I said nothing. From my pack, I pulled a length of rope and wound it around my waist. I then lay the other end in Pylos' hand and took the lead. The others noticed but did not comment. Pylos, for his part, took the rope, almost smiled and huffed his thanks.

In the evening, Cynte found us a small flat patch of muddy grass amidst a grove of dead trees. My calves and shins ached, and my whole being felt sore. I was sure I smelled like the worst of the bog, but knew I was in good company. None of us could clear the pungent smell of rot from our nostrils. We dared not make a fire this far into enemy lands, and I suspect even Pylos would have a challenge coaxing light and heat from the rotten wood all around. We ate a solemn and damp meal that tasted like mud but filled the stomach, and soon we were all quickly asleep.

Cynte woke us in the early morning fog. All night the swamp had rung with a mournful bullfrog dirge, slithering and sucking sounds, and the occasional unidentifiable dying cry of some distant creature. The constant but unpredictable swamp music had made for a restless sleep with frequent awakenings. I woke up feeling grumpy, and the cold and soggy breakfast mash did little to improve my mood. The others spoke little and wore the same sullen demeanor. Even Mryyn, whose spirit was usually indefatigable, was quiet and irritable.

Later in the day, after an endless and exhausting slog, Cynte had us stop out of concern for Vyyd. Mryyn had noticed at lunch that he had been sweating profusely, and asked him how he was. He had brushed off her concern. Now, however, he appeared much worse. His normally steady stride had become a shuffling stumble. He dripped with sweat despite the chill and had vomited twice along the path. Now that we stopped, it was clear that he was shivering and feverish. Vyyd still refused Mryyn's attentions until the evening when his consciousness began to lapse, and he slipped into a delirium.

Mryyn ordered Thom and me to undress him and redress him in the last dry cloak we carried. She cleaned him with some of our precious water, and while doing so found a long thorn slash along one thigh. The wound was purulent and severely inflamed. Brown and green mucus seeped from its depths. Even in his delirium, Vyyd winced in pain when the wound was touched. Mryyn explained that some of the swamp water must have gotten in the wound. Its foulness had caused the wound to abscess. The sickness now was in his blood.

Ull, for his part, was inconsolable. He lay chin on paws next to his master, whimpering softly. Several times, Mryyn had to push him away as he tried to sniff and lick the wound. His grime would not help the infection. Later, as Vyyd lapsed into an even deeper fever-wracked delirium and Mryyn was able to check the wound more thoroughly, she became concerned that perhaps a piece of thorn was buried in the wound. As she ran her hand along his thigh, I could see her band glow with translucent blue tracings.

"We need fire," she announced to no one in particular.

"I need to cut out the rot and cauterize the wound or Vyyd will certainly die."

Without any further discussion or debate about the risk of a fire, Pylos and Synnett set about coaxing flames from a small pile of rotten twigs. It was smoky and weak, but it was fire. After about a half an hour, the coals became hot enough and Mryyn set to work. She burnt her blade, and then cooled it in water.

Next, she carefully cut along the full length of the wound. The skin flapped open and from the center, a gush of heavy pus burst forth. Mryyn flushed the wound again with water and probed with the tip of the blade. I heard a scraping sound as the tip passed along something hard in the leg. Now, with patient care, while Thom and Synnett held Vyyd's writhing limbs, she adjusted the knife tip and angled it. With a sickening sucking sound, and a big gush of blood and pus, she popped out an inch-long thorn.

"Ahh," she sighed, "there's the bugger."

I felt like vomiting.

Next, she washed the wound well, sprinkled a white pow der into it that Pylos had handed her. The fire was now quite hot and cast a bright light. She stuck the blade deep into the coals until it glowed orange. Then with a sizzling and bubbling, plunged the blade lengthwise into the wound. Vyyd screamed and screamed with a cry that would wake the dead, then he seemed to pass out completely. Ull's howls, however, rose to an achingly painful lament.

It was at precisely that moment, when all our attentions were turned toward Vyyd's suffering, that a man stepped into the firelight.

Chaptyr 22

Synnett and Thom saw him first and lunged for their weapons.

The man, however, did not react. He lifted no weapon but took one further step into the circle of firelight, exposing his features. I heard Cynte gasp and his eyes turned toward her. "Hello, Cynte," he said softly with a small smile.

"Jaxx!" She bound up and embraced him. "I was fearful you had perished in the sands! Everyday I prayed it was not so, but after experiencing the horror of the sands myself, I had almost given up hope. It's been almost a year, how have you survived in this hell? Why didn't you come back? How did you find us?"

Cynte's questions came in a flowing gush. Fears, anxieties, hopes, doubts, all bottled inside her for so long, and now suddenly, this man from her past appearing like a ghost, and in the most unexpected of places.

For his part, this man Jaxx took it all quietly.

I saw now, as we all did, that Jaxx was not well. He stood leaning on a cane. His right leg looked thin, and his foot was crooked at the ankle. His skin was yellowish and hung loosely on his large frame. It was clear that at one time he had been quite muscular, but by some wasting disease, had lost much of his bulk. His features were hard and angled. Many small pock-marks scarred the skin of his cheeks. Curly brown hair and beard, now long and unkempt, framed this weathered face. Jaxx's eyes though, were a bright yellow green and seemed to flame in the firelight.

"You've made enough light and noise tonight to wake the dead. You're lucky I'm your only visitor so far. This place crawls with dark things you'd best not disturb."

Saying this in gentle reproach, mostly directed at Cynte as our guide, he then paused.

"But by Dyos, it's good to see your face, Cynte."

Jaxx directed us to snuff the fire, hide all evidence of its presence under the mud, and follow him. Thom and I lifted Vyyd, and as a group we slogged off after this mysterious man.

How anyone, even the best of trackers, could have survived the desert and this bog alone for months on end was beyond me. I found something vaguely suspicious about Jaxx's timely appearance. I was not wholly comfortable that we were doing the wise thing following a man we hardly knew into the darkness. Nonetheless, we had little choice, and I had come to profoundly trust Cynte's intuition and judgment.

As it turned out, our journey was surprisingly short that night. Jaxx led us slowly to a small knoll in the swamp, not a half hour's walk from where we had been camped. At its highest point, it rose at most ten feet above the waters. This was enough however, to make it reasonably dry, and to give it a commanding view of the surrounding mud flats. I now understood how

Jaxx had found us so easily.

On the edge of this knoll was a small cave, hardly large enough for our crew. Here Jaxx had made his home. It was a miserable pit of a place, but it had protected him from the rain and from prying eyes. I was stunned to see a large fresh skeleton of some giant lizard-like creature lying on the ground outside the cave. When Jaxx saw our curious looks, he responded by casually gesturing at the bone pile.

"It was the last tenant of my cave. He put up quite a fight when I tried to kick him out. Damn near chewed off my leg."

I, for one, was too stunned by this bit of news to inquire further. The others must have felt the same, for the story ended there.

Jaxx had us lay Vyyd on a crude thatch mat that appeared to be his bed. Ull curled up next to his master in an attempt to still his shakes. Vyyd's breathing was even now, and he slept deeply. Mryyn pronounced him stable enough but warned us he probably would not be moving under his own power for days yet.

"He's not the only one who will be dead if you keep heading where you are," Jaxx declared.

I found it strange that Jaxx already seemed to know where we were going.

"We have no choice, Jaxx. We've been called on this path by Dyos," Cynte said softly.

Jaxx smiled and nodded as if he'd expected her to say that.

"How is it you survived all this time, my friend?" Cynte asked. "I was sure when I found your bloody cloak that you had met a bad end."

"Indeed I have," Jaxx replied with a wide and bitter smile, gesturing broadly at himself and the grim surroundings.

"At least you're alive," Cynte said.

"Hunnh," Jaxx grunted. "This is hardly alive. Many days I have wished death had taken me in the desert and that I had never seen these hellish lands. This leg has made it impossible for me to escape."

His pain, as he spoke, was clear to all. Cynte seemed deeply saddened to see her brave friend so beaten and bitter. She reached out and hugged him hard and long.

"We're here now," she said softly, looking directly into his eyes.

Looking back at her, Jaxx suddenly seemed to see her for the first time. I began to wonder whether Jaxx thought he was in a dream, and was surprised to find that we were real. So many months of solitude must have waged terrible war on his mind.

Jaxx began to cry with heaping sobs. These cascaded out of him in waves of misery. After a time, he calmed and seemed to gather himself some.

Over the next hour or so, we heard his story of survival.

He had encountered a small pack of vulls just at the edge of the desert near where we had had to make our cliff jump. He fled into the hellish sands after a fight with the intention of looping back in the darkness. But the vulls pursued him deep into the desert, and he made the decision to continue deeper in hoping to find the other end. Like us, in the moment of greatest need, he had found the oasis canyon. He was delirious from thirst and had fallen down the rock fall badly breaking his leg. For many days, his survival was in question, but the fruit and water of the valley had given him strength. He fashioned a splint and crutches. Like us, he had decided to follow the river's course through the caves.

Over many days, in the pitch darkness of the caves, he had followed the river. However, his supply of torches had run out, and he was trapped like a blind man in complete darkness. He tried for days to continue on but fell so many times that he finally gave up and lay down waiting to die. He did not know whether he lay there for a day or a week. In his delirium, a faint light filling the chamber in which he lay suddenly surprised him.

"It was a group of demonym—four in all—black as pitch they were, and with red eyes that found me there near death." Jaxx said.

He went on to tell us how at first they seemed to fight over whether to kill and eat him on the spot, or whether to leave him for dead. Though they spoke some strange and guttural tongue, largely composed of grunts and growls, he was able to determine their general tone. It seemed this was some type of scouting contingent. The leader seemed to be arguing that Jaxx had to be taken to camp for torture and questioning. The fight grew so intense that the largest of the bunch, the one who was apparently the leader, stuck his pike into his aggressor's throat, effectively ending the argument. The victim squirmed around on the ground for a while, all the time gushing black-red blood and gurgling. Jaxx had watched in horror as the other three had not waited for his groaning to stop before they began cutting the creature up and eating his flesh raw. They seemed to completely ignore Jaxx as they enjoyed their feast.

Later, and without further discussion, one of the bloody men lifted him easily onto his shoulder, and they trudged off into the darkness. Two cycles they traveled thus. The demonym carrying him never seemed to tire. Each day, after walking many miles, they would stop, tie him up, and sleep for a couple of hours. Sometimes they would eat live rats that they found. Other times they would look at him hungrily as a meal missed. At no time did they try to communicate with him at all. During this journey, Jaxx slipped in and out of consciousness. They never fed him, but they let him drink his fill from the river.

One night, shortly after they fell asleep, Jaxx rolled into the river in an attempt to kill himself. They were camping near a low falls, and he just let himself get carried over in the rushing torrent. He struck something hard at the bottom of the falls and was knocked completely unconscious. When he awoke, he was lying on his back in the mudflats, near the exit of the cave, still bound.

"I must have floated a long way, or they must have assumed I'd drowned, as was my intention, or that I had somehow escaped on foot, for they never came after me."

Jaxx went on to relate the next year's struggle to survive in this dank swamp. His leg was too weak to travel far. He had no feeling below the knee and often could not control the muscles in his foot. He had survived on rainwater, birds, a rare rabbit, and the few swamp plants fit for consumption. His loneliness and hopelessness had been horrible, and he had begun to think that he was in some protracted nightmare, or that he had indeed died in the river and had awakened in some hell.

I watched Cynte during Jaxx's long tale, and saw her tears run silently. I could see her heart break for her good friend and mentor.

"This hidden perch has allowed me to watch my enemy though," Jaxx said, looking up.

"I have seen vast armies to the west and south heading into the caves. At night, there are sometimes long lines of torches, and the terrible howls of the vulls, and the growls of the demonym. I'll be honest, at times I am not sure any more whether I am seeing what is real or just dreaming terrible visions."

"We saw them too, Jaxx," I said. "We saw the armies on the march as well."

Jaxx sighed and nodded. He seemed to take small comfort in knowing his eyes still told him some truth.

During this time, Vyyd slept deeply, his breathing long and slow, Ull nearby. The cycles of sweats and wracking chills became less intense over the next day. We also slept during this time in long shifts, unable to go on until Vyyd recovered. Jaxx spoke to whoever was awake, always asking questions and looking off into the distance. At first I thought him rude or disengaged, but later I realized that his time alone had left him socially awkward and had done injury to his mind. At times, it appeared, we were just voices in his head. He asked endlessly about home, about Lord Pellanar and the others, but surprisingly little about our journey or why we had come.

Cynte spent a long time talking quietly with Jaxx, at times rubbing his hands, at times holding him while he wept. It was amazing that this man had survived the physical trials of the journey. It was even more astounding that he had now lived for over a year in this dank bog, sustained by its foul creatures. It was a testimony to his strength that he had persevered. Sadly, however, it was increasingly evident that the man Cynte had known had passed away long ago, leaving a horribly scarred husk of a man.

Vyyd awoke hungry as the sun rose on the second day. We shared what little we had left from the oasis stores. Jaxx left for a while without revealing his intentions and returned later with three long snakes as big around as his arm. I watched, astonished, as he fileted them expertly, skewered them with some yellow mushrooms, and roasted them over a sod fire. I had lost a good fifteen pounds of fat on this journey and craved fresh meat. The snakes were stringy and sour, but we left no scraps among us. I caught myself licking the last of the grease from my fingers and was saddened at my own desperation.

On the third day, Vyyd was able to walk with support, and we prepared to go. In truth, it was a pitiful bit of preparation, as we had essentially no provisions or supplies, and very little hope. Jaxx promised to take us a far as he knew to the north, less than a day's journey. He said that the swamp ended there and was replaced by a vast wasteland of cracked earth, stones, and a complete absence of life. I did not understand the purpose of this journey into darkness, nor Dyos' intentions. In truth, it was only the character of Dyos that I knew for sure, and that from Yakum's life and death. It was the memory of my encounter with Yakum; that last look he gave me as he was whipped, that tear he shed for me that moved my feet now. That alone was what kept me heading north, when all seemed hopeless and futile. As for my companions, I suppose it was their own encounters with the Master that kept them moving. We were not talking much by then.

So in the hot fog, we retied our sodden boots, re-bundled our few belongings, and stepped again off the small rise into the mud. We followed a winding path Jaxx knew through the swamp. Jaxx dragged his right foot and used a staff for support. Further back, Vyyd walked between Thom and Sennytt, his arms over their shoulders.

I saw several hoof prints in the mud, and asked Jaxx about them.

"This path belongs to boars, great tusked monsters. We best be praying we don't bump into one coming the other way."

He went on to relate how when he first arrived, he had tried to spear one of the monsters for a meal. The beast had twisted the lance in its tusks and thrown him a dozen feet into the water. Since then Jaxx had given them a respectful distance.

We made very slow progress because of the injured, but by late afternoon, the ground became firmer and rockier. Thorn bushes grew in great bunches. These impenetrable needle-sharp thickets required constant backtracking and ducking to negotiate. The trail had been made by creatures three feet tall and apparently immune to thorns. Though my skin had calloused on this long journey, I learned that I was not immune to them. At one point, as dusk was arriving, I crawled from a long tunnel of thorns, just behind Jaxx, to find myself in a wide open space surrounded by vulls.

They stood in a wide silent circle surrounding the small glade, thirty, at least. I was too shocked to sound any alarm, and as the others crawled two by two from the thorns, they quickly registered the same horror I had felt. In the center of the horde were two huge hellwyyn and a man on a great black horse. It was Desmodys.

I had never seen vulls so still and so quiet. They stared with those terrible red beady eyes, but made no movement. All of us, even Sennytt, surveyed the scene silently. Finally, Desmodys spoke. He looked as noble and righteous as ever astride his great stallion. "Nice of you all to join us," he said softly, a thin smile on his lips. "Oh, and well done, Jaxx."

I heard Cynte gasp at these last words as if she had been punched in the stomach.

We were suddenly, to a one, enraged.

Jaxx looked at our glares with defiance.

"How do you think I have survived so long?" he hissed. "Do you think it was easy, living here so alone, no hope of escape? Don't judge me. When they told me you were coming, they promised to save you, Cynte, and let us free together. He said we would be free to go if I just followed instructions..."

Cynte stared at Jaxx, a mix of horror and sadness on her face. Jaxx seemed to shrivel before her gaze.

Long moments passed.

"I will stand with my friends," she said finally, and stepped away from him symbolically.

Jaxx looked crestfallen.

"Well, it seems the lady will have nothing to do with you, Jaxx, my friend. What a shame," Desmodys taunted. "As for me, I always keep my promises. I will set you free."

He nodded with a smile, and an arrow hissed from the right. Somewhere hidden from our view was the demonym archer. It struck Jaxx in the neck.

"You're free to go," Desmodys said.

Jaxx grunted once, tried to speak, then fell forward into the mud.

Cynte screamed, "Jaxx, no!" and dove to his side.

Before I could grab my sword, even in the split second it took me to decide the fight was on, I heard Mryyn to my left unleash an arrow. I heard someone scream a scream of death in the shadows, confirming a hit, and then all chaos ensued and the vulls charged.

I swung with my sword at whatever came close, a blue rage suddenly overtaking me. I caught one vull between the eyes, another in the side as it leapt at Mryyn and a third on my return sweep, sheering its two front legs. Sennytt fought to my left, wielding an axe in great arcs, ripping flesh and clubbing heads. Even as I watched though, he took an arrow in the cheek, knocking him to his back, and the vulls were upon him. I dove into the fray swinging wildly. Thom too, joined me, cutting a vull in two with his great broadsword.

Thump! I took a thundering blow to the upper back, which sent me flying over the others. I rolled on impact, feeling broken. I lay paralyzed and gasping for air in the tall grass far to the side. I could not feel my whole left side. I felt as if I had been trampled by a bull.

Through dazed eyes, I saw the terrible hellwyyn who had hit me swinging a heavy club with deadly force. Thom took a glancing blow to the head but went down like a bag of rocks; he lay still. Sennytt, who was now free, slashed at the back of the hellwyyn's knee. It roared and stumbled onto one leg, but swung to the left as it fell and caught Sennytt full in the chest. I could hear his ribs break. He went down and was quickly swarmed by vulls.

I tried to move, and tried to breath. I rolled a bit to my left freeing my sword hand. A vull, mouth wide and dripping, lunged at me when it saw me move. I tried to get my sword up, but it was no use. I saw the jaws and could smell the stench of breath before the creature was knocked sideways. Ull crashed upon it snapping viciously at its neck.

Vyyd, Cynte, and Pylos stood in a group. Mryyn was down somewhere and I could not see her. Vyyd buried his sword in the hellwyyn's bent neck as it tried to regain footing. As he was trying to free his sword, the second hellwynn swung, narrowly missing his face. I saw, with wonder, as Pylos stepped forth blindly, swinging his staff. It caught the monster in the ear, causing it to turn in a rage. As it rushed him, Pylos raised his hand and threw something at the beast's feet. Yellowrock...

A great flash and a deafening blast filled the glade. The hellwyyn was blown in two. Chunks of flesh flew everywhere. A half dozen vulls were wiped out with him, as was Pylos. I saw him smile in the blaze of light, even as he fell. This was the first time I had ever seen him truly smile with joy.

For a moment it seemed that Pylos' sacrifice would turn the tide of the battle. I was able to regain my feet and reenter the fray. My left side, however, remained largely useless. I found Mryyn lying in the mud. She was bloody and unconscious. Her right arm lay at an angle. I saw Sennytt rise yet again from a mound of dead vulls. He presented a terrible sight. The broken arrow still stuck in his cheek, and he was growling so fiercely as he swung his sword that the remaining vulls seemed timid in comparison. Great splashes of vull blood filled the air around him.

I watched helplessly as Desmodys rode up behind him. I screamed a warning to him, but he did not hear me in his rage. Desmodys swung once from behind and nearly beheaded him. That great warrior fell forever onto the bloody grass. Desmodys casually wiped his blade on a loose cloth tied to his saddle. I charged him with a terrible roar, but never made it more than two steps.

In quick succession, an arrow went through my right shoulder, and a vull's jaws clamped down on my head from the left. I lifted my sword enough to pierce its throat, but we fell together. My face was crushed into the mud, and my breath was gone. I knew I was dying, but I was helpless to move. My mind floated above the glade for a moment, and all was still and silent as I looked down upon my fallen friends. Like a phantom, I floated over to Mryyn and whispered love in her ears. There was darkness, then silence, then nothing. For a long, long time, nothing.

I felt something roll me onto my back. Something foul, a bloody hand was in my mouth, scooping out the mud and clumps of grass. Vulls were all around. I saw Desmodys, still high on his mount. Not far away, Vyyd and Ull lay curled together, apparently dead, covered in blood. I couldn't move my head. I felt myself being lifted up. My head lolled back helplessly. I saw the grey sky. I saw Sennytt, Pylos, and Jaxx all in pieces. Mryyn was gone. Thom's sword was in the grass, but I could not see him. Bloody and unconscious, Cynte was being lifted onto a cart.

I watched this all as if in a dream. I could feel no body beneath me, just a heaviness. Blood dripped across my eyes, clouding my view. I heard my heartbeat far away; it seemed so faint.

I lay now on a hard surface, blackness all around. I opened my eyes one more time. Up in the rocks above the glade I saw him. Yakum stood there in the wooded dimness. Healthy and quite alive. He was looking at me. I tried to call out. He put his fingers to his lips to quiet me, then smiled softly. I felt free and still. I was not afraid.

Chaptyr 23

I tried, but I could not open my eyes. They seemed stitched shut, sticky and crusted. I licked my lips. They were dry and cracked, and tasted salty. My head felt like an aching bag of rocks. A terrible, immovable heaviness weighed me down. I lay still and tried to think, tried to remember. I concentrated on what senses were still working.

I realized I could hear now. There was a distant pulsing beat and harsh voices. I thought I could hear the banging of metal far away. The nature of the sounds, their bend across the distance, suggested some expansive place, a great emptiness. The pulse was earth deep and powerful. I had heard it before, but could not place the sound for a long time.

I lay and thought, and felt the beat. Then I knew. It was a forge. The blacksmith that Thom had worked in had pulsed like that. You could hear it if you stood a few feet away, and feel it in your chest. It frightened me to imagine the magnitude of the forge required to shake the very rock beneath me now. It must have been huge. It must have been filling the cavern.

I could feel the heat now too. Not in the air, which was stale and cool, but through the rock beneath me. It was unnaturally warm. I lay on rock—on my back—this I could tell now. I could smell moist earth, smoke, sand, stagnant water, and stale straw. Urine and my own unripe body filled my nostrils, too. And there was something more; rot, death, and old corrupted flesh filled my nostrils.

I tried to move again. My right side seemed cast in stone. I could lift my right forearm, though with great soreness and stiffness. My shoulder felt dislocated. I rubbed my face. It was thick with dried mud and blood. I licked my fingers and rubbed my eyes again, scraping away the crusts. I tried again to open them. The lids stretched and finally tore open to reveal a grey dimness all around.

After much blinking and tearing, my eyes began to focus. At first I thought I might be outside at night, but the air had an indistinct weight to it, and sounds seemed to reverberate off distant walls. I realized that I was lying on my back in some colossal cavern. I could not discern the ceiling in the darkness above. I turned my head ever so slightly and the bones in my neck cracked and ground together painfully. It appeared that I lay on a ledge of some sort, which dropped off about ten feet away into an abyss. Far, far away, through the dimness, I thought I could see some massive hanging stalactites, and some great cliff-like walls.

It took me a long time, and a lot of pain, but I eventually was able to pull myself up into a sitting position, and to fully survey my surroundings. I was stunned and frightened by what I discovered. I realized that I was perched atop a massive flat-topped stone pillar that was twenty feet in diameter. On the rough surface, there was a small amount of dirty straw some pebbles, bat droppings, and to my horror, scattered piles of bones. I crawled carefully to an edge and peered below. A terrible rush of vertigo ensued but quickly passed. Some distance below, a sullen grey mist floated and seemed to slowly swirl. A sudden nausea twisted my stomach, and before I could suppress it, I vomited bile into the emptiness. The abruptness of the purging and the dizziness left me feeling as if I were slipping off the edge of the pillar toward the mist. I shifted my weight and scrambled with my feet. My fingers dug into the rock, knocking several small pebbles into the abyss. As I steadied myself, and once again lay flat on the rock, I listened for some sign of their landing. There was none.

I lay for a long time, letting my heartbeat slow and the dizziness settle. As I lay on my side, I peered far off into the dimness. After a while, and with some twisting around, I was able to identify several other pillars like the one on which I lay, also sticking up from the abyss. They were widely scattered, perhaps a couple of hundred feet at the closest, randomly placed, and all roughly level with mine. To call them pillars was not entirely true, for they were far wider at the top, and surprisingly narrow at the neck. I presumed mine must have the same shape. Below that, I could not see at all for the mist was as thick and dark as coal smoke. Once again, I looked for a ceiling, but the dimness above seemed as dense as that below. I suddenly felt pitifully small in this colossal cave.

What had happened? How had I gotten here? How long had I been unconscious? My head was incredibly sore. There was one large patch of dried blood above my left ear. The tissue beneath was soft and sore but felt more like an injury a few days old than brand new. I carefully surveyed my body. I was badly beaten, and my joints were all aching. My right shoulder could barely move and felt like fire. I was sure I had a few broken ribs on my left side, and my mid-back was incredibly stiff and spasming. I had a wide assortment of cuts and scrapes, but these looked to be three or four days old.

My mouth was very dry. I knew I was dehydrated, and my stomach had that past-hunger emptiness that follows extended fasting. I had soiled my trousers long since, and my shirt was in tatters. I was alive, but in pretty bad shape. I felt horribly dirty, sticky, and pungent, but was so worn and hungry and exhausted, that I almost didn't care.

I tried to recall what had happened at the fight. I found it hard to believe that I had been unconscious for three or four days. Try as I might though, I could not recall anything after the battle. How had I ended up here, atop some pillar, deep beneath the earth? Why was I brought here? Most confounding of all, why was I not dead? I asked myself these and other questions again and again until my head hurt, but no answers came. I felt tired and weak, and began to feel an impossibly heavy sadness creeping over me. I tried to stretch my sore limbs, but it hurt too much. I lay back down to rest for a moment, but as the dimness settled upon me, I did not have the energy to fight it. I slept. No dreams.

I awoke on the same rocky bed but felt like something had changed. I looked around, but the same depressing emptiness greeted me. I sat up painfully again. It took all my energy. Then, I saw it. On the edge of my small perch sat a metal basket. A thin, ragged rope stretched upwards from it into the darkness. I could not see its end. I crawled painfully over to the basket. Inside were two rusty buckets. One held water—precious to me at that moment beyond all gold. I grabbed it and drank. I did not care whether it was poisoned or foul. I would welcome death as long as I could wet my throat. The water was warm, muddy, and had a metallic taste but was like heaven. I drank five gulps and promptly threw up. After that, I drank more slowly. It was a good-sized bucket, and was still half full. I saved the rest. The other bucket held some kind of stew. It stunk. It was thick and rancid. There were chunks of something in it and some pieces of bone. I made myself eat some. I knew I would die without food. I threw up two more times but ended with a bit more in my stomach than on the rock before me. I drank all the water I could hold and I used the rest to clean myself. I scrubbed off most of the dried blood and cleaned my drawers. I was still foul when I was done but felt much more alive. I put both buckets back in the basket. As if on cue, the rope suddenly became taut. The basket creaked, then started rising, swinging gently back and forth. I peered upwards but could see nothing. I watched as the basket slowly faded into the dimness. When it seemed impossibly small and far away—I guessed several hundred feet—I lost it in the gloom. I could not see its end.

Despite my terrible state, I could not help but be intrigued by this strange prison. Here I was, trapped somewhere deep beneath the earth on a small pinnacle of rock, being watched over by some hidden enemy far above in the darkness. Apparently they could see me, but I was blind to them. What a hopeless quandary.

I listened intently to the great space around me. Nothing. Nothing at all but the faint and distant pulse. I fancied that I could hear the mist swirling above and below. And then I heard a faint scream, high and painful. An even more distant echo followed. I knew that yell. Once before, I had heard Mryyn scream like that. She had been frustrated at her mother for some unfair disciplining, a rare outburst from a younger Mryyn. She had screamed and stomped her feet.

Mryyn was somewhere nearby, and she was alive! I knew this with a certainty that went beyond my senses. I heard it again. Longer, this time. Still so far away. I stood painfully and peered all around, trying to get an angle on the cry. The cavern,

I knew, played tricks with the sound. I heard some barely perceptible crying now. I stared and stared but could not see any
sign of Mryyn. Then finally, far off in the shadows, probably two
or three hundred yards away, I saw the faintest movement, the
dimmest shadow of a figure. I knew in an instant it was her, in
a way that lovers only know. She sat upon a pillar just like mine.
She was weeping. I jumped up and down and yelled until my
body screamed for mercy and my throat closed. She didn't hear
or see me, as far as I could tell. She never appeared to turn. She
never moved. After a long second try, my body gave out and I
fell down hard, almost rolling off the edge of my perch.

I cried now. I cried and cried. My hoarse throat screamed
silent curses. I pounded my fists until they bled anew, just to feel
the pain. I began to wonder if I were alive at all, or if I had died
in that battle. Perhaps this was my forever, my condemned eternity. Forever alone, forever in darkness, forever just out of reach
of all I loved. Then I recalled the buckets of food and water. The
dead don't eat. Someone was keeping me—us—alive, barely, but
we were not dead yet. This did not make me feel any better. As
I lay there, my anger and frustration was once again replaced
with an exhausted hopelessness, a persistent heavy, thudding
dread coupled with a terrible loneliness.

I fell asleep again. My sleep was now more fitful and filled
with dark dreams. Images of my companions lying in their
own blood, torn and mutilated, rushed through my mind. The
dreams were colored in somber greys, sickly yellows, and dried-
blood reds.

I woke again. I could not tell whether I had been asleep for an
hour or a day. I felt no sense of having rested. Pain and fatigue,
and a horrible misery filled me. The same endless, cavernous,
echoing greyness surrounded me. I peered far off to where I
had seen Mryyn before, but I could not see any form there now.
I wondered whether I had been dreaming when I'd seen her

before. Perhaps, my mind was slipping away, filling with phantoms and visions. I cried some more, but few tears came—more groaning sobs, really. I fell asleep again.

When I awoke later, the buckets were back. A little water, barely enough to wet my cracking lips, filled one bucket. The other held some more cold mash. I pulled the foulest bits out and threw them off the ledge, and then tried to eat the rest. I knew I had to eat if I was going to live. I was growing quite weak and thin. Try as I might though, I could not swallow more than two or three small bites. On the third bite, my teeth crushed something hard and, when I took it out of my mouth, I saw it was a rat's skull with flesh still on it and two wrinkled eyes. I pushed the rest away. Before too long, the buckets were once again slowly lifted skyward until I lost sight of them.

I surveyed my wounds. My scalp was healing, but a large gash on my right shoulder where the arrow had pierced was putrid and sore. It appeared to have been cauterized. Most of the rest of me was covered in bruises, scrapes, or dirt, but seemed to move reasonably well. My clothes were mostly tatters of cloth, hardly useful for warmth. My belt was gone. I had no boots. My feet were pale and abraded. They seemed foreign to me, as if they belonged to someone else.

I thought back to the fight in the marsh. I thought of my fallen friends. When I had last seen them, Vyyd and Ull had been laying together in the bloody mud, curled upon each other, companions even in death. Sennytt's massive headless chest arched up out of the mire, as if trying to rise for one last rally. Pylos, brave Pylos, now only tatters of cloak and bits of flesh flung afar. Jaxx, I thought, *you fool, you bloody stupid, pitiful fool. Look what sadness, what destruction you have wrought.* My friends buried in the mud among defyyl creatures, never to rise. I had seen Thom fall, but could not picture his final repose in my mind. Cynte and Mryyn had been in carts like me when I had finally lost consciousness.

I looked out across the cavern's great misty space at the other distant pillars and wondered if Thom and Cynte yet lived. Were they residing atop one of these lonely prisons? Why had we come here? Why had we ever left Duvall? Our reasons, our passion, the zeal that had driven us all seemed so distant and so faint now. I could hardly remember Yakum. Why had Dyos brought us all this way for this? Pain, loneliness, even slow, starving death—why? I had no answers. I hardly even cared. I was just tired and weak and ready to quit. I slept.

I awoke in a new place. Before I even opened my eyes I knew everything had changed. My head rested on a plump cotton pillow, and my body on a bed of feathers. I no longer hurt anywhere. My shoulders' ache had faded almost completely. I was in a room bright with candlelight. There must have been two score candles all alight scattered about the room on shelves, tables, and the mantle. A hickory fire danced in the hearth. The room was medium-sized, about twenty paces across and perfectly round.

I sat up, expecting the aches and pains I had come to know with every movement, but I felt well. My belly rumbled in hunger. Almost at the same moment, I noticed a table near the hearth piled high with food. There were bowls of fruit and loaves of bread, a platter of baked chicken, and sausages, grilled vegetables, a large carafe of wine, and a pitcher of water dripping with coldness. I was too stunned to move. What had happened? How had I come to be here? What of my pillar prison? How had my wounds all healed? Had I perhaps died? I looked down. I had been dressed in a white silk cloak, unbelievably soft, and finer than any I had ever seen.

I looked again at the table and noticed it was set for two. I thought suddenly of Mryyn, perhaps she was here too. Almost instantly, I heard a soft female voice. "Hello Pityr, I hope you slept well."

I turned to the voice. There, not two steps away, stood a woman. This was no ordinary woman, however. She was beyond beautiful. She wore a black gown, silken and tight to her shapely figure. Her hair also was jet black, brushed long, and shimmering in the candlelight. Her features were strong and powerfully alluring, even in my state. Her skin was pale but highlighted with rich colors. I had known street women that used paints to highlight their features, often with garish results. This woman had made already beautiful features, truly stunning. Her eyes were fiery green, the color of the sea south of Parthis, and the lids were shadowed. I had never seen a person with such brightly colored eyes. They looked almost feline. Her lashes were long and the color of midnight. Her nose was strong and upright. Her lips were generous, and glistened the brightest red I had ever seen. She smiled a smile of bright perfect teeth. Large red rubies hung from each earlobe. I realized I had not responded to her inquiry and sat gawking.

"I...I am sorry," I said. "I am just...just confused by all...all this," gesturing around me but never taking my eyes from hers.

I felt naked and embarrassed and completely confused by the whole scene before me.

"Oh Pityr, of course you must be confused," she replied with a gentle smile of complete sympathy and understanding.

She reached out with her hand and delicately stroked my cheek. I noticed her nails were long and painted the same rich red as her lips.

The skin on my cheek tingled at her touch. I caught my breath. My heart beat rapidly. Who was this woman?

As if she had read my mind, she spoke again.

"I am Allyre, Pityr. I am your ildyni." Her voice was just above a whisper, rich and achingly beautiful. She held me with her emerald eyes.

"What...what is an ildyni?" I asked hoarsely, barely able to speak.

She smiled and looked down alluringly, revealing the full length of her thick lashes. The crystal green of her eyes made me flinch with their intensity.

"I am your spirit woman Pityr, your ildyni, a dream come alive for you...a gift from the master. All this..." she said, sweeping the room with her hand, and ending with herself, "is yours to enjoy."

A range of sensations rushed through me at this moment. I had never known such intensity. Wonder and hunger, confusion and weakness, deep cravings, anxious fears, and over it all, absolute desire consumed me. I had been lifted from the depths of depravity and pain to soaring heights. I could barely control my passion. So intense were my feelings that they seemed to wipe out all hints of caution, all warnings of danger, all memories of things past.

As if reading my mind, Allyre leaned forward and put her lips a hairs-breath from mine.

"I am for you, Pityr," she said.

I could feel her warm breath combining with mine. My lips trembled. I yearned to touch those full red lips with my own and complete the bond. I knew I could never stop there. My blood was rushing too fiercely now, my senses far too aroused. I'd been deprived of touch for so long that my desires seemed to burst forth unchecked.

I suddenly thought of Mryyn. In the midst of all this opulence, I had all but forgotten my good and beautiful wife. I had forgotten my past and my friends.

Was it not good to enjoy this moment, to let its pleasures wash over me—even if it was just a dream? *Especially* if it was just a dream?

But now the memories came. I saw my wife on the day of our

wedding. I felt her touch. I saw her smile.

I leaned back from Allyre and stopped her slow advance with my hand.

"No, Allyre," I croaked. "I can't."

She looked at me inquisitively, with a hint of hurt. I thought I even saw a flash of green fire in her eyes. Then she smiled again and stepped back.

"Come." she said suddenly, and took my hand, dragging me from the bed. She held my hand and guided me over to the table.

"Sit," she said, and tucked the chair beneath me. She sat next to me.

"This is for you, Pityr. You may eat of it all."

"Allyre, how did I come to be here?" I asked. "Last I remember I was imprisoned on a shelf of rock, barely alive."

"My master brought you here," she said, her green eyes twinkling.

"Who is your master?" I asked.

She smiled.

"You will come to know him soon enough. He will be your master too," she replied. "Give me your hand."

I did as I was told, reaching out to her with my left hand.

"The other," she said.

She took my right hand in hers and I felt her nails stroking my palm. She leaned forward and brushed my ear with her lips. "Take off the band," she whispered.

I looked down at my wrist and noticed the band there. The jagged lines quiet and without color. I had almost forgotten that I wore it.

"Why?" I asked, also in a whisper. I could feel her chest touching me through the robe, and I could barely breathe.

"So that we may eat together all the riches the master has for us." I knew she spoke of more than just the plentiful food before us.

I shook with a terrible desire so powerful, I was sure I would burst. "I cannot remove it." I said.

"Yes, you can," Allyre whispered.

"You can remove it any time you wish." I felt her tongue lightly touch the cheek near my ears as she said this.

"Take it off, and we can share all this." Her fingers caressed my hand.

I began to feel a distant unease. Images began to fill my mind. I remembered Duvall. I remembered the moment I first saw Yakum on the forest path. I remembered chipping stone with him and building the arch. I remembered his smile and his eyes. I remembered his blood, and finally I remembered his death.

"No," I said, suddenly firm. "I will not remove the band."

Allyre looked suddenly hurt by my tone and maybe a bit angry, but she recovered quickly.

"Pityr," she said, her smile now a bit strained. "Come now, remove the band and we will eat together and be together, and together serve the master."

Her pleading tone made me wary. Some of the fire in me stilled.

Now I began to think more clearly as if I had been in a fog before.

"My friends?" I inquired. "What has become of them? Where are Mryyn, Thom, and Cynte?"

"Worry not about them," she said, now slightly angry. "My master is caring for them just as he is caring for you. He knows the needs of all his subjects."

I thought again of Yakum and felt his presence begin to fill me. I felt angry now.

"Whoever this master is of yours," I said, "I do not serve him. I serve Dyos. He alone is my master."

Allyre recoiled at the name of Dyos as though she had been

slapped.

Suddenly, the fog of desire was gone, and I knew who Allyre served. My anger grew. The band on my wrist began to dance with blue fire.

Allyre pushed my hand away abruptly as if she had been scalded.

"No!" she screamed. "You must not utter such things here!"

The memories now flooded me. I saw my friends in all their fullness. I felt Mryyn's wondrous joy fill me. I felt Yakum look at me across the square as he was being whipped. *I love my friends,* I thought. *I love my wife. I love my King and savior.* "Dyos is now and forever my king," I said

The band now burst alive in flame. My eyes saw with intense clarity. The food on the table began to rot and became putrid and green with mold. Maggots sprung from the rancid meat. Cockroaches crawled among the rot. I turned at Allyre's scream.

She began to change. Where before she was alluring and healthy, she began to appear sick and gaudily caked with paint. Her skin wrinkled before my eyes and began to shrivel. She clenched her face with hands that were now skeletal and grey, with yellow broken nails. Her scream was horrible. Her clothes became ragged and torn. She shrunk to the ground still screaming.

I heard the bed fall apart in a heap of dust and dirty rags. The candlelight began to waver, the fire tuned to coals, and then in a whiff of acrid smoke, the room went dark.

As the smoke faded, I found myself sitting anew atop the pillar of stone all alone.

I wailed. I wailed the wail of a dying man. But I did not die that day. Or the next, or for many thereafter. I wanted to. Many days I prayed for death to come and sweep me away. Other days, I didn't move at all, I just lay in a ball on the rock.

Really, there were no days or nights, just the same grey environment and the same hard rock. I measured my time by sleep and wake cycles and by the basket. Foul water and vile stew, always the same, always inedible.

I lingered. I weakened. I became skeletal. My mind wandered and faded and numbed. I heard cries in the darkness and thought occasionally of the others. But I could hardly remember them at all. Even their names began to fade from memory, to be replaced by more dull grey. The whole world became grey to me.

There were breaks.

Two more times I was taken up like before into the room. Each time it was different. I never saw Allyre again.

Once, I was alone in the room and could see below through the glass floor. I saw the others upon their pillars. There were Thom and Cynte and my wife, each curled in pain. I could see their faces as if I were close. Terrible, deadly loneliness, starvation, dread, even insanity filled their features and drooped their skin. My beautiful Mryyn had lost most of her hair. Her face was scarred by terror. Her eyes were black and vacant. She chewed on her fingers.

A man spoke to me in the room. I could not see him. He was beyond the light of the candles.

"You miss your friends, Pityr, and your wife." The voice was soft. It was a statement, not a question.

I did not reply

"You have the power, Pityr, to set them free.... They need not live like this." The voice continued softly, as if it broke the speaker's heart to see such pain.

"Look at them suffer... Let it end, my friend."

I sighed. "I am no friend of yours," I whispered.

"Come now, Pityr. We could be good friends yet. And they... could be free," the shadow replied.

I said nothing.

"Remove the band, it serves no purpose here... The past is gone. Far greater things await you when you serve me."

"I will never serve you," I said resolutely, my voice barely a croak.

"Pityr, don't be foolish," the voice said. "Look at them...Your friends will soon die. Why not save them. Free them from their pain. You alone choose their fate."

I did not speak for a long time. I looked far below. I watched those I love suffer. I thought of the square, and the long look Yakum had given me, as his blood ran. I knew now what he was telling me with that look... "You will suffer with me, you will die with me..."

"Goodbye, my friends. Rush forth to the great beyond. Dyos will meet you there," I said through tears.

I turned my back on the shadow. The third vision came sometime later.

I stood again in the candle-lit room. Where the hearth had been, there was now a great window. The room must have sat atop a great peak, for the view was as from a mountaintop. Light grey clouds stretched forever below. Far off into the distance, the sky seemed tinged with fire. A black line of smoke rose above the clouds before bending in the currents. The window blew open with a crash. A violent icy wind filled the room in gusts and the candles were extinguished in an instant. I felt myself torn to and fro. The wind pulled me toward the opening until my body leaned out of the sill.

In the strange way of dreams, my eyes now crossed the great distance toward the red sky and the pillar of black smoke, as if I'd flown. I still gripped the sill, and the wind still battered my face. But now, below me, as if magnified a thousand-fold, stretched a great battlefield. For a few moments, I knew not what I stared at. Then I recognized a few buildings.

I had never seen Duvall from the air, as a bird would see

it, but now I was sure that I looked upon its end. I was horrified at the mess below. Twice before when I had neared a seam, I had seen quick visions of Duvall's destruction, but this was far worse. The devastation was complete. Little remained of my home. The great stone wall had been burned away toward the north, and most of the northern town had been completely scorched. Swarm upon swarm of fell creatures were pouring into the town, like a great black tide. I could see a few remaining townspeople rising against the wave, but even as I watched, they were quickly engulfed and consumed. I looked toward the north, and I beheld a vast field of slaughter. I saw all of Duvall's fighting men spread across a field of blood. Not one remained to fight. Not one moved in the mud. Not a horse, not a man. The tide of black beasts—vulls, cy'daal, demonym—flooded the whole lowlands as far as the eye could see. Many fed upon the corpses. The whole land lay scorched by black fire, blood, plague, and death. Even as I watched the last few lives in town, a few women and children sheltering in a temple were dragged into the street and slain. The church was lit with black fire.

On a hill overlooking the town was a shadowed figure. It was Desmodys, his great arm outstretched toward the town, commanding its destruction. I tried to turn and close my eyes, but the wind tore at my head and whipped my eyes open.

"See my power, Pityr... I am unstoppable," the shadow spoke from behind me. "You see what comes. Even now my armies descend upon your home."

I could not reply through my wind-whipped tears.

"Speak now, and I will end this foolishness. I will turn aside my wrath," the shadow whispered. Remove the band, serve me, and all the Southlands are yours to rule as you wish. There is no need for their destruction. Come now, it's an easy choice." The words were almost gentle.

I heard the words of Yakum, even as I spoke them in reply.

"Dyos alone determines what will be, and what is to come. In him I lay my trust."

I closed my eyes. The wind stopped. The room was gone again. I fell to the hard rock. The grey mist settled. I knew now there would be no more visions. Soon, I would die.

CHAPTYR 24

Still, death came too slowly. More days passed, though it was hard to determine since the sun and the stars were a mere memory to me. I could no longer move at all now; I lay in a heap. My bones rubbed through my skin in places where my body touched the rock. My clothes had mostly rotted off my body. I did not try to eat or drink. The baskets stopped coming. I could no longer swallow. I panted, hoping any moment my breathing would stop. Surprisingly, I felt strangely more lucid than I had been, as if the past days had been filled with fog. I thought of my friends and my wife. I remembered them with love. Clear memories now flowed through my mind. They were rich in color and sound. I smelled the grass and trees, the horses, and leather. I smelled bread and wood-smoke, waterfalls, and snow. I smelled my wife's hair, and her breath, and the scent of our bodies mixed in love. I heard Thom's laughter, and the crickets, the creak of the saddle, the clang of hammer against stone... I dwelled silently, and joyfully with these rushing memories for a long, long time.

I lay on my back and stared into the grey. I knew it was my last day. My body was seeping into the rock beneath me, my mind into the grey above. And then I saw it.

Far above, circling in the grey mist, was the sylverhawk. I blinked. I knew my eyes were no longer reliable. But, there it still was. I heard its far away cry.

Dyos'Bri!

I could feel my wrist dance with responding fire. Fresh air filled my lungs with my next breath.

"Come," he said. "Come with me."

And then I suddenly had a vision of the truth. I saw my prison for what it was.

I watched the hawk sail off to the far pillars, and I knew he called the others. I rolled over slowly, peeling my bones from the stone. I would not leave my body here, I knew.

With all my strength, I rolled twice more. I was on the edge now. I heard the hawk's cry again. He swooped beneath me now into the mist below.

I rolled once more and I fell.

After a fall of less than ten feet, I struck the ground. Thick dry sand padded the fall. A swirling mist twisted a foot off the floor.

Even in my desperate state, I was stunned. For so long, I had expected a long fall to sudden death. Instead, I had fallen a mere seven feet, exposing the horrible reality of my prison. All along, it had been a prison of the mind. My imagination, my fears, my presumptions, my sin, had been the weapons by which the shadow had kept me imprisoned.

I could almost hear him laugh his dark laugh now, as I lay curled in the dust.

I learned forever in that moment that his battle against us—the people of Dyos—has always been and will always be one mostly of illusion. Much of the power Mael wields against us derives from our own confusion, fear, hopelessness, timidity, pride, and sadly, the lack of trust we have in our savior. He uses our minds and our faithless hearts against us, and often allows us to do his work for him.

My anger at my own foolishness and my own weakness is what saved me now.

I rose, not just to my knees, but all the way to my feet. I had not been vertical in many days, and my muscles had long ago given up trying. Now though, I was mad, and newly filled with anger and a passion that drove me forward. My body rebelled in pulses of vertigo and waves of weakness, but stayed up. I knew that no matter how intense my passions, my body would soon give out, and then I would never rise again. I therefore lunged forward in a stumble.

Before taking a step, I screamed for my friends. What came out was barely a whisper. My throat was as dry as winter leaves. Nonetheless, I heard a cry and then another.

Before long, we found each other, stumbling in the low mist, our heads, almost at the level of the plateaus that had so long been our prisons.

I came upon Thom first, then Mryyn, and finally Cynte. We embraced, crying hoarse, dry tears.

Thom and my wife were in bad shape, maybe even worse than I. Cynte appeared to be in the best shape. Together, we looked like a cluster of phantyms. Starvation, dehydration, and isolation had shredded our bodies and our minds beyond recovery. Mryyn was skeletal and had indeed lost most of her beautiful hair. Her face was a series of self-inflicted scratches and dried blood, and her lips were deeply cracked and fissured. Her left arm was twisted awkwardly at her side. I hardly recognized her at all until I looked into her eyes. Despite the grime, and a laceration that had torn one eyelid almost in two, I saw Mryyn's eyes. The fire was still there. She tried to smile but her lip bled with the effort.

We touched. I held her softly. It was like hugging a bag of bones.

"I am sorry," I whispered. "I am so sorry."

She put her head against my chest and could not speak. Thom and Cynte held us, too.

Thom, huge, seemed shrunken and crumpled. The flesh of his face sagged. One ear was missing completely—a mass of old blood and pus crusted against his scalp. His front teeth were gone, making him look suddenly ancient when he tried to smile. His left arm, his sword arm, was gone below the elbow. It was crudely tied with some old cloth and appeared to have been cauterized. Like Mryyn, only his eyes seemed alive, the rest resembled a walking carcass.

Cynte, at least, was recognizable. She had many healing lacerations, and the left side of her neck was missing a huge section of skin, but she was the steadiest on her feet. I know her training had not let her give up her fight for survival, during our long ordeal. I am sure she had forced the vile stew down every day. This discipline of hers had given her a slight edge. This edge now saved us all. Cynte took immediate command when she saw our horrid states, and it was her energy alone that drove us forth. I, for one, would have been content to die there with my friends, finally free from our imprisoned minds, but Cynte would not let us die yet.

She found us water. Somehow, by stumbling and dragging each other across the cavern, we reached a streamlet, and fell into its wetness. I do not know how Cynte had discerned its presence, but it was a last stroke of hope for this broken and spiritually crushed band. We lay with our faces half in the small stream for many minutes, slowly sipping its life-giving richness, and letting its coolness trickle across our scarred and ravaged faces.

I could not believe that in such a hellish place, this small trickle of life persisted. Despite all the terrible years of Mael's rule, and the devastation of the defyyl inflicted upon the land, life—at least the substance of life—persisted.

I do not know how long we rested there. Long ago I had lost all sense of time. Those faithful internal cycles, set by the sun and moon, had died in me ages ago. We drank. We washed, and we drank some more. We hugged and spoke volumes with our eyes. We wiped away each other's blood and grime, tear streaks, and pus. Mryyn touched us each for a long time, the blue fire dancing on her band. It seemed to revive her rather than tire her. I began to wonder what would come next. Though revived by the water for the moment, I doubted we would be able to move from that spot. Even as I was pondering this dilemma, the answer presented itself.

Out of the mist, a dozen black demonym appeared silently and surrounded us.

Clearly, they were going in for overkill. In our state, one of these hugely muscled creatures, bristling with weapons, could have finished the whole lot of us.

It seemed though, that their intentions were different.

They bodily and effortlessly lifted us and bound us together. A long rope was wound around our necks, tied, and then strung to the next person. We became a human chain, bound at the neck. During this whole encounter, they worked in silence, hardly even acknowledging our existence. It was as if they were roping goats. Occasionally, they grunted or growled at each other.

They led us away from the stream, along a winding course through the field of pillars. Atop many of them, I could see piles of old bones, some still hung with flesh. Clearly, we had not been the only prisoners this place had known. Eventually, we came to a wall, which towered up into the mist at an almost perfect vertical. In our sorry state, the walking was tough. A few times, I stumbled, and once fell completely from exhaustion. The ropes cut into my neck and strangled me. We helped each other the best we could. The demonym sometimes tugged us and grunted, but mostly just trudged forward in silence.

Finally, after what seemed like forever, we came to an opening in the wall and entered. It was dark but lit by widely spaced torches around every other corner. We came to several intersecting tunnels and made a half dozen turns. The demonym knew where they were headed; there appeared to be no indecision. With each turn in the tunnel, the air became warmer and warmer, and the faint pulsating I had felt through the pillar became louder. The demonym began to drag us when we stumbled. At some point, we intersected a much larger tunnel that seemed to be a main thoroughfare, and turned right to follow its course. It rose slowly at first, and then began a long and winding descent. All the time, the heat was intensifying, and the pulse was becoming more powerful. I could feel its throb against my chest now and saw the torch flames along the wall bend toward us with each beat. Despite being almost beyond caring, I tried to imagine what kind of forge could produce such power.

At last, we turned one final corner, and saw the answer before us. We entered a tremendous chamber, larger even than the pillar chamber. Like the former, its ceiling and distant walls were lost in darkness. With each step forward, my lungs had been sucking air. Now, however, my breathing stopped. I gasped at the horror before me.

Far ahead, in the middle of the chamber, was a colossal domed furnace. On the side facing us was a large opening. A terrible black fire burned within its depths. I had always loved the comfort and warmth of fire. I had always seen it as joyful, useful, and life-sustaining. What we saw before us now though, was the antithesis of all that.

This fire burned with black and blood-red flames. Though it gave off tremendous heat, it was strangely chilling and cloying. Whereas a normal hearth fire was comforting and cozy, these flames were sulfurous and nauseating. Pure, painful evil pulsed in waves from this monstrous forge. As we watched, one after another, demonym, cy'daal, vull, drolloch, and hellwynn stepped forth from the black depths of the fire. After each one came forth, still flaming and smoking, and black as pitch, it was led to a river, which cut across the chamber near the forge. Here, they were quickly dipped, billowing with steam, and then made to stand in long rows.

I was still in poor state, and my body was so weak, that it took me a long time to realize what I was witnessing. When it did finally hit me, I fell to my knees and covered my face, for the terror so overwhelmed me.

Here was the birthplace of the armies of Mael. Here within this defyyl-fire forge, the fellspawn of the Lord of Shadows were born. By its fire, they also were sustained in life. This terrible forge was the pulsing heartbeat of the dark world and its craven creatures. I realized, with agonizing horror, that I was watching the demonym loading the furnace at one end with dead bodies. People and animals, long dead and buried, were the source blood and flesh, the raw materials for Mael's fellspawn. I watched in horror as the bodies went in one end and, from the other end came demonym, vulls, cy'daal, drollochs, and hellwynn. To my horror I even saw some squirming prisoners being fed in the front end. The others saw the same thing. Together, the four of us cried and retched and screamed and covered our eyes against the evil.

I had felt the evil of Mael already in my short life many times, but I had never known until that moment, the magnitude of the evil. I felt crushed by it, consumed by it, and helpless before it. As I looked at the endless lines of dark creatures stretching across the chamber, I recalled the great armies we had already seen, and I was convinced we were lost. For so long, I had held just a whisper of hope that the forces of light and goodness would rise to conquer Mael's defyyl masses. But now, I knew, there were fewer people in the whole Southland cities than were dark beasts in this chamber now. Here stood only a fraction of the great dark armies. And there were more being birthed every second. We had come to the heart of Mael's kingdom, and it was terrifying beyond all imaginings.

If he were so powerful, how could Dyos have let his enemy get so strong? Somehow, the scales seemed all off. I had understood Yakum as the King returning to conquer the lands again for Dyos. But now his life seemed so insignificant compared to this massive throbbing army of evil before us. Even at his most powerful, I had never seen anything from Yakum that rivaled this. The sudden loss of hope immobilized me more than all my suffering.

I'd like to say that I remained faithful and strong to the end. That we—all of us—stayed the course in the face of overwhelming darkness, and won, but the truth is, we did not. All of us now lay weeping and completely defeated. Our final hope had been crushed.

For a few moments, the demonym let us lay there, perhaps gloating in our misery. More likely however, they were simply following orders. After a while, I saw another one approach from the direction of the forge. He was larger and even fiercer than the others, and he wore a band of red on each arm. The others bent as he approached. In obedience to his grunts, they lifted and dragged us the additional quarter-mile across the chamber until we came within fifty feet of the forge's opening, where the dead were being loaded. The agonizing, pulsating, black fire was unbearable at this close proximity, and we all lay facedown in the dust, trying to avoid its direct power. That was why, when we first heard the soft voice speaking to us in words we could understand, it did not immediately register. When I realized that someone stood before us, addressing us, I turned my head and peered through slit eyes.

There stood Mael.

I am not exactly sure what I had expected. Perhaps I had anticipated that if we had ever encountered Mael in the flesh he would be some monstrous black demon or some great-horned phantom. Over the last several months, we had heard so much of the Lord of Darkness, and had encountered so many of his horrid servants, and witnessed the effects of his devastating black touch. Here was the greatest of silvermages, conqueror of the seven Triliset kingdoms, the one who had released the Defyyl on all of Terras, the one whose power had caused the Ryft. Here stood the commander of all the terrible forces of darkness now arrayed before us. Mael, lord of the dead and the underworld. And he was a man. He looked younger than I expected. It seems absurd to characterize a man who has walked the earth for over a millennium as young, but I had expected someone ravaged by age. Mael's countenance was youthful and quite handsome. He was tall and had wavy black hair, thick black brows, and yellow-brown eyes. He was well-muscled and strode forward with a confident gait. His clothes were rich and well cut, all purples and dark reds in tailored neatness. He smiled a gentle smile as he spoke, the type you might give to a close friend you had not seen for years. His teeth were perfect and white, all in a row except for one of the incisors, which was turned just a bit off center. This slight deformity seemed, if anything, to add to his commanding allure.

I was so shocked that I quite forgot to hear what he was saying to us as he strode forward. Indeed, so unexpected was his appearance that I had no inkling that this was actually Mael. My friends seemed equally confused.

"Come, come," he said almost jovially. "No need to wallow on the ground, in self pity. Let us help you up." He signaled to the demonym at each side, and we were lifted bodily to our feet. The full frontal heat was scorching. I noticed not even a trace of sweat on Mael's well-groomed countenance.

"My poor friends, it has been quite an ordeal for you, has it not?" He looked at us with a soft pity that almost made me believe he cared. "Truly, you have done quite well and come so far. This, I must say for my enemy, he does know how to pick the persistent ones to do his bidding. Fools no less, but persistent fools to be sure."

His statement seemed to require no response, and we gave him none.

"Indeed, you are proving to be quite irritating in your persistence. Do you not know that you are doomed to failure and have been so since the first day you climbed the wall in Duvall and snuck off into the forest?"

We all looked at him with wide eyes.

"Yes, my stubborn friends, I have known all along of your little adventure. I have eyes everywhere. I must say, you have proved surprisingly resourceful and stubborn. Nonetheless, your little alliance is completely hopeless. Ever since you signed on with that rebel Yakum, your fate has been sealed. You have no concept of the power you are up against."

As he said this, his countenance changed briefly, and his eyes flared with a black fire, but just as quickly, it was extinguished.

I looked around the vast chamber and at the dark multitudes all around us. I looked through squinted eyes at the hellish black fire furnace before us.

Mael was wrong. I was beginning to grasp the extent of the

power against us, and it was colossal and terrifying.

"What did you hope to achieve, anyway?" he asked softly, his eyes probing in true inquiry. He again seemed like a caring friend. His voice tickled the ears like the whisper of a lover and gave the heart a tug.

The thought came from nowhere. I realized at that moment that Mael did not know why we were there. In truth, this not knowing bothered him, perhaps even scared him. It wasn't any power we wielded, or some great plan that scared him, but the simple irrationality of our journey. It had been faith alone that had brought us this far, and faith alone that had kept us alive. It was this faith that was disconcerting to him because he did not understand it. Actually, none of us could say why we were there, because we did not really know. We had followed the call of Dyos, a king we thought we could trust with our lives. But none of us knew the purpose of our journey.

When we failed to answer, I saw on his face a sudden flash of uncertainty. It was the same flash of indecision I had seen cross Desmodys' face when he had first seen Samuyl, my brother, rise from death.

Thom spoke now. He had that strange far away look again. I knew he was walking to the light.

"How is it that with all your power and all your wisdom, you do not know why we are here?"

I was surprised by the boldness of this question, but then quickly realized, we had nothing to lose at this point by being bold. I doubted we would be alive much longer.

Mael, for a flash, seemed uncertain, but he did not fall for the bait.

In calm control now, he smiled a most understanding smile. "There was a time when, like you fools, I believed in the good-ness of Dyos. But there is no true kindness in him. There is only hypocrisy and ceremony and drudgery and dry history. In my readings and my travels, I began to see the errors and fallacies of Dyos' plan. It is a reign built upon foolish weakness. It had to come to an end. I was the only one bold enough to stand up to him. The only one with vision enough to blaze a new trail. The only one with power enough to beat him." He said this motioning with his hand to the great cavern around us.

"And this is your vision for a kingdom?" Thom said sarcastically, also motioning to the cavern.

Mael grinned, showing his one bent tooth among the perfect row.

"Merely a means to an end. I have lulled the people into a spiritual sleep, even as I have grown in power. My armies spread across the earth and beneath it. It has taken me some time to regain my strength, but before long there will be none left to stand in my way. I am patient. The Lord of Shadows will be lord of all, and all left to be decided then will be who rules at his right and left hand." As he said this, he put each hand to the side extravagantly.

"If you are so powerful, how could it be that the four of us have survived so long even in the midst of your lair?" I challenged, stunned by my own recklessness. I felt as though my mouth spoke of its own accord. The others stared at me with wide eyes, recognizing my death wish while Mael chuckled to himself.

"You are awfully bold for one chained at the neck," he replied, still in control of his emotions. "Those Dyos marks," he said, pointing to our bands, "present a special challenge. Your resistance has surprised me. Alas, I have come to understand that only the fires of the defyyl will destroy those bands. Have no fear, the particular problem of your survival shall be quickly resolved. Now perhaps you grasp your fate?" His smile was sparkling as he said this. It really made him so appealing, as if he were doing us a kindness by revealing our end.

A palpable shudder ran through our group at these words. I had guessed at our fate as soon as we had entered the chamber. Nonetheless, a small part of me had hoped there was some other way, some other path than this horrid death. Worse than the concept of death was the idea of maybe coming out of the other side of the forge as fellspawn.

"Now you see the pure elegance of my vision. The obedient servants of Dyos, being transformed into useful servants for my armies—delightful in its perfection, no? Of course, there is another option. I am patient even with fools. If you revoke your alliance with this weakling Yakum and remove the bands, I will let you live and even give you a place of power in my kingdom. It is your choice. You can serve me as demonym fellspawn or perhaps cy'daal, or you can serve me as leaders in my kingdom. It's your choice: slavery or freedom."

One by one, we turned our backs on Mael now at these words, and stood together in a tight circle. The ropes on our necks chafed. We stared in each other's eyes and held each other close, and spoke silently with our eyes of our love and admiration for one another. Then I turned back and spoke for us all, all the while keeping my eyes on the Lord of the Defyyl.

"You have no power to give us freedom," I said. "You are a lord of slavery and oppression. Freedom is totally beyond you. We will complete our journey. We will serve Dyos, even if it means we must perish in the fire. This is the only way we will have freedom."

Now Mael grew venomous as he spoke. He gave us a pitiful, malevolent stare. His countenance had changed. For the first time I saw the haunting dark monster behind the mask. In his eyes, the emptiness was deeper than any seam, and in this abyss swirled a cold, unspeakable evil.

"So be it. You have chosen your fate! The source fires of Mael, the flames of the defyyl, will consume you, and you will serve me as fellspawn forever!"

Without another word, he signaled our arms and feet to be tied. The demonym silently complied. When this was done, we were bound at the neck, arms, and feet, and could barely shuffle. We were turned toward the great black fire forge. The purulent heat and the gaping black emptiness of its flames were agonizing.

We were pushed forward. The opening towered above us almost a hundred feet as the flames licked the stone arch and my skin began to blister.

"Faster!" Mael screamed. "Push them into the flames!"

The fires roared and throbbed. It felt like a stone mallet struck my chest with each pulse of the flames. I turned my head from the scorching abyss before me for one last look back, and I saw it.

In the high corner shadows of the cavern, in a sharp dive, was the sylverhawk.

I turned back toward the flames and lifted my right arm against the pull of the cords, and I saw the blue lightning dancing on my wrist.

The demonym beside us and pushing us began to smoke and bubble, and then, with a suddenness that shocked us all, they burst spontaneously into flame. But they had pushed us far enough. We stumbled into the depths of the forge.

I saw the white streak of the hawk sweep by my cheek and I felt the blue fire on my wrist ignite.

I heard Mael roar in anger and I smiled a very small smile.

The world exploded about us. There was a pulse of great blue fire, like a thousand bolts of lightening all at once. It began as a sudden spark among the four of us at our bound wrists. It traveled outward in a great shockwave that flattened all before it. The black defyyl-fire was extinguished in an instant. The mighty stone forge shattered like the finest crystal, sending ten-ton shards of flaming rock in every direction. In an instant, blue fire filled the great chamber and consumed everything before it. One second, Mael and the endless armies of fellspawn were there, the next instant, they were borne away in vapor. The explosion blasted giant stalagmites from the cavern's distant ceiling, and a million tons of mountain fell upon the burning debris below.

We stood together in a shield of blue, watching the pure might of Dyos, and feeling its power course through us. Above our heads, the sylverhawk flapped its wide wings and great boulders fell all about. Fires and smoke filled the chamber as far as the eye could see, but we remained untouched. The pulse of Dyos'Bri was all consuming, and I felt myself slipping away in its wondrous embrace. Never had I known such aching love, such a powerful sense of absolute freedom. My mortal sinner's heart could not handle the intensity. I found myself falling to the stone, wanting to bury my face in the dust. The others fell as well, our binds long since burned away. At the last moment, when I knew a second longer would kill me, I heard the wings of the hawk fade and the blue fires quieted. The glory dissipated, and I slipped into unconsciousness.

Chaptyr 25

Sometime later, perhaps an hour, perhaps a day, we awoke to a wasteland. We lay amidst great piles of scorched and steaming stone. In places, the heat had been so intense that vast quantities of rock had liquefied into pools, and then hardened again. Light shone from above in thin shafts where the ceiling of the chamber had completely collapsed. Fires still burned, and white smoke wound upward through these shafts of light. I saw no evidence of the great armies of cy'daal, vull, and demonym, except a fine grey ash that seemed to coat everything. We sat on a plate of sparkling black obsidian maybe twenty feet round, untouched by even the tiniest flake of debris.

We sat in a silent huddle, too overwhelmed to speak or move. Truly, there was nothing worth saying at that moment. The experience was beyond the power of words.

After a long time, Cynte rose unsteadily to her feet. One by one, and without even a whisper, she helped each of us rise. She grabbed Thom's hand and slowly began shuffling away, leading us silently to the river. It too was filled here and there with giant boulders, and it ran grey with ash, but it was moving. Without hesitation, we stumbled and splashed into the warm water until only our heads were above the flow. Holding hands, we let the gentle current float us slowly along until we passed from the chamber altogether.

The river wound through low damp tunnels and around great bends. We floated in the silence of absolute emotional and physical exhaustion. I think I may have even dozed a few times as I floated. The water was warm and buoyant and even gently caressing in its muddy embrace.

At long last, the tunnels opened into a vast cave, with a more turbulent pool. One end of the cave was wide open, and I could see stars. I heard waves and smelled salt and seaweed. This was where the river met the sea. We bobbed in the brackish turbulent pool; low waves lifting us gently, and then dropped us back down as they rolled by.

I heard the noise of wood on wood, at first far away, then closer. I heard what I could have sworn was an oarlock creaking close by. I couldn't see a thing. I couldn't think. I could barely stay conscious. I thought for a second I saw a torch loom above me, but figured I was dreaming. Then all of a sudden, I felt two strong hands grab me and lift me bodily from the water. I fell onto the hard wooden floor of a boat. A torch was indeed burning in an iron rack on the bow of the boat, and by its light, I saw Thom, Cynte, and Mryyn also huddled on the floor of the small craft. As I turned my head, I saw Vyyd, an oar in each hand, and at his feet, a curled up Ull.

"Hi Pityr," he said.

And that was when I fainted again.

I am not sure, when it was that I became more aware. I was

barely aware of being propped up by strong hands, having my body massaged and tended to, and of being forced to eat and drink. My mind slipped and wandered endlessly during this time, and I was never sure if I was awake or dreaming. All the time, I remember the slow rise and fall of the boat, and the creak of the oars.

At some point though, my body responded to the care it was receiving. Finally, on what I found out later was the third day, I awoke to a red sunset. The sun had set moments before; its last red rays had shown upon my face and brought me back. The sky now was dark blue to the west and red-orange and green in the east. I was propped against the bow in a sitting position. Thom and Cynte were curled together on the floor of the small wooden craft. They appeared to be asleep. Mryyn was sitting on a box talking quietly with Vyyd.

And so it was apparently real—I had not been dreaming after all. Vyyd and Ull were alive. Once they realized that I was awake, Mryyn came and helped me move my stiff body. She gave me water and some fresh fish. Her arm was in a cloth sling. I hugged her for a long time in silence, and then together we shuffled and sat with Vyyd at the stern where he was manning the rudder. There was a small makeshift sail that seemed filled with wind, though I could not feel a breeze. The water was black in the failing light. The stars were winking brightly in the west. I held Vyyd's head between my hands, looking into his eyes and smiling at him. He looked remarkably well. I pulled him into a long hard embrace. I had so many questions I didn't know where to begin, but Vyyd knew, and told his story without prompting.

"Ull woke first. I don't know how long before I did. I think though, that it had been two days or more since the battle, judging from the smell, and the state of the bodies. He was licking my wounds when I awoke. He'd dragged me out of the mud somehow, and the two of us were in tall grass. I could barely move. My leg was broken pretty badly at the shin, my ribs were cracked, and my head felt like it had been put in a press. I had lost a lot of blood. Ull seemed in pretty good shape except for several bad cuts and a broken foot. Our immediate concern was for water. Fortunately, by some stroke of luck, we found two abandoned water bags in the carnage. This kept us alive until it rained heavily the night after I awoke.

"Oh, my friends, what painful days those were. How alone I felt. Were it not for Ull, I would not have even tried to live. I could see clearly that Sennytt and Pylos were dead. I had seen Jaxx take the arrow in his throat, and knew he was dead. I had no idea how the four of you had fared though, until I was strong enough to move about the battlefield, and examine it thoroughly. There were over thirty bodies on that field, and by then the swamp had made a mess of them. I wasn't able to figure out what had happened to you four until I found cart tracks some ways away. I understood then that I had been left for dead. I wished at that point, that I had died and escaped such a horrible place.

"It took about ten days before I could move much beyond a few steps. We had to get away, for the wild pigs and various other vermin had discovered the carnage, and were regularly trying to scavenge. Ull did a good job of keeping them away and even killed a few to keep us alive. Eventually, the scavengers became more and more persistent, and more numerous, as the stench worsened. I thought I heard some much larger creatures in the night, and did not want to stay around to meet them. I did my best to bury our friends. It was the first time I had cried since my family was killed.

"We slogged through the swamp heading west for three days. We made a pretty ragged pair, and our progress was painfully slow. I did not know where to go, but I knew that somewhere to the west lay the ocean, and the only chance we had lay there.

To be honest, I had come to the conclusion that our mission, whatever it was, had failed. I figured—please forgive me—that the four of you would never survive long in Mael's clutches. I had seen the wounds you all had taken in the battle, and knew you were likely headed for torture. I am sorry my friends, but I had given up the fight, and was having a hard time trusting Dyos any further. I did not know what I would do next, but I had clearly lost the will to fight. I wanted only to get away from my shame.

"After three days, I came to some tidal flats. Here, we were able to catch some crabs and fish, and even some birds. Water was abundant, and I was even able to find a few late season berries. We made it to the beach six days after leaving the swamp. After all the suffering we had seen, I cannot tell you the sense of freedom and peace that overwhelmed me when I stared out into the great sea. We rested here for many days. I made a shelter in the high dunes at the edge of the sea. Nothing revives the body like salt water and the sound of the waves. After almost a full cycle of the moon, I was able to remove the splint I had fashioned, and after a while, throw away my cane.

"By the end of this time, we were fully recovered physically, and I had come a long way back from the edge of insanity. I was, however, still emotionally numb, and nowhere closer to any plan for the future. I think I would have been content never to move from that beach again.

"One night there was a storm. It raged all through the dark night; the waves crashing relentlessly and the wind roaring. I slept fitfully; worried our shelter would be overtaken by the sea.

"I dreamed I saw a sylverhawk. It sailed far above me in great circles. After several rotations, it flew off to the north. I could see it in my dreams as if its wings were my own. I sailed high above the storm along the coast. Then I dove toward some tall cliffs. Here, I found a small cave at water level, and disappeared inside. I awoke in a sweat, but with a strange peace upon me. I did not understand the dream's significance but knew it had come from above.

"In the morning, the storm was gone, and the sea was like glass. High up on the beach, not thirty feet from my shelter, was this boat, perfect in every respect, including intact oars. I know that there is no luck in all the world that works that well. I understood now that the boat and the dream were connected, and that once again, I had a mission.

"For two days, I stocked the boat. Ull had become quite proficient at catching sea birds. We even found some nests with eggs. Fish were plentiful and the rocky pools had snails and crabs by the heaps. At the next peak tide, by the change of the moon, we pushed off and set a course north along the coast as I had seen in my dream.

"For three consecutive days, we followed the shoreline, pulling into the beach each night for rest, and to collect more provisions. Sometime during the third night, I heard a terrible rumble, louder than any thunder. It came in a clear star-filled sky from several miles north in the mountains. It was followed by a blazing flash that shot beams of blue into the night. It lasted several minutes then faded.

"In the morning light I could see a pillar of black smoke far off, but otherwise, nothing unusual. I had a sense from my dream that I would reach the cave that I had seen in my dream this day. Indeed, by nightfall, I saw the entrance. Further inland I could still see a faint whisp of smoke where the flash had occurred the night before. As I had been instructed in the dream, I rowed into the cave. I had no idea what I would encounter. To be honest, the thought that I might find the four of you never even crossed my mind. I thought you were all long gone. Imagine my surprise when, after only an hour or so, the four of you come floating down the river half dead. Mryyn has already told me your incredible story."

Here, Vyyd stopped speaking and put his hand firmly on my shoulder. I could see a gentle empathy in his eyes.

"Now you can rest my friends," he said softly. "I will take care of you now."

I was still incredibly weak, and even my short time awake had left me feeling ready for more sleep. Mryyn looked equally exhausted. She took my hand and, together we lay on the hard deck not far from Cynte and Thom.

Holding my wife close again was like the first time. I had so forgotten the touch of another. Our breathing became deep and synchronous. Mryyn was asleep within seconds. I looked at the great swath of twinkling stars above. How good it was to see the sky again. My mind started to fade with exhaustion. In the last second, before I passed into unconsciousness, I remembered a question that had been on my mind ever since I had awoken.

"Vyyd, where are we headed?" I asked in a tired voice.

"Rest, my friend, we're following the sylverhawk west across the sea," he whispered.

For four more days, we sailed a fair sea, heading always west, the wind behind us, the rising sun ahead. Vyyd had brought plenty of provisions and water. We were all deeply scarred, physically and emotionally. During these days however, we began to slowly heal. We talked some but mostly sat in silence, comfortable just to be close. I could not put into words the horrible emotional journey of the last few months. Thankfully, I did not have to because my friends had experienced it all with me. It would be years before we could each talk in detail about our journey. We did, however, mourn our friends Pylos, Sennytt, Toss, and even Jaxx, and remembered their ultimate sacrifice. We wondered where we were headed. We trusted Vyyd's instincts, and Dyos'Bri's guiding. It was a strangely peaceful time.

We woke on the fourth morning to a dense fog. It was as if

a cloud had fallen upon us in the night. The fog glowed slightly pink from a hidden sun. The water was still and the same color as the fog. There seemed to be no wind now, but the sails remained full, and a hand into the water confirmed we were, in fact moving at a good pace. There was no noise. I could not escape the sensation that we had left the sea all together now, and were sailing through the sky amongst the pink clouds. The mood on the boat remained hushed and expectant all through the day. The fog never lifted, and if anything, the strange floating sensation deepened.

Suddenly, and without warning, the bow struck soft sand, and the boat ran almost soundlessly onto a beach. We could not see or hear anything other than the lapping of small waves, and a quiet wind in the mist. Indeed, we were forced to keep a hold on each other as we stepped off the boat and onto the sand. The shroud of fog was so dense we were afraid of losing each other.

"Where are we?" Mryyn whispered, since a whisper seemed the only appropriate way of communication.

"I do not know," Vyyd said. "None of the maps I have ever seen in Parthis show any lands west of the Fyre Islands. We passed those to the north two days ago."

"Could we have circled north and east?" Mryyn asked.

None of us had really been paying attention to our course, trusting Vydd to lead this section of our journey.

"No. We've been heading due west for days," Thom said. "I've been watching the stars."

"Thom's right," Vyyd agreed. "It's been due west for nine days, my friends."

Together we pulled the boat up the sand and turned it on its side. We huddled together in a tight group, ate the last of the provisions, and drank the remaining water. The sun was setting somewhere beyond the fog. Strangely, even after much time had passed, it never grew darker. Vyyd suggested that perhaps a full moon had come with the sunset, but I had watched the stars for a long time the night before, and there had been only the tiniest sliver of a moon. The violet mist glowed. I could barely see the iridescent faces of my friends in the dim light.

The fog was strangely intoxicating. I began to feel heavy and tired. Voices were dulled and seemed far away. I was clearly disoriented and a bit dizzy. My eyelids drooped. I grabbed Mryyn, who was closest. She was also slipping away. She looked at me for a moment, and then, as if giving up a well-fought battle, closed her bright eyes. She slumped in my grip, and I let her slip slowly to the ground. My own weariness grew. I wanted to speak, to cry out to the others, to warn them, but I was too tired to speak. I should have been afraid, but somewhere in the back of my mind, I knew all was well. None of the usual alarm bells were ringing. I was sure there was no danger. For the first time in a long time, we were safe.

I heard Thom's snore. Vyyd and Cynte were quickly succumbing as well. Ull was curled in a tight ball.

I smiled, and dove finally into the lavender mist. I felt as if I were falling into a feather bed. I was asleep before I hit the soft sand.

"Pityr, wake up. Look... Pityr..." Mryyn was shaking me awake. So deep and fulfilling had been my rest, that for a moment I refused to open my eyes or respond. "What?" I said, rolling over.

"By the light of Dyos!" Thom gasped.

I opened my eyes to a brilliant day and a sight beyond my wildest dream. The sky was a blazing blue, the water azure and like glass. The beach was pink with gold sand that glistened like powdered gems. It stretched from the water's edge perhaps two hundred yards, and there met a wall, unlike anything I had ever seen. The wall stretched seamlessly a thousand feet into the sky, and as far down the beach in both directions as I could see. So smooth was its surface that it seemed to be made from white glass. A closer inspection revealed fine blue electric fires dancing in its milky depths. It almost appeared to be pulsating.

We moved slowly toward it, our heads bent backward, trying to see its upper limits. Cynte reached forward and touched it cautiously. At the point of contact, I saw her band spring to life with responding blue fire.

I touched it, too. My band also glistened with sparks of azure flame and my arm and whole body trembled with power. I felt its rich and comforting fire surge within me. Like a cleansing flame, it pulsed through my veins.

"It's the same," Thom said.

I saw him staring at his wrist.

"What...?" I asked. But before I could finish my question, I understood what he was saying.

The wall and our bands were made of the same substance. Both had been forged from the same milky white material. Whether it was stone, glass, or ceramic, I knew not, but was sure they were of the same.

I stepped back and looked skyward. Not a seam, not even the tiniest irregularity marred its perfect, glistening surface. At its peak, so far above, light seemed to pour over the wall. I realized now, that there was no sun in the sky. Rays of violet gold and white light that breached the wall lighted all the land and the sea and the sky. The view was stunning and left us all breathless.

"Listen," Mryyn whispered.

"Music," Vyyd said. His eyes were alight with joy and he was smiling. I realized I had never seen him smile before.

Then I heard it too. Far away. Barely on the edge of the senses, it was there—a chorus of thousands, rich and alluring. The melody sailed on the rays of light and seemed to fill the air like a wind.

Ull barked loudly, again and again, and went bounding

down the beach toward the water. We all turned to see what had caught his attention. A figure sat at a fire, his back toward us, a little way down the beach. He wore a white cloak and was stoking the flames with a stick.

"Where did he come from?" Thom inquired. "He wasn't there a few minutes ago."

I suddenly realized I did not know how long I had been staring at the glistening wall, watching the dancing lights, and listening to the spectral melodies. It could have been hours.

Ull reached the cloaked figure and skidded to a halt. His bark ended abruptly. The figure reached out with one hand and patted him enthusiastically. Ull danced around excitedly and repeatedly licked the strange man beneath the hood.

A sudden impossible ache filled me, and I found myself, along with the others, running toward the figure at the fire.

At the last minute, he turned toward us and swept back the hood.

I began to cry with joy and long dormant pain.

Yakum spread wide his arms, and met us all with an enveloping hug.

To a one, we were sobbing, and unable to speak. All the pain and fear, all the burdens of so many months, were released. Regrets, failures, sins, doubts, hopelessness, were washed away like so much debris. I gasped for breaths between sobs of joy. I fell to the sand at the foot of my King, joyous at last, to be where I belonged.

Yakum reached down, and one by one lifted us into an embrace.

"Oh, my friends," he said. "Well done..." His smile was shimmering and perfect. His face was alight with joy, regal and glorious. "It has been a long journey, I know... So much pain, and loss..." He said the rest with his eyes. He knew the pain. He, above all, understood. Our King had been there too.

"Come, my friends, and eat," he said turning and holding his arm wide. "It will make you well." Before us, several large fish grilled on the flames. Fresh rolls bulged from a pan on the edge of the coals.

My stomach was suddenly rolling. I was still wiping away my tears, as were the others. We dropped to the sand and sat around the fire. Yakum expertly skewered the fish and handed one to each person. The aroma was wonderful.

"Father, thank you for all this..." he said softly, spreading his arm wide, indicating the food and all of us. "Your kindnesses never ends."

We ate with a hunger of the soul and were fed deeply. Something in that food, in that fish and bread and wine, and in Yakum's softly smiling presence, was magical. Its nourishment was transforming.

I knew then, that it was the spirit of Dyos'Bri somehow feeding us through the food. The very presence of the King was flowing in our veins. Where the power of Dyos'Bri had been focused externally, he now healed inwardly. The darkness, the pain, the disease, hunger, fear, and doubt that had so long filled me, was washed away in a flood of blue light. It was as if I had been drowning a hundred feet below the water's surface, suffocating; my lungs crushed, dying slowly. With a sudden thrust, I had been yanked to the surface, gasping, filling my lungs with new air, every breath a brand new rush of life. For the first time ever, I was alive, with an altogether different kind of life within me.

I looked at the others and watched them undergo the same transformation as me. I saw Mryyn heal before my eyes. Her face so brutalized by pain, suffering, starvation, and injury, was infused with light. With each bite, her wounds faded, her smile deepened, her eyes glistened. Her broken arm straightened like a dry flower soaked in rain. Whereas before, she had appeared so painfully thin and ragged, she now shone with vibrant health, and appeared more beautiful than I had ever seen her.

I watched in wonder as Thom's severed arm reformed and moved as if it had never been injured. His ear was suddenly there again. Tears ran down our faces. Tears of such joy and yearning, I cannot even express. And Yakum shared it all with us. He too cried through his smile. He fed us each, hugged us with strength, spoke whispered, private words to each of us.

"Where are we?" Thom asked for all of us once our tears had finally stopped.

"You sit just beyond the walls of your long home," Yakum replied softly.

We all looked again toward the glistening walls, and to great rays of violet and gold light, dancing a thousand feet above. The melody of a billion distant voices floated on the wind.

"It's not quite time just yet..." he said with a soft smile. His eyes were on Mryyn, Cynte, Thom, and me. "It will seem but a blink of an eye before you will arrive again on these glorious shores."

"As for you, Vyyd," he said, turning to look in his eyes. "Your wife and sons await you even now, beyond the wall. Your friends Synnett, Toss, and Pylos long to greet you, too."

Vyyd gasped for breath. Fresh tears of longing and joy poured forth. He grasped Yakum in a fierce embrace and sobbed.

"Truly?" he asked, joyful expectation filling his face.

"I am sorry that the hurt has gone so deep....and lasted so long..." Yakum said as he held Vyyd in his arms. "Never again will you know such things..."

A fresh burst of sobs shook our friend.

"What now, for us?" Thom asked when Vyyd's sobs had ebbed.

"You must each return to serve your King a while longer in the darklands," Yakum replied. "He abides within you all now, the defyyl has been torn away. You will know what you must do. You are Ayili now, each marked by the bands, which bind you to me. The people of Duvall, your families, your friends, need you yet. It is the way of Dyos to free one through the love of others, and all through one." He said this as he touched his own chest.

I stared at Yakum. I remembered the night. I remembered the whip. I remembered the table. I remembered the beast. I remembered his blood and his death. I understood now the victory.

For a long time we lingered at the fire. We enjoyed the companionship of our King for a while. We talked and laughed and shared the painful memories. We ate more and spoke of things to come; some too great to tell. Sometime, a long time later, the light became more violet, and far off out to sea, a great wall of mist rose. And we knew it was time to say goodbye.

"Serve well, my friends," Yakum said as he rose from the sand.

"When you come again to these shores, I will be waiting here for you, and together, we will step beyond these walls, and you will no longer need to dream or hope, for you will know finally why you were made."

We hugged Vyyd a long goodbye and we each patted and kissed our faithful companion, Ull.

Without another word, they turned and walked up the beach, and around a distant bend. Ull was jumping and barking and dancing in circles, the last we saw of them through our tears.

The wall of mist rolled silently upon us, until once again our world was a translucent, glowing like a purple cloud. With it came the irresistible dreamless sleep of peace.

CHAPTYR 26

I woke to a perfect blue sky as I lay on my back. I had the sense of having slept deeply. I sat up and looked around. At first, I was completely disoriented, and then with a surge of joy I knew where I was. A long time ago, our journey had begun right in this spot.

There was the stone table, a pile of broken marble. From this heap, a great tree had risen to life. Its tentacled roots twisted into the huge rock pile and gripped it like a hand holding a fistful of pebbles. The tree's giant branches arched skyward, laden with verdant loads of leaves. Upon the ground where the blood of Yakum had been cast, thick mossy grass now grew. My friends all lay blissfully asleep in its caress. Some of the tree's great roots twisted away toward the area of scorched stone where the seam had been. Like the stitches of some gaping wound, the roots had sealed the sore closed.

The whole scene was so radically transformed from the horror of death and blood it had been that I was moved to quiet tears. I let the others sleep for a while. Though I was suddenly eager to see what remained of Duvall, I was, for the moment, content to dwell in this beautiful valley. I peered at my sleeping friends. They had been fully restored physically. There were no more broken bones, amputations, lacerations; no sign of the prolonged suffering and starvation. I looked with wonder at Thom's left arm, which was as whole and sound as the day we had left Duvall. Mryyn and Cynte were shimmering with beauty and health as they breathed the deep breaths of restful sleep. Indeed, had I not seen the white bracelets on the wrists of my sleeping companions, I might have considered all my painful memories, one long night of bad dreams.

Yakum had healed us well and deeply. I knew not what mystical powers had transported us back to this place. I had no recollection at all of anything beyond the iridescent purple mist and the beach. Strangely, it did not matter to me. I had seen enough miracles already in my short life that I was growing accustomed to them. I almost laughed aloud when I thought back to that naive young man I was just a bit ago. How skeptical of even the simplest supernatural ideas I had been. Now, what I had seen, what I had done, what had been achieved within me and all by the hand of my King... Who could have conceived of such amazing things and brought them to life but the mind of Dyos?

Now for the first time in thousands of years, the power of the defyyl was broken. The people of all the Southlands were no longer slaves to darkness and hopelessness and fear. As the result of sacrifice of Yakum, they were free to know and love, and live for Dyos, and once again to have their hearts filled with Dyos'Bri. But those who survived would need to learn and to make the journey of faith for themselves. This is why Yakum had sent us back, why the struggle for us was not yet done. We all longed to follow Yakum, Vydd, and Ull beyond those white walls, but we also wanted to bring our families and friends and all our neighbors with us beyond the purple mist, and that meant we had work yet to do here.

They each woke one by one to the wonder of the transformed valley and the joy of restored health. We lingered there long past when we knew it was time to go. Thom, Mryyn, Cynte, and I shared a prayer for what lay before us. Finally, we left the sun- dappled shadows of the great tree and headed out of the valley on the path toward Duvall. As we crested the first hill, we saw a great pillar of black smoke rising from the hills beyond. Now we ran.

We traveled the long winding path through the woods. All around us were signs of massive destruction. The forest had been trampled flat, the undergrowth tilled by the crush of thousands of feet and hooves. Even some of the larger trees had been felled to make way for the great siege carts, which had left ruts in the soil a foot deep.

A closer inspection however, showed evidence of early regrowth. Small saplings were already breaking through the crushed undergrowth. It seemed like a season had come and gone since the great armies had passed this way. I was suddenly concerned that we were too late. The war must have ended long ago. The others too, noticed the signs and we ran all the faster.

At last we broke out of the woods and ran through the grassy hills. The black smoke was once again in clear evidence and seemed to be coming directly from Duvall. Another three minutes of sprinting brought us over the last hill, and Duvall lay before us. The sight was shocking.

"By Dyos!" Thom blurted upon cresting the hill.

"How...?" Mryyn tried to formulate a question, but was at loss for words. Cynte and I stood stunned.

Duvall was hardly recognizable, but not in the way we had first feared. As I peered over the valley, I could not believe my eyes. Everywhere, there were signs of battle and destruction, but the town itself was relatively untouched. What had once been a sleepy village walled in by stone was now somehow a city. As far as the eye could see, new construction stretched. Houses, halls, streets, and new marketplaces had overwhelmed the old town boundaries and now filled the valley, rim to rim. And everywhere people were at work. Thousands upon thousands crawled all over the valley, hard at work, building, transporting, selling, clearing, mining, planting, and even casually congregating. In the middle of the old village, a great fire burned in a pile of rubble. This was the source of the pillar of smoke we had seen. Few people seemed to be paying attention to the blaze as if it were deliberate. I realized that it was located in the old town square, roughly where the Consul Hall had been. As I looked for my landmarks, I realized that the Hall itself was the pyre. It had been destroyed and was burning steadily, which made no sense to me. The Hall had always been the focal point of Duvall and the center of consular authority. I looked again across the valley at the full scope of new building and busy energy. So much had changed in such a short time.

In my most hopeful dreams, and my most terrible nightmares, I had never conceived of a Duvall like the one before me now. I had hoped that some remnant would survive Mael's army. I had even dared to dream that among them, would be some of my own family. But this was unbelievable and truly inexplicable.

"Look," Thom said pointing across the fields at a flag atop a newly constructed hall.

"That's a Triliset flag," Cynte said in wonder.

We all had seen the red flag with the silver Triliset before, but it had been in the great hall of Aelikos. Now it flew above

Duvall.

And then, like a wave, revelation came upon us in unison. Thom was the first to voice the new truth. "They came from the mountains," he said. "They came to help, and to escape, and to defend. Lord Pellanar had fulfilled his promise."

Just then, three horsemen galloped from our flank and took positions before us. They each wore swords and were strangely dressed. A Triliset marked the red cloth on each chest.

"Who might you be?" the leader in front inquired. "The scouts saw you coming out of the forest to the north. We don't get travelers from there."

So unprepared were we to be confronted in this way, that none of us could answer at first. As we stood still, I realized we were appearing more and more guilty and peculiar. I was just about to answer when one of the soldiers in the rear spoke up.

"Is that you, Thom?" he asked, peering over my shoulder at Thom.

Thom leaned around the leader's horse and looked at the soldier and I saw his smile suddenly appear.

"'Tis I, Brayn," Thom said. "Rose from the dead."

I realized that the soldier in the rear was Brayn Terr. He had been a fellow apprentice with Thom in the smithy.

"Where have you been? Its been nigh on three years since you disappeared."

From there, it all happened quickly. After an abbreviated summary of our journey, the three horsemen escorted us into town. Nothing had prepared us for the wonders that encountered us there. We were led into the presence of Harkion and Karolyne and several town leaders. Our families were summoned, and the day became filled with tears of joy and celebration. Long stories on both sides were told, and wonder after wonder.

We were encouraged over and over again to tell our stories,

and all, including Lord Pellanar listened with wonder. Many in Duvall, especially our families, already knew some of the story. Lord Pellanar and his people, of course, had filled them in on all of the events that had brought us as far as Aelikos, but none had know the details of our journey beyond. We in turn, came to hear the incredible events that had occurred since our departure from Aelikos. Lord Pellanar himself related the incredible tale.

Less than a month after we had left the blessed valley of Aelikos, it had been overtaken by the endless legions from the north. Pellanar and his people had known that the northern armies were coming, and had spent a great deal of time preparing both defenses, and an escape. Before the invasion, five thousand soldiers, and most of Aelikos' women and children had been sent southward toward the lowlands. For ages the sacred valley had existed in secret security, but that time was finally gone. Pellanar was aware that no amount of defense could protect Aelikos from Mael's wrath for long. So great was Mael's dark power that he would never stop until the valley, and the mountains all around, were but a heap of rubble. Nonetheless, even Pellanar had not foreseen the awesomeness of the black power that Malthanos brought down upon the remaining residents of Aelikos. Over half of the seven thousand remaining soldiers were wiped out in one day by a force of demonym, fellspawn, cy'daal, and vulls numbering in the tens of thousands. They swept over the mountains, and arose through seams deep in the cliffs that none in Aelikos even knew existed. Desmodys led Mael's armies weilding black fire that melted rock, and blasted whole mountainsides.

Less than a third of those remaining escaped southward, and they brought with them their Lord Pellanar, who was mortally wounded in direct combat. Their best healers were barely able to keep him alive for the journey, and his recovery took over a year. The Lord lifted his shirts to show me the large ragged scar across his abdomen at this moment in the retelling.

And so the remnants of Aelikos, about eight thousand strong, straggled and hobbled into Duvall about a month later. They were met with both shock and fear. Messengers had been sent well ahead, with as many wagon-loads of provisions and weapons, and Duvall was as prepared as it could be. Nothing, however, could prepare a town to double its size overnight. All were aware as well, that Mael would not stop with the destruction of Aelikos, but would soon follow to wipe the Southland peoples off the map.

Messengers were sent off to Parthis and other small Southland villages, and day after day more stragglers came to the now bursting town. By early spring, the town had grown to almost thirty thousand people, but more than half were women, older people, and children. New walls were raised, scouting parties were organized, defenses were strengthened, all for what most felt would be a hopeless last stand against Mael's black tide of wrath.

One day in early summer, two scouting parties failed to return, and the town was alerted to prepare. By nightfall, a wall of black figures blotted out the northern horizon, and a million torches lit the air. But the night was silent. The first light brought a horror beyond all reckoning. As far as the eye could see across the hills to the north, west, and east of Duvall, were demonym, vulls, cy'daal, giant hellwynn, and other fellspawn, all standing erect in absolute silence. A force of at least fifty thousand strong encircled Duvall. Even the most war-hardened soldiers in the streets cried out in terror.

All day they stood without moving. Dark clouds laced with a peculiar green lightning crackled in the air and the town was frozen in terror. As darkness fell, a giant black-cloaked figure stepped forward. The armies parted before him, bowing at his feet.

A horror-stricken town listened with chilling clarity as he spoke to them. They recognized his voice all to easily. Desmodys had returned.

"Bow, people of Duvall. The true king has finally come to subdue his slaves. Those who bow at my feet now will be spared and permitted to serve him. The fire of death will consume all who choose to stand against me. No one else but I can save you now."

Thirty thousand people listened in stunned silence, and almost six thousand heads bent in shame. They had been used to obeying Desmodys and they did so now. At his call, they left the confines of Duvall to bow before the ambassador of their new king, Mael. Among them were men and women, leaders and peasants, soldiers, and more than a few of the Exarchate. The remnant looked on, brokenhearted and defeated, as their weaker brethren bowed.

The great black figure of Desmodys spoke again. "Very well. The rest of you have chosen a pain-filled death."

With that came a black lightning bolt that blew open the northern wall of Duvall. Thunder like none ever heard before rocked the valley. A great cry of death arose, and the fight was on.

After his initial demonstration of black fire, Desmodys stood back on a rocky prominence, and let his armies destroy. And destroy they did. The people who had bowed before Mael were the first to be slaughtered. As a result of their shame and shock, they hardly put up a fight. They learned the true nature of the one they served. For their loyalty, their blood was spread across the plain until it was ankle-deep, and not a body was recognizable. Then the demonym turned their attention to the town.

Though the remaining defendants fought valiantly, they were hopelessly outnumbered. Soldier after brave soldier fell into the bloody mud. For five hours, the brave soldiers of Duvall, Parthis, and Aelikos held back the swarming black tides. Finally, as the orange moon rose, the town was breached, and demonym and vulls poured into the gap. From somewhere near the center of town, a rush of black bodies appeared. How they had sprung up in the center of town was not at all clear. Harkion Pellanar, along with some of his best, held them at the gap for a while longer. Then, just as they were broken, something extraordinary happened

There was a deep rumble through the earth that shook the whole valley. Desmodys, who had been gazing down upon his vile deeds with delight, screamed as if he had been burned. Thousands upon thousands of fellspawn suddenly crumbled like dry dirt, and fell to the ground. A silence followed deeper than any known before. No one could speak or believe their eyes. Shortly, there came from the north a great cold gale that lasted an hour. It roared through the town with a deafening ferocity. And the armies of Mael, reduced to dust, blew away on the wind.

When the sun rose again, nothing remained of the dark armies but thousands of fallen weapons, dried blood, and the smell of burnt sulfur. Desmodys' body alone lay like a sacrifice on the barren plain. His head had been severed by a lone soldier. All were at a loss to explain this unbelievable event. Who had struck this impossible blow against Mael's dark forces? For a long time the people were in shock, unable to do more than huddle in small groups and whisper. Was it some kind of strange trick, or a trap, perhaps? But all knew Mael had needed no traps. Within the hour, he would have overtaken the last fighters. What then, had happened?

Somehow, on the moment of total annihilation, the darkness had been broken, and the creatures of darkness destroyed. The horrible foreboding and oppression that had weighed upon the land for so long had suddenly lifted.

It took weeks to bury the dead. The "unfaithful" masses were buried first in tragic ceremony. The heroic fighters and townsmen who had taken the first blows were buried on a northern hill in marked graves with military honors. The dust of the darkest creatures, all that remained of Mael's terrible armies, was loaded into carts, and dumped into the old quarry, where it perpetually smokes to this day. Desmodys' corpse joined them there.

The town began to rebuild. Harkion's people, who had survived, and all the Southlands' remnants, joined to begin a new city. Many more people flooded in from distant farms and Southland villages. The people of Aelikos had brought with them their greatest artisans, scientists, alchemists, architects, craftsmen, and visionaries, and a new Duvall began to rise from the dust. The first new Triliset city in a millennium.

During the raising and rebuilding, one of the first buildings to go had been the old Exarchate Court, the secret fortress of the consul. It was the very same building in which Yakum had been imprisoned and tortured. The people of Duvall had been deceived by the consul. They felt betrayed by the consul's leadership, many of whom they all had seen bowing to Mael on the eve of the battle. What they had been blind to before, the people now saw with a sudden brutal clarity. The consul had all along been a tool of the enemy, to dull the hearts of the people. The murder of Yakum had been a terrible mistake. He alone had warned the people of the Exarchate's duplicity.

The true face of the consul was revealed even more clearly when the destruction of the Exarchate Hall uncovered a seam built right into its lowest basement. All along, right in the heart of Duvall had been a vein of horrible darkness, veiled in ceremony and religiosity. This also finally explained how a regiment of demonym and voles had suddenly appeared in the heart of

Duvall during the heat of battle, and how Desmodys had traveled to the northlands secretly. The fury of the people was horrible toward the surviving consulors, and it was only the hand of
Harkion, which stayed the populace from a complete purging.

Those consulors who had known nothing or who repented
with sincerity were allowed to survive. Those who, through trial
were exposed, were banished forever from the city and left to
fend for themselves in the wilderness.

The more the people uncovered, the more they realized how
complete the planning for their destruction had been by their
enemy. Why then, had they failed? Who or what had broken
this great dark power at the peak of its strength?

Only Harkion and a few of his closest advisors remembered
the small band that had left many months before, headed for
the heart of darkness. Only they dared to hope the amazing
events of that day had a link to these few young warriors who
had followed the call of Dyos'Bri. But even they did not dare
to hope that these Ayili warriors had survived their encounter
with the enemy.

Mryyn, Thom, Cynte, and I listened with stunned silence as
the story as Lord Pellenar spoke, finally realizing how significant our journey into Mael's lair had been. We finally came to
understand how important the destruction of the black fire furnaces had been. The defyyl- fed fires had been the life-sustaining power behind his colossal armies. We had never grasped
this, but of course, Dyos had known all along and had selected
us for this task.

We stood in the hall now as unlikely heroes, embarrassed by
the attention and celebration directed toward us. And celebrate
we did. Surrounded by family and friends so long missed, and
the newfound friends of Aelikos, the celebration lasted for days.

Each of us was given a position of honor by the people of
Duvall. I was to head a new army of banded silver-white war-

riors: Ayili'nosterlei. Like the four of us, the white knights were selected by Dyos alone. Each would journey by faith, often into the darklands, specifically by the call of Dyos'Bri, where they would find the Triliset box, be banded, and join the ranks. Some, with the lightning engravings, would join the white knights or Nosterlei, others who would return with the delicate waves of Mryyn's band, become a part of the Ayili'mynili—the renowned healers. Still, others would become scouts and trackers under Cynte's leadership. Finally, those with the bands of inscription like Thom's, would join the Ayili'veritai, the wise men and truth seekers, those who hear most clearly the voice of Deos Bri.

These, as you know, became the new heroes. They lived on to combat Mael's slow new rise from the ashes, fought the great battles since waged, and courageously met all the new struggles of the Fourth Age—the Age of Hope. It is their story now

Chaptyr 27

The first shades of yellow and orange lit the western sky through the trees when I finally stopped speaking. The fire had burned down to mere cinders. For a long time now, my voice had been weak and just above a whisper. My breathing had become raspy and strained. Jonam, for most of the night, had been bent forward trying to hear every word. I knew he felt himself among this heroic band through every step, every defeat, every great victory. I could tell it was hard for him now to come back into his own world. He rocked back in his seat, stiff and sore. He looked hard at me, and seemed shocked at my frailty. I know I looked as I felt - empty, as if the telling had drained the last few drops of life from me.

"Thank you, Pater," he said quietly, reaching out to touch my shoulder with affection. "Now I believe I have the courage to follow the King's call for my own life. I was fearful, I am ashamed to say."

"Do not be ashamed, my son." I replied. "Anyone who does not approach such a costly journey with trepidation, is a fool. But forget not the character of your King. As you journey alone, his will be the light that sustains you when all seems hopeless. It is the journey that makes the Ayili, not the band."

With these final words, I spoke no more.

We sat together for some time, just looking into each other's eyes. Finally, my young warrior rose stiffly, stretched, and wound the blue cape once again around his shoulders. The Triliset markings looked crisp in the morning light. He mounted his horse without another word and sat there for a moment.

"I love you, Pater," he whispered.

I smiled softly in reply.

Jonam twisted the reigns, kicked his feet, and the horse cantered from the glen.

I peered up into the high leaves. The dawn light was yellow and purple. Mist rose off the grass as the sun touched the dew. I hadn't told Jonam, but I could not move anymore. Sometime during the night I had lost the last bit of feeling in my legs, and now my arms were numb. I took a deep breath. I was sure I could smell salt water and wet sand as the sun rose higher. The morning mist danced around me. The wind in the leaves seemed to be singing to a far-off tune.

My palm tingled now. I felt Mryyn's hand in mine. It had been too long. Her voice whispered sweetly in my ear. Her warm lips brushed my cheek.

"I've missed you, Pityr," she sighed.

The mist swirled now, wonderfully purple. I could feel the sand between my bare toes. She was beside me now. The great sheer wall was there. It rose to the sky.

We walked hand in hand slowly up the beach. The gate was open. The light was glorious. Yakum stood there waiting with his kind smile that I had grown so used to over the years.

"Welcome home, Pityr," he said.

The End

THE END

Appendyx

Note: it is common in old Terrasian to substitute "y" for "e"or "i" in many words especially names. For the convenience of modern readers most words have been translated to modern English but the names have been kept in their original form.

Here follows a description of common terms for the modern reader

Aelikos - the mountain city inhabited by the remnants of the seven Triliset cities. Harkion Pellanar is their Lord. Population: approximately 24,000.

Allyre - An ildiyni sent to seduce Pityr.

Ayili - The silver-white banded. Those chosen through special trial to serve Dyos with their lives. They include the following:

Ayili'nosterlei - Renowned warriors

Ayili'mynili - Healers

Ayili'veritai - Truth-tellers or wise men

Pathfynders - Scouts. One must be chosen by Dyos and banded during a personal journey of self-sacrifice and service to the King.

Aster Sypiros - The greatest mage of the Consul of Mages during the Old Age. He turned to the dark magics in pride and released the defyyl on all Terras. He was thus transformed into Mael—Defyyl Lord.

Cynte Lass - The three-mark north-tracker and banded Ayili from Aelikos.

Cy'daal - A small thin vile creature that rides the vulls in battle. Their saliva is deadly to all causing the dregs, a slow rotting and brain-wasting disease.

Defyyl - The evil bane released on all Terras by Aster Sypiros— later Mael. It acts like a veil to block the minds and hearts of all people to the truth and love of Dyos'Bri.

Defyyl fire - Or black fire. The Vel'bri furnace fires of Mael that are the lifeblood of all fellspawn. Also occasionally used as a weapon by Mael and his servants in war. It can melt rock.

Defyyl Lord - Mael

Demonym - Black skinned man-like fellspawn standing about seven feet tall and heavily muscled. They serve in Mael's armies and are powerful warriors.

Desmodys - Head of the Exarchate Consul in Duvall—the religious and political leaders.

Duvall - The largest city in the Southlands. Population: approximately 20,000

Dyos- Creator of the entire known universe, right King of all peoples, Lord Almighty.

Dyos'Bri - Breath of Dyos, a living manifestation of Dyos' illihi power.

Dyos'Lei - Light of Dyos, Dyos' son and chosen sacrifice. In human form, known as Yakum.

Fellspawn - Describes any of the many vile creatures born of Mael's defyyl fires. The raw materials for these creatures are typically derived from corpses of people and animals, and from live slaves.

Harkion Pellanar - Lord of Aelikos

Hyss- A monstrous skeletal bird born of Mael's defyyl fires with a scream that turns the heart black often irreversibly.

Illihi- The power of the creator Dyos in two forms; Vel'bri - earth power, all physical and atomic forces that make up the universe infused by Dyos at creation, and Dyos'Bri (Breath of Dyos) the personal, spiritual touch of Dyos comprising all morality, truth, hope, purity, and holiness.

Ildiyni - A spirit manifestation, often evil and often quite appealing and seductive. Created by Mael to serve him and lure others into his service.

Jaxx - A renown north-tracker, friend of Cynte.

Jonam - Pityr's grandson.

Katheryn Pellanar - Lady of Aelikos

Mael (also known as Malthanos) - The Defyyl Lord. Fallen great mage Aster Sypiros.

Mryyn - One of the three adventurers from Duvall. Later, Pityr's wife. Later Ayili'mynili.

Parthis - A small Southlands city. Population: approximately 11,000

Pityr - The first Ayili'nosterlei. Teller of the tale recounted herein.

Pylos - Renown mage of Aelikos. Blind to visible light but able to see Illihi power.

Phantyms - Cat-like creatures made of vapors, able to inflict injury but immune to weapons. Only appears in misty Northland valleys and only at night.

Seam - A surface fissure to the dark under realms of Mael. Located all over Terras, these fissures allow rapid access to the surface for Mael's fellspawn creatures.

Sennytt - A great and huge warrior who joins the expedition to the Northlands from Aelikos

Silverhawk - The occasional physical manifestation of Dyos'Bri.

Soll-Pajj - A great prophet of Dyos. Leader of the Ayali'vinn silver warriors of the ancient age who conquered the pagans, bringing forth the age of the Triliset kingdoms.

Solyss - The colossal beast of the defyyl, which is its physical manifestation. Helped to break the chains binding Mael in the Temple.

Stone Table - Traditional sacrifice table at the seam at the foot of the Breach Cliffs. Usually used to feed the Solyss those judged irredeemable.

Terras – The known world.

Thom - Pityr's best friend. One of the three from Duvall to head north. First Ayili'veritai.

Tos - Renown stonemason. Pityr's employer. Joins expedition north. Ayili.

Triliset - An ancient symbol combining a triangle and a seven-sided star. It represents the seven ancient kingdoms ordained by Dyos, interwoven by the three persons Dyos, Dyos'Bri, and Dyos' Lei.